I0554022

Smith's
MONTHLY

Every Month Original
Novels, Stories, and Articles

USA Today Bestselling Writer
Dean Wesley Smith

TABLE OF CONTENTS

SHORT STORIES

SMITH'S MONTHLY ISSUE #37

All Contents copyright © 2016 Dean Wesley Smith
Published by WMG Publishing
Cover and interior design copyright © 2016 WMG Publishing
Cover art copyright © by Philcold/Dreamstime.com

The Writings and Opinions of
Dean Wesley Smith

Introduction
Into Year Four

That seems like a mind-numbing thing to me, that this monthly magazine is going into year four.

And at the same time I am very proud of this. Parent of a small child proud.

One of the reasons this is still going is the support from you fine folks on Patreon. Without that monthly support, I doubt this magazine would have continued. So thank you all.

And I thank you in the back of each issue as well, as I have done for the past two years.

I also want to thank the subscribers. It took a mighty leap of faith to believe I could do this for long enough to make a subscription worthwhile. I hope to keep repaying your faith.

Thank you all.

So now, what is happening in this first issue of the fourth year of the magazine?

And what do I see for this project going forward?

Second question answered first. I see this magazine going for one-hundred issues, which means at least six more years. I kind of find that a crazy and perfect goal.

After that I got a hunch it will keep going on, but I'll decide in six years.

It's crazy enough that one writer will do a monthly magazine of this size and fill it all. But it will be very, very crazy if I can do that for one hundred straight months.

So stay tuned there.

What I hope to have in the issues? A lot more original novels and even more original short stories. I also plan on more nonfiction books and more serial novels.

In other words, more of what I have done so far.

I keep thinking of doing an issue or two of only short stories, but so far the novels have maintained their place as the anchor of each issue. So we shall see on that as well.

Can't tell I don't really know what is going to be in each issue until I put

Thanks for the Support

Dean Wesley Smith

it together, can you? Sort of like editing any magazine.

On my blog, on the right side and down just a little bit, you can follow the progress of the next three issues of *Smith's Monthly* coming up as I put the pieces together. And as the magazine goes through the publishing process.

What is in this issue? A really expansive new Seeders Universe novel. I didn't think that universe could get much bigger and then I wrote *Starburst*. The universe got a lot bigger.

And there are four never-before-published short stories in this issue as well, plus the first third of one of my writing books.

So onward into year four I go. Again, thank you everyone for coming along on this ride. I hope to keep giving you as much entertaining fiction as I can every issue.

Cheers.

—Dean Wesley Smith
October 28, 2016
Lincoln City, Oregon

Coming Next Issue in *Smith's Monthly*

HEAVEN PAINTED AS A SUNSET

A Ghost of a Chance Universe Novel

NUMBER THIRTY-EIGHT
NOVEMBER, 2016

Original Stories,
Novels, and Articles

DEAN WESLEY SMITH

HEAVEN PAINTED AS A SUNSET
A Ghost of a Chance Novel

USA Today Bestselling Writer

DEAN WESLEY SMITH

THE HOUSE AT THUNDER ROCK

A Thunder Mountain Story

Duster Kendal found a newly built cabin along a trail just south of the old mining town of Roosevelt, Idaho.

But the cabin never existed before in 1905.

The cabin should not exist. Period.

Another time-travel puzzle in the acclaimed Thunder Mountain series.

The House at Thunder Rock
A Thunder Mountain Story

ONE

May 2nd, 1905
Monumental Valley

DUSTER KENDAL CAREFULLY worked his horse up the muddy, narrow wagon trail between the rushing waters of Monumental Creek on one side and the steep rock-covered hillside on the other. The sun was still hours from reaching the bottom of this narrow canyon and he could see his breath in the morning air.

He had on his long, oilcloth duster, a heavy shirt, jeans, and boots. His head was protected from the occasional shower by a wide-brimmed cowboy hat. The morning air had a bite to it, but he felt comfortable.

In fact, he felt the most comfortable here in the Old West, just riding his horse and exploring. He loved his original time in 2020, but he liked it back here in the past more.

Around him the spring melt was in full force and the stream looked dangerous and downright angry. Pockets of snow still covered the ground under the trees and the upper peaks were completely still snow-covered.

Everything smelled fresh and new and damp. The dry pine smell of the summer still a month or more away.

Sometimes he wondered why anyone had built a wagon road between Thunder City and Roosevelt. The mountains above him towered thousands of feet into the air and in places this valley was barely big enough for the stream and a trail, let along a wagon road.

Ahead of him about seven miles, the wagon road ended at the bottom of the steep hill going up to the Monumental Summit Lodge. Only a very dangerous trail led up that hill. The lodge at the summit was where he was headed now. He knew that the trail opened in two days, so he would stay the night in Roosevelt, maybe play a little poker, and then ride on. He was looking forward to getting back into his room at the lodge.

Behind him the wagon road had gone past the tiny mining town of Thunder City and all the way down to where Monumental Creek emptied into Big Creek. From there only a trail led onward. This time of the year that trail was the best way to get into this valley, coming down through the mining town of Big Creek and then up this wagon road.

He had been in Denver playing poker for a few years, since the construction of the lodge had finished. He planned on staying in the lodge for a few weeks and then heading back to Boise to the Institute and then back to 2020.

He was just a mile above the small mining town of Thunder City and still a few miles from Roosevelt when he came around a sharp bend in the valley and saw a large log cabin that flat couldn't exist.

Or at least in his other hundreds of times up this old wagon road, the log home had never existed.

The house sat perched on a flat area above the roaring waters behind a tall rock formation called Thunder Rock. Everything in this valley had been named Thunder this or Thunder that because of the tall mountain at the headwaters of Monumental Creek called Thunder Mountain.

Thunder Rock looked more like a pile of stones than one rock and it towered over the valley.

But now a newly built log home sat right behind it, cut slightly into the hillside. A wagon trail led off the main trail and up to the home.

In the hundreds of time-lines that Duster had ridden this wagon road, just as he was doing this morning, never had there been a home there, especially one built on such a large scale and with such wonderful craftsmanship.

Nothing about this home looked like it originated in 1905, although he doubted anyone of this time would even notice. More than likely if anyone did notice, they would just think it was built by someone from the East. People from the East just did things differently than Westerners, or so everyone out West believed.

But Duster didn't need to even go up to the house to know it didn't belong here, that it was a home from another time.

He kept on riding, going by at a normal pace. He was half-tempted to go up and just knock on the door, but there were far too many things that could go wrong doing that.

Too many timeline problems.

He saw no activity around or in the house other than the slight drifting of smoke from the stone chimney.

Looked like he was going to cut his stay at the lodge short. He needed to get back to 2020 and figure out just what was going on. Because at no point in history had anyone built that cabin there before.

At least in the thousands of years of history that he knew about.

Two

November 16th, 2020
Boise, Idaho

DUSTER CAME UP out of the lower crystal caverns to the larger cavern they called the living room. It was massive, the size of a normal school gym. They had put groups of couches and chairs around the middle of the floor and a large group of furniture facing a large stone fireplace.

At the moment the fireplace was burning, giving the cavern a warm feel and a faint tint of burning wood.

Along one wall of the cavern they had built a large kitchen counter. When he had left ten minutes before, his wife Bonnie and historian Dawn Edwards were sitting at the counter eating a light lunch.

They were both still there. And both still eating.

He had spent almost twelve years in the past but been gone for only a few minutes here. One of the many things he loved about traveling to other timelines.

Bonnie heard him come into the cavern and turned and smiled.

Damn he had missed her. He always did. They often spent generations, sometimes lifetimes apart in the past, but here, in this time, they were always in love and he wouldn't trade her love and partnership for anything.

Besides that, she was the smartest woman he had ever met.

Bonnie didn't look a day over thirty, but both of them had lost track of how many years they had lived. She was a couple inches shorter than his six-foot at five-ten and her long brown hair was pulled back and tied today, accenting her wonderful smile and face.

Dawn was much shorter than Bonnie, but also had long brown hair. She and her husband, Madison, were Duster and Bonnie's two best friends and had traveled in time almost as much.

"How long this time?" Bonnie asked as Duster came up to her and gave her a hug.

"Twelve years," he said. "We got the lodge built again in that timeline."

"And you played a lot of poker in Denver, right?" Bonnie asked.

He laughed. "Of course. But I ran across one new thing while heading up Monumental toward the lodge in May of 1905. Someone had built a house behind Thunder Rock."

Both women looked intently at him.

"There has never been a house there," Dawn said.

Duster nodded.

Dawn and Madison had spent many, many lifetimes in the Monumental Summit Lodge, living there all year, raising families in different timelines. They loved it there and the only reason Dawn was here right now was for a Institute founder's meeting tomorrow. Then she and Madison would take a helicopter back into the lodge for the winter.

"And it's not just any house," Duster said. "It's modern-looking. No one of that timeline would notice, I'm sure, but I could tell."

"Someone from here built it?" Bonnie asked. "Why?"

Duster shook his head. "I have no idea, but my question is from when did they go back and build it?"

Bonnie and Dawn both nodded to that.

At the moment there were only twenty travelers jumping into other timelines to the Old West. But they all knew that one hundred years in the future, that number would be over fifty, and by 2320, the number of travelers would be over two hundred who used the crystals and moved in and around other timelines.

But Duster and Bonnie had set up a system that a traveler could only go back one hundred years. So a traveler in 2120 could only come back to today. No way could anyone from that time, without express permission, move back into the Old West and build a cabin.

And what really puzzled Duster was why build it there? In just a few years, that valley would be mostly abandoned after the dying town of Roosevelt was wiped out by a mudslide turning the valley around it into a lake.

Only the Monumental Summit Lodge would remain to eventually become a modern tourist attraction fifty years later.

"We need to talk with Parks to see when in the future that was authorized," Bonnie said.

"Finish your lunches," Duster said, moving around behind the bar and heading for the bathrooms. "I need a shower after that ride."

"Yeah, we noticed," Bonnie said.

"Nice homecoming," Duster said, laughing but not turning around. "Call Parks. Tell him we're coming."

Three

November 16th, 2020
Boise, Idaho

DUSTER SAT ACROSS from Director Parks next to Bonnie and Dawn. Parks was as tall as Duster and often dressed exactly the same. His job was to run the Historical Research Institute through the four-hundred-plus years that it existed in time so far. And Duster was shocked he could do it so well.

The office was in what would have been a large upstairs bedroom in the Institute's Victorian mansion main building. The mansion sat above the main cave on Warm Springs Avenue in Boise. They had built the place and the entire underground facility in 1880 and kept it looking the same. The old light fixture that hung in the middle of the room now held modern bulbs and the walls still looked like they had the wallpaper from the 1880s although Duster knew that everything had been kept fresh every decade.

A huge oak desk filled the center of the room and Parks sat in a high-backed chair behind the desk. This office looked exactly the same in 1880 when it was built and in 2320 in the future.

Parks always looked right at home behind the desk and always in control. He had short hair he kept in almost a military style cut and a smile that reached his dark eyes often.

Bonnie and Duster had picked him to run the institute through time and it was the best choice they had ever made.

Duster, Bonnie, and Dawn sat in comfortable chairs facing Parks and Duster told Parks what he had seen.

Parks just frowned.

Duster did not like the look of that frown at all.

Parks pulled open a laptop on his desk and his fingers flew over the keys as Duster, Bonnie, and Dawn watched in silence.

Finally Parks shook his head and said, "I have no record of that happening at any point going forward. Are you sure it was built by a traveler?"

"Not completely sure," Duster said, "I didn't stop, but the building had structural details not even used or figured out until this time. Not even back in the Midwest and East."

"And even if it was one of our travelers," Dawn said, "building it there, at that location, would make no sense. Almost no one traveled that way for decades and even today very few go that far down Monumental except to see the old ruins of Thunder City."

"And if they built it to be completely alone," Bonnie said, "there are many side canyons no one goes up that they could have easily built in."

"No," Duster said, "they built the home to be seen and on a major trail for the time. And until I saw it in that timeline, it did not exist in any of the others."

The four of them sat there in the office silently, only the sound of a November wind rattling the big windows of the mansion behind the heavy drapes.

Finally Parks stood. "I'm going to jump forward to 2320 and check records there and all the way back. This happened at some point if one of our people did it. I'll find the record of it."

"In the meantime," Duster said, "I'm going to jump back to June, 1905 into the same timeline and go knock on the door."

"I'll go with you," Bonnie said. "I'm dying of curiosity. Besides, we haven't been back to 1905 together in some time."

  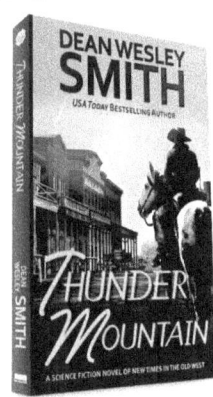

Now Available
from all your favorite booksellers
in trade paper and electronic editions.

Duster nodded and the four of them headed for the elevator to take them to the caverns.

There had to be a reason for that cabin. They were going to find out what it was.

Four

June 10th, 1905
Monumental Valley

DUSTER AND BONNIE had taken a leisurely three-day ride from the Institute in Boise up to the Monumental Summit Lodge. There they had spent a few days with Dawn and Madison in the lodge, telling them both what was happening.

The Dawn and Madison in that time-line was not the same Dawn of the time-line they had left from, so she didn't know.

It was a wonderful few days with wonderful food, a few drinks, and a lot of laughter between friends.

Then as the weather cleared at sunrise on the 10th of June, Bonnie and Duster headed down the trail toward the old mining town of Roosevelt.

In many timelines, they had had a home in Roosevelt for the years the town existed, but not this timeline.

They reached Roosevelt at eleven in the morning and had lunch at a wonderful café next to the general store. The general store had often been run by other travelers as well, but again not in this timeline.

They made it to the new cabin just before one in the afternoon. The sun filled the valley with light and the creek was much lower now than it had been when he had gone by the first time.

They dismounted on the main wagon road and walked their horses up the steep wagon trail to the cabin. They tied them off on a nearby shrub.

No one came out of the home to greet them and there was no smoke from the chimney this time.

"It is new," Bonnie said, noting the freshly cut logs and what looked like chinking that seemed to still be setting.

"And new construction not of this time," Duster said, pointing to where logs had been cut together on a corner.

"They didn't try to hide that," Bonnie said.

"That's what bothers me," Duster said.

They moved up onto the wooden front porch and Duster knocked on the plank door.

The sound was hollow.

There were drapes over the windows, but no real signs of anyone here. The area around the cabin had been trampled down by construction, but not by regular living.

Duster banged again on the door.

Nothing moved.

So he glanced at Bonnie and shrugged and then pushed open the door.

The inside was an empty shell. No rooms, no kitchen, nothing.

Even most of the flooring hadn't been put in past a small area near the front door.

"What the hell is going on?" Bonnie asked, standing beside Duster and looking around.

Her voice echoed in the empty shell of a home.

"I have no idea," Duster said.

This was not how you built a log home. The insides were always part of the entire support structure. The roof on this would never survive even one winter of snow.

He turned and went back outside and around to the back. There was no stable there in the hillside.

Nothing.

No one had built this cabin to live in.

Bonnie came up beside him, glanced at where a stable should be and where a food storage area should have been dug into the hillside.

"No one was ever going to live here," she said.

Duster nodded and turned back to the front of the cabin so he could see the road below.

"Someone knew I would be coming along this road in May of this year," Duster said, "in this timeline and they built this for me to see."

Bonnie nodded.

"And they made it clear enough that a traveler had built it," Duster said, "that I had to tell you and Parks and then investigate. Why is the question?"

Bonnie stared at the road below in silence for a moment, then turned and said, "What were your plans in this timeline before you saw this?"

"I was going to spend a week at the lodge, then head back to Boise," Duster said, starting to see where she was going with the question.

"And instead you came straight back, right?" Bonnie said.

Duster nodded. "Forming an infinite number of timelines where this wasn't here and I didn't go straight back."

Bonnie nodded. "And every decision we made and Parks made and is making in the future is splitting timelines because you saw this cabin."

"I'll be go to hell," Duster said, looking back at the fake cabin. "This is an experiment."

"A timeline experiment," Bonnie said, nodding.

"I'll bet that someone at some point in the future is trying to track timeline creation," Duster said.

He shook his head and looked around at the peaceful valley below the fake cabin. "I am in awe of the attempt."

"It's going to take some real computing power," Bonnie said, "even beyond our capabilities of 2320."

"You think we built this cabin?" Duster asked, glancing at his partner. "You think we are going to do this experiment?"

She shook her head. "We have far too many smart people working for us and along the same lines of math we started. One or two of them will do this at some point in the future."

Duster laughed. "Damn, those results are going to be interesting to see. How many numbers of timelines did my seeing this one fake cabin create?"

"How many timelines were created and then went back into a main timeline?" Bonnie asked. "That will be fun information as well."

"How many alternate timelines is Parks creating by investigating this instead of doing what he would have done?" Duster asked.

This excited him more than he wanted to admit. A real math challenge.

"And how many timelines are we creating," Duster said, working through more, "by taking this trip back here together instead of doing what we would have been doing in other timelines?"

"Infinite numbers of futures changed because someone came back here and built a fake log cabin," Bonnie said. "What a brilliant idea."

Duster actually felt charged up for the first time in a long time about math, his and Bonnie's first real passion. Math was how they discovered that going to another timeline was even possible.

"Let's go back and see if Parks can figure out who did this," Duster said.

Bonnie leaned into him and kissed him. "You know he won't find out."

Duster looked up into Bonnie's wonderful brown eyes and knew she was right.

"He won't know yet," Duster said, nodding, completely understanding what she was saying, "but as the Institute moves more into the future, at some point we will all know."

"And when that happens," Bonnie said, "we might actually know how many seemingly unlimited timelines you created by seeing this fake cabin here in 1905."

Duster nodded. "That will be fun."

They took their horses and walked back down to the main road and then saddled up and headed back up the valley toward the Monumental Summit Lodge.

That night Duster knew that they would have a wonderful venison steak dinner with fresh potatoes and sautéed mushrooms and talk about all this with Dawn and Madison.

And then in a few days they would head for Boise to see what Parks had found, even though they both knew it would be nothing.

And Duster had no doubt that by the time he and Bonnie reached Boise, that fake cabin would be torn down by the travelers who built it and no sign that it had ever been there would remain.

The fake cabin was the control point.

The fake cabin was the stone tossed into the calm pound of time in an experiment to calculate the ripples created over time, no matter how small or large.

What a fun experiment. He couldn't wait until the mathematician who would do that experiment was born. He knew it had to be sometime after 2320.

And now he would be watching for that person and waiting for the time when computing power caught up with this experiment.

And more than anything, he would be waiting for the results of how much he had changed all of history because one day he happened to pass by a fake cabin.

Now Available
from all your favorite booksellers in trade paper and electronic editions.

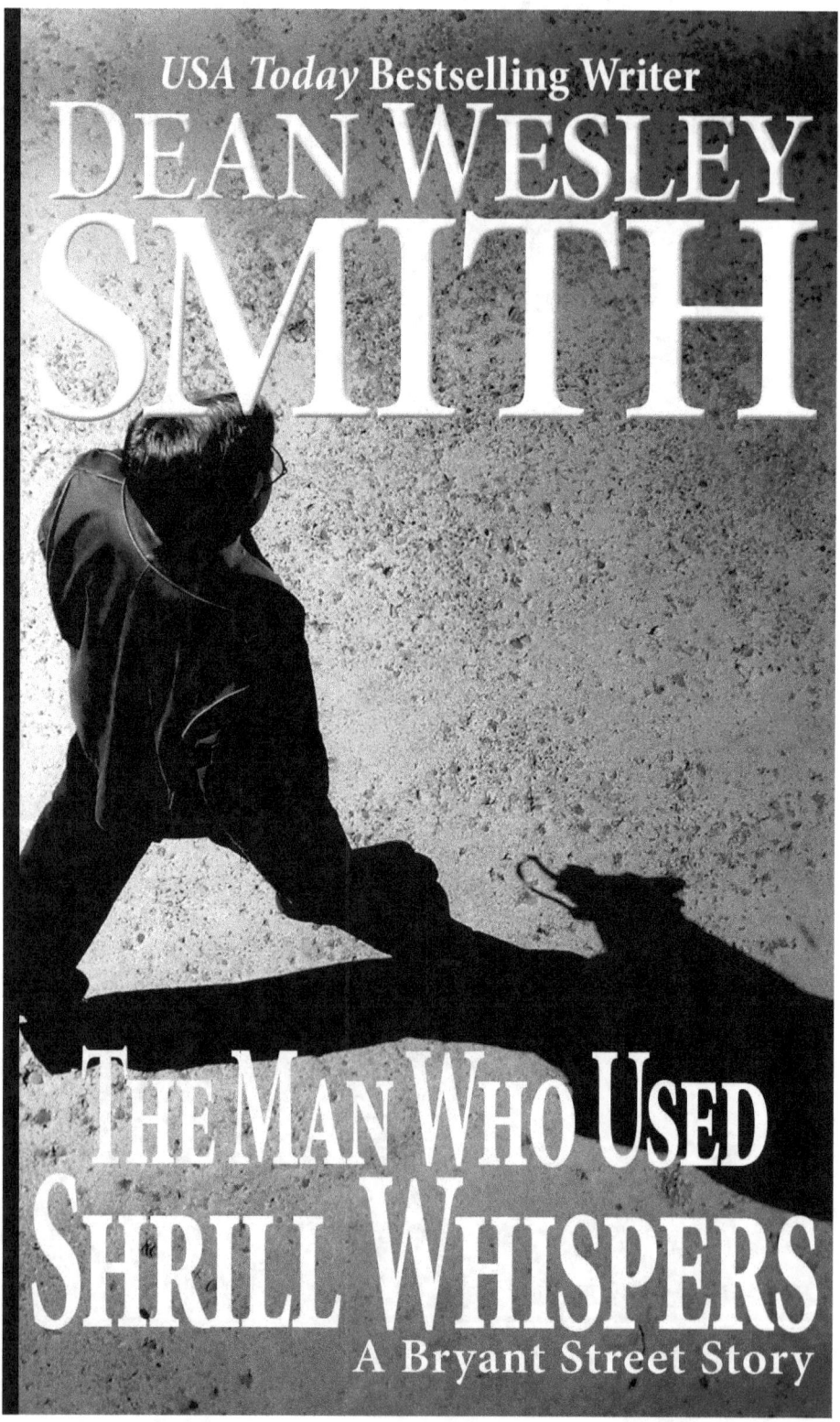

USA *Today* Bestselling Writer

DEAN WESLEY SMITH

THE MAN WHO USED SHRILL WHISPERS

A Bryant Street Story

Byant Street exists in that subdivision where reality tips over into the absurd.

Accountant Frank Filby and his one special skill live on Bryant Street. He knows everything about everyone in the entire subdivision. Keeps track.

Frank thinks of himself as the god of the subdivision.

Another twisted Bryant Street story where reality sometimes means little.

The Man Who Used Shrill Whispers
A Bryant Street Story

FRANK FILBY HAD a talent.

Or a skill.

Or maybe it could be called a gift. He didn't know. Early in life he had considered his talent, his gift, a curse and his mother had tried to cure him of it by first beating him and then taking him to doctors for drugs.

All it cured him of was talking about what he could do.

Frank Filby could hear the thoughts of someone in emotional pain. That was his gift.

It seemed everyone had emotional pain.

He called what he heard a shrill whisper.

Shrill because emotional pain always seemed shrill to Frank. Whisper because that was what the thoughts from others sounded like to him inside his own head.

Now, at the age of thirty-five, Frank lived alone in a three-bedroom ranch on a suburban street smack in the middle of a subdivision with exactly one thousand, two hundred and seven homes, his home not included.

Simply driving out of the subdivision to get to a local grocery store took him numbers of twists and turns that confused many, but that he knew by heart.

For a living, Frank worked alone, in an office in his home, doing online accounting. He was good at it and had steady clients that kept his bills paid and extra legal, taxable money building up in his many bank accounts.

During week-day business hours, even at home, Frank wore a dress shirt with a blue bowtie, brown slacks and comfortable loafers. His hair was thin and he kept it trimmed close to his head. He stood five-ten and was very thin, even though he ate three meals a day.

After hours and on weekends he wore a darker blue long-sleeved dress shirt and darker slacks and tennis shoes.

To a stranger coming in, Frank's home looked perfectly maintained and cleaned and he never left dishes out in the sink or clothes anywhere but in his walk-in closet where he dressed every day.

Strangers never came into Frank's house. In fact, since he had bought the house ten years earlier with an inheritance from his mother's estate, no one had ever been inside his home.

His business office was in a small bedroom to the right of the simple living room. The office had a simple wooden desk, a simple chair, and a computer with a printer and scanner.

A few accounting and business and tax books filled a small bookcase under the room's only window.

The living room had a reading chair, a long brown cloth couch, and a large-screen television facing the couch.

He watched news every night from three channels and nothing else. He loved the news for all the stories about all the ugly things humans were capable of doing.

He read only books about human nature, human psychology, and human feelings. Those books were his passion because they helped him understand his gift better. The few hundred books that he owned on that topic were arranged neatly on a large bookshelf unit on one wall behind his reading chair.

Every night, just after the sun had set, Frank went for a walk.

The subdivision had wonderful sidewalks and Frank made sure to smile at anyone he saw during his nightly walk. Neighbors even waved at him. He found that ironic.

Over the course of two weeks, he walked in front of every home in the subdivision. Then he would start the pattern over.

He had been doing this for ten years.

He had never missed a night no matter the temperature or weather.

In what would have been a family room in his house, behind a locked door, Frank had a large map of the subdivision on a wall.

Every house was numbered and in a large file cabinet beside the map was a numbered folder for every house.

A massive oak desk sat in the middle of the room facing the map and two large-screen computers sat on the desk. A high-backed leather office chair sat behind the desk.

Here, at this desk, after he came home from his walk, Frank recorded the information his gift had brought to him.

The file on each home in the subdivision contained exact information about each resident in the home. Names, likes, dislikes, birthdays, social security numbers, bank account numbers.

Everything.

And most importantly what each person in each home liked, hated, was feeling, and wanting.

And all the misdeeds of each person as well in the house, from the petty to the large.

His gift allowed him to listen to the close emotional thoughts of a person inside a house as he walked by.

He could listen to their shrill whispers and learn everything about them.

And sometimes he did something about what he heard. Mostly he just listened and recorded in the files.

Mostly.

At least at first.

As the years had gone by, Frank found himself thinking he was like a god of the subdivision, an all-powerful, all-seeing entity that knew every secret, every lie, every small detail of every person who lived in his subdivision world.

And over the last few years he had started to use that information in various ways, often to solve a problem which created more emotional stress that then allowed him to enjoy his gift better. This week he had sent blackmail e-mails to five husbands and six wives in the subdivision.

Those e-mails were what he called his "monthly affair tax" for those having an affair and living in his subdivision. He considered an affair a petty crime, so he charged them accordingly.

Each e-mail had been from an untraceable address, even by the best hacker, and he told each person to give exactly three thousand dollars to a charity account of their choice and send him a copy of the receipt. Otherwise he would tell the partner or spouse of the affair.

He never kept the "monthly affair tax" for himself.

But he did enjoy the extreme emotional turmoil the letters always caused, which made his walks past that house even more enjoyable for a few months.

Extreme emotional stress made a person's thoughts clear as a bell to him. Their whispers almost became like clear conversations over a phone.

Every night after his walk, he came back refreshed, feeling charged as he recorded every detail in the files.

Twice in the last year he had managed to stop a wife beater and once two years before he had stopped a wife from killing her husband. Both times he had done it through very detailed, anonymous tips to the police.

Six times in the last year he had stopped child abuse. He loved bathing in the emotional torture of an adult, but children were off limits as far as he was concerned. His mother had done enough damage to him.

For the child abusers in the family, the worst crime there was as far as he was concerned, he had a very simple solution. He killed them, just as he had killed his mother. Not in exactly the same way, of course, but in creative ways for each one.

Last month, for the abuser named Harry three streets over at 2910 Harper, Frank had simply hacked into his computer and put on his screen a subliminal flashing image that repeated to Harry that he was a worthless human being over and over and should take the gun in his closet and blow his brains out.

It took two weeks, but finally Harry did, leaving child porn up on his computer for everyone to see.

For the white-collar criminals who cheated at their work, Frank simply took their money, moving it from their bank accounts to his when it was the most incriminating for them.

And what Frank found most interesting is that by all national statistics, this subdivision had no higher or lower crime rate than any other. Frank often wondered if there were others like him, gods of neighborhoods, keeping the world a better place to live.

He hoped so. But he had no desire to meet any of them.

But as with many gods, Frank had a weakness.

He didn't know he did until four months after Johnny Aimes moved into a house five doors down from Frank.

Johnny's house, also on Bryant Street as was Frank's home, was along Frank's walking route to get to a larger part of the subdivision.

So Frank walked past Johnny's home five nights per week.

Johnny was also an accountant, a man with serious computer skills and very, very little emotional issues. Johnny was two inches taller than Frank and had short hair. He kept his new home looking perfect from the outside, as Frank did with his.

Frank had very, very little information on Johnny since the man seemed to just be serene. Without emotional distress, Frank could not get any shrill whispers from Johnny.

Then four months in, Frank got a sense that something was causing Johnny some distress.

And it took Frank two nights of walking past Johnny's home to discover from the whispers that the cause of the distress was Frank himself.

Johnny was in lust with Frank.

Johnny had seen Frank on his nightly walks, waved at Frank a few times and Frank had smiled at him. And now Johnny was working to stop himself from imagining Frank without clothes on.

And fighting to keep himself from going to the window to watch Frank walk past.

At first, Frank had laughed that off, but as Johnny's emotional distress got stronger over the lust, Frank could read his mind and see the images very clearly.

Disturbing images, yet erotic images. Frank had never felt that directed at him and he honestly didn't know what to do.

Johnny had investigated Frank, knew that he was single, that he worked at home, and that he had never been married.

Those details had excited Johnny even more and now he was working on a way to actually meet Frank and talk with him.

Until Frank had discovered that Johnny's imaginations were erotic, Frank had never considered himself a sexual being in any way. But clearly if he leaned at all, it was toward another man.

And Johnny's mind was giving Frank a clear roadmap of what that kind of relationship would be like.

Then one fine evening, in the middle of one of Johnny's elaborate fantasies about himself and Frank, Johnny slipped. He dropped his mental guard slightly, just enough to let Frank catch a glimpse in Johnny's mind of the real intent.

Johnny had the same talent as Frank.

Exactly.

The sex stuff had all been a ruse to try to disrupt Frank.

And Frank had been an open book to Johnny with each night's walk. Frank being conflicted on the sexual interest had allowed Johnny to get into Frank's mind.

Frank continued on his walk as if nothing was wrong, blocking Johnny from any access besides the surface of Frank's brain. Once Frank was back at home, he checked all his computers.

Only his accounting office computer had been compromised. More than likely

Johnny hadn't got deep enough yet in Frank's mind to see his real office in the old family room.

But Frank checked every detail just in case.

Clean.

Then, carefully, very carefully, he explored into Johnny's computer, and found fairly quickly that Johnny had a second computer as well.

And that was when Frank got the shock of his life. Johnny had been in contact with an organization of others like Frank, others who could read minds, who controlled areas like this subdivision all over the world.

They controlled massive corporations and governments as well.

Actually, from everything Frank could tell with careful searches over a few days, the main corporation behind everything called itself Deep Water Lives, Inc. It was a huge corporation and they had noticed that the normal crime rates were slightly off in this subdivision.

Frank had started involving himself in other people's lives instead of just watching. That had been his mistake.

They had discovered Frank ten months earlier, which shocked Frank more than he wanted to admit. He had been so very, very careful.

But not careful enough and that was why Johnny was here. They had sent Johnny to either bring Frank into the organization or to deal with him.

Frank was not a joiner. He was a god of his own world and that was exactly how he wanted to remain.

He had no desire to be some corporate lackey standing where he was told and doing what he was told.

So making sure to keep his mind blocked completely, he stayed in his routine

for the next week while planning his next move. Turned out his move was simple.

He sent an e-mail to the president of Deep Water Lives, Inc., and the chairman of the board. If they did not back away and pull Johnny from the subdivision, Frank would ignite every gas line in the entire subdivision and blow the entire place off the map.

Frank could do that. Easily.

From his laptop while sitting two miles away.

And the people in charge of Deep Water Lives knew Frank could do that.

Johnny was loading things into an SUV the next evening when Frank walked past.

Johnny nodded to Frank.

Frank smiled and waved back.

Frank's problem was solved.

He was again the god of his own world. All powerful.

Six nights later, what appeared to be a stray bullet from a nearby robbery gone bad, struck Frank between the eyes while he was on his walk.

When the police went into Frank's home the next day, they found only a regular family room where Frank's planning room used to be.

Frank was buried without anyone attending his funeral under the conditions of his will and his money went to charities.

A god had died, but no one on Bryant Street knew it or cared.

Two weeks later Johnny moved back into the house he had just left and a month later started regular exercise runs around the Bryant Street subdivision.

And the balance in the subdivision remained.

~

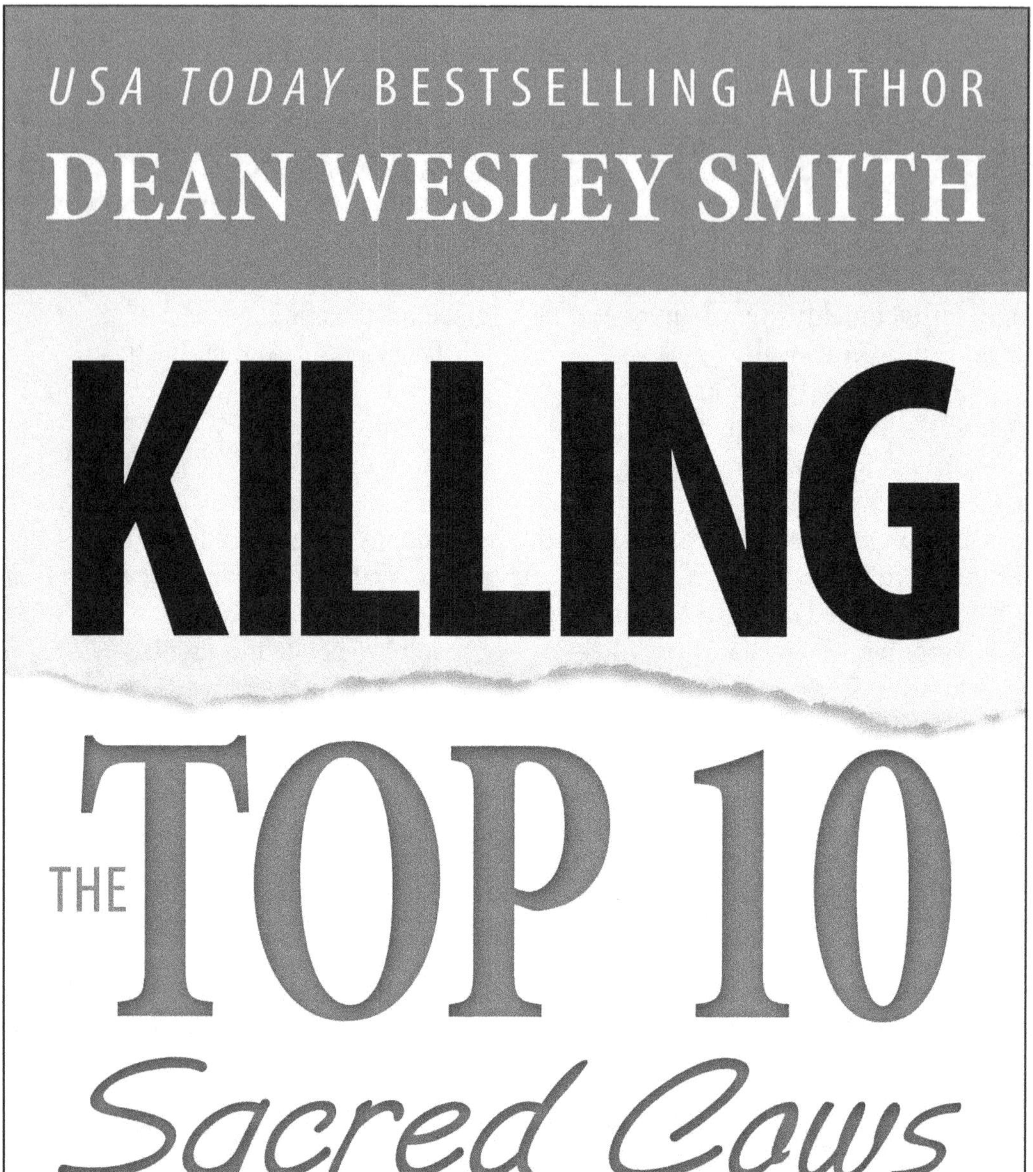
USA TODAY BESTSELLING AUTHOR
DEAN WESLEY SMITH
KILLING
THE TOP 10
Sacred Cows
OF PUBLISHING
A WMG WRITER'S GUIDE

The publishing world continues to evolve, but myths about who can make a living as a fiction writer maintain a life of their own. Whether you pursue traditional or indie publishing success, you need to know the pitfalls and traps that undermine many writers' careers.

In this WMG Writer's Guide, USA Today *bestselling author and former publisher Dean Wesley Smith addresses the ten most damaging myths that writers believe in modern publishing.*

Killing the Top Ten Sacred Cows of Publishing
A WMG Writer's Guide

Part 1 of 2

INTRODUCTION

IN 2010 I started doing short blog posts about the myths that hurt fiction writers that I had seen over my forty years in publishing. I honestly have no idea why I started these articles, but right from the start I called the myths of publishing "Sacred Cows."

Over the next few years I wrote upwards of 50 "Sacred Cows" knocking down one myth or another, or at least attempting to. And then two years ago I went back and updated some of the myths as indie publishing started to take hold.

Then, over the last two months of 2013, I updated these ten again, picking what I thought were the ten most damaging myths that writers believe in modern publishing.

An Important Note About This Book

In this book, I am only talking about commercial fiction. Nonfiction often has similar problems, and fiction written as a hobby has yet a different set of problems and myths.

But for this book, I am talking to writers who want to make a living with their fiction and sell a lot of copies, either through traditional publishers or through their own indie press.

So Who Am I to Try to Kill These Myths?

I think at one point or another since 1974, I fell into one or more of these myths, sometimes more than one at a time. Before I fell for the rewriting and writing slow myth, I wrote and sold two short stories and a lot of poetry in 1974 and 1975. Then I went down into the myths taught by college classes and didn't sell a thing for the next seven years.

Once I finally got out of those myths in 1982, I sold professionally over 200 short stories and wrote far more, and I have sold traditionally over 100 novels and written even more. I am considered one of the most prolific authors working at the moment.

During the years I was also an editor, starting as the first reader and publisher for Pulphouse Publishing in 1987, then staying a publisher as well as editing some lines for Pulphouse. I also helped my wife, Kristine Kathryn Rusch, at times as a first reader for *The Magazine of Fantasy and Science Fiction.*

In 1995 I started an almost three-year run as the fiction editor for *VB Tech Magazine.* Then in the late 1990s I also went to work for Pocket Books as the fiction editor for *Star Trek: Strange New Worlds.* I did that for ten years. Now I am one of the executive editors for Fiction River and often edit a volume myself. I was nominated five times for the Hugo Award for my editing.

And during all those years being a publisher and editor, I got to talk a lot with writers coming into the business. And all of them were dealing with one myth or another. Often a myth had them stopped cold.

In the late 1990s, Kris and I also started to teach, trying to help professional writers who were stuck to move forward in their careers. We've been doing that, as well as teaching online, since. Many, many of the writers we've helped were stuck in the myths.

So I hope this book helps you with your writing. I'll be happy to answer questions on my website at www.dean-wesleysmith.com. And I am writing more Killing the Sacred Cows chapters there, so stop by and join in the fun.

Two Important Points

I will repeat this over and over throughout this book. But I want to be clear right up front here.

1… Every writer is different.

2… And if you can't enjoy your writing, what is the point?

Now off into the myths of fiction writing. There are a lot of them.

In this book I've tried to take a pretty good shot at the top ten.

Enjoy.

—Dean Wesley Smith
January 5, 2014
Lincoln City, Oregon

Sacred Cow #1
THERE IS ONLY ONE RIGHT WAY TO DO ANYTHING IN PUBLISHING

"THAT IS THE only way to do it."

How often do writers in this business hear that phrase? Some writer or editor or agent telling the young writer to do something as if that something was set in stone. Nope.

The truth is that nothing in this business is set in stone.

Nothing.

And everything is changing so fast, what might have been true three years ago is very bad advice now.

For example, three years or so ago a wonderful new professional writer in one of the workshops here e-mailed a well-written query with ten sample pages and a synopsis of the novel off to an editor in New York from the workshop. The next morning she came out of her room smiling. Overnight, the editor had asked to see the entire book. So being am imp, I went to that publisher's website and printed off the guidelines, which said in huge letters *"No electronic submissions and absolutely no unagented submissions."*

Lucky for her she hadn't bothered to look at the guidelines, or listen to all the people who said she needed an agent, or believed there was only one way to get her book read at that company.

Now, I would have asked her why she bothered even going to a traditional publisher.

Nothing in this business is set in stone. Nothing.

Of course, that little story about not looking at guidelines will cause massive anger to come at me I'm sure.

As will my question as to why she even bothered with a traditional publisher.

So before you go tossing bricks at my house because you need a rule to follow, let me back up and try to explain what I am saying here. And what I will be saying throughout this book. Then you can toss the brick.

All Writers Are Different

Perfectly good advice for one writer will be flat wrong for the writer standing beside him.

Some writers feel for some reason that they need an agent. Some writers need the control of indie publishing, but for some other writer that control would scare them to death. Some writers know business, other writers need help figuring out how to balance a checkbook and wouldn't understand cash flow in a flood of money.

So how do writers learn? And how can those of us who have walked this publishing road help out the newer professionals coming in? Carefully is my answer. But now let me try to expand on that.

How do writers learn?

1) Take every statement by any WRITER, including me, with your bull detector turned on. If it doesn't sound right for some reason, ignore it. It may be right for the writer speaking and wrong for you. And for heaven's sake, be extra, extra careful when you listen to any writer who is not a long distance down the publishing road ahead of you. Some of the stupidest advice I have ever heard has come from writers with three or four

short story sales talking on some convention panel like they understand the publishing business and think that everything they say is a rule.

In fact, I get that all the time in e-mail. Honestly. Some beginning writer with a couple novels published is insistent that I am doing something wrong. I might be and I always keep an open mind and look at what they are saying. But most of the time it's the writer telling me in no uncertain terms I need an agent or need to publish in traditional publishing as they did. (I guess they forgot to look at my bio with over a hundred traditionally published novels behind me.)

So, when some advice doesn't feel right, check in with yourself and ask yourself where the concern is coming from. Is the concern that some advice isn't right in conflict with something you learned in school from someone who wasn't a writer? Or does the advice just not feel right for you. Check in with yourself on each thing you hear.

2) Take any statement by any EDITOR and run it through a very fine filter. Ask yourself why they are saying what they are saying, what corporate purpose does it fill, and can you use it to help you?

Remember, editors are not writers.

And they only know what they need in their one publishing house. Editors have the best of intentions to help writers. Honest, they do. But they often do not understand how writers make money, and most think that writers can't make a living, since all they see are the small advances to writers they are paying. Just nod nicely when they start into that kind of stuff and move on.

And remember, they always have a corporate agenda. It's the nature of their job and who they work for.

3) Take any statement from an AGENT with a giant saltshaker full of salt, then bury it with more salt. Then just ignore it. Agents are not writers; agents can't help you rewrite, and they only know about six or seven editors and nothing at all about the new world of indie publishing.

In this modern world, agents work for publishers, not you. If any agent is flat telling you that you must do something, and it sounds completely wrong to you, my suggestion to you is RUN! Remember, agents have an agenda. It is not your agenda. It is their agenda.

The day of agents in publishing is dropping away, finally. They are working for publishers or becoming publishers. So be careful when listening to what they are saying. There are many alternatives to needing an agent in this new world.

So how do writers learn?

—By going to lots and lots of conferences and listening to hundreds of writers and editors and taking only the information that seems right to you. This takes years. Think of it like going to college for four years. And after that the learning never stops.

—Read lots and lots of books by writers and only take what seems right for you.

—Read and follow lots of different publishing blogs, from publishersmarketplace.com to thepassivevoice.com to writer blogs like Kristine Kathryn Rusch's blog and Joe Konrath's blog. And then only take what information seems right to you.

—Learn business, basic business, and apply that to writing as well. Writing is a business, a very big business. Keep learning business and contracts and copyright as you go along.

—And keep writing and practicing and getting your work out to readers to get reader feedback.

How Can Professional Writers Help Newer Writers?

1) Professional writers, keep firmly in mind that your way, the way you broke in might be wrong for just about everyone else in the room listening to you. Especially today, when the world of publishing is shifting so fast it's hard for anyone to keep up. A story about your first sale in 1992 as a way to do it just won't be relevant in any real way to a new writer in 2014. Be clear that you understand that.

And remember, slush piles are gone. Writers are going directly to readers these days more and more. And then editors find them and make them offers.

And remember, the contracts you saw in 1990 and 2000 don't exist these days. Advances are much, much smaller and terms much, much worse. Don't give contract advice unless you see the contract and understand what the young writers are seeing. You will be stunned at what publishers are offering young writers these days.

2) Keep abreast of what the newer writers are facing. I get angry at times because newer writers keep accusing me of having some advantage. I don't, really. I have years more of practice, sure, and I have more work in inventory, and I understand business better than most, and I have a better work ethic than most writers on the planet.

But even with all that, I still have to get my work to readers in some fashion just as everyone else.

There is no secret road to selling to readers (or editors) just because you have done it before. I wish like hell there was, but alas, if it exists, I haven't found the entrance ramp yet. So to help myself, I keep abreast of what newer writers are facing, I help teach them how to get

through the starting gate and become better storytellers, so I also know how to do it with my work. Duh. I learn from newer writers as I teach them.

3) Stay informed as to the changes in publishing and don't be afraid of the new technology.

Bragging that you belong to the Church of Luddite or that you won't touch any Apple product or that you hate smartphones sure won't instill a lot of confidence in the newer writers who live with this modern publishing world and use the new technology. And wishing things would go back to the way they were just doesn't help either.

And for heaven's sake, understand sampling and indie publishing and cover design and blurb writing and apps and all the basic skills needed by writers these days.

Newer Writers Need Set Rules

Writers, especially newer writers are hungry for set rules.

This business is fluid and crazy most of the time, and the need for security screams out in most of us. So in the early years we writers search for "rules" to follow, shortcuts that will cut down the time involved, secret handshakes that will get us through doors. It is only after a lot of time that professional writers come to realize that the only rules are the ones we put on ourselves. In my early years I was no different.

Writers are people who sit alone in a room and make stuff up. The problem we have is that when we get insecure without rules, we make stuff up as well.

When we don't understand something, we make something up to explain it. Then when someone comes along with a "this is how you do it" stated like a rule, you jump to the rule like a drowning man reaching for a rope. And when someone else says "Let go of the rope to make it to safety," you get angry and won't let go of that first safety line.

In all these chapters, that's what I will be trying to tell you to do: Let go of the rope and trust your own talents and knowledge.

When I first wrote these chapters online over almost three years ago, my suggestions caused some very "interesting" letters from writers mad at me for challenging their lifeline rules.

The desire for safety and rules is one of the reasons that so many myths have grown up in this business.

Rule upon rule upon rule, all imposed from the outside. Most are just bad advice believed by the person giving the advice at the time.

The key is to let go of the rope, swim on your own, and find out what works for you.

If you believe you must rewrite, write a couple dozen stories and get them out to readers without rewrites to see what happens. If you are having no luck finding an agent, send it to editors instead. Or better yet, indie publish it.

If you think you can't write more than 500 words a day, push a few days to double or triple that and see what happens. Push and experiment and find out what is right for you.

Will it scare you? Yes. But I sure don't remember anyone telling me this profession was easy or not scary. Those two things are not myths just yet.

Okay, all that said, here are a few major areas where following rules blindly can be dangerous to writers. I will talk about these in coming chapters. But for

the moment, I want to touch on them right here because they are major.

1) "You must rewrite."

This is just silly, since writing comes out of the creative side of our brains and rewriting comes from the critical learned side.

Creative side is always a better writer. But again, this is different for every writer no matter what level. Some writers never rewrite other than to fix a few typos, others do a dozen drafts, and both sell. Those professionals have figured out what is best for them. But if a younger writer listens to someone who says you MUST rewrite everything, it could kill that writer's voice. This rule is just flat destructive. Keep your guard up on this one. Experiment on both sides and then do what works for you, what sells for you.

2) "You must have an agent."

This is such bad advice for such a large share of writers these days, it's scary.

These days there are many ways of not using or needing an agent.

—Using an intellectual copyright attorney is one way. Cheap and you don't have to pay them 15% of everything.

—Doing it yourself is fine as well.

—Indie publish it and let editors come to you.

3) "Editors don't like (blank) so you shouldn't write that way."

I can't begin to tell you how many thousand times I have answered questions like "Can I write in first person? Editor's don't like that." No rules, just write your own story with passion and then figure out a path to get it to readers.

If the readers don't like it, they simply won't buy it. No big deal. Stop worrying about what editors or agents want and write what you want. And then let readers decide.

Be an artist. Protect your work and don't let anyone in the middle of it.

Think for yourself, be yourself, write your own stuff. No rules.

4) "It's a tight market so you need to do (blank)." or "I need to figure out a way to get my fiction noticed in the noise."

You want a secret? It's always been a tight market and there has always been noise.

Right now there are more books being published every year than ever before, more markets, more ways for writers to make money. This silly "tight market" statement always sounds so full of authority coming from some young agent or editor. And it will drive a new writer into doing a dozen rewrites on a novel for someone who really doesn't know what they are talking about and couldn't write a novel themselves if forced to at gunpoint.

Again, my suggestion is stop letting others into your work and get it to readers. Let readers find it.

More WMG Business Books
from all your favorite booksellers
in trade paper and electronic editions.

Truth: Publishing and readers are always looking for good books and new writers. And it has always been tight in one way or another. And there has always been noise.

Focus on what you can control such as how much you write, the quality of your own work, and where and how you get it to the most readers.

A Brand New World

Right now publishing is going through some major changes, all rotating around distribution for the most part. Writers have been so shut out with the system in New York that they are turning more and more to taking control of various aspects of their own work with indie publishing. POD and electronic publishing is allowing authors to become both writer and publisher and electronic distribution is allowing readers to find more work from their favorite writers, often either new work, dangerous work, or work long out of print..

This new area of publishing is quickly becoming full of "rules" and future myths. For the longest time publishing your own work was looked down on by "the ruling class" (whoever they are). Now, except for a few holdouts in the basements of the Church of Luddite, writers are taking the new technologies and running with them.

Common sense: It takes a lot of practice to become a professional-level storyteller. You may think your first story or novel is brilliant because you rewrote it ten times and your workshop loved it, but alas, it might not be. In this new market, just as in the old one, the readers will judge. Let them, either through traditional channels or indie publishing.

And then write the next book and the next and keep working to become better. Keep writing and learning.

It's called "practice" which is a term most writers hate.

Now I'm Taking the Rope Away

As I said above, writers tend to have this fantastic need for rules. We all want to make some sort of order out of this huge business. And actually, there is order if you know where to look and how to look. So instead of giving you rules, let me help you find order without myths and rules.

1) Publishing is a business. A large business run by large corporations in traditional publishing or your own home business when you are indie publishing. But it is always a business. If you remember that, learn basic business, understand corporation politics and thinking, learn copyrights, most everything that happens anywhere, from bookstores to distributors to traditional publishers, will make some sort of sense. Don't take anything personally. It's just business and that is the truth.

2) All writers write differently. And that includes you. My way of producing words won't be correct for anyone but me. So instead of listening to others looking for the secret, just go home, sit down at your writing computer, and experiment with every different form and method until you find the way that produces selling fiction that readers like and buy. Find your own way to produce words that sell.

3) Learning and continuing to learn is critical. This business keeps changing and the only way to stay abreast of the changes is to go out and keep learning and talk with other writers and find advice that makes sense to you and your way. Go to workshops, conferences, conventions and anything else you can find to get bits of learning. Read everything you can find about the business and the craft of telling great stories.

My goal has always been to learn one thing new every week (at least). I've been doing that since my early days and it has worked for me, and kept me focused on learning. Find what works for you.

I know those three things don't seem to give you any secrets, don't really show you the path to selling and getting readers to really want your work. But actually, they do. And if you just keep them in mind and don't allow yourself to get caught in strange rules and myths, you will move faster toward your goal, whatever that goal in writing may be.

It's your writing. It's your art. Stop looking for the secrets and stand up for your work.

More WMG Writers' Guides
from all your favorite booksellers
in trade paper and electronic editions.

Trust your own voice, your own methods of working. Get your work to editors who will buy it. Or indie publish it and let readers buy it. Or both.

And if your methods are not producing selling work that readers love, try something new.

Keep learning. Keep practicing your art.

The only right way in this business is your way.

Sacred Cow #2
WRITING FAST IS BAD

OR SAID IN myth fashion: WRITING SLOW EQUALS WRITING WELL.

Or the flip side: WRITING FAST EQUALS WRITING POORLY.

This comes out of everyone's mouth at one point or another in a form of apology for our work. "Oh, I just cranked that off."

Or the flip side... "This is some of my best work. I've been writing it for over a year."

Now this silly idea that the writing process has anything at all to do with quality of the work has been around in publishing for just over 100 years now, pushed mostly by the literature side and the college professors.

It has no basis in any real fact when it comes to writers. None. If you don't believe me, start researching how fast some of the classics of literature were written.

But don't ask major professional writers out in public. Remember we know this myth and lie about how really hard we do work. (Yup, that's right, someone who makes stuff up for a living will lie to you. Go figure.) So you have to get a long-term professional writer in a private setting. Then maybe with a few drinks under his belt the pro will tell you the truth about any project.

In my Writing in Public posts this year, I am doing my best to knock some of this myth down and just show what a normal day in a life can produce, even with me doing a bunch of other things at the same time.

My position:

NO WRITER IS THE SAME. NO PROJECT IS THE SAME.

And put simply:

THE QUALITY OF THE FINAL PRODUCT HAS NO RELATIONSHIP TO THE SPEED, METHOD, OR FEELING OF THE WRITER WHILE WRITING.

That's right, one day I could write some pages feeling sick, almost too tired to care, where every word is a pain, and the next day I write a few more pages feeling good and the words flowing freely and a week later I won't be able to tell which day was which from the writing.

How I feel when I write makes no difference to the quality of what I produce. None. Damn it, it should, but it just doesn't.

And I just laugh when a myth like this one attempts to lump all writers into the same boat and make us all write exactly the same way book after book after book.

No writer works the same, even from book to book or short story to short story.

In fact, as you will discover watching me over this year of writing in public, I don't do any story or novel similar to any other.

Talk to any writer, and I mean privately, and you will discover that one of the writer's books was written quickly, maybe even in a few weeks, while another book took the writer a half year to finish and he was deathly ill during half the writing time. And you, as a reader,

SMITH'S Monthly

reading the two books, would never be able to tell the difference.

But yet, traditional publishing, college professors, and just about anyone who even thinks about the writer behind the words has a belief system that words must be struggled over to be good.

Well, yes, sometimes.

And sometimes not.

Sometimes a writer gets into a white-hot heat and a book flows faster than the writer can type, getting done in just a number of days or weeks. And sometimes it just doesn't work that way.

Sometimes a writer has a deadline to hit and pushes to hit it, spending more hours in the chair, thus calling it writing fast. Some writers think and research a book for a few months, then write it in a few weeks. Some writers spend a month or two on a detailed outline, then take a month to actually write the book. Some writers start with a title, some write chapters out of order and then put it all together like a puzzle.

And on and on and on.

Every writer is different. Every writer's method is different

There is no correct, mandated way to write a book. Just your way.

The Myth of Writing Slow to Write Better Actually Hurts Writers

There are two sides of our brains. The creative side and the critical side.

The creative side has been taking in stories since the writer started reading, knowing how to put words together at a deep level. The critical side lags far, far behind the creative side, learning rules that some English teacher or parent forced into the critical mind.

The creative side is always a much better writer than the critical side. Always. It never switches, no matter how long you write.

Long-term (20 years and up) professional writers have learned to trust that creative side and we tend to not mess much with what it creates for us. Of course, this lesson for most of us was learned the hard way, but that's another long chapter for another book.

A new writer who believes the myth that all good fiction must be written slowly and labor-intensive (called work) suddenly one day finds that they have written a thousand words in 35 minutes. The new writer automatically thinks, "Oh, my, that has to be crap. I had better rewrite it."

What has just happened is that the wonderful writing the creative side of the mind has just produced is then killed by the critical side, dumbed down, voice taken out, anything good and interesting removed.

All caused by this myth.

And professional editors in New York are no better, sadly. I once got a rewrite request on a major book from my editor. I agreed with about nine-tenths of the suggestions, so I spent the next day rewriting the book, fixing the problems, and was about to send the manuscript back when Kris stopped me.

The conversation went something like this:

"Don't send it, sit on it a few weeks," Kris said, looking firm and intense, as only Kris can look.

"Why not?" I asked, not remembering at that moment that the myth was a major part of traditional publishing.

"The editor will think you didn't work on it and that it is crap," Kris said.

32

"But I agreed and fixed everything," I said, starting to catch a clue, but not yet willing to admit defeat.

Kris just gave me that "stare" and I wilted, knowing she was completely correct.

I held the rewrite for three weeks, sent it back with a letter praising the rewrite comments and a slight side comment about how hard I had worked on them, even though I wrote most of another book in the period of time I was holding the rewrite. Story ended happily, editor was happy and commented on how fast I managed to get the rewrites done, all because Kris remembered the myth and how it functions.

Now, let me do something that just annoys people. I'm going to do the math.

The Math of Writing Fast

This chapter when finished is going to be around 2,000 words. That is about 8 manuscript pages with each page averaging 250 words per page.

So say I wrote only 250 words, one manuscript page per day on a new novel.

It takes me about 15 minutes, give-or-take (depending on the book and the day and how I'm feeling) to write 250 words of fiction. (Each writer is different. Time yourself.)

So if I spent that 15 minutes per day writing on a novel, every day for one year, I would finish a 90,000-plus word novel, a large paperback book, in 365 days.

I would be a one-book-per-year writer, pretty standard in science fiction and a few other genres.

15 minutes per day equals one novel per year.

Oh, my, if I worked really, really hard and managed to get 30 minutes of writing in per day, I could finish two novels in a year.

And at that speed I would be considered fast. Not that I typed or wrote fast, just that I spent more time writing.

God forbid I actually write four pages a day, spend an entire hour per day sitting in a chair! I would finish four novels a year. At that point I would be praised in the romance genre and called a hack in other genres.

See why I laugh to myself when some writer tells me they have been working really, really hard on a book and it took them a year to write? What did they do for 23 hours and 45 minutes every day?

The problem is they are lost in the myth. Deep into the myth that writing must be work, that it must be hard, that you must "suffer for your art" and write slowly.

Bull-puckey. Writing is fun, easy, and enjoyable. If you want hard work, go dig a ditch for a water pipe on a golf course in a steady rain on a cold day. That's work. Sitting at a computer and making stuff up just isn't work. It's a dream job.

Spend More Time in the Chair

Oh, oh, I just gave you the secret to being a "fast" writer or a "prolific" writer. Just spend more time writing.

I am the world's worst typist. I use four fingers, up from two, and if I can manage 250 words in fifteen minutes I'm pretty happy. I tend to average around 750-1,000 words per hour of work. Then I take a break. I am not a "fast" typist, but I am considered a "fast" writer because I spend more time writing than the myth allows.

That's the second thing that makes this myth so damaging to writers. It doesn't allow writers to just spend more time practicing their art. In fact, the myth tells writers that if they do spend more time working to get better, they are worse because they produce more fiction.

Writing is the only art where spending less time practicing is considered a good thing.

In music we admire musicians who practice ten or more hours a day. Painters and other forms of artists are the same. Only in writing does the myth of not practicing to get better come roaring in.

We teach new writers to slow down, to not work to get better, to spend fewer and fewer hours at writing, to not practice, and then wonder why so many writers don't make it to a professional level.

Writing Slow Equals Writing Better is a complete myth, a nasty sacred cow of publishing that hurts and stops writers who believe it.

—The truth is that no two writers work the same and no book is the same as the previous book or the next book.

—The truth is that writing fast is nothing more than spending more time every day writing.

—The truth is that there should be no rule about speed relating to quality.

—The truth is there should be no rule that lumps all writers into one big class. There should only be your way of writing.

We No Longer Have to Wait for Traditional Publishers

For the last few decades, unless a writer wrote under many pen names, we were forced by the market to write fewer books per year. But now, with indie publishing, we can once again write as much as we want.

And we can write anything we want.

We can sell some books to traditional publishers, we can indie publish other books and stories. Or as I am doing, we can create our own market and indie publish almost everything.

The new world has lifted the market restrictions on speed of writing. Now those of us who actually want to sit and write for more than 15 minutes per day can publish what we write in one way or another.

And being fast, meaning spending more time writing, is a huge plus with indie publishing. We are in a new golden age of fiction, especially short fiction, and just as in the first golden age, writing fast (meaning spending more time at your art) will be a good thing also for your pocketbook.

Be Careful!

Sadly, this myth is firm in the business, so writers who spend more time in the chair and who write more hours have to learn to work around the myth. We must learn to play the game that teachers, editors, book reviewers, and fans want us to play.

And if you decide you can spend more hours every day writing and working on your art, be prepared to face those who want you to write the way they do. Be prepared to face those who want to control your work. Be prepared to face criticism from failed writers (reviewers) who can't even manage a page a day, let alone more.

This speed myth is the worst myth of an entire book full of myths. Caution.

The best thing you can do is just keep your speed and your writing methods to yourself. Don't write in public as I am doing. You're an artist. Respect your way of doing things and just don't mention them to anyone.

Also, I beg of you that if you believe in the myth, please don't do the math about my age. I sold my first novel when I was 38 and have published over 100 novels. At one book per year, I must be at least 138 years old.

After my hard, single-page-of-writing every day, I sometimes feel that way.

Yeah, right.

But I stand by that story except when I am writing in public on my blog. (grin)

Sacred Cow #3
YOU MUST REWRITE TO MAKE SOMETHING GOOD

THAT'S ONE OF the great myths of publishing. And one of the worst and most destructive to fiction writers.

First off, I want to repeat clearly what I said in the previous two chapters in different ways:

No writer is the same.

Let me repeat that with a few more words.

No writer works or thinks the same way, and there is no right way to work. Just your way.

That includes speed of writing, style of writing, and most importantly, how you handle rewrites of what you have written.

So, to make sure we are all speaking the same language, let me define a few terms that Kristine Kathryn Rusch and I have used for a long time now, and I will try to use in this discussion.

REDRAFT: That's when you take the typing you have done and toss it away, then write the story again from your memory of the idea. When you are redrafting, you are working from the creative side of your brain.

REWRITE: That's when you go into a manuscript after it is finished in critical voice and start changing things, usually major things like plot points, character actions, style of sentences, and so on. When you rewrite like this, you are working from the critical side of your mind,

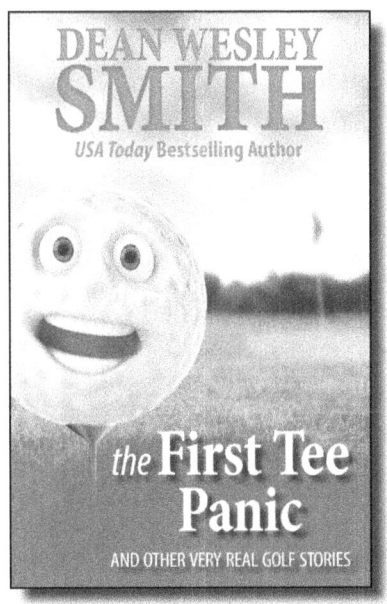

This often comes from fear or from workshop advice.

TOUCH-UP DRAFT: When you run through a manuscript fixing small things, things you wrote in notes while writing, things your trusted first reader found. Often very small things or typos. This draft takes almost no time, often less than half a day for a full novel, sometimes only an hour or so.

SPELL-CHECKING DRAFT: Since so many of us work with our grammar-checkers and spell-checkers off, we need a spell-check draft, often done before the manuscript is given to a first reader. This often takes an hour or so for a full novel.

Now, let me say right up front here that I am a three-draft writer. Most long-term pros that I have talked to in private are "three-draft" writers. Not all, since we all work differently, but a vast majority of the ones I have talked to use a process very near mine.

My process:

First draft I do as quickly as I can, staying solidly as much as possible in my creative side, adding in things I think about as I go along, until I get to the end of the draft. Again, I try to write as fast as the project will allow since I have discovered a long time ago that if I just keep typing, the less chance I have to get in my own way and screw things up.

Second draft I spellcheck and then give to my trusted first reader.

Third draft I touch up all the things my first reader has found and then I mail the novel or story.

If my first reader hates the story, I toss the draft away and redraft completely.

That's my process. I am a three-draft writer. (Unless I need to redraft, then I am a six-draft writer.)

More Basic Information About Writers

There is a way of describing and dividing writers into two major camps. Taker-outers and putter-inners.

In other words, a taker-outer is a writer who over-writes the first time through, then goes back and takes things out.

As a putter-inner, I write thin (my poetry background still not leaving me alone) and then as I go along, I cycle back

---

More WMG Writer's Guides
from all your favorite booksellers
in trade paper and electronic editions.

and add in more and then cycle again and add in more, staying in creative voice, just floating around in the manuscript as I go along. Some people of this type make notes as they go along and then go back in a touch-up draft and put stuff in.

Okay, so terms done, on to the major topic.

So, What's the Great Myth About Rewriting?

First, our colleges and our training and New York editors and agents all think that rewriting can make something better.

Most of the time that is just wrong.

Flat wrong when it comes to fiction. It might be right with poetry, or non-fiction or essays, but with fiction, it can hurt you if you believe this completely and let it govern your process.

Secondly, it makes writers think there is only one "right" way of writing.

And that if you don't fit into that way and rewrite everything, you are doing something wrong. That kind of thinking kills more good writers' careers than I can imagine, and I can imagine a great deal. And I have watched firsthand it kill more writer's dreams than I want to remember.

All writers are different, so sometimes a writer works with a ton of rewrites. Sometimes a writer just does one draft.

A Wonderful Conversation With a Master

One fine evening I was having a conversation with Algis Budrys about rewriting and why so many new writers believed the myth. He shrugged and said, "They don't know any better and no one has the courage to tell them." So I asked him if he ever thought rewriting could fix a flawed story. His answer was clear and I remember it word-for-word to this day: *"No matter how many times you stir up a steaming pile of crap, it's still just a steaming pile of crap."*

If you ever worry about not "fixing" a story because you didn't rewrite it, just put that quote on your wall.

So, as an example, let's take some new writer hoping to write a book that will sell at some point. This new writer does the near-impossible for most new writers and actually finishes the book. That's a huge success, but instead of just sending the book off and starting on a second book, this poor new writer has bought into the myth that everything MUST be rewritten before it can be good. (It makes the new writer feel like a "real writer" if they rewrite because all "real writers" rewrite.)

All beginning fiction writers believe this myth, and you hear it in comments about their novel like "Oh, it's not very good yet. Oh, it needs to be polished. Oh, it was JUST a first draft and can't be any good."

I even hear that come out of some newer professional writer's mouths. I never hear it from long-term pros (over 20 plus years making a living).

Of course, for the beginning writer, the first book just isn't very good most of the time. Duh, it's a first novel. It might be great, but it also might be crap. (Let me refer you back to Algis Budrys' comment.) More than likely the first book is flawed beyond rescue, but the writer won't know that, and the first reader won't be able to help "fix" anything besides typos and grammar.

So, what is the new writer to do at this point with a finished novel?

Simple. Mail it to editors or indie publish it yourself.

That's right, I said, "Mail it or publish it."

Awkkk! Has Dean lost it?

I can just hear the voices in your heads screaming now...

"But, it's no good! It needs a rewrite! It might be a steaming pile of crap. I can't mail something that's flawed to an editor!"

Or you indie published writers are thinking...

"I can't publish a book that's flawed or readers will hate me!"

And thus the myth has a stranglehold on you.

The great thing about editors is that we can't remember bad stories. We just reject them and move on.

Most of us, over the years and decades, have bought so much, we have a hard time remembering everything and everyone we bought. So you have nothing to lose by mailing it and everything to gain, just in case it happens to be good enough to sell.

And if it isn't, WE WON'T REMEMBER. Why? Because we didn't read it. Duh.

And readers of indie published books have a wonderful thing called "sampling." And taste. If the book sucks, oh, trust me, no reader but your family will buy it. And at that point you don't have a "career" to kill anyway. (Future chapter on that myth.)

Just because the book is bad doesn't mean someone will come to your house and arrest you if you mail it or publish it. Editors do not talk about manuscripts that don't work and readers never buy or read them.

Honestly, no one can shoot you for publishing it.

So get past the fear and just mail it. Or publish it. You have nothing to lose and everything to gain. (What happens if it is wonderful and will make you a million?)

One true thing about writing that is a firm rule: There is no perfect book. (No matter what some reviewer wants to think.)

(Also, there is a very true saying about writers that I will deal with in another chapter. Writers are the worst judges of their own work. Why is that? Because, simply, we wrote it and we know what was supposed to be on the page. It might not be, but we think it is. We just can't tell. A future myth chapter.)

If You Don't Rewrite, How Can You Learn?

You have to write new material to learn. No one ever learned how to be a creative writer by rewriting. Only by writing.

More WMG Business Books
from all your favorite booksellers in trade paper and electronic editions.

So, after the story or book is in the mail or published, start writing the next story or book, go to workshops and writers' conferences to learn storytelling skills, learn business, and meet people.

Study how other writers do things.

But keep writing that second story or book.

And then repeat.

Trust me, the second one will be a lot better than the first one, especially if you just trust yourself and write it and don't fall into the myth of rewriting.

When the second one is done, go celebrate again, then fix the typos and such and mail it to an editor who might buy it or publish it yourself, and then start writing again.

A writer is a person who writes.

Rewriting Is Not Writing

Yeah, I know what your English Professor tried to tell you. But if your English Professor could make a living writing fiction, they would have been doing it.

Putting new and original words on a page is writing. Nothing more, and nothing less.

—Research is not writing.

—Rewriting is not writing.

—Talking to other writers is not writing.

And what you will discover that is amazing is that the more you write, the better your skills become. With each story, each novel, you are telling better and better stories.

It's called "practice" (but again, no writer likes to think about that evil word).

Well, if you want to be a professional fiction writer, it's time to bring the word "practice" into your speaking. On your next novel, make it a practice session for cliffhangers. Mail the novel and then work on practicing something different on the next story or novel. And so on.

Follow Heinlein's Business Rules

I believe that a writer is a person who writes. An author is a person who has written.

I want to always be a writer, so I have, since 1982, followed Robert Heinlein's business rules. And those rules have worked for many, many of us for decades and decades.

His rules go simply:

1) You must write.

2) You must finish what you write.

3) You must not rewrite unless to editorial demand.

4) You must mail your work to someone who can buy it.

5) You must keep the work in the mail until someone buys it.

Those rules do seem so simple, and yet are so hard to follow at times. They set out a simple practice schedule and a clear process of what to do with your practice sessions when finished. But for this chapter, note rule #3. Harlan Ellison added to rule #3. "You must not rewrite unless to editorial demand." *Harlan addition: And then only if you agree.*

And, of course, if you indie publish, substitute "publish" in #4 for "mail" and let reader's buy it. And then for #5 just keep it for sale.

Speaking of Harlan, many of you know that over the decades he has tried to prove this point (and many others) to people. He would go into a bookstore, have someone give him a title or idea, then on a *manual* typewriter, he would sit in the bookstore window and write a short story, taping the finished pages on the window for everyone to read.

He never rewrote any of those stories. He fixed a typo or two, but that's it. And many of those stories won major awards in both science fiction and mystery and many are now in college text books being studied by professors who tell their students they must rewrite. But Harlan wrote all first draft, written fast, sometimes in a window while people watched him type every word.

I know, I was going to publish a three-volume set of these award-winning stories written in public back when I was doing Pulphouse Publishing. But alas, he was still writing them, a new one almost every other week at that point, and the book never got out before we shut down. He's done enough since then to fill two more books at least.

Every writer is different.

If you want more on Heinlein's Rules, I did an almost two hour lecture (15 videos) on how and why Heinlein's Rules work and how they worked for me over the decades. It's under the lecture series tab if interested.

So, How Come Rewriting Makes Stories Worse Instead of Better?

Back to understanding how the brain works.

The creative side, the deep part of our brain, has been taking in story, story structure, sentence structure, character voice, and everything else for a very long time, since each of us read our first book or had a book read to us. It's that place where our author voice comes from, where the really unique ideas come from.

The critical side of the brain is full of all the crap you learned in high school, everything your college teachers said, what your workshop said, and the myths you have bought into like a fish biting on a yummy worm. Your critical voice is also full of the fear that comes out in "I can't show this to friends." Or, "What would my mother think?" That is all critical side thinking that makes you take a great story and dumb it down.

In pure storytelling skill level, the critical side is far, far behind the creative side of your brain. And always will be.

So, on a scale of one-to-ten, with ten being the top, the creative skills of a new writer with very few stories under his belt, if left alone, will produce a story at about a six or seven. However, at that point the writer's critical skills are lagging far behind, so if written critically, a new writer would create a story about four on the scale. So take a well-written story that first draft was a seven on the scale, then let a new writer rewrite it and down the level comes to five or so.

I can't tell you how many times I have seen a great story ruined by a number of things associated with this myth.

For example, take a great story, run it through a workshop, then try to rewrite it to group think. Yow, does it become dull, just as anything done by committee is dull. (Workshop myth coming in a future chapter.)

I helped start and run a beginners workshop when I was first starting out. None of us had a clue, but we were all learning fast. I would write a story a week (all I could manage with three jobs at the time) and mail it, then turn it into my workshop for audience reaction.

That's right, I mailed it before I gave it to my workshop. Why? Because I had no intention of ever rewriting it. I followed Heinlein's Rules.

And I sold a few stories that the workshop said failed completely, which taught me a lot, actually. If I had listened to them, I never would have made some of those early sales.

If you would like to see a first draft of one of my early stories, pick up Volume #1 of *Writers of the Future*. I was in the middle of moving from Portland to the Oregon Coast, actually packing the truck, when my then-wife, Denie, asked me if I had the story done for *Writers of the Future* that Algis Budrys had told me was starting up. I said no, the mailing deadline was the next day and I didn't have time.

Thankfully, Denie insisted I go finish it while she packed. I didn't tell her that I hadn't even started it yet and had no idea what to write.

I put the typewriter (electric) on a partially dismantled desk on top of a large box, sat on the edge of the bed, and wrote the story from start to finish having no idea what I was writing or where the story was going. Three hours later I finished the story called "One Last Dance" and mailed it on a dinner break.

That's right, it was a first draft on a typewriter. No spell-checker, no first reader, nothing.

Algis Budrys and Jack Williamson loved it and put it into the first volume, and because of that story, I ended up meeting Kris a couple of years later after Denie and I had gone our own ways. I also got lots of wonderful trips and money and a great workshop from that three-hour draft. And now, twenty-nine years later the story is still in print and I'm still proud of it.

All because I had the courage to write and mail first draft. Because I followed Heinlein's Rules.

I trusted my creative skills, I trusted my voice, and I was lucky enough to have someone who gave me support at that point in the writing.

Another Example: Every year for years, editor Denise Little and I would prove that same point again to early career writers. We forced them to write a short story overnight to an anthology idea and deadline, and those quickly-written stories were always better than the ones the same writers wrote over weeks before the workshop. And many of those stories, first drafts, have been in published anthologies out of New York.

The problem was that even though Denise and I harped on that lesson for years, most of those writers would then just go home and right back to rewriting, making their stories worse. That's how powerful this myth is.

The creative side is just a better writer than the critical side, no matter what the critical side tries to tell you.

Remember, the critical side has a voice of restraint and worry. But the creative side, as Kris likes to say, is your two-year-old child. It has no voice of reason and no way to fight. But if you let the child just play and get out of its way and stop trying to put your mother's or father's or teacher's voice on everything it does, you will be amazed at what you create.

One More Point

Every writer is different, granted, but I have only met a few writers who really, really love to rewrite. Most find it horrid and a ton of work, but we all, with almost no exception, love to write original stuff.

If you can get past the myth of rewriting, writing becomes a lot more fun.

Following Heinlein's Rules is a ton of fun, actually. And you end up writing and selling a lot of stuff as well.

However, this myth is so deep, I imagine many of you are angry at me at this moment, and trust me, even if you get past this myth in private, out in public you will need to lie.

That's right, I just told a bunch of fiction writers to lie. Go figure.

Maybe you don't need to go as far as Hemingway and tell people that you must write standing up because writing comes from the groin or some such nonsense. (He loved screwing with new writers minds.) But you do need to hide your process.

I know one writer who at writers' conferences tells people with a straight face he does upwards of ten drafts. I knew better and one day, in private, I asked him why he said that.

He just shrugged. "I like making my audience happy, so I tell them what they want to believe about me. It makes them believe my books and stories are worth more if I tell them I rewrote them ten times."

In other words, even though the reality of professional fiction writing is often few drafts, readers still believe we must rewrite because they went to the same English classes we did. Duh.

So, out in public, you will hear me say simply that I am a three-draft writer. It's the truth. I write a first draft, I spell-check the manuscript as a second draft, and I fix the typos and small details my first reader finds as a third draft.

And after 100 plus novel sales and hundreds of short story sales, it seems to be working just fine.

For me, anyway.

Every Writer Is Different

If you are rewriting and not selling, try to stop rewriting for a year and just mail or publish your work. You might be stunned at what happens.

Just remember, the writing process has nothing to do with the finished work.

Never tell anyone you "cranked that off" or that it's a "first draft." Let them

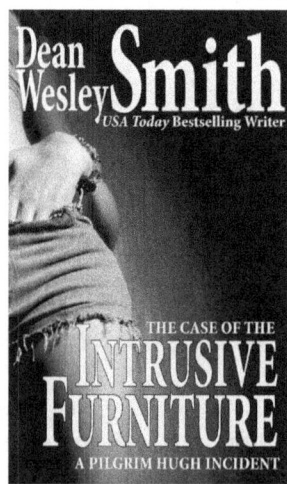

Three Pilgrim Hugh Incidents
Available at your favorite booksellers.

believe you worked like a ditch digger on the story, rewrote it 50 times, workshopped it a dozen times, and struggled over every word for seven years. Won't hurt your readers.

But getting rid of this myth for yourself sure might help your writing.

And make writing a ton more fun as well.

Sacred Cow #4
YOU MUST HAVE AN AGENT TO SELL A BOOK

IN THE WORLD that now has indie publishing as a viable path, that myth is just flat silly. But alas, the myth is very real and a foundation belief for a lot of writers who only want to go to traditional publishing.

To be clear, I like agents as people (for the most part) and have no desire to bring them harm. Most of them are decent people who love books. But there are a few out there who think nothing of taking a writer's money. However, most do try their best in a very tough new world.

The problem is that their place in the profession is going away quickly. I used to call agents the "wart on the butt of publishing" since they have no real job in the process of writing and publishing a book. But now that "wart" is about to come off completely.

But even with the place of agents in publishing fading fast, in the last 20 years the biggest myth that has blown up into a damaging myth is that you need an agent to sell a book. And the myth is holding on and killing many great dreams of writers.

Needing an agent to sell a book in 2013 is, of course, complete hogwash. But I have no doubt some of you reading this are already resisting this idea. You want someone to do the dirty work for you, to do the research, to just "take care of you" so you can just write. Yeah, that's going to happen. And in a way it will. They will "take care" of what little money you have and then kick you to the curb.

And even worse, the false myth that you need an agent to sell a book overseas or into translation or into movies has gotten worse since indie publishing started up, trapping many, many writers into thinking they needed to give a part of their work away to some scam agent. That part of this myth is also total hogwash.

All overseas contracts are in the language of the author and very, very simple and direct. Agents are the ones to make them complex and take a part of your money, if not all the money.

And for Hollywood, you need a Hollywood attorney if someone comes calling and is serious. The old joke used to be that the actress was so dumb, she slept with the writer. The joke is now that the actress was so dumb, she slept with the agent. Literary agents in Hollywood are long gone from a value position and lawyers have mostly taken their place, just as is slowly happening in book publishing.

Warning: The biggest place for scams with all agents and agencies is in overseas money. Most authors, even big names, never check money owed them with the overseas publisher as to how much they are supposed to be getting.

So to explain this "Agents Must Sell Books" myth clearly, I need to back up just a touch and run through some history to get to why this myth even exists and then move on into how to fight it.

Basic History

Book agents came over from theater and movies from 1900-1950. They were used by fiction writers to help with the contracts, to get the books into movie and early television (in New York) and overseas, and to go get the coffee. They were simply a lower-level employee used by writers to do some of the busy work.

It never occurred to most fiction writers to have an agent sell a book for them except in very unusual circumstances. Writers worked directly with the editors, and the idea that anyone needed to be in the middle of that was just thought of as silly.

But then, as the industry got bigger through the baby-boom years, fewer writers lived near New York and thus mailing manuscripts to editors started to become the norm. Editors and writers still worked together, and the agent did the deal, negotiating the contract, helping with contracts overseas and in Hollywood. But up until the early 1990s, book deals between editors and writers were often done across a dinner table with a handshake, with the agent left to handle the calls with the contract department later.

In fact, about twenty of my early novel deals were done over dinner up into the mid 1990s. I basically sold my first novel sitting in a bar, talking with an editor friend while waiting for a meeting with a person who would be my agent for the next seventeen years.

In those days editors had power to make deals as well. That is long gone now.

Also in those days, in the big New York publishers, there were rooms and rooms full of what is called "slush."

Now the term "slush pile" came from the early days of publishing. An editor usually sat at his desk and writers brought him work. But when the editor was gone and the office door closed, the writer still wanted to leave the manuscript, so they tossed it through the small window over the door. The top of the door is called a transom, so thus the term "over the transom" came into being.

When the editor returned to the office and pushed open the door, the manuscripts on the floor would be pushed into a pile which looked a lot like a pile of dirty New York snow. Thus the term "slush pile" came about.

In the early 1980s, publishers tried to slow down the growing wave of manuscripts coming at them by putting requirements on guidelines that no manuscript be sent unless it was solicited. A simple thing to ignore, and it stopped only the really stupid new writers.

Huge rooms of book manuscripts filled New York buildings and many, many assistant editors were hired to dig through the slush to find the gems among all the trash. And many, many major writers you read today came out of those slush piles.

Then in the 1990s, lots of things happened in publishing, not the least of which was a complete distribution system collapse. Publishers had to cut back, larger presses ate smaller ones, and at the same time New York real estate prices went up and up and up. Publishers could no longer afford the huge rooms full of slush, or the assistant editors to wade through it all.

At this point in time, agents were doing more and more for writers, and the top writers had very powerful agents, simply because the agents worked for the top writers. (Agents always used to get their power from their clients. They have no power on their own.)

Also, writers became more of an unknown to publishers, a vast sea of people with a computer and a stamp who thought they could write and should be rich even though they had never spent any time practicing their craft or even learning how to spell. Very few of these new writers ever thought of going to a writers' conference and actually meeting an editor, so editors became somewhat fearful of the nutballs out there.

And trust me, that fear was founded in reality. You ain't lived as an editor until you've had the FBI come and interview you about a writer making threats through the mail. Death threats because of rejections were fairly common, folks. I personally got three or four over the years.

Something had to be done to stop this massive wave coming at the money-worried publishers and overworked editors. So someone, somewhere, came up with the idea "Let the agents handle it."

So onto the guidelines of every publisher went the simple line. "No unagented manuscripts accepted." Even though most editors were still buying from writers without agents, or manuscripts from writers where the agent had not sent it in.

But every new writer believed that guideline, for some reason, without thought or reason or understanding of how publishing worked. Even editors at the time were surprised how well that one simple line worked to turn away the uninformed.

Thus, for the last fifteen years or more, agents have been getting buried with the vast amount of slush. Older agents went into hiding, knowing their job wasn't to read slush, and new scam agents popped up everywhere, taking advantage of this new guideline from publishers by milking the writer of their money and crushing their dreams.

It makes me very, very sad to think of the number of incredible books we have all missed because of this stupid one-sentence guideline.

Who Fights for the Writer?

Let's step back for a second and look at the relationship of agent/editor/writer/publisher in 2013.

First: A writer sells a publisher a manuscript and there is a contract between the publisher and writer. In simple business terms, the writer produces a product and goes into a partnership with a publisher to produce and distribute the product.

(In indie publishing, you are your own publisher, which makes it very simple.)

Second: The editor works for the publisher. Paid by the publisher, represents the publisher's needs.

Third: The agent used to work for the writer and fight for and represent the writer's needs. That's the belief, but sadly, it is no longer the truth.

Now, even though an agent gets paid by taking a percentage of the writer's work, the agents actually work for the publishers. Remember, the agents were the ones that accepted the outsourcing of the slush pile by the publishers. The agents can always find new writers these days. The agents can't find new publishers with (in their belief system) only the big five left.

This new relationship with publishers allows young agents to think they are the boss over writers. Of course, no long-term writer think this, and no respected, longer-term agent thinks it either (but there are only a few of those left anymore). Beginning writers and early professionals fall into this trap, and even go so far as to rewrite a book on demand of their agent.

If you are rewriting a book for an agent, just stop. For heaven's sake, indie publish the draft you mailed them first and get on with your life.

Agents can't buy books.

And keep this in mind very, very clearly if you are rewriting for an agent. If the agent could write, they would be, instead of taking 15% of what a writer makes for writing. Yet beginning writers and young professionals who don't understand how the business really works fall into this ugly rewriting trap all the time. This has gotten so bad, I try to not even listen when some poor sucker of a writer is telling me happily that they "got" an agent and are rewriting their book. Just turns my stomach.

So in this new world.

—Traditional publishers believe that writers are a dime-a-dozen and the publishers don't even want to bother with the writer's manuscripts.

—Editors work for the big corporation, thinking only bottom line.

—Agents work for the publishing houses, vetting slush and trying to keep their five editor-friends happy.

The writer is outnumbered and alone. Three parts of the old process now work for the big corporation. No one (but an attorney, if the writer is smart enough to hire one) is on the writer's side.

But we have a new secret weapon: We don't need any of them anymore.

And honestly, that's driving them nuts.

Who Can Be an Agent?

Can you have a business card printed up for you? Then you can be an agent. Actually, skip that, you don't even need a business card.

Can't Get Enough of Poker Boy?
These stories and more are
available at your favorite booksellers.

Anyone can be an agent. Anywhere.

There are no rules, no regulations, no training. The old joke is "What does it take to become a book agent? Stationery."

Yet new writers put their entire business, their entire dreams, their entire hopes for a future on someone who only needed stationery to get started.

See how silly this all is? And sad.

And what is even more scary is that writers give these total strangers all the money from their work and the paperwork that goes with that work. And then wonder why they get ripped off.

Here is how it really works when put in real world terms.

You go to a hotel and meet a total stranger. They agree to take months of your work and sell it, then you trust this total stranger after they have sold your work with getting you all the money from your work and all the paperwork for that money. You don't know the person.

And only in publishing do otherwise sane and smart business people think this sort of thing makes sense.

Literary agents are not regulated at all. (We all have watched in the financial world and how well unregulated people do with money.) Yet new writers, without research, hire an agent and give them control over all their income.

If you don't think the Madoff types also live in the agent world, you are sadly kidding yourself. And they make a fortune, mostly off of big name writers who can't be bothered to keep track of their own money. Not kidding.

"My Agent Is Good" Myth

Every professional writer I know who has an agent (and has yet to discover the agent is taking their money or stopping deals or not sending in books) thinks their agent is the exception. It's the "I believe you, Dean, but it doesn't apply to my agent" syndrome.

The "My Agent is Good" myth is deeper than any of these myths combined. Only when a writer gets

Can't Get Enough of Poker Boy?
These stories and more are available at your favorite booksellers.

screwed or their money taken or they are dumped by their "perfect agent" for asking for something to be done, does the writer finally step back and understand. Sometimes. But sometimes the writer just runs to another agent and starts again. The myth is that deep.

If you think your agent works for anyone but themselves and the publishers in 2014, you are really, really deluding yourself.

But, of course, your agent is the exception... right?

And keep this question firmly in mind...

How does my agent pay to live in New York, have an office, have employees, on 15% of book advances that have declined by factors of ten over the last few years?

Answer: They can't and won't for long.

So when it comes down to paying their mortgage and buying food vs. sending you the money a publisher sent to them on your latest royalty (remember they have all the paperwork), they will pay their own mortgage and buy the food with your money. They will think you won't notice it being late for a month or so. And then when you don't notice at all that you didn't get that royalty statement from Germany (or your US publisher because you are writing and can't be bothered,) they just "forget" to get around to sending the money to you.

So unless you are talking with every one of your publishers, and know exactly when every penny is coming to you and how much, your "Perfect" agent will stay in business on your back. Sorry. Just reality.

And big agencies are the worst at this, folks. Far worse, because they have

accounting departments and the agents in big agencies usually get a base salary.

You get your money stolen, you have no one to blame but yourself. You gave a perfect stranger all the control of your work, your money, and the paperwork with that money. You deserve what you get or don't get, I'm afraid.

Solution?

We live in a wonderful new publishing world where agents are just flat useless.

Their place in the industry is fading away and they know it, which is why so many of them have set up publishing arms to "help" their clients out of even more of their rights and money. That's right, every major agency now has a "publishing arm" to scam their clients by taking 15% for work the writer could easily do themselves and faster and better.

So back to the point of this myth. How do you sell a book to a traditional publishing house without an agent?

Two ways here in 2014, and not one of them involve an agent.

First, indie publish your book and then keep writing. Sure, there is a slight learning curve of covers and blurbs and such, but if your books get traction, traditional publishers will come calling and you will be able to actually negotiate a contract with some clout because they want your book. And you will know what your book is worth.

This happens every day now.

But a warning. If your book is making $3,000 per month for you in indie publishing, you might not want to sell it or any book for a $10,000 advance for the life of the contract. (grin)

Second method, mail the book directly to an editor. This has sort of come around to where it was when I started off. You must meet editors and be a nice business person and talk with them directly.

You need to go out and meet some editors at writers' conferences and conventions. So while all your idiot friends are crowding around the agents, make an appointment with an editor and pitch your book. Know ahead of time what the editor publishes and be nice. Let me stress the be nice and professional part.

If the editor gives you a card and asks you to send the book, you are in the editor's door and on their desk without an agent. You have become one of their writers.

Oh, wait, one more way...

Third: DO BOTH AT THE SAME TIME. Why wait around with your book when indie publishing won't hurt it in anyone's eyes in New York?

Just a thought.

One final point on this:

New writers today are *still* flooding agents with manuscripts and great books and writers are being lost in this ugliness. This myth will only go away over time, more than likely the next twenty years or so, as writers take back control and start realizing there are more ways to get into traditional publishing than by giving away part of their work.

I've sold over a hundred novels to traditional publishers and I sure can't see myself going back until traditional publishers stop some of their contractual practices, but that's another article. But if I did go back, I sure wouldn't use an agent.

Traditional publishing is in a period of major transition. It will survive, but not in a form we would recognize now, or with many of the names that are now in business.

Agents will not survive. At least the non-scam ones.

Sacred Cow #5
BOOKS ARE EVENTS

(Or put as clearly as I can...)

ALL BOOKS NEED TO BE EVENTS, NEED TO BE SOMETHING SPECIAL

HOGWASH, OF COURSE. All books must be written as well as the author can write the book, but just because the author spent blood and sweat on the book, or the author wrote it in twenty days, doesn't make the book either special or not special. And it certainly doesn't make it an event.

Hard and fast rule about writing:

THE PROCESS AND EXPERIENCE OF THE AUTHOR IN THE WRITING OF THE BOOK HAS NOTHING AT ALL TO DO WITH THE FINAL QUALITY OF THE BOOK.

If you put that on your wall, you will always have a defense against many of the things I'm going to talk about in this chapter.

When is a book an actual event? Let me answer that question before I move on to other areas of this topic, the deadly areas and the areas that are hurting many writers and indie publishers.

1) A book is an actual event when an author finishes his or her first novel.

Now, that's something special and should be celebrated with friends and family with a good dinner, maybe cards, flowers, something special like a cake. Finishing a first novel puts the writer in a very small minority of writers. Most writers talk about writing, but never find the time to write, let alone to do what it takes to write an entire novel, working for weeks or months to do it. Finishing a first novel is a small event. Celebrate, then put the novel in the mail and get started on the next one.

Kevin J. Anderson sent me a great card after I finished my first novel. On the face of the card are four pictures of a very small mouse pushing a huge elephant up a steep hill. When you open the card, it shows the mouse, sweating, with the elephant at the top of the hill, and at the base of the hill is a herd of elephants just waiting. The caption says, "Great work! Now, do it again."

Spot on the money.

2) Publishing a first novel is an actual event. In the old world of traditional publishing it most likely wasn't your first novel written, but it will always be considered your first novel from that publication forward. My first novel is *Laying the Music to Rest,* which was the third book I wrote. That first publication should be celebrated, and I remember I did. It is very special, and that specialness needs to be acknowledged by both the author and everyone around them. That is an actual event. Enjoy it!

So Why Is Making a Book an Event So Bad?

About a hundred different reasons, so let me start slowly into the thinking that kills author after author on this myth. And frighteningly enough, this is the myth that I fight the most. This myth has cost me years of my writing career.

Years. And I am not kidding.

And I am watching it kill indie writer after indie writer already in this new world.

In the Beginning...

None of us start out as novelists. No one. Sorry, doesn't happen.

We all learn to write in school, from teachers, from hundreds of people along the way. And often writers start by writing poems, short stories, things like that, even when starting into fiction decades after they learned to write their first sentence. Novels are those big, complex things in a beginning writer's mind that need to have a ton of time spent on them to do correctly. (See the myth about writing fast.)

And all believe we must write the book from word one to the last word because that's how readers read them. And that must take time and effort and be really hard because it seems complex. And almost magical.

Why do we all have this belief? Because before starting to write novels, we all read novels, and they seemed complex, they seemed long, they seemed just flat hard to do. We built them up to be something really special before we even wrote word one of a novel.

So here comes something like the November novel challenge that happens every year. Thousands and thousands of people manage to write at least 50,000 words in a month or less. Many of them found it easy, many of them had a blast doing it. But alas, to most of them the book they produced can't be any good because it was fun to do, it was easy to do, and gasp, it was written quickly.

The thinking is that novels have to be hard and complex and thus because it was fun and easy and quick, it can't be good. In other words... A novel must be an EVENT in the writing process.

Total hogwash, of course. Back to the only solid rule in writing.

THE PROCESS AND EXPERIENCE OF THE AUTHOR IN THE WRITING OF THE BOOK HAS NOTHING AT ALL TO DO WITH THE FINAL QUALITY OF THE BOOK.

Book as Event thinking puts thousands and thousands of great books into drawers every December 1st because the author had too much fun writing it.

Not kidding.

Writers don't mail books or indie publish the book because they enjoyed writing it.

This myth is that stupid. And that deadly.

It Must Be Perfect.

Book as Event really hits right here, kicking in the myth that everything must be rewritten to death before it can be good. A book must be worked over and over and over to make it "perfect." Hogwash, simple hogwash.

So how do you write a novel? Simply do the best you can every day during the writing, finish the book, fix the mistakes a trusted first reader finds, and mail the thing or publish the thing and start the next book.

There is no such thing as a perfect book and the more you work to make a book perfect, the more you turn it into a polished stone with no character or voice. Leave your book rough, leave your voice alone, mail the book to an editor or indie publish the book and do another.

Repeat after me....There is no perfect book.

Never has been, never will be. *And you certainly won't write the first one.* Sorry.

Senator Ted Kennedy had a great quote that my wife has on her wall in her office. "Never let perfect be the enemy of the good."

But...but...but...

Yeah, I can hear you all starting into that thinking. So let me start with a few of the doubts I can hear creeping into this.

Doubt #1. "If I don't write a perfect book, it will be rejected in this tough market. Or readers won't buy it even if I discount it to 99 cents."

Wrong. Books are bought for story. Sure, keep the spelling mistakes and typing mistakes down to a minimum by having some trusted first readers and a good proofreader, but your story won't be rejected for a few bad sentences if the story is kick-ass. Novels are simply stories, nothing more. Write a good story, get it out for readers to find, write another.

Doubt #2 "But I want my story to be perfect, my characters big, my plot flawless."

To do that, you have to trust your subconscious, and *that part of your brain only functions in fast, first-draft mode.*

You come at your book from critical brain, and you'll end up writing like your first-grade teacher, without voice or anything original left in the book.

There are many more doubts, many more. I know, I've had them, and fell for some of them along the way. But for the moment, back to the bigger topic.

This Is Too Hard.

If you feel that way in a book, you are trapped in a myth somewhere, more than likely Book as Event.

When did writing a story become hard? It's not, no matter what authors want to tell you at conventions and writers' conferences and on their blogs. And I have done a chapter on this as well coming up.

The truth: Writing a story is fun.

And those of us lucky enough to do it for a living have the best job in the world, period. I sit alone in a room and make stuff up and people pay me large sums of money to do that. And readers buy my stories and sometimes even write me fan letters. What is so hard about that?

But when it starts feeling hard, when the voices start creeping in that the story sucks while you are writing, that the plot doesn't work, that even your first-grade teacher will hate you when they see the crap you are writing, then guess what? You are trapped in Book as Event myth.

A book is not an event. It is just a long story. Nothing more. And nothing less.

Tell the story, move on to another one. And have fun. You could be digging a ditch in the rain.

It Must Be Art.

Oh, heavens, if that is your thinking, you are lost. Way, way deep in Book as Event.

If you think every book you write must be art, stop writing now, which more than likely you already have. There is no such thing as the "Great American Novel" anymore, and I sort of doubt there ever was, actually. I have a hunch that was a myth made up way back.

The truth is that in traditional publishing every month thousands of publishers and imprints must fill a monthly list. Those lists must be filled to keep the machine of publishing going. And now, with electronic publishing, the slots needed for novels is increasing even faster.

No book will climb above that crowd, at least not as art. Your book may climb above it as a bestseller, but if you are thinking you are writing art, I'm sure you look down your nose at bestsellers. Go study the history of the books that are considered art today and you might have a hope of getting over that, since most of the books studied as art today were the bestsellers of their time.

Art needs audience.

If you are selling your book that took six years to write to 200 people, you are not writing art. Sorry.

(Oh, that's going to make some people angry. Sigh…)

To Sell More Copies, My Book Must Be Bigger.

I have to admit, I fell for this one as well for a few years, as did most of publishing because of the collapse of the distribution system in the mid 1990s. I even taught a class here on the coast in how to write a "Big Book." Worst class I ever taught, and most destructive to writers. Sorry, those of you who took it.

A story just is what it needs to be.

Some stories are small, some fit in niches, some sprawl large and wide. Whatever you want to write, let your story be what it wants to be. Then when you are finished, figure out how to market it and get it to readers. Then get started on the next book.

I Have to Promote My New Book...

This comes from Book as Event myth as well.

I have a chapter later in this book on promotion. Promotion thinking has come solidly into indie publishing because no one really knows what works. So writer after writer on blog after blog talk about how they promoted their new book. That just makes me shudder, to be honest.

Not a one of these "indie promotion specialists" trust their own book to be good enough to attract readers. They all assume that because they did promotion their book sold. Wow, what little understanding of readers these people have.

Books don't sell because you promoted it. Books sell because they are good stories readers want to read. Nothing more.

I am a believer that more writing promotes writing better than anything artificial an author can do. Just because you finished a novel doesn't mean you have to spend six months promoting it. Why not spend those same six months writing the next one or two novels?

Yet this Book as Event thinking is causing writer after writer to stop writing and promote their last book. What a waste of time.

And if you really want to know how to promote a book that won't kill your writing and help you understand what is a waste of time or not, Kris and I have put together an online promotions workshop. If you are having trouble clearing this myth, you might want to take that workshop.

But remember one thing about promotion to an extreme: It's like walking through life backwards, always looking back and paying attention to what you have done in the past, not what you are going to do in the future.

Face forward.

Remember, writers are people who write. Authors are people who have written (and are now promoting).

Be a writer.

Eating the Elephant

That's what Kris and I call the problem writers have when they can't seem to start something. If you were standing beside a well-cooked elephant and your task was to eat every bite of the huge thing, you would say you couldn't do it. But, actually, you could. One bite at a time, over a period of time.

Novels are the same thing. They are mostly impossible to hold completely in your mind, so when starting it looks like a huge task (book as event again) and thus it's just easier to not start, easier to keep outlining and plotting and researching and doing all those things that are not writing.

The key is to just start, write so much per day, stop when you find the ending, and then mail it or indie publish it. (Yup, sort of like many of you do in the November challenge.)

This problem stops all of us at times. Even someone like me who has sold over 100 novels to traditional publishers, and written more than that number. I have a sign over my computer that says simply "Trust the Process" and it's right beside another sign. "Write Scenes."

Scenes I can hold in my head. Write a scene, then write the next scene, and trust the process as the days and weeks go by.

Summary

This topic is so huge, and this problem so big, that I'm sure I'm missing areas of it. I will try to cover those areas in other chapters along the way.

But in short, the myth of Book as Event is the underlying problem most writers face all the time.

It's easy to start building up a book into something more than it really is, especially when people ask "How's your book coming?" That question sort of underlines that the book is an event, and that it is the only book you have in you.

I once had a guy come up to me and say, "I hear you have a book coming out?" That year I had eleven novels coming out, just about one every month. So I said, "Sure do."

Being a nice guy, he said, "I'm looking forward to reading it. What's the title?"

I said, "Which one?"

He looked puzzled, like it didn't make sense that I had more than one book coming out. To him, and to most folks, writing and publishing a book are huge events, so how could it be possible to have more than one?

When I tried to help him and said, "I have five books in the next five months coming out," he looked horrified.

Right now, quickly check in with yourself.

—Do you feel horrified by the idea that I published eleven novels in twelve months one year?

—Do you think that because I did that, those books must automatically be bad?

If those thoughts passed through your mind, then you have an issue with the myth of Book as Event.

And that myth will stop you in one way or another, at one point or another.

So, if you just finished a book and are making up excuses to not mail it to editors or not get it out indie published because you had too much fun writing it, because it came too fast or too easy, or it needs a massive rewrite, you really have issues with Book as Event thinking.

Just because a book is fun to write, just because you wrote it fast, just because you don't think it's any good, doesn't mean it's a bad book.

In fact, it usually means it's a pretty darned good book.

Have fun getting it published.

And then get writing on the next one.

To be continued...

Now Available
from all your favorite booksellers in trade paper and electronic editions.

USA *Today* Bestselling Writer

DEAN WESLEY SMITH

A
Mary Jo Assassin
Story

DEATH IN THE MORNING

Mary Jo hated her most recent job of killing a woman named Bonnie Malak. Something felt off.

So Mary Jo, with her lover and fellow assassin, Jean, decided to figure out what seemed out of place.

Sometimes a job to kill might not be on target.

A Mary Jo Assassin Story of love, death, and friendship.

Death in the Morning
A Mary Jo Assassin Story

One

MARY JO USUALLY loved mornings. The fresh promise of a new day at hand, the savoring taste of freshly brewed coffee, the smell of eggs and ham.

This morning wasn't that much different from her normal mornings. She went through her daily ritual of shower and getting dressed. Jean, Mary Jo's partner, lover, and roommate, didn't much go for mornings, so she normally slept in and it wasn't until hours later that Jean usually crawled out of bed.

But this morning, because Mary Jo was at a critical point on a job, Jean got up and cooked her breakfast. They had learned that working together was so much more fun than working alone, so they shared everything, and Mary Jo was glad they did.

Especially today.

There was something about this job Mary Jo had been hired to do that bothered both of them and neither of them could put their finger on the problem.

Today they would find out what exactly was happening.

Mary Jo came out of the New York City penthouse apartment's main bathroom and into the modern kitchen where the sound of ham sizzling greeted her along with the thick, rich smell of freshly brewed coffee.

She had just entered heaven.

Mary Jo loved how Jean normally looked in the mornings, her blond hair pulled back, her perfect body tucked into a thin cotton robe. But this morning Jean had gotten dressed in Levi's and a silk blouse and tennis shoes, her working clothes. She had actually gotten up ahead of Mary Jo, which in their two years together had almost never happened.

Mary Jo thought Jean the most beautiful woman Mary Jo had ever seen. Jean said the same about Mary Jo. There was no doubt they were a striking couple from all the looks they got when they went out in public.

Jean, at five-three was two inches taller than Mary Jo. Jean had blonde hair and striking green eyes while Mary Jo had short brown hair and deep brown eyes. What Mary Jo loved was how they fit in each other's arms perfectly. In fact, last night, they had spent an hour in each other's arms naked in the hot tub going over every detail of Mary Jo's job today.

Both of them were professional assassins, both had done their job for over a thousand years, but as best they could figure, Mary Jo was about a hundred years older than Jean.

Neither one of them could imagine doing anything else but be an assassin.

But this last job Mary Jo had been hired to do just bothered them both and

they had learned over the centuries to listen carefully to that gut sense that something was wrong.

Today, they were going to find out what was bothering them exactly.

Mary Jo hugged Jean from behind as Jean stood at the stove, then went and poured herself a cup of coffee.

Jean already had one for herself on the kitchen table that looked out over a garden area.

Mary Jo sat and took a sip of the wonderful flavor, then watched Jean move as she cooked. By the way she was moving, it was clear to Mary Jo that Jean hadn't thought of what was wrong yet.

The job, on the surface, had appeared simple.

Mary Jo had been hired through normal channels by a man named J.D. Sones, a multi-millionaire head of an information company. Mary Jo got the standard one million up front, two million on completion. The job was to kill a woman by the name of Bonnie Malak.

But after five months of looking, Mary Jo could see no connection between Malak and Sones. No business, no past love affair, nothing.

The two had never crossed paths as far as Mary Jo and Jean could tell.

What bothered Mary Jo most was that Bonnie Malak looked like an assassin herself. Short, in shape, clearly in no need of money, living alone just off Broadway in a penthouse apartment. She moved like an assassin and seemed to have few friends and no enemies, the perfect way an assassin lived.

She also seemed to have a history under the Malak name that felt a little too perfect in places.

Sones, on the other hand, had made many enemies over the years. There were a lot of reasons to want Sones dead, but no reason to want Malak dead.

And that bothered both Mary Jo and Jean.

When they had told a third assassin friend of theirs, Susan, she had thought the same thing. Susan lived about eight blocks away and the three of them had worked a number of jobs together.

They trusted each other.

Susan was going to help today as well.

So today they would all find out exactly what was happening. And why. Mary Jo had no problem killing anyone. It was what she had done for more than a thousand years.

But she had always tried to make sure she killed the right person.

Bonnie Malak did not seem to be the right person.

Two

THE FIRST PART of their plan had gone like clockwork. Mary Jo bumped into Sones "accidently" as he came out of his 5th Avenue apartment elevator into the underground parking of his building.

She had been going in and pretended to trip on the edge of the glass airlock door leading to the elevators. Sones had caught her.

The accident allowed her to stick him lightly with a small amount of a very powerful drug that would knock him out in about thirty seconds.

He made it to his Mercedes sedan, got behind the wheel and passed out. Since his door was closed and his windows tinted, no security cameras could see that.

Earlier, Susan had managed to get into the car without any security seeing her and was waiting in the backseat of the car. She quickly pulled him over into the back seat, then climbed into the driver's seat and put on a chauffeurs-style cap even though Sones never used a chauffeur. She got the car out of the building just as a normal driver would.

Jean was to meet Susan in the underground parking of an apartment they had rented just for this day and take Sones up to the apartment and tie him up in one bedroom.

Mary Jo's next job was to get Bonnie Malak to the same apartment.

They had all figured out, after watching Bonnie for some time, the best way would be to just level with her and invite her.

All three of them were sure she was an assassin, but short of talking with her, there was no way to know. There certainly wasn't a membership number or something. Assassins were all trained by an ancient order and worked on their own, for the most part.

So in the preparation for today, all three of them had made sure they had watched her a number of times in an obvious way that an assassin would pick up on if she was good.

As they had watched her, Bonnie had become a creature of habit and would have been an easy target for Mary Jo. Bonnie sat at the same time every morning in the window seat of a deli three blocks from her apartment. A simple sniper shot from a nearby apartment window would have done the trick.

Mary Jo was fairly certain that Bonnie would know that.

Bonnie was a strikingly beautiful woman about Mary Jo's age. She had bright green eyes, red-tinted short hair, and freckles across the bridge of her nose.

Mary Jo went into the deli and ordered a cup of black coffee at the counter without looking at Bonnie. The place smelled wonderful of fresh-made bread combined with a rich, thick smell of bacon. When she took her coffee over to the table, she was actually surprised at the power and beauty of Bonnie up close.

"Is this seat taken?" Mary Jo asked.

Bonnie looked up and smiled. "For you, it is always available."

Bonnie indicated Mary Jo should pull out the chair and sit across from her in the window.

Most of the people walking by outside were on the way to work. The day was going to be a beautiful spring day with the snows and cold of winter now forgotten.

"I'm Mary Jo," Mary Jo said, holding out her hand.

"Bonnie," the green-eyed woman said, smiling. "But you already know that."

"I do," Mary Jo said, nodding.

"You three have been watching me now for four months, you for longer," Bonnie said. "I've been wondering why, actually."

"You're a target," Mary Jo said simply. "We wanted to let you know we were there to see what you would do."

Bonnie nodded. "Thanks for not filling the contract just yet. Can I ask who took it out on me?"

Mary Jo was impressed that Bonnie was taking the news so calmly. Chances are inside she wasn't calm, but on the outside she was doing what any trained assassin would do and not show any emotion. And also, chances are, she had figured it was something like this.

"J.D. Sones," Mary Jo said.

Bonnie slowly shook her head. "No memory of anyone by that name."

"We didn't think so," Mary Jo said. "We could find no connection at all. We have Mr. Sones under wraps. Would you like to meet him, get to the bottom of all this, before we decide what to do with him."

"I would love to," Bonnie said, nodding. "Thank you."

The two of them headed out of the deli and up the street. Mary Jo knew that in disguises, Jean and Susan were both watching her every move. She couldn't see them, but she knew they were there.

The three of them did not take any chances that didn't need to be taken.

After three blocks of walking in silence through the morning crowds, about a half block from the rented apartment, Bonnie turned to Mary Jo. "You are being very trusting of me."

"Why would you say that?" Mary Jo asked.

"I don't see the two others that helped you."

Mary Jo laughed. "You are not supposed to see us unless we want you to see us."

"I had heard rumors you three were that good," Bonnie said, nodding.

Mary Jo didn't much like that she had a reputation among assassins. But she liked that she was known for being good at her job.

After doing it for over a thousand years, she should be good at it. Otherwise, she would have been dead a long time ago.

Three

MARY JO LET Bonnie into the two-bedroom apartment on the fifth floor of the walk-up. The buildings next door were so much taller and so close, little natural light could get into the place.

And the furniture was nineteen-sixties beat-up. There was even a bottle candle on one end table that had been lit so many times a black circle had formed on the ceiling above it.

The place had a cloying smell of far too much pot and cigarettes.

Mary Jo let Bonnie enter first.

Bonnie glanced around and nodded. "I like what you did with the place."

Mary Jo smiled and let the door stand open as Jean came through behind her.

"This is Jean," Mary Jo said.

"Wonderful meeting you, Bonnie," Jean said, smiling. "Wow, anyone ever tell you that you are a real stunner?"

"Wow, you are right about that," Susan said, coming in behind Jean. "I'm Susan."

Bonnie smiled at Susan. "You're not so bad yourself."

Mary Jo was pretty convinced that Susan actually blushed a little.

The four of them went into the kitchen. The counters were old and needed repair, a couple of the empty cabinets had lost their doors, and there was a square wooden table to one side.

Bonnie sat down on one metal kitchen chair and Susan sat across from her while Jean and Mary Jo remained standing. Mary Jo could feel a little tension, but not as much as she had expected.

Jean pulled out a cell phone and quickly dialed a number. Then she said, "Freyja Mist."

Mary Jo knew that Jean was calling the ancient order of assassins. She just gave them her assassin name. The order didn't even have a name, but it had recruited all of them way back in time and trained them. It still kept track of all its members. Mary Jo had not contacted them in sixty years, but Jean had no problem calling them when information was needed.

Jean waited, then nodded. "We think we are talking with another member of the order who has been targeted by a client. Can you confirm that this person is an assassin or not?"

"Your name?" Jean asked Bonnie after a moment.

"Sunshine MorningBee," Bonnie said.

Mary Jo knew that the name meant that Bonnie was a younger member of the order, clearly recruited in just the last few hundred years or so.

Jean repeated the name and listened, then nodded and said thank you and hung up the phone.

"Confirmed," Jean said to Mary Jo.

Mary Jo reached down into a cabinet where they had stored a laptop and pulled it out and opened it on the table in front of Bonnie. "So this is the man who is tied up and still out cold in the bedroom."

Mary Jo showed Bonnie a picture of Sones.

Bonnie shook her head. "Never seen him before nor do I know the name."

Mary Jo ran through Sones' company dealings and again Bonnie just shook her head no.

Then Mary Jo put up a picture of Sones' wife. She was an attractive woman with black hair and dark eyes.

"Oh, shit," Bonnie said, glancing around at the three of them. "I had a wonderful affair with her about a year ago. It lasted for two months and she said her husband was getting suspicious so she broke it off. She said her name was Gretchen Hunt. I knew she was married but didn't care that much. She was a great time, if you know what I mean?"

"Gretchen Hunt Sones," Mary Jo said, laughing.

Susan turned the computer so she could see the picture of Gretchen Hunt

Sones. Then Susan looked right at Bonnie. "Think she would be up for a threesome?"

This time it was Bonnie's turn to slightly blush. But then she smiled and said, "Never hurts to ask."

Susan just smiled back and Mary Jo could tell that Susan and Bonnie were making a real connection.

Mary Jo glanced at Jean who just smiled and raised an eyebrow.

"So husband wants to kill wife's lover," Bonnie said. "Gretchen was a wild one. I wonder how many other former loves of Gretchen he has killed?"

"I suppose we could ask him?" Mary Jo said, glancing at her watch. "He should be waking up about now."

"I would love to," Bonnie said. Then she looked at Mary Jo. "I know we follow our contracts and all that, but any chance I can buy my way out of the one you have on me?"

Susan, Jean, and Mary Jo all laughed. "We never go against another assassin for any reason."

Now Available
from all your favorite booksellers
in trade paper and electronic editions.

Bonnie seemed actually relieved. "I thought I remembered that in my training and that was why I trusted you would come to me to tell me why you were all following me."

"You trusted right," Susan said, smiling at Bonnie and turning her toward the bedroom. "We work alone, we work together, but we never target each other."

"I've never worked with another assassin in three hundred years of doing this," Bonnie said.

"Well," Susan said, "you are in for a real treat then."

Mary Jo and Jean just laughed and followed them into the bedroom.

Four

THE BEDROOM ONLY had a bed with a stained old mattress on it and a dresser that had one drawer missing. Sones was tied to the frame of the room's small closet, sitting on the floor, his hands tied behind his back. A black zip-tie held his legs together at the ankles

He had on an expensive silk suit, black dress shoes, and black dress socks. Mary Jo wagered Sones never thought that he and his expensive silk suit would end up on a dirty apartment floor.

All of them stood in silence and watched as Sones slowly came to.

At first he looked worried and confused.

Then he saw the four of them standing around in front of where he was tied and he looked scared.

Then he recognized Bonnie and got angry.

Red in the face angry.

Confusion, fear, and then anger. The three phases of a hostage waking up.

They all followed exactly the same pattern, some slower than others. Mary Jo had seen it more times than she wanted to think about.

Good old Sones was one of the fast ones, going through all three phases in less than a minute.

He fought for a second at what tied him to the closet frame, then realized that was fruitless and squared his shoulders and glared at Bonnie.

"You think he seems a little angry?" Bonnie asked, smiling at Susan.

Mary Jo laughed. She was starting to like this young assassin more and more.

Susan just laughed as well, as Mary Jo went over to the old dresser and picked up what looked to be a small dart. Then, as Sones struggled, she moved over and jabbed him through his fine silk suit into his shoulder.

"What did you just give me?" he demanded.

Mary Jo wasn't going to tell him it was an ancient and very powerful truth drug that made it impossible to not answer questions directly.

Mary Jo put the dart back on top of the dresser and returned to her spot near the foot of the bed beside Jean.

Jean took out a pad of paper from her back pants pocket and a pen and opened it. "I'm ready."

"Ready for what?" Sones demanded.

Mary Jo counted to ten, then with a smile at Jean, she turned to Sones.

"Why did you hire someone to kill this woman?"

For a second Sones struggled as the drug took complete hold. Then he said flatly, "She had an affair with my wife."

"You think that is worth killing over?" Mary Jo asked.

Sones again said simply, "Yes."

The drug had taken the fight and the anger out of him. Inside she knew he was screaming, but outside he was calm and without emotion.

"Have you had other women or men killed that your wife had an affair with?"

"Yes."

"How many?"

"Six."

Bonnie sucked in her breath but said nothing. She clearly knew that only one person could ask the questions with this drug.

"Does your wife know you do this?" Mary Jo asked.

"No."

"Have you had others killed besides those who slept with your wife?"

"Yes."

"How many?"

"One."

"Who was that?" Mary Jo asked.

"My former business partner, Adam Hoss."

"So you have had killed seven people. Correct?"

"Yes."

"Do you have hidden bank accounts?"

"Yes."

Mary Jo glanced at Jean who nodded.

"Please give each bank name and country and account name and password associated with that account."

They all stood and listened and Jean wrote as quickly as she could as he calmly listed account after account, mostly in off-shore banks.

Finally he stopped, sitting calmly on the floor, staring straight ahead.

"Do you have a mistress?" Mary Jo asked.

"No," he said.

That surprised Mary Jo for a moment until she finally realized the next question. "Do you have a boyfriend?"

"Yes."

"Do you have more than one?"

"Yes."

"How many?"

"Three."

Bonnie just shook her head.

Mary Jo was feeling the same disgust. The man thought nothing of killing his wife's lovers, but kept three himself.

"Do you pay for your boyfriends' apartments or condos?"

"Yes."

"Please give us the addresses and your boyfriends' names."

Sones listed three names and addresses and Jean wrote them down, shaking her head the entire time.

"Do you think you are hypocritical," Mary Jo asked, "killing your wife's lovers but having lovers of your own?"

"No."

"Why not?" Mary Jo asked.

"No one touches my property without my permission."

"You consider your wife your property?" Mary Jo asked.

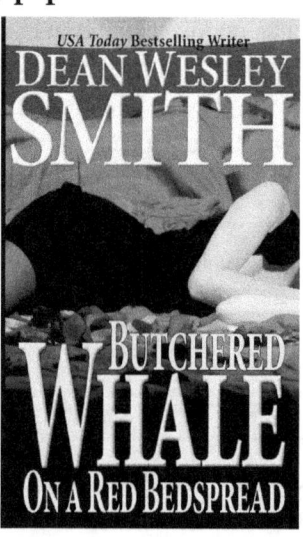
"Yes."

Mary Jo had seen this for centuries, but seeing it again here, in this modern city, just disgusted her. She had been a man's property a thousand times over the centuries. He had usually ended up dead fairly quickly.

Mary Jo knew the drug would start wearing off at any moment, so she indicated they should all go back out into the kitchen and they silently did.

"Wow, that's a piece of trash that needs to be taken out," Susan said.

"Yeah," Bonnie said, "and I'm afraid if we let him go what he might do to his wife after all this."

"No one said anything about letting that excuse for a human go," Jean said as she sat down at the table and opened up her laptop.

Mary Jo nodded. "Bonnie, do you have an offshore account we can land some money in? You can move it later."

"Sure," Bonnie said.

Susan knew the drill and helped Bonnie give Jean the account number and then Susan gave Jean her account number.

"Wow, this guy is loaded," Jean said after a moment. "I'm going to leave him a few thousand in each account. Make it look like he might be returning to the account."

Mary Jo nodded and watched Jean work. Mary Jo was so in love with Jean that sometimes she couldn't believe it. She could just sit and watch her for hours and enjoy every second.

Jean's fingers moved quickly over the keys. Mary Jo had no doubt that any of the other three of them could do what Jean was doing, but it would take them a lot longer. Jean was stunningly good at computers and financial accounts.

After just fifteen minutes, Jean smiled and said, "All of us are about forty million richer and the scum in there is a lot poorer.

I made sure none of the money could be traced to us, but after a day move it again and spread it out."

"I think I really like working with you all," Bonnie said, smiling. "So what do we do with the scum in there?"

Jean looked up at Mary Jo and smiled. "How about we do a wicked witch on him?"

"Drop a house on his head?" Bonnie asked.

Mary Jo, Jean, and Susan all laughed and Susan hugged Bonnie around the shoulders.

"No, we're thinking of melting him," Susan said.

Bonnie laughed. "I like that a lot. And I can learn another trick. Perfect."

Five

MELTING SONES WAS actually very easy.

Susan and Bonnie went and found a large metal garbage can and got it up into the apartment without being seen. The thing smelled of old wine bottles and some distantly remembered Chinese food.

At the same time, Jean went back to her and Mary Jo's place to get the bottle of acid.

Mary Jo, in the mean time, sent letters to the three boyfriends of Sones telling them that they needed to get out quick, take everything that wasn't nailed down, and vanish. Sones was under Federal investigation.

Then Mary Jo made sure that Sones will left his wife Gretchen all his assets, including the three boyfriend apartments, all his stock and cash in his regular accounts, and the penthouse apartment that they lived in.

Sones was going to vanish without a trace and that will and personal instructions left her everything and in charge of

it all. It would take some time before she could declare him dead, but Mary Jo had a hunch no tears were going to be spilled by Gretchen on any of this.

In fact, all of the research they had found about Sones over the last months showed that he had no real friends. He would not be missed.

So when Bonnie and Susan got back with the garbage can, laughing at something as they carried it, they took it into the bedroom. Mary Jo followed.

Sones now looked panicked.

"I can pay," he said. "Anything you want."

"We already have all your overseas money," Bonnie said. "Gretchen is going to get the rest."

As Bonnie kept Sones focused on her, Mary Jo once again stabbed him in the shoulder with a dart.

He was out cold in less than a second.

Then she tossed the dart and the one she had used earlier into the bottom of the garbage can.

Then Bonnie and Susan hefted Sones into the can head first, making sure to tuck in his legs and expensive shoes.

Then all four of them used pitchers Jean had brought from their apartment to fill the can about a third full of water from the bathroom and kitchen. More than likely, at some point along the way, Sones drowned.

Nobody cared enough to check.

Then Jean poured about half the bottle of acid into the garbage can, put the lid on the bottle, put the small bottle into her pocket, and stepped back as the acid combined with the water.

Mary Jo went over and opened up the window and then they all left the room, closing the door behind them.

It was going to smell like dry cleaning for about a day in that room.

But in a very short few minutes there would be nothing at all left of Sones.

And the acid would vanish as well in about an hour, leaving nothing more than a three-inch layer of thick sludge in the bottom of the can that would harden like a rock in a few days.

Mary Jo glanced at Jean as they left the bedroom and headed for the door of the apartment. "A good morning. Anyone up for brunch since it's still a few hours before lunch?"

"I know a perfect place about five blocks away," Susan said.

"Hanson's," Bonnie said.

"Hanson's," Susan said, smiling at Bonnie.

"I'm buying," Bonnie said. "It's the least I could do for you guys not killing me this morning."

"Never would have happened," Mary Jo said. "But you can still buy."

At that, Susan and Bonnie went out into the hallway. They were totally focused on each other.

"Young love," Jean said, smiling at Mary Jo. "Isn't it wonderful?"

"It is," Mary Jo said, smiling at the woman she loved. "And after brunch, when we get back home, I'll show you some real young love."

"Oh, that sounds like fun," Jean said. "Can we skip brunch?"

Mary Jo laughed. "I think the kids need some company on their first date, don't you?"

"If they make it to lunch without spontaneously combusting," Jean said.

"I know that feeling," Mary Jo said.

"I'm feeling it right now just looking at you," Jean said, laughing.

Mary Jo kissed her and then they followed the other two assassins down the stairs.

Mary Jo loved how this had all turned out. A problem solved, money made, a clean death done, and the woman of her dreams beside her.

Just about as perfect a morning as any assassin could ask for.

Mary Jo Assassin Short Stories
available from all your favorite booksellers in trade paper and electronic editions.

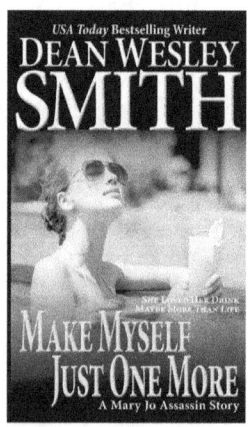

Now Available
from all your favorite booksellers
in trade paper and electronic editions.

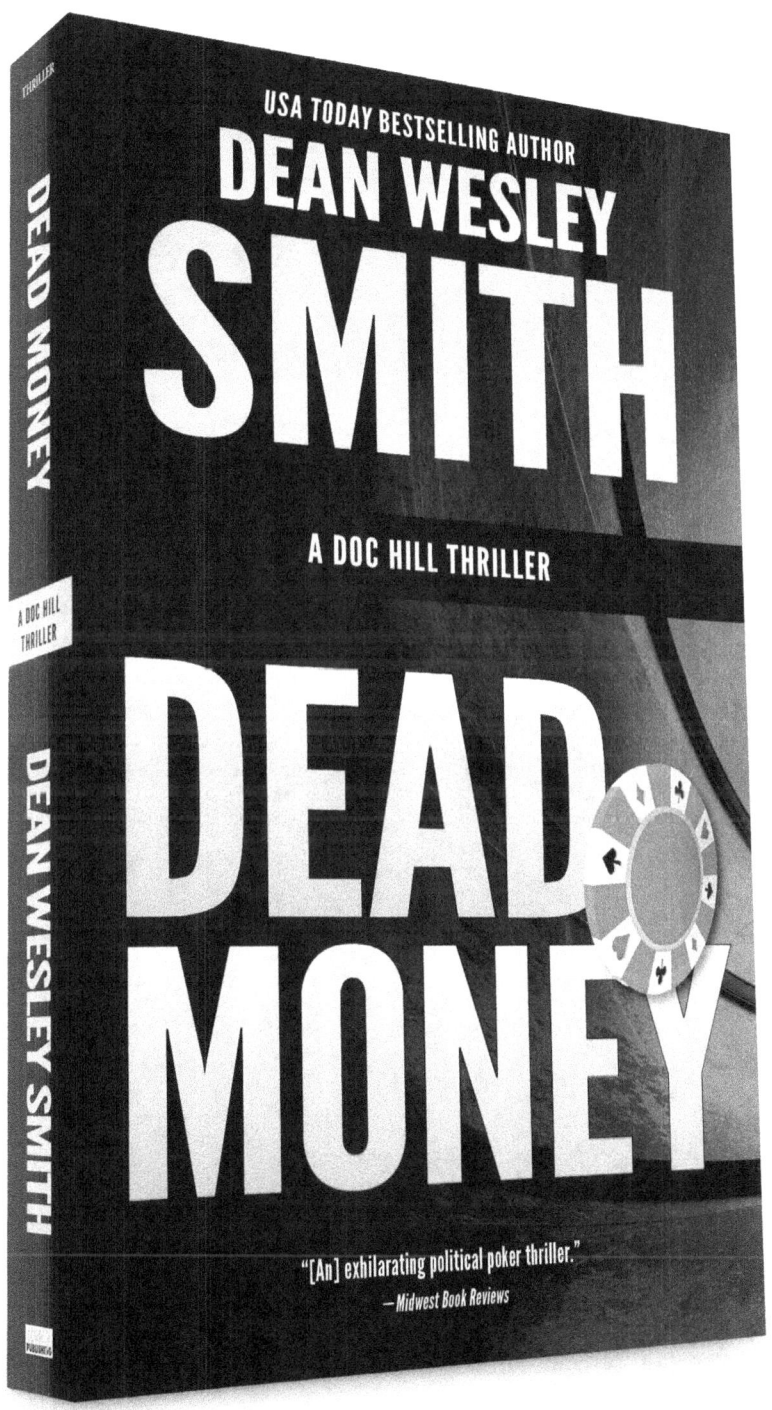

USA *Today* Bestselling Writer

DEAN WESLEY SMITH

HE MEANT NO HARM

In the near future, subdivisions sat dead.

When Dennis Phipps goes to clean out his grandmother's old home in a dead subdivision, what he finds will change his life.

A short story of a man reliving his past.

Sometimes the old saying about the past should remain in the past rings frighteningly accurate. Especially for Dennis Phipps.

He Meant No Harm

DENNIS PHIPPS, GRANDFATHER, father, and normal retired citizen meant no harm. At least that was what he kept telling himself.

It started as he was cleaning out his grandmother's home. The late summer day was hot, with temperatures promising to be in the high nineties before the heat was finished. And his grandmother's home had no climate controls, so he had come out early, right after sunrise, while the cool of the morning still held.

Grandmother Judy had died at the age of one hundred and three and had lived mostly on her own until a year or so before the end. He had always admired her for that.

Her home in a once upscale subdivision had been the family home of generations. It was a single-story, four-bedroom ranch-style house, decorated from the time when his grandmother had been young in the 1960s.

Now, in 2080, almost all of the homes around hers had been long abandoned as the population of the country and the world shrank and moved into the cities. Some of the homes along his grandmother's street had already started to fall down.

He had no doubt from the rotted smell of wood and mold inside her home and the water that had flowed through the old roof and down the walls in numbers of places, this house wouldn't be far behind.

Her home had once been painted white with brown trim, but all that had weathered away years before. She had refused to move into the city with him and his wife, even though she had never met her two great-great-grandchildren. She actually never did, which Dennis thought was sad.

So twice a week he had taken old-fashioned ground transportation and gone to see her, taking her food and whatever else she might need.

The old-fashioned cars had been the only way to even get into the subdivision. And even that was a task at times after storms in the winter. The last winter she lived out here, he had had to hire help clearing the road to her house.

Dennis, in the last thirty years of his grandmother's stay in the old house, had put in a solar-powered generator so she at least had heat and light. That generator had stopped working a few years back which had caused her to get sick and they had put her in elderly care at that point.

He hadn't been back out to her house since.

Dennis's parents had both died and he was the only grandchild close enough to take care of his grandmother.

He honestly hadn't minded. He was now retired and didn't see his own kids or grandkids enough. Besides that his grandmother's stories she told with each of his visits brought back lots of memories of another world, what seemed to be a safer, more carefree world when he had been a kid and visited her.

Back then, in 2020, the subdivision had been thriving, with green lawns and families everywhere. Now there was nothing green, nothing much left alive here, actually. He would have to check if he thought about it, but his grandmother

might have been the last person alive on this entire street. More than likely in this entire subdivision and this part of the reclaimed wilderness around the city. It wouldn't have surprised him.

Eventually, the plans were for the government to go in, knock down and bury everything that was left in subdivisions like these, plant trees and let nature reclaim it all.

So as he dug through her things, deciding which few small personal things to take back with him into the city and which to just leave to rot, he found what had been a brightly-colored box tucked in the top of one of the side bedroom closets. It stuck out of a larger cardboard box.

A box of old fireworks.

The images on the box of colored explosions sent Dennis back to the days when his grandparents and parents would all get together for the 4th of July holiday. They would cook outside in the backyard, sit in the shade, and then as it got dark, they would set off fireworks.

This was back before fireworks were banned throughout the world when certain groups around the world started using them, combining their explosive strength somehow, to cause real damage and terror and death for whatever cause they might have been fighting for.

Dennis remembered that the ban happened when he was twelve. He had been disappointed until his father showed him images of mangled people, hands and legs gone, lying in the streets, killed by explosives made from seemingly harmless fireworks.

He had never thought about fireworks again until today.

Now he held an entire box of the illegal things in his hands.

Dangerous things, actually.

But still things that brought back another time, another era, when he was a kid and explosions were thought of as a form of celebration, not a way to bring death.

He took the old box out onto the old pavement in front of the house and carefully started pulling some of the contents out. He had no idea if explosives became more dangerous with time or not, so he was going to go carefully.

The box said they had been manufactured when he was eleven, right before the ban. He was now eighty-one, so that meant they were seventy years old.

This box had been sitting on that high shelf in the spare bedroom closet for seventy years. Amazing, just amazing.

He supposed he should just call the authorities and they would send someone to take care of all of it.

He would do that in a minute.

But first it couldn't hurt to just look at what was in the box if he was careful.

He pulled out what seemed to be a package of regular common fireworks with all kinds of strange names on the packet. It looked like an assortment you could buy back then in almost any store. He had that memory from his childhood.

He remembered walking the aisles with his father and wanting to buy them all, but his father saying no, they already had all the fireworks they would need for the holiday.

Under that colorful package were a fist-full of metal sticks labeled sparklers. He put them to one side of the box, then pulled out what looked like an old packet of eggs his grandmother used to get. It said on the outside Cherry Bombs.

He opened the carton and saw twelve of the small red things. They were round with a fuse sticking out of the top where a cherry stem would be.

"This is amazing," he said. For the first time in a long time, he was feeling like a kid, ignoring the warming sun on his back and head.

There were three other cardboard cartons in the bottom of the box labeled M-80s. He had no idea what they were, but they looked dangerous.

He carefully put everything back in the box.

The feeling of being a kid again was like a drug. He had loved those years when his parents were alive and when his grandmother hosted wonderful family events.

Those had been the great years.

He stood and stared around the dead and brown neighborhood. It was amazing that when this neighborhood was full of people, all the neighbors played with these sorts of things for fun every year.

He had played with them himself.

What would it hurt if he just tried one of them for fun before turning the entire box in to the authorities.

He would be careful.

He went back into the house and dug through his grandmother's kitchen drawers until he found some old wooden matches that still seemed to light. He remembered she had used the matches to light candles when the power went out before he got her the solar-powered generator.

He went back out into the heat of the morning and looked at the contents of the box, holding the box of matches in one hand.

"What would be fun to try?"

The warm breeze took his words away over the ruins.

Again he looked up and down the street. Nothing was moving. Only a slight breeze stirred the dead grass and dead shrubbery and brown trees.

He decided that the safest bet would be to just do a sparkler.

He remembered as a kid holding one of those in his hand and running around the backyard waving it in the air.

He smiled at the memory and took out a sparkler. He was too old to run with it, but it would be fun holding it again, remembering being young.

Then he lit a match and put it against the end of the sparkler.

It didn't want to take, sizzling for a moment, then suddenly bursting into sparks all around him.

Some of the sparks hit the hand with the match in it.

It startled him and he went to hold the sparkler away from himself more and stumbled.

He dropped the lit sparkler, along with the matches, including the lit match, right into the box.

"Oh, no," he said.

He quickly bent over the box to dig the sparkler out. But he couldn't tell which end to grab the sparkler on and another sparkler was sizzling.

Then the matches in the box of matches ignited with a whooshing sound.

He tried once more to grab the sparkler.

The explosion rocked him back and into the middle of the old street where he hit the back of his head hard on the concrete.

He had no idea how long he lay there, clearly unconscious, but when he came to, the front lawn of his grandmother's house was in flames, her house was in flames, and the slight breeze was blowing the spreading flames to the next abandoned home.

Two unexploded M-80s were in the street beside him.

He tried to move, then realized he really couldn't.

His one hand was mostly gone, his arm was bleeding, and he could feel blood running off his face.

His pants had been blown off the front of his legs as well and he could tell his skin was burned.

He looked like a victim of a bombing that his dad had shown him when he was twelve.

He tried to tap his emergency medical band and phone, but it had been on his wrist, the wrist that was now missing.

Blood was pooling around him in the street as the fire crackled and got larger.

He lay there, staring at the M-80 beside him, feeling himself start to get faint.

He really hadn't meant any harm. They were just kid's fireworks from back when he was a kid.

He had meant no harm.

He had just wanted to feel young once more.

At least that was what he kept telling himself over and over as the neighborhood he used to love slowly caught fire and he bled to death in the street.

He had meant no harm.

Now Available
from all your favorite booksellers
in trade paper and electronic editions.

More Bryant Street Stories
available from all your favorite booksellers in trade paper and electronic editions.

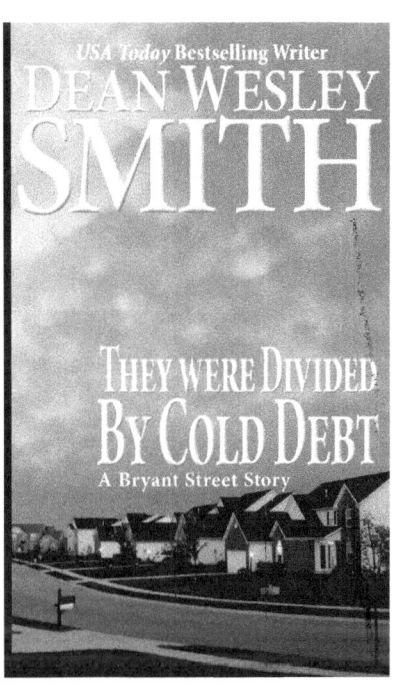

USA TODAY BESTSELLING AUTHOR

DEAN WESLEY
SMITH

STARBURST

A SEEDERS UNIVERSE NOVEL

Exploring the vastness of space: The mission of the massive Starburst ships.

Chairmen Cole and Echo of the Starburst ship Star Trail get wrapped up in finding lost ancient cultures.

And in the process find far more than they ever could imagine.

Starburst takes the vast Seeders Universe and expands it yet again beyond where humans dare go.

Starburst
A Seeders Universe Novel

For Kris

Section One
The Mission

Prologue

"ECHO, CAN'T YOU just relax a little?"

Echo glanced around at her best friend and lover, Cole Lemmon, as he followed her up the center of the deserted suburban street. The day was hot and Cole was sweating, staining his white T-shirt around the brown straps of the backpack he carried. His longish brown hair was damp where it stuck out from under his Yankee's baseball cap.

His handsome face was flushed even though they had only gone four blocks in distance.

She was hot as well, which was why she had been walking fast, trying to get them to their starting target before they stopped or the heat got them. It normally wasn't this hot in Portland, Oregon, or at least that's what some long-time residents of the area had told her earlier.

She was wearing jeans with tennis shoes, a sleeveless blue tank-top with a sports bra under it, and she had her short blonde hair under a Dodgers baseball cap. Sweat was running off her neck and down her chest and she desperately needed a drink of water.

She had her Smith and Wesson pistol in a holster on her hip and Cole had a small twenty-two saddle rifle tied to the side of his backpack. It had been years since they had gone anywhere in this city without those guns, winter or summer. They both had admitted they would feel naked without them, even though they could teleport away from any problem at an instant's notice.

But now, after three years mostly living on the surface of this planet, trying to help the residents recover from a horrid disaster, she and Cole had decided it was just easier to act like locals instead of Seeders. And locals all still carried guns, for the most part.

On both sides of the suburban street around them, the houses were like tombstones for the people who had been killed inside of them when the Big Death happened five years before. The once-green lawns where children had played were brown and had long turned to tall, dry weeds. The house windows were dirty and almost every house had drapes pulled, at least on the lower floors.

Weeds and grass had started growing in patches of dirt along the street and up through cracks in the concrete. What had been perfect lines of lawns, driveways, sidewalks, and street were now blurred as Mother Nature slowly took back the neighborhood.

Echo had seen a projection on how in fifty years a neighborhood like this would be completely overgrown, in one hundred years it would be all plants and piles of rubble, and in five hundred years it would be almost impossible to tell what had been here.

Just as Mother Nature had killed most everyone on the planet one day with a burst of electromagnetic waves from space, she now was slowly reclaiming the planet.

The Big Death had hit at a little after eight in the morning here in Portland, so most people in this neighborhood were either at work or taking kids to school or some such thing.

Cole and Echo had come to this planet as part of the Seeders reconstruction program. They had been a couple for almost fifty years. Cole was just over two hundred years old while Echo had just gone past one hundred. One of the wonderful things about being a Seeder was that you never aged.

But she was sure that this task, being on this planet, was aging them both. She knew, without a doubt, that no matter how long they lived or how many planets they visited, they would never forget this.

Seeing death every day and living in the middle of it did that to a person.

They lived together in the city of Portland, Oregon, worked together both on the local newspaper, and searching for the dead, and she couldn't imagine being without Cole through any of it.

They also had a nice apartment on their base Seeder ship, *Silver Moon*, but these days they seldom jumped back to that place. Here in Portland they had adopted two wonderful cats and she actually liked the home better here with the cats. When they left this assignment, she planned on taking the cats with them.

She looked around at all the empty houses. This neighborhood hadn't been cleared yet, which was the process they were sent to start.

They were to inventory the bodies in every home along the street and mark from the outside which homes had bodies so the removal crews could come and take the bodies to the new cemeteries.

And in each home she and Cole were to look for information as to who lived there and double-check it with their database, even those houses without bodies.

The ultimate goal of the Respect Project was to give everyone who died in the Big Death a proper resting place and a record of their existence for the future, including where they had lived and what they had done for work.

It was almost an impossible task, but everyone in the five now-growing new cities around the country, which included Portland, and the new national government, were committed to the task.

Both Cole and Echo thought it a wonderful task and worth every minute they spent doing it. It would be part of the rebuilding of the civilization on this planet.

"We can start anywhere, you know?" Cole said. "How about we start here, work back to the truck along both sides, then cool down and bring the truck to here and go the other direction?"

Echo stopped and glanced at an address still visible on the side of one of the homes. From what she could tell, they were about halfway along the long subdivision street. Cole's idea was a good one.

They had to get out of the sun. It was only ten in the morning and this day promised to be far too hot to stay out in the sun for very long.

She nodded. "Good plan."

"Thank you," Cole said, stopping and taking off his pack, letting it drop to the concrete in the middle of the street.

They had been going out four mornings a week to catalog houses and bodies in the vast subdivisions that surrounded Portland. It had bothered her some at first, nosing into people's personal homes, but then she had grown numb to it. After all, the people they were investigating were all dead.

The thing she could never look at were the children's bodies, often in cribs. Every time they found a home with a child, Cole took that house on his own, even though they had clear orders to always stay together. Not that there was anything dangerous in these old subdivisions besides slowly rotting wood.

This subdivision had lots of signs that children lived in these homes, from swing sets visible in the backyards, to small bikes and other toys left near the front doors.

She really never wanted children and Seeders seldom had children, actually. Cole had no desire for children either. But that didn't mean she could stomach seeing a dead child. There were some things she would draw the line at.

Period.

She took a long drink of semi-cold water that tasted wonderful and then handed the bottle to Cole, who took a drink and sighed. Around them a slight breeze kicked up filling the air with faint noises of houses creaking and dry brush rustling. The sounds did nothing to break the death silence of the subdivision.

"Let's go get snoopy into people's lives," he said, handing her back the bottle of water.

"That one first," she said, pointing to a light blue house on her right. "Let's do two on that side, then two on the other side, as we work back to the truck."

"Sounds perfect," he said, smiling at her and picking up his pack.

She loved everything about him, his dark eyes, his solid build, and his strong arms. But mostly she just loved that smile.

Somehow, over all the years of living now in the middle of death, that smile of his had kept her sane.

They headed up the front sidewalk of the two-story home that must have been very nice in its day for this time in this planet's history. The drapes were pulled and more than likely the front door was locked. Both of them had been trained before they started this job to pick a lock. Cole was slightly faster at it than she was, but only by a second or so. They hadn't found a lock so far that had stopped them.

The people in charge of the Respect Project wanted all the homes to be respected, if possible, even though eventually they would all just rot away. Echo was fine with that as well.

Cole left his pack on the front step and took out his rifle, slinging it over his shoulder before bending down and picking the front door locks. Thirty seconds later he stood and pushed the door open.

The smell of mold and dust and something with a slight tang greeted them and they both stepped back out of the smell and pulled out their cloth masks and tied them over their mouths and noses. That smell with a bite meant there was a body in the building.

They always wore masks when a body was in the building.

The masks also helped them with the dust. They went through about a dozen of the masks a day, maybe more on a hot day like today.

Even though there was some light filtering through the drapes and from a back window in the kitchen beyond the living room, they both clicked on flashlights. When they first started out doing this job, they had both tripped over various things in homes that they just hadn't seen in dim light. So they took no chances now.

Echo panned her flashlight around the living room. More of a formal room that didn't look much used. A layer of gray dust dulled down all colors in the room.

Moving slowly to not kick up too much dust from five years of no one moving around in here, they headed for the kitchen and the family room beyond.

Echo was relieved to see no sign of children's toys around the family room.

Cole slowly opened some drawers near the family dining area. Often families left personal information in drawers near a kitchen table.

While he was doing that, she turned and opened the back door leading into a two-car garage. There was one car there. And a spot for a second one. Tools were in their places on the walls.

Nothing else of interest.

"One car left," she said as she went past Cole and toward the rooms to the right of the big living room. One looked like a guest bedroom and was as sterile as the living room. Whoever lived in this house believed in keeping everything in its place. Even after sitting abandoned for five years and layers of gray dust making everything pale, that feeling of "in its place" was clear in this home.

It made her wonder what the residents of this home had been like. Clearly different than her and Cole. Their large apartment in a building in the downtown area was always awash with clutter of various types, mostly books. They were both just comfortable in that.

And their apartment on board *Silver Moon* was the same way. Cluttered and comfortable.

She would not have been comfortable in this place. It felt sterile and even more dead than most homes she had been in, as if this home had been dead before the Big Death hit.

"Anything?" she asked.

Cole shook his head. "Nothing. Drawers in perfect order, but no bills, no letters, nothing. More than likely all that is in a study someplace from the looks of all this."

With Cole leading, they headed upstairs.

The light was brighter upstairs as most of the back windows in the home had the blinds open. They all looked out over a lush backyard that had held a pool. Echo had no doubt it had been beautiful in its day. And from the looks of the house, the lawn would have been mowed perfectly and the pool more than likely cleaned twice a week.

At the top of the stairs a hallway lead the length of the house. It had a number of closed doors. Echo had a hunch behind one of those doors would be the body they knew was in here from the faint musty smell. The smell had a slight tang to it after five years, but it wasn't a smell that was easy to miss.

And now that they were upstairs, the smell was thick.

And even though it was still fairly early, this upper area of the house was already heating up. Any body they did find would be well mummified in this kind of heat.

A mummified body was a lot better as far as Echo was concerned than a body torn up from animals. Not all animals had survived the electromagnetic pulse. Dogs and rats and mice had been killed, but cats had survived. And with a cat trapped in a home with a dead human, they ate the dead human when they got hungry enough.

There were no signs this home had cats, so the body would be mummified and look moderately human even after five years.

The first two doors were to small bedrooms with no occupants. The rooms had been furnished with small single beds and just left. One room was painted pink, one blue.

Clearly the rooms had been meant for future children that had not arrived yet.

And now never would.

The third door was to an empty bathroom and the next door was to a master bedroom and bath, also empty. The bed was made perfectly.

Now Available
from all your favorite booksellers in trade paper and electronic editions.

There was nothing out of place in this entire house. Echo found that amazing and very closed up and creepy.

The next door on the other side of the hall was to a study with a big desk.

"Got it," Cole said, moving to the desk and file cabinet that would let them know who had lived here.

There was one more door at the end of the hall and that meant it had the body in it.

Echo went to it and opened it slowly, making sure to not stir up any dust as she did so.

The blinds were open in the room and it was a fairly large family room that also did not look used in any way. This room had a large screen television, a number of couches, a game table, and plush carpet.

It had been designed to be comfortable, but clearly not made comfortable.

Everything again was in perfect position. Nothing was used. It was as if the people living in this house had just existed in it and never really lived in it.

There was a door off the family room that was closed. More than likely that was where the body was. They had found many bodies, since they started this job, in various stages of bathroom routines.

Cole came in behind her. "This is the home of Ben and Cathy Freeman. He worked at a pharmacy downtown and she was an RN."

Cole held up his digital pad. "We already recovered his body when they cleaned the downtown area."

"This place sure looks like they were planning for kids," Echo said. "Clearly didn't get the chance."

Cole glanced around and nodded. Then he pointed to the door. "You want me to look and see who is in there?"

"We both will," she said.

Slowly she opened the bathroom door to keep the dust from swirling while both of them shined their flashlights into the small bathroom.

What she saw stunned her and took her a moment for her mind to wrap around.

What had been a fairly attractive, thin, brown-haired woman lay in the bathtub face up. She had mummified, but she still looked pretty good, with her long brown hair fanned out on the back of the tub over her.

And her face was calm in death. Very calm.

What had really surprised Echo was that the tub water when it evaporated had left an ugly brown stain.

It took her a moment to see why. Both of the woman's wrists that were crossed over her chest had been slashed.

A razor blade lay on a napkin on the edge of the tub.

"Now that's a first," Cole said beside Echo in the bathroom door. "More than likely she cut her wrists right before the Big Death hit."

On the counter was a note card standing up with the name "Ben" on it.

Echo looked at it, then glanced at Cole. Clearly that was Cathy Freeman's suicide note.

Cole shrugged, meaning she could read it or not. Up to her.

Echo wasn't sure if she wanted to read it, but at this point she felt she had no choice.

She picked up the note and opened it. Then read it aloud as Cole held his flashlight so she could see.

Dearest Ben,

I am so sorry for the mess I have left you. I have tried to keep this clean and simple and plan this in a bathroom we seldom use.

I am so sorry that I cannot bring the children into the world we so hoped to have. I could no longer look at the deadness in your eyes and the disappointment I felt every time we made love. My passing here will allow you to move on, to find a new wife, to be happy, and finally have and raise the children you so wanted.

Please don't be mad at me, love. This is for the best. Remember me to your children when they are old enough to understand. Have a wonderful life.

Love Always,
Cath

Echo carefully replaced the suicide note on the counter.

"Let's get out of here," Cole said, gently touching her elbow. "We got all we need from here."

Somehow Echo nodded and turned and followed Cole out of the family room and down the hall past the future children's bedrooms, then down the stairs and out into the hot air of the dead subdivision.

Cole marked the house, picked up his pack, stuck his rifle back in it, and led the way to the street.

She pulled off her mask and tucked it in her pocket, letting the warm air work to clear her mind.

They stopped in the middle of the street, both with their backs to the house they had just been in.

After a moment, Cole gently touched her arm. "You all right?"

"Honestly," she said, turning to look into his worried dark-blue eyes. "I think I'm done for the day."

"I agree," Cole said. "Too hot anyway. So what are you thinking?"

She looked into the eyes of the man she loved, the man that had helped her survive more death than she ever wanted to think about. "I am thinking about a long cold shower in our air-conditioned apartment."

"We are on the same track with that," Cole said, smiling.

"Then maybe a few hours in bed making love to you."

At that, his eyebrows went up and he looked at her, clearly puzzled.

"After all this death," she said, sweeping her arm around to indicate the dead neighborhood, "I just want to feel close to you, to be alive."

He smiled bigger than she had remembered him smiling in a very long time. "Perfect, just perfect."

She kissed him, then took his arm and together they headed up the hot street of the dead subdivision.

It would be a day she would never forget.

And this assignment on this mostly dead planet would also never be forgotten. No matter how long she lived.

Chapter One

(Over 400 years later)

CHAIRMAN COLE LEMMON stood next to the big command chair on the Starburst exploration ship *Star Trail,* leaning against the wide rail that separated the lower level from the next level of command.

He wore his normal jeans, dress shirt with the sleeves rolled up, and running shoes. He had on a blue ball cap with the brim pushed back off his forehead. He sipped on his normal morning cup of coffee, black and strong, as he watched the stream of data flowing over the massive screen in front of him.

He had longish brown hair, a square face, and looked to be in shape, with wide shoulders and a smile people said could calm an entire room.

In front of him, the main screen in the command center filled an entire thirty-foot-high wall and was twice that wide. At the moment, the wall was covered by flowing reports from the thousands of scout ships ahead of *Star Trail*, doing surveys of galaxies, two ships per galaxy.

He had watched these reports now every morning for over fifty years, since *Star Trail* had launched from the Milky Way galaxy. He never grew tired of it because he knew that at some point one of those scout ships would find something very special in one of those galaxies.

Maybe even a growing alien race, which excited him more than he wanted to think about.

Behind him in the command center, thirty of the best people he and his life partner, Echo, could find were at their stations. They were the main command crew. The command center was always manned with three different shifts covering different times of the day.

The command center was the beating heart of *Star Trail*.

The massive room was built like a large amphitheater. The chairmen's command chair, actually two chairs molded together, was on the lower level. Two steps up behind the command chair and the wide railing were four stations, with their second in command, JP Horshaw, to the right.

The next level up had eight stations and the level around the back wall and top had another eighteen stations. At this time of the day, with all the reports flowing in from all the scout ships exploring galaxies, all stations were occupied.

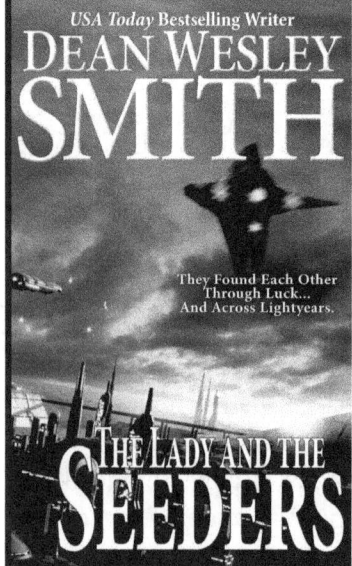

Everyone was busy, each with a specific task of not only keeping *Star Trail* and the three million souls on board safe, but studying in detail every report flowing in from the scout ships.

This was part of his morning ritual. He flat loved it. And the strong, black coffee in his mug.

Echo, his co-chairman, liked to exercise first thing in the morning, something he couldn't imagine doing. They were both runners and he liked to run later in the day, usually through some of the thousands of parks and forests covering millions and millions of square kilometers inside the ship.

There was one thing good about their conflicting exercise schedules. One of them was always in the command center during most of the day. They did each lunch and dinner together every day. They got a lot planned over those meals.

And they made sure they had time together every evening, even if to just sit and read.

With over three million Seeders on board, at first he had felt the responsibility of all those people more than he wanted to admit. Now he understood it.

He still felt it, but he understood it as well, which helped.

Star Trail was shaped like a giant bird soaring through space, with a pointed nose and wings frozen in place. It was so massive that every year the crew had a ten-person relay race that covered the nine thousand kilometer distance from the tip of the ship to the tail and then back to the tip. Every Starburst ship had the same relay. It had become a tradition for all of them.

Cole loved running in it because he saw parts of his own ship he would never have a chance to visit personally. His favorite run now was through the massive forests that covered millions of square kilometers. It made him feel for just a time that he wasn't inside a space ship.

"Chairman," *Star Trail* said, *"Incoming message from Star Fall to all Starburst ships. Priority One."*

Star Trail's voice was feminine and precise while remaining warm. He liked the voice a great deal. And when in the command chair it felt like *Star Trail* and he and Echo were almost one at times, the wonderful aspect of being chairmen of a Starburst ship.

"Have Chairman Guinn report to the command center at once."

A moment later Echo appeared at his side. Her short blonde hair was matted to her head in sweat and she had a towel over her shoulder that she was using to wipe off sweat from her face. She must have been in the last part of her exercise routine. She liked to do sprints. Another reason they seldom ran together.

To Cole she looked as beautiful today as the day they had met all those hundreds of years ago. She was about five-four, with a thin build that didn't really show how strong she was. She had dark blue eyes like his that could be both warm and harsh.

He never tired of looking into those eyes.

"What's happening?" she asked as she finished wiping sweat from her face and neck and let the towel drape over her shoulder.

He shrugged. "Priority one message from *Star Fall*. *Star Trail*, please put *Star Fall* through on the big screen when they are ready."

Around them the command center fell silent as everyone listened and watched.

Star Fall was another Starburst ship that had left the Milky Way at about the same time as they had. *Star Fall* had been one of the three ships to lead the successful war against a run-away genetic experiment that threatened all of the human space. Cole and Echo had only gotten involved in that war toward the end as the chairmen of *Star Trail.*

After the war, the Starburst program of sending out fourteen massive ships to explore in all directions through known space started. *Star Trail's* intelligence and personality was moved into the new, far larger ship they were in now.

The Starburst program had really shown benefits no one would have expected. In the last year or so, *Star Fall* had discovered the abandoned home of all humanity and Seeders, something no one even knew had existed. The massive area of space had also been the home of the two other intelligent races in known space, the Gray and the Cirrata.

Cole and Echo and all the other Starburst ships and crews had watched the unfolding story of exploring the old abandoned worlds and then finally meeting the ancients who had stayed behind in the old home center.

So now, with *Star Fall* contacting them and all the other Starburst ships, there was no telling what was happening. But Cole had a hunch it would be exciting.

On the big screen in front of Cole and Echo the familiar faces of four people appeared. The couple on the right and slightly back were Chairmen Matt and Carey of *Star Fall.* Both had wide smiles and seemed very much relaxed, which made Cole instantly drop one level of worry.

The two that faced the screen head on were Chairmen Ray and Tacita. They were over four million years old and before the discovery of the ancients, Ray and Tacita were thought to be the oldest Seeders alive. They had been the chairmen of the very first Seeders' mother ship to ever start to seed humanity in another galaxy.

Turns out they had also been seeded by the ancients and helped along for a period of time.

Cole and Echo sort of thought of them as grandparents, even though both looked not much older than any other Seeder. Tacita had short, black hair and eyes that seemed to cut through a person and Ray wore his gray hair long and down his back.

Cole had no idea how anyone could live four million years, but he had every intention of trying.

"Chairmen," Ray said, smiling and nodding.

Cole knew that all of the thirteen Starburst ship's chairmen's images were on a split screen in front of Ray and Tacita.

"Data will follow this message about a discovery that has just been made," Ray said. "In short, it seems our branch of the Seeders is only one of six hundred different Seeder groups the ancients started over four million years ago."

Cole glanced at Echo who was just shaking her head. He couldn't even fathom that number. Over a billion galaxies had been seeded since Ray and Tacita started and each galaxy had billions and billions of human worlds.

That meant out there in the vastness of space there might be almost six hundred more Seeders groups working at the same pace.

Incredible.

And at a scale impossible to imagine as far as Cole was concerned.

Did the Seeders ever do anything on a normal scale?

Ray went on. "The information being sent to you is the locations, adjusted for galactic shift over the four million years, of the other seeded groups. Unlike with our group, which was the closest to the old home worlds, the ancients have not made contact with any other groups in four million years due to the vast distances involved. We were the only ones they stayed around and helped past the first Seeder ship."

"They don't know what's happened to the ancient seeded groups," Echo said softly.

Cole felt his stomach twist up. The history of the Seeders, this branch of Seeders at least, had been full of near-disasters. Not counting the major war they just had barely won. No telling what had happened to the other groups.

"So our new mission for the Starburst program is to find those other groups," Ray said. "We will decide on a group by group basis if contact will be wanted or required."

Ray took a deep breath and with a nod from her partner Tacita kept going. "The distances are so great to these other groups that even our five-hundred-year missions would have not reached the closest one."

Cole shook his head. He had tried to understand the distance they planned on traveling on the five-hundred-year Starburst mission. To say that all the other Seeder groups were far beyond that was impossible to grasp.

"So we need all Starburst ships," Ray said, "to pull in all scout and military ships and return on a direct course toward the Milky Way Galaxy at top speed. We will meet each ship within a year with a construction fleet to do upgrades on every Starburst ship."

"Upgrades?" Cole asked softly so only Echo could hear. He had no idea what kind of upgrades were possible.

Ray smiled, more than likely seeing the puzzled looks on every Starburst ship's chairman's faces.

"We will revamp the drives on every ship to a top speed of trans-tunnel forty-two and boost the shields to match. All information is being sent to you. Study it as you get turned around and headed back at full speed. We will be in direct contact with every ship over the next few days as to upgrade schedules."

With that the screen went back to scrolling data coming in from all the scout ships.

"Data being received from Star Fall," *Star Trail* said.

Cole stared at the big screen for a moment, then glanced at Echo. Around them the command crew had broken into talking.

"How fast is forty-two?" Echo asked, glancing at Cole. "We can already go by an entire galaxy in an hour at a fourteen trans-tunnel speed."

Cole had no idea. Trans-tunnel drive opened a tunnel outside of space to allow ships to travel faster than light through

the tunnel. Someone, a long time ago, had realized that if you opened more tunnels inside of already open tunnels, the speed increased by factors.

Before the war, it had taken a ship fifty years to get between galaxies. By the end of the war, the trans-tunnel drive at fourteen trans-tunnels opened inside of each other had allowed travel time between galaxies to be cut down to only hours.

For the last fifty years they had been traveling at trans-tunnel eight and had gone by millions and millions of galaxies.

Forty-two would mean they could get between galaxies in seconds for all he knew.

How far out were they going to go to find these other Seeder groups?

The idea of that kind of distance just scared him more than he wanted to admit.

Chapter Two

(Seven years later)

CHAIRMAN ECHO GUINN felt relieved, finally, that they were about to get started outward again. Exploring again. The last seven years had seemed to really drag more than any other stretch of years in all her life.

Instead of a constant thrill of exploring, going forward, they had reversed course for almost a year, then stopped for six years as all upgrades were done by fleets of repair ships as well as in factories onboard *Star Trail*.

Most of the crew had managed to get back numbers of times to their home galaxies over the repair time, but she and Cole had stayed onboard the entire time. This was their home, their life.

But they had taken some down time to explore the vast wild areas on the ship and to rest.

Now she stood beside Cole in the command center watching the big screen. *Star Trail* and all the thousands of smaller ships onboard had been modified and tested for the new top speed and with shields that could plow through the center of a planet and not even notice.

The thousands of military ships on board had been upgraded with new weapons systems and cloaking capabilities as well.

They were finally ready to go once again.

Outward into unknown space.

It had been decided a year ago that the Starburst ships, of which there were now twenty, since six new ones had been built and crewed over the last seven years, were to head directly toward the closest Seeder areas.

Star Trail was to be the first to start out, with the others heading in different directions over the next few months. They had over six hundred other Seeder groups to find. And the vast distances in the universe those six hundred were spread through wasn't possible to even imagine.

But to Echo, the speed they would be traveling also wasn't possible for her to imagine.

The plan now was to not explore the galaxies they passed along the way, but just head at near top speed for the closest Seeder location. Even with the new drive at trans-tunnel forty, the trip would take eight months to reach the closest Seeder area.

Galaxies would flash past like so many dots. Over the last seven years, they had developed ways to take sensory readings of all the galaxies as they went by, at least the closest ones. And if something seemed interesting, the plan was that a scout ship with a military escort would launch and go back to take a look.

Star Trail would remain at forty trans-tunnel speed, but the scout and military ships dropping back would chase *Star Trail* down after their survey was done by going at maximum speed of trans-tunnel forty-two.

It would take the scout ships a few months to catch up if they spent a full day surveying a galaxy, but they would.

She and Cole figured that in the billions of galaxies they would flash past, they would only deploy a few-dozen scout ships. That's how dead the universe was of intelligent life.

But what had everyone scared and excited was what they would find when they reached the Seeders area. *Star Trail* would be the first to do so of all the Starburst ships.

And that worried Echo more than she wanted to admit even to Cole.

"Ready?" Cole asked Echo.

He smiled that wonderful smile of his that she never grew tired of, but she could tell from his eyes that he was as worried as she felt.

She nodded and together they turned around to face their command crew.

"Scout ships with military escorts ready to launch?" Echo asked.

"They are," JP said.

JP was their second in command and the most efficient person Echo had ever met. He was shorter than her five-four height, but she had no doubt he was a lot stronger. He had a bald head that he kept shaved on purpose. He looked slightly round, but Echo doubted there was an ounce of fat on the man.

"We're going to flash past where we were seven years ago in about an hour," Cole said. "Sensing systems on line and ready? If so, here we go. Stand by."

He glanced at Echo.

She smiled at him and took his hand as they turned around and sat down in their command chair.

The chair molded in around them, giving them complete contact with *Star Trail.*

Heads-up displays appeared around them showing them the complete status of the ship. Echo loved sitting in the command chair with Cole. It felt like she was even closer to him than any other time. The two of them and *Star Trail* felt almost like one unit.

"*Star Trail,*" Echo said. "If all systems are go, take us to trans-tunnel forty."

"*Jumping to trans-tunnel drive now,*" *Star Trail* said.

Both Echo and Cole watched every detail that came across the screen in front of them for the next hour until they went past the point they had turned around seven years before.

"*All scanning systems working and online,*" *Star Trail* said.

Echo could see that they were scanning a hundred galaxies to each side of their path. She didn't want to leave just yet as she watched the tally of thousands of galaxies flashing past, the number adding up more and more.

"*Scout ship and military ship launched,*" *Star Trail* reported.

Echo had seen that. The scout ships with military escort would launch automatically at the first sign of any life in a galaxy.

"Show us the data that caused that launch?" Cole said.

The image of a small spiral galaxy appeared on the screen. The data showed a clear sign of a medium-advanced civilization that had once tried to expand to a number of star systems but it seemed to be now extinct.

But it was worth a closer look, Echo had no doubt.

"At the old speed we wouldn't have run across that galaxy for another thirty years," Cole said.

Echo just watched the data as thousands and thousands more galaxies dropped behind them.

Not only was the space between galaxies vast, but most galaxies never gave birth to any intelligent life at all. And when it did, it rarely survived.

Humans, the Gray, and the Cirrata had somehow beaten the odds.

Echo wondered if they would find more races that had.

She wasn't sure if the idea scared her or excited her.

Chapter Three

(Eight months later)

COLE STOOD BESIDE Echo near their command chair and watched the scans coming in from in front of *Star Trail*. They were now close to the location of the Seeders that the ancients had launched here. If the Seeders had come this direction with expansion, there might be galaxies in this area.

But so far no signs of any kind of life in any of the galaxies ahead.

Around them the command center worked at an almost silent intensity, only talking in hushed tones when needed.

Star Trail was at trans-tunnel twenty now, moving past galaxies one every minute. That was slow enough for the scans ahead to really work.

And *Star Trail* was also shielded completely. No one would be able to see it coming. Cole and Echo had decided to take no chances.

Almost all scout and military ships were on board at the moment as well.

Over the last eight months they had launched thirty-nine scout ships with military escorts to get closer readings on galaxies with possible life. All but five of those ships had caught up with them and were now back on board. The scout ships had found very little. Mostly just either growing cultures that had yet to leave their home planet or dead cultures that had managed to spread out a little before going extinct.

The other five scout ships would catch up within the next day at this speed.

Now everyone stood ready. No one knew for what, but they were all ready.

The other nineteen Starburst ships were also watching, as well as the ancients remaining in the old home area.

Cole and Echo had spent a lot of time poring over the old records from the ancients of this group of Seeders. The last contact this group had had with the ancients had been just under four million years ago, just as the Seeders had started to move out of their home galaxy and into others.

Six thousand, two hundred of the ancients had stayed behind knowing they would never see their home worlds again due to the slowness of the ships and the vast distance. No one believed that many of them would still be alive. But Ray and Tacita had lasted four million years, so it was possible.

Very possible.

From what Echo and Cole could see, there seemed to be nothing at all that made this group different from the early years of Ray and Tacita. But Ray and Tacita had the ancients helping them for centuries. This new group had no outside help at all other than the six thousand ancients embedded in the culture.

And four million years was a very long time.

Cole just hoped they would find a large, galaxy-spanning culture of humans that had been seeded.

But as each galaxy flashed past and there was no sign of any form of life at all, Cole got more and more worried. In twenty minutes they would approach the home galaxy of this branch of Seeders.

Cole felt the clock just ticking down as they got closer and closer. And around them the tension in the command center seemed to expand like a weight pushing down on the air.

No one in the control room around them said a word. Echo stood absolutely still, her hands behind her back, her intense gaze on the big screen in front of them.

Cole shifted his weight from foot to foot, like he was getting ready to take off running. He felt like he was swimming through the silence like it was deep water pushing him down.

Finally, with just a dozen galaxies left to go before the home galaxy, *Star Trail* said simply, *"Signs of terra-forming in the approaching galaxy."*

It seemed that everyone in the room exhaled at once.

"Stop near the edge of the galaxy," Cole ordered.

A few seconds later *Star Trail* said, *"Holding position."*

"Human civilizations?" Echo asked as she and Cole both stared at the data flowing over the big screen in front of them.

"No," *Star Trail* said.

Then Cole saw the data coming in that twisted his stomach.

"The Gray fill the arid areas of every terra-formed planet and the Cirrata cities fill the oceans," Cole said softly. "No signs of human inhabitation."

Echo nodded.

Cole could see that the scans were showing millions of Gray ships and Cirrata ships in flight throughout the galaxy. They all seemed to be moving at the old pre-war Seeder ship speeds that would take them weeks to get across a galaxy and years to get between even the closest galaxies.

"Dispatch fifty cloaked scout ships with military escorts," Echo said. "Surround this galaxy and get any information possible. Stay cloaked."

The ships had been standing by, ready to launch, and within a minute *Star Trail* reported all ships launched.

"Let's move on," Cole said, working to keep his voice calm.

Echo nodded.

He knew there were many explanations for what they had just found. In their area the Gray had home galaxies as well as living on all human worlds. And so did the Cirrata. And Gray and Cirrata had joined each group that the ancients had seeded. So seeing the Gray and the Cirrata was no surprise. They were supposed to be here. But so were the humans.

It bothered Cole that there was no sign of human inhabitation.

Bothered him more than he wanted to think about, actually.

On a direct path to the original seeded galaxy were eight other galaxies. They found the same at each. Bustling and seemingly healthy Gray and Cirrata civilizations filled each galaxy.

No humans.

Not even signs after four million years that they had been on any planet. Of course, after that long, there would be no signs left.

Cole and Echo left scout and military ships at each galaxy to do intense scans and gather information.

Then they flashed into a holding position near the original seeded galaxy.

The same.

No sign at all of humans.

Just Gray and Cirrata.

"Something went horribly wrong here," Echo said softly as the data came in.

Cole only nodded.

"Star Trail," Echo said, "Can you scan for any extremely ancient signs of human civilizations."

"There are signs," Star Trail said. *"But nothing remains."*

"Can you estimate, within a range, how far in the past the humans vanished?" Cole asked.

"On only preliminary data," Star Trail said, *"approximately three-point-five million years ago. Possibly longer."*

Cole glanced at Echo who was looking as shocked as he felt.

"Star Trail," Cole said. "Recall all ships."

Echo nodded. Then she said softly, "This is out of our hands now."

"Exactly," Cole said. "The Gray from our area will need to make contact here if contact is even desired."

He had a hunch the Gray and the Cirrata that worked with them and the ancients wouldn't make contact. From what he could tell, this culture was stable. No point in bothering it now.

They would do a full scan of all the galaxies this culture occupied.

If the humans had actually vanished over three million years ago, there would be no evidence of what happened. This might be a mystery that might need to remain a mystery.

Chapter Four

ECHO AND COLE had just finished lunch in their apartment when *Star Trail* said simply, "Chairmen Ray and Tacita request a conference."

Echo sipped on her coffee as Cole said, "Put them through here."

Their apartment was large, with two offices and a large bedroom and walk-in closets. The kitchen was wonderful, state of the art, and their dining table was huge, usually half-covered in books and work pads. Echo loved everything about it.

The living room was sunken and had soft couches and walls full of books. A stone fireplace filled one wall of the living room. They spent a lot of time there either reading or watching movies.

The place had a college clutter level, as Cole liked to call it. Mostly just books either just finished or to-be-read.

Their three cats, direct descendants of one of the cats they had found on one of their missions on a destroyed planet, napped in different areas of the living room. All three were shades of orange and white. None of the cats had even bothered to come into the dining room to join them for lunch. Typical cats.

There was a screen over their dining table and it flickered as *Star Trail* made connection with Ray and Tacita back in the Milky Way Galaxy.

As *Star Trail* had traveled the vast distance from the Milky Way, they had dropped off small stations, all pre-built and staffed with a crew of ten each. The stations were actually fairly large and comfortable with furnished apartments for hundreds and restaurants and a few bars on each station. The crew of each station rotated in and out every few weeks.

Seeders could teleport long distances, but not as far as *Star Trail* had traveled. Not even chairmen who could teleport the farthest could make that length of jump.

So they called the trail they had left of small stations breadcrumbs and any Seeder on board *Star Trail* could jump from station to station back to the Milky way if needed, stopping to sleep and eat at any station along the way. It normally would take three days to make the journey, but it was possible and many of *Star Trail's* crew were doing it at any given time.

Considering that there were over three million people on *Star Trail,* Echo was surprised that breadcrumb trail of stations wasn't more crowded than it was.

Star Trail had dropped over eighteen hundred breadcrumb stations. Those stations also allowed new crew to join *Star Trail* from the Milky Way and easy communications over the vast distance as well.

Every Starburst ship was creating a breadcrumb trail out into the distances of space. Echo actually considered those trails to be one of the most important things they were doing. On board *Star Trail* they had six factories that covered many, many square kilometers, working at full speed to build the stations and get them ready to drop.

At any given point they had over a hundred stations just waiting with more being built and completed right down to the furniture. They were built on a pace of one station per five hours. Every Starburst ship had the same capability.

Here in this culture of Gray and Cirrata, they would drop off a much larger and very shielded station for those wanting to come and research and watch this culture as well as a smaller station near each occupied galaxy.

After a moment, as Cole cleared off the last of their dishes from the wonderful French Dip sandwiches they had had for lunch, Tacita and Ray appeared on the big screen behind their dining room table.

"Ancients have any idea what happened here?" Cole asked.

Echo was hoping that they did.

Both Ray and Tacita shook their heads. Echo could tell that both were very bothered by what had been found. As was everyone on board *Star Trail*. They had gone looking for long lost cousins and found them all dead or missing. That would clearly upset anyone.

It wasn't doing her any good at all, that's for sure.

"We have something you should know about that we have just been told by the ancients," Ray said. "The mother ships of the Seeders of four million years ago all had hidden tracking devices built into them."

Echo shook her head as Cole laughed.

"Four million years is a long time for a ship to survive," Cole said. "Let alone a tracking device to still work."

"Ask *Star Trail* if she could survive that long?" Tacita said.

Echo said, "*Star Trail,* could you survive in space for four million years in your old mother ship form? Before you became a Starburst ship?"

"Yes," Star Trail said. *"It would not be difficult."*

"Shit," Cole said, standing and facing the screen.

Echo moved over to stand beside him.

Ray and Tacita looked extremely serious.

"When the ancients pulled back from the area you are in, the Seeders there had three mother ships," Ray said. "Their names were *Sun Hawk, Sun Hunter,* and *Sun Heaven.*"

"Find them," Tacita said, "And we may find out what happened to the Seeders and humans in that area of space."

"We are sending the information to *Star Trail* that would be needed to track them through long distances," Ray said. "And through the years."

"Good luck on this," Tacita said.

And the screen went blank.

Cole laughed and went back to the sink to put the dishes in the dishwasher.

"What's so funny?" Echo asked. She clearly didn't find any of this funny.

Four hundred years earlier they had been stationed on a human planet mostly wiped out by a rare electromagnetic pulse. Their work for those years had never left either one of them and now here they were finding another culture destroyed. This was bringing back memories of those years for her and she knew it was for him as well.

"I was kind of hoping," Cole said, "that we could just move onward and leave this mystery for someone else to solve."

Echo agreed with that. She had been hoping the same thing.

Desperately hoping to get away from what seemed to be massive death of more billions of humans than she ever wanted to think about.

But that wasn't going to be the case, clearly. Somewhere in this vast area of space were three Seeder mother ships.

Very, very old ships.

Now the question was where.

Section Two
The Search

Chapter Five

ECHO HAD COME up with the idea that the best way to start to find three four-million-year-old Seeder mother ships was to map the area they had seeded.

Cole liked the plan only because it would give them more data, not because he thought it would help them figure out where the ships were in this vast area of space.

Star Trail had scanned the immediate area around the home galaxy and found no trace of the three ships. So they had launched eight hundred scout ships with military escorts to go out from the center and discover which galaxies had been seeded.

Now Cole stood next to the command chair, sipping his morning coffee, watching as the results started to come in from the scout ships.

No sign of any human in any galaxy had been found in three days of exploring outward. That really bothered him more than he wanted to let on. Something horrid had happened and they were sitting here with a ship full of three million Seeders, basically human in all respects except for a few genetic details. Somehow they needed to figure out what had happened.

"Star Trail," he said, "please put on the large screen a three-dimensional map of the galaxies that were seeded. Make the seeded galaxies green, the ones not seeded or that we have not explored yet white."

On the big screen thousands of green dots appeared surrounded by many more white dots. A clear pattern was emerging from the exploration.

The three mother ships had gone in three different directions from the home galaxy.

Just as Ray and Tacita's ship had done from their home galaxy, the seeded galaxies formed a trail as the mother ships jumped from one seeded galaxy to the next closest galaxy.

Three trails led away from this home system, each with hundreds of galaxies. About as many as could be seeded in a half-million year's time. But now the scout ships were starting to find the end of the trails. That much was becoming clear as well.

Whatever had happened had spread from galaxy to galaxy. How was that even possible?

Cole knew of nothing that would even make that possible.

Cole sipped on his coffee and watched as ship after ship reported in, firming up the map on the big screen. All three original Seeder mother ships had made about the same progress and all three had clearly stopped at about the same time.

Star Trail was constantly scanning through every scout ship for any sign of the three mother ships.

Nothing.

Echo appeared beside him. She was freshly showered from her morning exercise and smelled faintly of apricot shampoo. She had on a white blouse with her sleeves rolled up and jeans.

She had two cups of coffee in her hands, handing him a fresh cup.

He smiled and said, "Thanks."

It was part of their normal morning routine, one that he loved. Just being beside Echo made him happy no matter what they were doing.

"I see the map is almost filled in," Echo said.

"Afraid so," Cole said. *"Star Trail,* approximately how many galaxies did the three Seeder mother ships seed?"

"From the pattern," Star Trail said, *"the total will be just under eight thousand galaxies."*

"Thank you," Cole said. Then he turned to Echo. "There had to be over a billion human planets in each one of those galaxies. How did that many humans vanish? We need to find the answer to that."

Echo nodded, staring at the big screen. "We need to find those three ships or at least what happened to them."

Cole suddenly had an idea. *"Star Trail,* would you contact Ray and Tacita and have them ask the ancients if the three mother ships might have known about the ancients' existence even though their crew did not."

"Question sent," Star Trail said.

"What are you thinking?" Echo asked.

Cole just shrugged. "If those three ships didn't know about the ancients, they would act one way. If they knew, they would act another way. That's all."

Echo smiled. "Very good thinking."

"On this puzzle we need all the help we can get," Cole said. And he believed that.

As they watched, the scout ships sent back in reports from beyond the last seeded galaxy. No sign of any seeding and no signals at all.

On the screen now were the results of over a half-million years of Seeder work, now only occupied by the Gray and the Cirrata. And there was no doubt that after over three million years, neither of those cultures would be able to help at all even if contacted.

The Gray and the Cirrata didn't live as long as Seeders. In fact, normal Gray and Cirrata had life spans not much longer than humans. No chance after three million years of any memory that would help would survive.

Now Available
from all your favorite booksellers in trade paper and electronic editions.

Cole doubted they even would remember another culture built their worlds for them.

Cole glanced at Echo. "I suppose we need to take the next step."

She nodded. Then said, *"Star Trail,* please show at scale a three-dimensional representation of how far the three mother ships could have traveled at their top speeds since the last galaxy was seeded here."

A sphere appeared on the large screen. Billions of tiny dots, each representing a galaxy filled the sphere.

Cole just shook his head. That was a vast, vast area of space and those three ships or the remains of them could be parked anywhere in it.

"Star Trail, are any of the other ancients-planted Seeder cultures close to this sphere?" Echo asked.

"No," Star Trail said simply.

Once again Cole was shocked at the vastness of space.

"How long at trans-tunnel forty would it take scout ships to reach the edge of that sphere from here?" Echo asked.

"Three weeks," Star Trail said.

Cole just stared at the vast sphere, shaking his head. It would have taken those mother ships three and a half million years to travel what *Star Trail* and all the scout ships could now do in three weeks.

They stood in silence as the command crew worked around them and more and more information came in from the scout ships.

Cole knew what they needed to do next. He and Echo and their top command crew had talked it over and then presented the idea to Ray and Tacita who had agreed.

"Seems it is time to start the mini-starburst project," Cole said.

The project simply put was to launch almost every scout ship they had, about eight thousand, all with military escorts, in a starburst pattern from *Star Trail*, all going at top speed outward to the edge of where the three ships might have gone, all searching for the signals from the three ships.

Ray and Tacita had assured them that the signals would still be functioning even if the ships had been destroyed.

Cole just hoped that was right.

Echo nodded. *"Star Trail*, call in all ships. We launch the mini-starburst project tomorrow."

Cole stared at the sphere on the screen in front of him. That was a vast amount of space to search. And his biggest worry was that they would find nothing.

He almost dreaded that more than he dreaded finding the ships.

Almost.

Chapter Six

THE ANSWER CAME back from the ancients on the question Cole had asked. The three lost ships might have known about the ancients. And for one large and glaring reason. There was a chance there had still been ancients alive at the point the humans vanished.

Cole just shook his head. He and Echo had completely forgotten that one not-so-small point. The ancients had stayed behind with this group and more than likely would be on the mother ships.

When they got the answer, he and Echo had been just finishing up dinner in their apartment. Cole had made them

a spicy taco salad and they both had been sipping on some sort of special beer.

They liked to have a drink every evening to relax, usually right after dinner before going to their offices to work or moving to the living room to watch a movie. Neither of them drank more than one glass of wine or beer or one cocktail a day, but they enjoyed the ritual of it more than anything.

And they had made a game out of making the drink appropriate to the meal as much as possible. Tonight they were sipping on a beer that tasted so light and watery that Cole actually didn't much care for. But one of the command crew had told him it went well with tacos and taco salad.

He honestly wasn't so sure and from the way Echo sort of stared at the light golden color of the beer, she wasn't sure either.

"Saved from the beer by work," Cole said, pushing his still-full glass toward the center of the table.

"Thank heavens," Echo said, laughing and putting her glass beside his. "Tasted like colored water. Bad colored water."

"Tequila next time with tacos," Cole said. "Margaritas."

"Now that I would drink to," Echo said, smiling.

He loved it when she smiled. They were both under stress and the idea of having to find three mother ships that each had had over a million people on board bothered them. But they still managed to stay level, she more than he, of that he had no doubt. She was the rock in the relationship.

But she thought he was, so it seemed to work out fine.

Now the answer they had gotten back from the ancients changed how they needed to look at everything.

"*Star Trail,*" Cole said, "Could you please find out the top speed of the ancient ships when this area was seeded."

"*The ancient seeding ships that came here used trans-tunnel twenty,*" *Star Trail* said.

"You think the ancients might have helped them pick up speed?" Echo asked.

"If they were running from something," Cole said, "I sure would."

"*Star Trail,*" Echo said, "would you please ask through Ray and Tacita if any of ancients left here knew the locations of the other seeded groups closest to this one? And also get an exact list of the ancients left with this group if they have it. Their specialties if any. That sort of detail."

"*Contacting Chairmen Ray and Tacita,*" *Star Trail* said.

"What are you thinking?" Cole asked, smiling at his beautiful partner.

"Four million years or so ago the ancients started building a new home, didn't they?" Echo asked. "About the time this expansion started."

Cole nodded. That was at least what they had been told. All this was information that *Star Rain* and the other Starburst ships had found out when they made contact with the ancients left in the old home area of space, an area abandoned much like what they were finding here.

"And a million years ago the ancients supposedly all moved to that new home, wherever it might be," Echo said. "Right?"

Cole sort of felt a shock hit his system. "You think all these humans on these billions of planets simply packed up and left?"

Echo shrugged, but kept smiling. "The ancients' home area of space was millions of times larger than this area. It would be possible. Remember, Seeders never think small and ancients make us look like ants in their universe."

The ancients had built a massive structure they called "The Center" that was their home. It was five spinning rings and the entire thing was larger than the Milky Way Galaxy. Cole had seen and studied pictures of the place and still couldn't grasp its size.

Cole thought for a moment. Her idea made as much sense as anything they had come up with so far. And he liked the idea of the humans moving a lot more than something killing them all.

He reached for her hand. "Leave the dishes. Let's go back to the command center to do some calculations."

She nodded and a moment later they appeared near their command chair. Behind them the second command shift was working and no one seemed in the slightest bit surprised that they had arrived. They often came back to work at odd hours.

Cole looked up at the data flowing over the big screen. Almost all scout ships had returned. Everyone was preparing for the big launch tomorrow.

"*Star Trail,*" Cole said, "would you please show a sphere on the big screen with the distance the three mother ships might have traveled at trans-tunnel twenty in three-point-five million years."

A large sphere appeared that seemed to be filled with a film of white. Cole knew that every tiny dot that made up that film in that sphere was a galaxy. He couldn't even imagine the distance he was looking at. Numbers never helped him grasp such massive distances.

"Show with bright green dots," Echo said, "the other close areas seeded by the ancients if any are inside that sphere."

Many, many green dots appeared in one area of the sphere. Too many for Cole to count quickly.

"*Star Trail,*" Cole said, "please show the location of the Milky Way Galaxy with a bright white dot in relationship to this sphere."

A bright white dot appeared on one edge of the sphere.

Cole just stared at all of this.

"Shit," Echo said softly.

Cole looked at her. She seldom swore. She was intently staring at the sphere.

"*Star Trail,*" Echo said, "please show the ancients' old home world area of space as a bright red dot, keeping everything as best you can to scale."

The sphere shank just slightly and a bright red dot appeared.

Cole was starting to understand where Echo was going.

"*Star Trail,*" Cole said, "keeping everything as best you can to scale, show the other locations of all the seeded ancient cultures."

Over six hundred green dots appeared forming a half moon. The sphere included numbers of them.

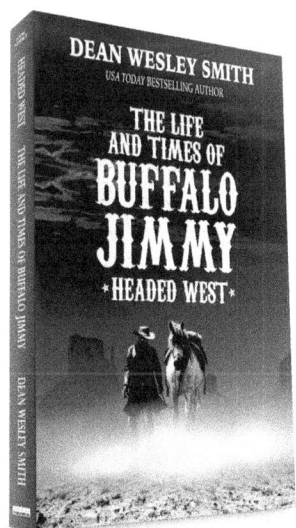
"Look where the Milky Way and all of our seeded galaxies are," Echo said.

Cole just stared at the screen.

The pattern was very, very clear.

The Milky Way was directly between the ancients' old home worlds and the half-moon of six hundred seeded cultures.

And now, for the first time, Cole understood why the ancients wouldn't tell anyone where their new home was.

They were afraid of something.

They were afraid of something in these cultures they had seeded.

Cole glanced at Echo. Her beautiful blue eyes were huge as she stared up at him.

"What the hell is going on here?" she whispered.

He just wished he had an answer for her.

Chapter Seven

"WHY WOULD THE ancients hide tracking devices on the mother ships?" Echo asked, staring at the big screen in front of them. They had gone over and over everything they knew during the last hour and all it did was confuse them even more.

"I don't know, but we have got to tell the other chairmen," Cole said.

"Not the ancients," Echo said.

"No, from now on out they are out of the loop until we understand more."

Echo nodded. She agreed, but she wasn't sure exactly what they needed to tell the other chairmen. Granted, the pattern of the seeded areas was alarming at best.

And what worried her more than anything else was that the one Seeders group the ancients spent a few million years helping was the one directly between the ancients' old home worlds and where the other groups had been seeded.

That group standing like a wall was the Milky Way Galaxy Seeders. Their group.

It sure made the fact suspicious that the ancients wouldn't tell them where their new home area of space was located. And it sure brought more possible reasons for the ancients moving from their old home besides outgrowing the old area.

But what was happening here?

What could the ancients possibly be afraid of over millions of years?

So many questions, no sign of any answers.

She and Cole had spent the next hour, after discovering the pattern, working with the command crew to get more data. But there just wasn't much they could do.

At that point *Star Trail* said, *"List of the known ancients left in this area has arrived. Also, the ancients here knew the locations of the other seeded groups."*

Everyone in the command center heard that and just stood silently.

Echo didn't know what to think. But she knew her stomach was twisting which usually meant they were into something over their heads.

Cole just stared at the big screen shaking his head.

"I think we have two choices," Echo said, finally turning to face him.

Cole nodded.

"We go ahead with the mini-starburst search mission tomorrow as planned."

"Second choice?"

"We head at top speed for the next seeded area."

Cole nodded. "I think we have a third choice."

She looked at him with a frown, but indicated he should go on.

"We wait for two days until *Star Ray* arrives at their destination. If there are no humans left there, we know something bigger is going on and we head on to the next seeded area. If they find a normal seeded culture with humans, we do the mini-starburst search pattern to look for the ships here."

She nodded. She liked that plan.

"Who knows," Cole said. "That seeded area is inside the distance the three mother ships might have traveled. Maybe *Star Ray* will find them there."

She looked at Cole and smiled. "You really don't believe that, do you?"

He laughed. "Not a chance in hell. Just trying to stay positive."

She shook her head and kissed him and then they went back to sifting through all the data that had come in.

It was going to be a long two days of waiting that was for sure.

Chapter Eight

YESTERDAY, COLE AND Echo had decided to tell the other chairmen on the other nineteen Starburst ships their theory in a vast conference call. The big screen in the command center had shown all the other couples and their expressions as Cole and Echo laid out the patterns.

Cole found it amazing how many of the other chairmen jumped right to the same point he and Echo had gotten to. Something far, far larger was going on.

No one had any idea what, but it seemed clear something had happened four million years ago to cause this pattern.

Everyone agreed to not mention this at all to Ray and Tacita yet, since it was all just strange supposition and worry. Besides, Ray and Tacita were directly connected to the ancients.

One chairman pointed out that it had been the ancients who helped them get the faster speeds to go find out what was happening with these other seeded areas.

"Free scouting missions," another chairman had said and everyone nodded to that.

The agreement was that nothing would be said until *Star Ray* reached the next seeded area within reach.

So now Cole stood beside Echo, watching the feed coming in from *Star Ray* as it approached the home galaxy of an ancient seeded group. Lisa and Jaden, the two chairmen had their image in the lower corner of the feed.

Cole liked them both. He and Echo had spent time with Lisa and Jaden as their two ships were being overhauled.

Lisa stood almost six feet tall and was thin as a post, with long black hair and piercing green eyes. She loved to pull pranks on people and her laugh was infectious.

Jaden was Lisa's height but didn't look it because of his wide shoulders and shaved head that gave him a tough look. He had hands that looked like they could crush anything, but it turned out he was gentle and one of the smartest people Cole had ever met.

Over the years of the refitting of their ships, the four of them had made it a habit to go out every week to a different restaurant, sometimes light-years distant from where they were living. The four of them had made it a game and great fun to never repeat a restaurant. And they found some wonderful food and some wonderful experiences, often tied into not-so-wonderful food.

Cole missed those dinners and the diversity of being able to find so many different forms of restaurants. It was partially why he and Echo changed their meals regularly and experimented with both food and drink. They had grown to like it.

And Echo often talked with Lisa and Jaden about a meal they had made. If he and Echo had best friends in this new world, it would be Lisa and Jaden, even though at the moment, the two ships were impossible distances apart.

Just as happened with *Star Trail*, Lisa and Jaden found terra-formed galaxies about eight galaxies away from the original galaxy. But no evidence of human life.

Over the next few hours as *Star Ray* approached the home galaxy, it became clear that it would repeat what *Star Trail* had found.

And when the home galaxy of that group of Seeders was scanned, it also showed only a stable society of Gray and Cirrata, but no sign of humans.

"That group also had three mother ships as well," Cole said, glancing at Echo who looked more worried than he had seen her look before.

"So we now have humans completely missing," Echo said, "from more billions of human planets than I want to try to imagine."

"What in the world happened?" Cole asked.

At that moment *Star Trail* said, *"Ray and Tacita are asking to speak to all ships."*

"Link us in," Echo said.

After a moment Ray and Tacita's faces appeared on the screen. They waited until all chairmen on all twenty Starburst ships were linked.

"The situation that *Star Ray* has found scared the ancients we are in contact with," Ray said.

"There is much they are clearly not telling us," Tacita said.

Cole was shocked at the anger clearly coming from Tacita. He always thought of her as cool and calm.

"Ask them what they are afraid of," Cole said.

"And why they won't tell us where their new home world is at," another chairman said.

"We did," Ray said, his voice cold.

"They said nothing," Tacita said.

"So we want every ship to be prepared," Ray said. "Full military alert as you move forward."

"We no longer believe the Seeder ships are lost or that anything happened to the humans in those galaxies," Tacita said. "We believe they all moved for a reason we do not yet understand."

"A reason having to do with why the ancients put them out there in the first place," Ray said. "We will continue the build up forces here and try to get answers from the ancients."

"Be on high alert," Tacita said.

Ray nodded and cut off the connection.

Cole felt shocked. Around them the command crew stood in silence.

"Feels like the world just shifted," Echo said.

Cole could only nod to that.

"*Star Trail*," Echo said, "are all the scout and military ships on board?"

"*All ships are on board*," *Star Trail* said.

Echo glanced up at Cole and he nodded. They needed to get moving now.

"*Star Trail*," Echo said. "Top speed for the next seeded group location."

"And inform the other Starburst ships and Ray and Tacita of our movement."

"*Entering trans-tunnel drive*," *Star Trail* said. "*The other ships have been notified. Star Ray will be jumping to full speed in two hours after leaving breadcrumb stations behind. It will also head to its next destination.*"

"Thank you," Echo said. "Continue scanning for the mother ship signals."

"Just over four weeks to our next stop," Cole said. "It's going to be a long four weeks."

Echo said nothing to that. And he didn't blame her.

Chapter Nine

ECHO WAS SURPRISED at how busy they had been in the last four weeks. Turns out the four weeks hadn't seemed to take that long after all. Almost every day one of the other Starburst ships approached their first target ancient seeded culture.

And every seeded home galaxy and culture was the same. All had spent a half million years seeding, then all humans and Seeders alike had just vanished, leaving thriving Gray and Cirrata cultures on the terra-formed planets.

And the three and a half million years since that point had effectively erased all traces of what might have happened or how it happened.

All the chairmen had conference called every day as new data came on board. It was actually Lisa and Jaden that came up with the idea that started to narrow down some things.

They had laid out all the known ancient seeded home galaxies in this area of space. They knew that at least twenty of them had been abandoned, since all twenty Starburst ships had found the same thing.

So Lisa and Jaden had tried to figure out among all the seeded areas what would be the center point if they were all migrating to one major spot.

Once the lines were drawn it became very clear where these cultures' new home worlds would be.

Since the ancients really liked to build large home areas, if all the populations had moved to that one area, it wouldn't be surprising.

The reasons, on the other hand, were unknown, and why the ancients wouldn't even talk any more about what was being found made no sense to anyone.

Star Trail was within one day of arriving at the second seeded area when Echo decided to ask *Star Trail* a question. It really wasn't a question she thought would have any meaning, but was just curious.

She and Cole were standing near their chair in the command center and the main shift was working around the room.

"Star Trail," Echo said, "Assuming ark ships the size of a Starburst ship, how many such ships would it take to evacuate one normal human planet?"

"Assuming a population of six billion humans on a planet," Star Trail said, *"assuming three million per ship, it would take two thousand ships of this size to evacuate a planet."*

Cole sort of shook his head at hearing that and then asked, *"Star Trail,* would the resources be available in each solar system to build that many Starburst-sized ships?"

"Yes," Star Trail said. *"If the military and scout ships were not also built at the same time."*

"So per galaxy we are looking at a billion planets times two thousand ships per planet," Echo said. She couldn't even grasp that number.

"Even with round trips," Cole said. "That's just not possible. Even at the scale the ancients worked at."

Echo nodded. "We are missing something major."

Cole nodded and the two of them stood there staring at the screen watching the scanning data come in. Neither one of them had a clue what they were missing.

Nothing about any of this made any sense.

And it hadn't from the beginning.

Echo could feel her tension climbing. In less than twenty hours they would be at the second seeded home world. So she offered to cook them a good dinner and let them try to get some sleep.

Or at least rest.

She had just taken out some freshly made rolls from the oven and put them in a basket to go with the fresh turkey and gravy and stuffing she had made when she finally realized what they had been missing.

Cole was sitting at the kitchen table sipping on a glass of red wine when she put the rolls down in front of him and pointed at them.

He smiled up at her. "They smell wonderful. You want me to eat one?"

She laughed. "I do, but first take one and break it open. Don't burn your fingers."

He took one out of the basket and over his plate he broke it open, then took a deep sniff of the wonderfully smelling fresh bread.

"Now put it back in the basket," she said.

"This some sort of kinky form of torture," he said, laughing but doing as she said.

She pointed to his plate. "What do you see there?"

He glanced down. "Breadcrumbs. I have…"

Then he stared at the crumbs for a moment, then smiled at her.

"You think they used a breadcrumb-like network to move all those people?"

She nodded, smiling.

"We eat first and then see if we can work out where the network would be exactly," Cole said, pushing his glass of wine away.

Echo had to admit, the dinner was good, but never before had they eaten so quickly and left such a mess in their kitchen when they jumped back to the command center.

Chapter Ten

COLE HAD *STAR* Trail work on figuring out where a breadcrumb trail would be from the Seeded area they were approaching that would lead to where they were guessing everyone had gone.

A dotted line appeared from the group of galaxies ahead.

Cole just stared at it. If the group ahead turned out to be as expected and that all humans had vanished over three million years before, they would search for that breadcrumb trail. Signs of it might still be in existence.

Echo stared at the image, nodding, then she asked a question Cole hadn't even started to think about.

"Star Trail, how long would it take to breed the Seeder genes into dominance in everyone in a planet's population?"

At that question the entire command center around them dropped to silence as the idea of what she had just suggested struck home.

"Approximately two-hundred-thousand years," Star Trail said, *"assuming a normal population of four billion per planet. But as the Seeders genes became dominant the population would stabilize, since children are unusual in Seeders. So assuming a population of one billion per planet at full Seeders gene dominance, less than one-hundred-thousand years."*

"Would that be possible to do?" Cole asked.

"Yes," Star Trail said.

Cole felt his stomach just clamp up around the wonderful dinner he had just had.

"They are here and watching us," Echo said softly.

"We have been played for the fools," Cole said, understanding exactly what she was saying.

They were pawns in a much larger and very ancient fight among ancients. And she and Cole had just come in thinking they would find backwards Seeders cultures.

"Star Trail," Cole said, "Get all Starburst chairmen and Ray and Tacita on a conference call."

"Working," Star Trail said.

It took almost a full minute before everyone was linked together. Some of the chairmen had clearly been in bed. All the Starburst ships had agreed to run on the same schedule, so even though this was evening, some early-to-bed types had already retired.

"Ray, Tacita," Cole said, "are you away from the ancients?"

"We are in the Milky Way on our mother ship," Ray said, nodding.

Cole nodded and went on to explain their theory of the breadcrumbs trail of evacuation and what they had discovered on the timeline to create entire planets of Seeders.

Some of the chairmen just looked angry at the idea.

Then Cole said to Ray and Tacita. "I believe we have been played by the ancients in some ancient fight. And I don't much feel like being the pawn anymore."

All of the chairmen on the screen nodded to that.

Ray and Tacita nodded.

Cole knew exactly what needed to be done and needed to be done instantly.

"Suggestions?" Ray asked.

"Chairmen, please go to your chairs and close down this discussion to only ourselves," Cole said. "No command crew please."

Everyone nodded and Cole and Echo moved to their chair and sat down, letting the chair close in around them.

"Star Trail, please remove this discussion from the large screen, contain it only here," Cole said.

"Done," Star Trail said.

All other chairmen were linked in including Ray and Tacita.

"I believe we have two things we need to do quickly," Cole said. "We need to first, without drawing attention to what we are doing, find a number of the breadcrumb trails and figure exactly where the new home worlds will be."

"Agreed," Ray said and all the other chairmen nodded.

"We need to monitor all communication back along our breadcrumb trails of all of our crew," Cole said.

There were audible gasps from some of the other chairman.

"You suspect that crew on each ship is spying for the ancients?" Ray asked.

"No," Cole said. "I believe there are ancients on these ships with us. They are Seeders, as we are."

"Star Trail," Echo said, "Is there any way to tell the difference between an ancient and a Seeder from our seeded group?"

"Yes," Star Trail said.

"Are there ancients on board this ship now?" Cole asked, surprised at *Star Trail's* answer.

"Yes," Star Trail said. *"Just over seven thousand."*

Cole looked at the shocked faces of the chairmen on his screen. "I'm sorry

for this but we have to know. *Star Trail*, would you please have each Starburst ship check to see if any chairmen of a Starburst ship is an ancient."

Star Trail said after a moment. *"Every chairman taking part in this conference is a Seeder from the Milky Way Galaxy group. But every command crew on every ship has an ancient."*

Cole was about as angry as he could be. And clearly, looking at the faces of the other chairmen, he wasn't the only one. Being a pawn in someone else's game was never fun.

"So what do you suggest needs to be done?" Ray asked. He also sounded angry and from the look on Tacita's face she was about to explode.

"We send them home," Echo said. "We would have welcomed them if they had been honest with us from the start, but we can't trust hidden spies. We clear each ship of them quickly."

Everyone agreed.

"And we set up monitoring systems," Tacita said, "along each breadcrumb trail to each of our ships so no ancient can come through."

"All of our ships will be set up to monitor any communication as well that might be suspicious," another chairman said.

"We will pull all of our people back from the old home world of the ancients as well," Ray said.

Cole nodded to all of that. But he had one more thought that he hated.

"The ancients put tracking devices on every Seeder mother ship in these seeded areas," Cole said. "All of our ships need to be completely checked as well for such a device."

Every chairman nodded.

"Good luck on the purge, everyone," Cole said.

And with that he cut the communication and he and Echo, still in their command chair, went to work on how to escort each ancient off the ship and back along the breadcrumb trail.

It was going to be a very long night.

Chapter Eleven

ECHO WAS THE most saddened to learn that their second in command, JP Horshaw was an ancient. But she was happy to see that he was the only one on the main command crew who was.

They decided to first get with the head of the military. All of his men and women were cleared. It seemed the ancients did not do well in the military.

They next invited JP to their apartment. They had three armed military personnel standing guard and *Star Trail* put a shield around their apartment after JP jumped to their dining room. The shield that wouldn't allow him to jump away or contact anyone.

So Echo and Cole both cleared off the remains of their dinner dishes and had JP sit at the dining room table.

They offered him a drink and he picked his normal coffee. Many, many times over the last decades of time the three of them had sat at this table and talked and planned. JP had been with them from the start.

"So we have a question," Cole asked, sitting across from JP

Echo sat at the table and the three military guards were out of sight in the bedroom and hall and living room area.

She couldn't look JP in the eye. She felt completely betrayed and very angry.

"Why didn't you tell us you were an ancient?" Cole asked.

JP jerked, then nodded and sat back.

"You know we would have welcomed you aboard in the same way," Echo said.

"I know that," JP said. "But we all have our missions."

Echo didn't want to hear that, not in the slightest.

"So now that you will be leaving us," Cole said, "you want to give us a hint about your mission?"

"To report back as to what you found," JP said, shrugging.

"We have already been doing that," Echo said. "Why the secrecy?"

"Because," JP said, "those in charge do not believe that a younger society such as yours can deal with having ancients around."

"Well," Cole said, "they are right about that, because you old folks can't be trusted, clearly."

JP nodded. "It sure appears that way, doesn't it?"

"So what in the world has your people so afraid of what we are going to find out here?" Echo asked.

"Exactly what you are finding," Cole said. "The ancients who were put out here to seed these cultures all believed that humans should be simply bred out of the equation."

"Ancients do not?" Echo asked.

"No," JP said. "We would approach the Seeders in different cultures and worlds that appeared naturally and give them the opportunity to have their Seeder genes become active or remain as humans. Many, in fact most, chose to stay human. And the Seeder genes remained a rare occurrence."

"So what do you expect we will find when we locate this central home of this batch of Seeders?" Cole asked.

"We honestly do not know," JP said. "That's why so many of us are on these ships."

"Couldn't trust the kids, huh?" Cole said.

"Pretty much," JP said, nodding. "Not even enough to tell you we were here."

"Well," Echo said, "seems you all can go back to hiding in your new home, wherever that might be."

Echo didn't even try to keep the contempt out of her voice.

"Yup," Cole said, standing. "Seems the kids now got to go it alone without adult supervision."

He moved over and nodded for the military escort to come in.

Echo stood, staring at someone she had trusted for decades. "Your people might just want to worry about which side the kids decide to take when this is all said and done."

JP's face went white and he nodded.

A moment later JP and the three military men were gone.

And five hours later every ancient on board *Star Trail* was gone, headed along the breadcrumb chain under guard back to the Milky Way and then back to their own worlds, she was sure.

After this, she doubted the ancients would be much welcome anywhere outside their own space, now that ships and security measures were set to scan for them.

After the last ancient was gone, the real search began for anything any of them might have planted, any tracking device, any communications device. Anything.

Star Trail was a vast ship that held over three million people and hundreds of thousands of other ships. That detailed search took them ten long days.

And it found hundreds of issues. For days, the anger and resentment to the ancients who had been tossed off the ship was almost at lynch-mob levels.

Eventually it calmed down as everyone slowly came to realize their world, *Star Trail,* was safe now. And that the other Starburst ships were safe. And all the ships back in the human galaxies were quickly becoming safe as well.

But that boiling anger at the ancients wasn't going to go away any time soon.

If ever.

Seeders lived a very long time and had perfect memories and Echo would never forget. She doubted anyone else on this ship would either.

Every Starburst ship had the same issues and all ships compared notes back and forth when something was found to make sure the same thing was found on every ship.

For the ten days, every Starburst ship had just stopped and held positions.

Every inch on the outside of *Star Trail* was scanned and the workings of all the screens and all the trans-tunnel drives were evaluated to make sure nothing could be traced in any fashion.

One minor adjustment had to be made to the trans-tunnel drives of every ship. The upgrade to clear out a traceable problem had been sent to them from the Milky Way scientists. That adjustment took out a clear signature of the drive and also allowed them to increase all speeds to trans-tunnel forty-four.

As the search and adjustments were going on, every Starburst ship set new protocols on anyone coming and going through the breadcrumb trail. And every inch of every ship inside each Starburst ship was constantly scanned and rescanned.

Echo hated the new security measures, even though most on board the ships would never notice them. But after ten days and all the traps, tracers, and other things they had found installed by the ancients, she was glad the new measures were in place.

It was very disconcerting when those you thought were your friends had suddenly become an enemy.

Chapter Twelve

COLE HAD MANAGED to keep his anger in check for the ten days of sweeps, changes, and new security measures. And now, as he stood beside the command chair drinking his morning coffee and studying reports as they came in over the big screen, he felt as if things might return to normal again.

Echo had decided she desperately needed her morning exercise and her routine as well. So she wouldn't be here for another twenty minutes at least.

He took another sip of his black coffee and then said, "*Star Trail,* please put on the big screen a logical meeting point for every possible direct breadcrumb trail from every seeded galaxy region the Startburst ships have explored so far."

"Parameters of the request?" Star Trail asked.

Cole thought for a moment, then said, "A large area of space with a vast cluster of galaxies, to start with. That area would need to be away from the Milky Way Galaxy in general, beyond all of these seeded areas we know about in relationship to the ancients' old home area, and approximately equal distant from most of the seeded areas the Starburst ships have explored so far. Show the seeded areas as green dots that we have explored and dashed lines as logical bread crumb paths to a new central home area of space."

Behind him the command crew went silent as they all watched. Cole had no doubt they all needed to get past what had just happened. Looking and thinking about the mission ahead was one way to do that.

It seemed that almost everyone on the ship had known or been friends with an ancient. And a number had been married to an ancient. Two spouses chose to go with their partner. Three broke off the marriage when the ancient partner left.

Everyone on all the ships had healing to do, some more than others.

The image on the screen showed a vast area of space. The galaxies looked like faint mist on the big screen with twenty green dots in a half-moon shape.

Dashed red lines left each green dot and met in an area far, far beyond the green dots.

"Scale, please," Cole said. "Show as a bright orange dot the Milky Way Galaxy."

The image shifted down in scale slightly and a bright orange dot appeared near the bottom of the screen. Seemingly very close to the green dots.

"Using the distance from the Milky Way Galaxy to the first seeded area we reached, how far away is that possible area?"

"Eleven-point-three times farther," *Star Trail* said.

Cole was stunned at that distance. "At trans-tunnel twenty, the speed of the old ancient ships, how long would it have taken them to reach that location from the location of the first seeded area?"

"Over six hundred thousand years," *Star Trail* said.

"At trans-tunnel forty-four," Cole said, "how long will it take us to reach that location?"

"Slightly under a year," *Star Trail* said.

He then had *Star Trail* show all of the six hundred seeded areas and with the same parameters to locate an area and show it.

Same area worked for all six hundred.

"Are there secondary areas closer?" Cole asked. "If so, please show them."

"There are no other secondary areas closer that contain the mass and cluster of galaxies that would be needed to support the large number of human planets seeded in the six hundred areas if this pattern holds."

Cole just nodded and stared at the big screen and then tried to even comprehend the distances involved.

"So now we need to find the breadcrumb stations, if any of them still exist," Cole said. "To see if this theory has any validity."

He stared at the image for a moment longer, then said, "Thank you, *Star Trail.* Please resume with the reports on the main screen."

Around him the sounds of the command center going back to work slowly filled the room. He just stood, leaning against the railing, sipping his black coffee and staring at the reports of repairs and scans being completed.

If the ancients who seeded these areas had actually moved to that distant location, it was clear they were very afraid of the main ancients.

The seeded cultures had used distance as a shield.

Unimaginable distances.

Then it dawned on Cole one thing they had been missing. Just as they had now sat up scanning for any ancients getting near this area or any area they were near, these areas they had just explored might have been monitored, even though abandoned.

That's what he would have done if he was that afraid of something coming after him.

And clearly, these ancients who had seeded these areas were very afraid.

For the next five minutes, he worked over ways of finding those scans, then when Echo arrived and handed him a fresh cup of coffee, he thanked her and indicated they should sit in their command chair.

She looked at him with a puzzled look, then set her coffee down and joined him in the command chair.

It closed around them and brought up the screens. Again he felt closer to her in this chair than at any point, almost as if the connection through *Star Trail* connected their minds in some way.

"*Star Trail,*" Cole said before Echo could ask him any question. "Please make sure this conversation is not monitored in any fashion."

"*Understood and complying,*" Star Trail said.

"*Star Trail,*" Cole said, "since by genetic development we were able to tell the slight difference between ancients and our seeded group, would it be possible to tell if we had any of the newly seeded groups on board?"

"*There was a high percentage chance that many of the ancients we removed were of the new groups,*" Star Trail said.

That stunned Cole and he sat back slightly.

"Because we removed all crew with ancient traits and the newer seeded groups would have the ancient traits?" Echo asked.

"*All personnel were removed whose traits did not match the Milky Way Galaxy group of Seeder traits that started in Chairmen Ray and Tacita's home world and on their Seeder ships,*" Star Trail said. "*The origin of such differences was not taken into account.*"

Echo nodded. "So they might have been other branches of ancients or they might have been from this area. Correct?"

"*Yes,*" Star Trail said. "*There would have been no way to distinguish the differences.*"

Cole felt a relief. That problem didn't need to be faced again with the safeguards they now had in place.

But his biggest worry still faced them.

"*Star Trail,*" Cole said, "using the information that the ancients gave us to track the

---

Some Classic Dean Wesley Smith Stories
Available at your favorite booksellers.

hidden sensors on the old ancient mother ships, would it be possible to detect if we are being scanned without knowledge?"

"Yes," Star Trail said.

"How long would it take to make the adjustments to equipment to discover any such scanning or tracking?" Echo asked.

"Thirty minutes," Star Trail said.

"Please make the adjustments and search for any scans," Cole said.

"Also use any of the technology found planted on this and other ships by the ancients and adapt it to find scans," Echo said.

"Understood," Star Trail said.

Then, for the next thirty minutes, Cole showed Echo what he had come up with as a possible location for where all the humans on all the planets had gone.

"At that distance they could not use ships," Echo said, nodding. "And if they were all bread to be Seeders, the bread-crumb trail would be the only logical way."

"Only one problem," Cole said. "If I was afraid of the ancients as much as these groups seem to be, I would not only go a long distance away, but I would destroy any evidence of any breadcrumb trail leading in any direction."

Echo could only nod to that. "So the ancients that we have met moved their massive home area farther away in fear of something from this group."

Cole nodded.

"And this group possibly built a massive home area an incredible distance away in the opposite direction."

"Sure starting to seem that way," Cole said. "What in the world were they afraid of about each other?"

"You know," Echo said, "I used to think space was vast and impossible to explore. But now I feel like everything has tightened down and we are stuck between two ancient fighting groups and we don't even know why they are fighting."

"Both groups seem to be doing a lot more running than fighting," Cole said.

"And for that I am grateful," Echo said, smiling.

Cole very much was as well.

Section Three
The Discovery

Chapter Thirteen

ECHO WAS RELIEVED that they were not being scanned by any of the groups. At least as far as *Star Trail* could tell and the other nineteen Starburst ships had also worked to develop scanning to see if any of them were being scanned.

They were not.

So the next step was to start to search for any sign of a breadcrumb trail from any of the seeded areas. But Echo didn't give a lot of hope in that search. Even in open space, three and a half million years was a very long time.

But Cole felt that with all twenty of the Starburst ships searching, they would find some sort of evidence, if it was there, that the Seeders had used breadcrumb trails to move all of the humans on these planets.

"Nothing," Cole said one week after the search had started.

Echo could feel the frustration in his voice as she arrived from her morning workout routine and handed him a cup of coffee.

Around them the command center hummed with its normal morning ritual and the reports flowing over the big screen now were search reports from thousands of scout and military ships dispatched from the twenty Starburst ships.

While she had been running, she had had a thought about the search and had expected this kind of result. They had been making some assumptions that clearly were wrong.

"Let's assume," she said, "that as the evidence points out, the Seeders from this area wanted to leave no trace as to where they were headed for the first group of ancients to find them."

Cole nodded.

"So we are assuming that they would have planted permanent breadcrumb stations as we did," Echo said.

Cole nodded again, then looked at her.

"My gut sense is that they used ships as jump stations with no intention of ever returning back to this area of space," Echo said.

"When the last person jumped past, they simply took the ship to the new home," Cole said. "I think you might have something there. It would explain why we are finding nothing. I was about to go back to the theory that they had all died off."

Echo felt her stomach twist at the thought she had when he suggested they all died off. She immediately went back to the memories of that planet she and Cole were stationed on with all the dead.

That had been their hardest assignment before being tapped to be chairmen of a mother ship and then a Starburst ship.

So just maybe this branch had died off. They seemed to be in a war with the ancients. Anything was possible.

She glanced at Cole. He was staring at the reports on the big screen in front of him, nodding.

"I need to talk with you," she said, pulling him toward their command chair.

He glanced at her, then nodded and they sat down, letting the chair close in around them.

"Something wrong?" he asked.

"I hope not," she said.

She wasn't sure exactly how to frame her question, so she started with a basic question. *Star Trail,* it is my understanding that Seeders can live for a very long time. Correct? Millions of years if circumstances allow."

"Yes."

"And that comes from a sequence of dormant genes in Seeders that can be activated. Without being activated, the Seeder would simply live a normal human lifespan. Correct?"

"Yes," Star Trail said.

"Would it be possible to scan the data from each ancient that we found on board and that the other Starburst ships found on board their ships and determine if anything about that long-life sequence was altered in any of them to reduce the lifespan? And altered in a way that would not be easily noticed or discovered. Possibly by a form of damage."

"Yes, it would be possible," Star Trail said.

"Please do so," Echo said. "While you are calculating that, please give me the standard birthrate for Seeders with activated genes."

"One child for every two-hundred-thousand Seeders," Star Trail said.

Echo knew that Seeders seldom had children. She didn't realize it was that seldom. There were a few births on the ship every month, but not many. Six of the children born on *Star Trail* had been born human with no Seeder's genes, so they and their parents had gone back to the Milky Way to give the child a regular life on a planet.

"Are you thinking that the ancients somehow altered the genes of the other ancients who came to this area?" Cole said.

"It would kill them off just as easily as fighting them," Echo said. "Given enough millions of years. Remember, JP said the ancients were worried about entire planets being bred to be Seeders only."

She hated the idea. That was why she had to clear it out of her head. And she had to make sure that everyone on board this ship was safe as well. At this point she put nothing past the ancients.

They wouldn't think of it as killing, only shortening already long life spans.

Damn she hoped she was wrong.

Chapter Fourteen

COLE SAT WITH Echo in their command chair, the command center around them completely blocked out, talking over possibilities as *Star Trail* scanned all the data collected from all the ancients they had kicked off the twenty Starburst ships.

He really hoped Echo was wrong, because as they waited, they ran over certain possible outcomes. And nothing either of them could think of sounded good.

Finally *Star Trail* said simply, *"I have the results of the question you asked."*

"Please summarize those results for us," Cole said.

"Two percent of the ancients removed from the Starburst ships had their Seeder genes damaged slightly, all in a similar and distinct fashion."

"Are the genes of any Seeder on this ship damaged in a similar fashion?" Echo asked a half second before he could.

"No," Star Trail said.

Cole let out the breath he didn't realize he was holding.

Beside him Echo nodded and looked relieved as well.

"So we had spies from these seeded groups on our ships as well," Cole said.

He wasn't sure how that was possible, but it sure seemed to be a logical assumption.

Echo nodded. "More than likely living with our group of Seeders since these groups started their big move over three-and-a-half million years ago. If we are right about where they moved to, the distance would be too great at the speeds they had to make it worth sending back spies."

"Star Trail, would you please trace all movements of the ancients with the damaged genes during construction and while here," Echo said. "I would like to know if they met with each other or tried to contact anyone outside this ship."

"Understood," Star Trail said.

"Star Trail, do you have a theory of how the genes were damaged?" Cole asked.

"A long exposure to a low level of a certain type of radiation emitted by older trans-tunnel drives. The problem would have been easily remedied."

"Would the damaged genes be hereditary, passed down to Seeder children?" Cole asked.

"Yes," Star Trail said.

"What is the affect of the damage on a Seeder?" Echo asked.

"None," Star Trail said.

Cole just felt shocked.

"None at all?" Echo asked, clearly as shocked as he was feeling.

"The specific damage I have found in the genes would have no affect at all on the Seeder," Star Trail said.

"So why did the ancients do this?" Echo asked, more to herself than Cole or *Star Trail*. "Assuming they did such a thing on purpose."

"I have no theory as to the motivation," Star Trail said.

"They did it on purpose," Cole said, nodding. "I am sure of that." The reason was dawning on him and he hated it.

Echo looked at him. "Why?"

"They branded them," Cole said. "Just as we could kick the ancients off this ship by seeing the difference in our genes, they needed a way to track anyone from these groups."

All Echo could do was nod.

The ancients purposely damaged millions of people simply so they could be tracked.

Cole was really starting to hate the ancients.

Chapter Fifteen

ECHO AND COLE sat over the dinner she had cooked. Chicken breasts in a light garlic sauce with steamed potatoes and some corn. She had to admit, this meal had turned out better than she had hoped. The sauce was a lot lighter.

The evening felt normal, which Echo loved. Even their cats were asleep in their normal places in the living room area.

It now had been a month since all the ancients had been kicked from all the Starburst ships and safeguards set up through the breadcrumb trail back to the Milky Way to let none of them through again.

Everything on all twenty Starburst ships seemed to have returned to a normal pace and the loss of friends and the hurt of being betrayed was fading. Seeders never forgot

anything, so the memory wouldn't leave any of them. But they could get past it.

And it seemed most were.

Echo could feel herself putting the hurt and loss of JP away.

As of today, fifty-two of the seeded areas had been explored by the twenty ships. All of the ancient seeded areas were exactly the same. The human populations had vanished a long, long time before. At almost the exact same time in history.

"We're wasting our time now looking at all these seeded areas," Cole said, finishing off the last of his chicken. Then he pointed to his empty plate. "That was wonderful."

He took a sip of the oaked chardonnay she had picked out to go with the sauce and dinner and nodded, holding up the glass. "And this is perfect as well."

"Thank you," she said, smiling. "Going to have to remember how I did that sauce."

"Please," he said.

"So what do you suggest we do next?" Echo asked, finishing off the last of her chicken as well and letting it sort of melt in her mouth.

"I think we pull in all scout ships," Cole said, "and all twenty of us head for the first logical location where we think all these people would have gone."

She nodded and sipped her wine. She liked the idea, but it worried her on a number of levels, not the least of which was what they would find when they got there. Assuming they figured out correctly where millions of galaxies of humans had vanished to.

"Not agreeing?" Cole asked.

"Not disagreeing," Echo said. "Just worried. Feels like there is something we are missing."

She had no idea what that might be, but everything about this entire mission felt off.

"I agree," Cole said, taking a sip of his wine and then standing and starting to clean up the dishes. She just sat and sipped on her wine.

"What is haunting me is that Ray and Tacita said that the ancients were scared when we discovered no humans here," Echo said. "It was what they had been afraid of."

"That bothered me as well," Cole said as he moved the dishes toward the dishwasher near the sink. "But why I have no idea."

Cole worked in silence as she sipped on the wine.

Finally she asked, "Think we should check in with the other chairmen tomorrow to see if they think we should all spend a year going even deeper in space?"

"I do," he said. "But if we are going to do it, I think we should all meet up in this area of space and go as a fleet."

She nodded. "One more ancient seeded area will be reached tomorrow. If no change, we contact everyone."

"If one of them doesn't contact us first," Cole said, smiling. "Got a hunch we're all having this same conversation."

"I have a hunch that you are right," she said, laughing.

And he was.

The next morning, while she was still running along the edge of one of the ship's many forests in her morning exercise routine, *Star Ray* reached yet another abandoned seeded area of galaxies. Thirty minutes later Chairmen Lisa and Jaden called for a conference call and included Ray and Tacita.

Echo was called to the command center and when she appeared there, Cole was laughing.

"Great minds think alike," he said to her, then turned to the big screen. "*Star Trail,* please add us into the conference link with the other chairmen."

It took only another fifteen seconds before all the Starburst chairmen and Ray and Tacita were on the big screen. Twenty boxes. In each image Echo could see the command center crews behind the chairmen.

"I would imagine we have all been talking about this," Jaden said. Since he and Lisa had called the gathering, it was his place to lead it. His smile was wide and his shaved head almost gleamed in the light around him. "What should we do next is the big question?"

Ray nodded. "There is little doubt now that all seeded areas will be found abandoned by their human populations."

"Are we all pretty much in agreement with where we think they all went?" Jaden asked.

Echo nodded and beside her Cole did as well. All the chairmen on the screen nodded as well, without exception. She liked that they were all in agreement on this.

"On a direct path to the assumed target location," Lisa said, "It would take one year. But Jaden and I have another suggestion."

Jaden nodded. "*Star Ray,* please show the image of the suggested exploration paths of each Starburst ship. Show each location now with a green dot, show the target location with a red dot. Show the paths with a dotted line."

An image filled the screen replacing all of the faces of the other chairmen. It was a three-dimensional image of what looked like a sphere, but not a perfect sphere, more like a pumpkin shaped ball, with all the lines coming back in together at the red dot.

Echo could see the line from *Star Trail* leading off into unknown space and then circling around and back to the red dot of the target.

"We're out here to explore," Lisa's voice came over the image. "That's what these ships were built for. We think we should go exploring for some years on the way to our target. See what's out there."

Echo loved that idea. It sent a thrill of excitement down her spine just thinking of it.

Beside her Cole was nodding as well.

"That plan is being sent to all of the ships now," Jaden said as all the images of the chairmen appeared back on the screen.

"How long would it take to get to the target with these paths?" Ray asked.

"At trans-tunnel forty," Jaden said, "and dropping scout ships where we find interesting galaxies, it would take five years. At trans-tunnel thirty-six, which would allow scout ships more time along the way, it would take just over ten years."

Ray and Tacita both nodded.

"This plan would explore a vast area," Lisa said. "An area we really haven't even looked at in the slightest."

Almost all the chairmen on the screen were nodding.

"I suggest everyone study the plan and the details we have sent," Jaden said. "We meet again at the same time tomorrow morning."

Everyone nodded.

"Good," Jaden said, smiling. "See everyone tomorrow."

And the screen went back to scrolling reports.

Around them the command center started buzzing with excited conversations.

Echo turned to Cole, who was smiling.

"What do you think?" she asked.

"I love the ten-year plan," he said, smiling. "And I find it exciting again. Just exploring into the unknown."

"Getting reports from twenty ships exploring into the unknown," Echo said. "I find this idea wonderfully exciting."

"Star Trail," Cole said, giving her a hug and then turning to the big screen. "Please put up the image sent from *Star Ray* on one side of the screen and the data on the other."

Echo turned to the command crew behind them. "I want all of you studying this as well and any problems or opinions you might have before shift change today."

Everyone nodded. They all looked as excited as she felt.

Suddenly what had been missing was now back. This was a ship for exploration and exploring they were going again.

Finally.

Chapter Sixteen

COLE WAS JUST about to head out on his afternoon run. He and Echo and the rest of the command center crew had gone over all the details about taking all twenty Starburst ships out to explore. Everything seemed fine and sounded exciting. There was no telling what might be out there in those millions of galaxies they would pass.

But something still felt wrong.

He leaned against their command chair, just staring at the large screen and information came over it giving him no help at all. Echo paced, just thinking, clearly not completely convinced at all either. She did that when she was bothered.

So he decided to do what a college professor had suggested he do when in doubt: Question all basic assumptions.

The first basic assumption was that one group of ancients was afraid of a second group of ancients. He could see no reason for that assumption. Nothing.

Sure, they had sent spies on this mission, but that didn't seem to be out of fear but more out of trying to find out what had happened out here.

The groups they were searching for had left ancient space over four million years ago. What kind of grudge would last that long? But Seeders did have the ability to remember just about anything.

So he decided to ask a question he should have asked back when the ancients were on the ship.

"Star Trail, what was the average age of the ancients who were on this ship?"

"Two hundred and six thousand years."

Echo snapped around and looked at him, frozen in mid-pace.

"Repeat that please," Cole said, not really sure if he had heard the answer correctly or not.

"Two hundred and six thousand years," Star Trail said. *"That is approximate to the nearest year."*

"What was the age of the oldest and what was the age of the youngest?" Cole asked.

"Seven thousand and four years was the oldest," Star Trail said, *"the youngest was ninety years of age."*

Cole just felt shocked. In all his years as a Seeder he had never thought to ask some really basic questions about living.

"What is the overall average age a Seeder will live to?" Echo asked.

"One thousand, three hundred, and eight years old," Star Trail said. *"Again that is an approximation of the average rounded to the nearest year of the data I have."*

Silence filled the command center.

Complete and heavy silence.

Cole always felt that if lucky, he could live for millions of years. Now he understood suddenly it was going to take luck.

A lot of luck.

"What is the average age of the Seeders on this ship?" Echo asked.

"Four hundred and sixty years."

"Main cause of death of Seeders?" Cole asked as he tried to get his mind working again.

"Accidents," Star Trail said.

Cole nodded to that. They had had many, many deaths on *Star Trail* from accidents since they launched. It always seemed tragic, but it happened so often he hadn't thought much about it. After all, they had three million people on board.

"Second main cause?" Echo asked.

"Suicide," Star Trail said.

Cole again nodded. They had had numbers of those as well, but usually when someone started developing suicidal traits, they were sent back to the Milky Way for help.

Echo was looking almost haunted.

The silence around them felt unnatural. Clearly none of their command crew had thought to ask these basic questions either.

But now Cole needed another piece of information.

"Star Trail, with the information you have, how many Seeders, by percentage, will live to one million years of age? And beyond?"

"One-point-three percent," Star Trail said.

Now Cole knew what happened to the ancients they were looking for out here. But he had to hammer the nail in the coffin home just to make sure in his own mind.

"Star Trail, how many humans with Seeder genes would be born on a normal planet of four billion population in ten years?"

"Approximately one thousand every ten-point-six years with a four billion population base."

"You multiply that by billions of human planets in any seeded galaxy and you have a lot of Seeders," Echo said. "Most don't have their Seeder genes activated."

Cole nodded. "Especially counting the fact that just in our group we have seeded a couple hundred thousand galaxies."

"Exactly," Echo said.

"Star Trail, how often do Seeders have children after their Seeder genes are activated?" Cole asked.

He knew the answer, but he needed to hear it one more time.

"One child per every two thousand Seeders," Star Trail said.

Cole nodded.

Echo looked pale. A number of the command crew gasped lightly.

If these groups of Seeders had been stupid enough to breed only Seeder genes in the entire populations of these planets and activate them all, then they really did just die out.

They would not have had the human population bases to continue seeding, either, since seeding requires taking base material from a seeded planet and moving it to the next planet.

Very, very few Seeders would have lived long enough to be alive now.

But the real question was could they have been that stupid?

He didn't believe they could have been. Something else had happened.

And where had all those mother ships gone?

Chapter Seventeen

ECHO NOW UNDERSTOOD why the massive numbers of galaxies that had been the ancients' home world were empty. It wasn't because they had all moved out to a big new home. The ancients had told them that those galaxies had been only populated by Seeders and the home center had only had Seeders in it as well. Hundreds and hundreds of billions of Seeders.

And that the ancients had stopped exploring and seeding new galaxies with humans millions of years earlier.

The ancients had died off as well.

They didn't have a big new home. They had an empty old one the ancients were trying to keep maintained so that humans could once again live in it.

How could the ancients have been that stupid? What could have happened?

But now she knew that what they were facing wasn't two warring factions of ancients. They just had one faction, the original ancients hoping against hope that the other groups had survived. No wonder the ancients had feared exactly what the Starburst ships had found.

"We need to talk with Ray and Tacita," Echo said. "Get them to confront the ancients with this."

"And we need to tell all the chairmen this theory," Cole said.

Echo nodded. She knew Cole was calling it a theory, but it was the only theory that explained what they had found. In both the ancients' home area of space and in these seeded areas.

"Star Trail," Cole said. "Please ask all other Starburst ship chairmen to join us in a conference call. And invite chairmen Ray and Tacita as well."

"Invitation sent," Star Trail said. *"Links are coming live."*

"On the main screen," Echo said.

Within three minutes the other forty chairmen were present on the screen. Their command center crews were all watching behind them.

Cole glanced at Echo and she nodded that he should start.

"Matt and Carey," Cole said, "when you discovered the ancients' home area of space, it was clear that they had all left the planets about the same time in history. Correct?"

Matt and Carey both nodded.

"And when the eight of you talked with the ancients," Cole said, to the eight chairmen who had originally met the ancients, "they alluded to learning while trying to build a new home? Correct?"

All eight nodded.

"They would not, in any fashion, tell us where the new home was," Ray said. "Even though we had been friends with a few of them for a very long time."

"Because they were embarrassed," Echo said.

"Why would they be embarrassed?" Tacita asked.

"Because they had to move back in with the kids," Cole said. "Their new home was with us."

"And we just kicked them out of it," Echo said. "For the moment at least."

The puzzled expressions on the forty faces on the screen almost made Cole smile.

"None of us did the math," Echo said.

Now the puzzled expressions just deepened.

"When you were talking with the ancients," Cole said, "didn't they say that all their home worlds had been only full of Seeders?"

"They did," Ray said, nodding.

"So let's do some math," Echo said. *"Star Trail,* what is the average lifespan of all known Seeders?"

"One thousand, three hundred, and eight years old," Star Trail said. *"Again that is an approximation of the average rounded to the nearest year of the data."*

Cole nodded. Those were the exact words Star Trail had said when they first asked the question.

"Star Trail," Echo said, "how often do Seeders have children after their Seeder genes are activated?"

"One child per every two thousand Seeders," Star Trail said.

"In other words," Echo said, "doing the math, a planet of one billion Seeders would have a population of only five hundred thousand in one thousand years. And a thousand years after that only two hundred and fifty."

Stunned shock covered the faces of the chairmen.

A couple chairmen were nodding.

"It would be delayed by the small percentage of Seeders who lived past the thousand years," Echo said, "but not much."

"Those original home worlds of the ancients were not left for some bright shining home," Cole said. "The ancients mostly died off. Plain and simple. They stopped seeding human populations and they simply died off."

Ray was now nodding as well.

"They would have had no programs to seed humans without seeding human planets to start with," Tacita said. "If they stopped seeding human planets, that would have been lost."

Everyone was nodding. They all knew that the seeding programs were generated from galaxy to galaxy from previous human and animal stock. Once the ancients stopped seeding and only brought in Seeders, they were doomed.

Echo knew it was too stupid to imagine, but the evidence sure pointed to that reality.

"Chairmen Ray and Tacita," Cole said. "I think you need to confront your ancient friends, get the truth out of them, and if they tell you the truth, we need to invite the old folks back into our society."

Nods from most of the chairmen on the screen.

"We still have the problem of the vanished mother ships in all these seeded areas," Echo said. "Where did they go? And why? If the ancients are out in the open, telling the truth, they might be able to join us again and help us figure that out."

Ray and Tacita nodded.

"We will return with the truth quickly," Ray said.

With that they clicked off.

"Everyone check our math on this," Cole said. "We'll be back as soon as Ray and Tacita get us some real answers."

With that the screen went back to showing scrolling data about the status of the ship overall.

Echo turned to Cole. "Well, so much for a big exploration mission firing up."

"Yeah, back on the search again for missing ships," he said.

"And I really don't want to know what we will find in them," Echo said.

And she didn't. But what she really wanted to know was why and how the ancients would not understand the repercussions of activating all Seeder genes in a population.

There was no chance they were all that stupid.

Something else had happened and that unknown something scared her more than the idea of finding giant ships full of dead bodies.

Chapter Eighteen

COLE WAS STUNNED that he had barely started into his morning coffee when Chairmen Ray and Tacita called a conference call.

"Star Trail, please have Chairman Guinn report to the command center."

Echo appeared at his side a moment later, a towel around her neck. She was sweating, but not much, so she must have just started into her routine.

"That was fast," she said, wiping off her face.

"Guessing they didn't get anything," Cole said. *"Star Trail,* please add us to the conference link and display it all on the large screen."

The other chairmen appeared on the screen as behind Cole and Echo the command center fell to silence. What they were about to discover might change what they would all be doing over the next decade or two.

"We are sad to report," Ray said after everyone was connected, "that your theory as to what happened to the ancients is correct. They were keeping their big center functioning in hopes we would fill it once again, this time with humans."

Cole felt like he had been punched in the gut. It was one thing to have that idea as a theory, but to have it actually happen was another matter.

"Didn't they understand what would happen?" Echo asked.

"They did," Tacita said. "They had programs to up the birthrate among Seeders that eventually failed and at first they were still seeding human galaxies and bringing in Seeders."

Ray nodded. "There was that. But they did not count on one major change. Seeders starting living shorter lifespans."

Tacita nodded. "When we were born, over four million years ago, the lifespan of a normal Seeder was over a million years."

"There were fewer of us in any human population as well," Ray said. "But as galaxy after galaxy of billions of planets were seeded, the lifespan of a Seeder started to reduce. Slowly at first, but as the years went past Tacita and I and many others studied the problem. We found nothing wrong or any solution."

"And neither did the ancients," Tacita said. "But it spelled their doom. That's why they were so interested and sent so many along on these missions, in hopes of finding growing human and Seeder cultures besides ours."

"How many ancients are left?" Cole asked.

"Fifty million," Ray said, "most living in our culture and on one planet just outside the old home worlds. They rotate in and out

of the command moon for the large center, keeping it maintained and waiting."

Cole just was stunned. A proud group now living in the bones of their greatest construction, doing everything in their power to keep it going in hopes someone would inherit the old home.

"So I suggest we lift restrictions on the ancients," Echo said.

"Everyone agreed?" Ray asked.

Cole watched as all chairmen nodded. No dissent or hesitations.

It seemed that now the forty chairmen of the twenty most powerful ships in all known space were the ruling body of humanity. At least for decisions like what to do with the old human culture now camping with them.

"So did you ask them about the missing mother Seeder ships?" Echo asked.

"We did," Ray said. "They have no idea and are worried."

Cole suddenly had an idea. "When these groups out here realized their mistake on activating all Seeder genes, would they have eventually returned to get more human stock to start the seeding process over?"

"Yes," Ray said. "The ancients have done that exact thing on the other side of their home area of planets. The have seven Seeder ships now going."

"Where did they get the human stock?" Echo asked.

"From our seeded planets," Ray said, shaking his head. "That was another thing they were very embarrassed about. They had to sneak in and take from planets enough animal and human stock to restart seeding."

"So there is a chance the old ships from these groups are still out there seeding?" Echo asked.

"Yes," Ray said, nodding. "There is a chance."

Cole just stared at all the faces. He had a hunch most of them were thinking the same thought he was.

How did they find them now?

Section Four
Back on the Search

Chapter Nineteen

ECHO STOOD BESIDE Cole next to their command chair and studied the information coming in. All attention had now been focused back on finding the lost mother ships.

Echo and most of the chairmen were convinced that the old Seeder ships, over eighteen hundred in total from the six hundred areas, would not have gotten faster. That kind of advancement was done when not worrying about their very survival.

So it would have taken the ships about sixty thousand years to return to where they could have gotten the right seed material to start the seeding over.

And then another sixty thousand years to return to their original areas. But so far, none of the ships had been found anywhere near their original areas. So they had gone somewhere else.

Echo had no idea why they would do that.

At that moment, behind them, a familiar voice said simply, "Permission to resume my duties?"

She and Cole spun around to see JP standing there beside his station, looking worried.

Silence had fallen over the command center as everyone watched.

Echo felt a surge of joy at seeing him again. She stepped up to his level, moved over to him and gave him a massive hug.

When she let him go, Cole, smiling from ear to ear, shook his hand.

"You may resume your duties on one condition," Echo said, staring at the man she and Cole had trusted for decades.

"Anything," JP said.

"No more secrets," Echo said. "We are all Seeders and are all in this together. Agreed?"

"Agreed," JP said.

Echo thought the smile would hurt him. In all their years she had never seen him smile like that before. It made her heart feel light.

Around them the command center broke into cheers. JP was not only well respected, but well loved by everyone. It was wonderful to have him back.

After everything had settled back down, Echo turned to JP. "We are trying to figure out where all the mother ships went. Your culture had to borrow from our culture to start new human seeding, what would these groups have done?"

"They would have left one area human only," JP said. "In our worlds around the center, we had already made our mistake by pulling in Seeders from many seeded planets. When we stopped seeding and then our birthrate experiments failed, and the lifespan dropped, the human cultures we had seeded were too advanced for us to get new material."

"But you had our culture close by, thankfully," Cole said.

"We did," JP said. "Thankfully."

"Did these groups out here know that?" Echo asked.

"No," JP said, shaking his head. "There was no contact. But being this far out, the logical thing would be to depend on one area to remain human seeding."

"Is there any record of any ultimate goal these six hundred groups had?" Cole asked.

"To build a second Center," JP said, "a second home world."

Echo turned back to the big screen. *"Star Trail,* please put up that center location we have all figured would be their destination. Show it with a red dot and show the six hundred plus seeded areas with green dots."

The image appeared on the big screen.

"Now which green dot would be the closest to that red dot?" Cole asked. "Show it brighter."

Echo had an idea and if she was right, this was going to turn out a lot better than anyone could have hoped.

"Star Trail," Echo said, "Assuming eighteen hundred mother ships, all seeding at a normal rate for their time, how long would it take to seed every galaxy in a hundred galaxy diameter path to that red dot from that closest green dot?"

"Approximately three million years," Star Trail said. *"That has a variable factor of a hundred thousand years in either direction."*

"Could we all be that lucky?" JP asked quietly.

"Only one way to find out," Cole said. "Let's talk with the other chairmen and go exploring."

Echo loved that idea.

Especially with JP back at their side.

Chapter Twenty

COLE AND ECHO stood facing the giant screen as the other chairmen linked in. They had also included Ray and Tacita.

After everyone was linked in, Cole started off. "After consulting with Commander Horshaw, an ancient who we are very happy to have returned to duty with us, we believe we might have an answer."

Cole turned and nodded to JP, who nodded back.

"We believe," Echo said, "that the groups out here would have left one group seeding only humans as a back-up, sort of a seed group if you will."

"The groups here had an intent to build a second major home, a second Center," Cole said. "We believe they would have left the most central group as human seeding."

"And they would have picked the area we have studied as a possible future home," Echo said.

"So if they started from the most central seeded group, the ones assumed to have humans, and seeded humans all the way in a hundred galaxy diameter area with all eighteen hundred plus mother ships, they would have reached their new home in three million years."

Echo said, "Show the diagram of what we are talking about please?"

An image appeared on the screen with a wide band leading from one green dot to a bright red dot. The wide band was a hundred galaxies wide.

The more Cole thought about this, the more he was convinced it was right and logical. Of course, he had thought that about a number of other theories so far on this mission and all of them had been proven wrong.

On the big screen most of the chairmen were nodding.

"It will take us over three weeks from our location to get to that seeded area. But it would take *Star Ray* only three weeks."

Lisa and Jaden were both nodding.

"I would suggest," Ray said, "That all ships head there. At top speed."

"Why?" Echo asked a fraction of a second before Cole could.

"Because the ancients at the center believe that might have happened as well," Tacita said.

"Since your first discoveries," Ray said, "they have been searching for any records, any information about the overall mission of the different ancient Seeder groups. They always intended, from what can be found, to build civilizations with Seeders only."

"But they wanted to keep one area seeded with humans," Tacita said, "to account for what they figured would be a decrease in populations."

"Just as the ancients here discovered," Ray said, "the declining lifespan of Seeders combined with the failed attempts at increasing birthrates would have spelled the doom of the original idea."

"Unless it didn't," Tacita said.

Cole had no idea what she meant by that.

"Either way," Ray said, "that center group will hold a lot of answers."

"Everyone in favor of heading at top speed for that center group?" Cole asked the gathered chairmen.

All nodded.

"Approach with caution and undetected," Ray said.

"See everyone shortly," Cole said, smiling at the rest of the chairmen.

Then he cut the connection.

"Star Trail," Echo said. "Are all scout and military ships on board?"

"Yes," *Star Trail* said.

"Go to full speed," Cole said. "Let's go see what we can find this time."

This excited him. Again they were moving, looking for answers in the unknown. That was what this ship had been built to do and for one, he was very glad they were back doing it.

Chapter Twenty-One

ECHO HAD MANAGED to keep herself busy for the past three weeks. This morning both she and Cole had taken their coffee and snack bars instead of breakfast to the command center to watch the feeds coming in from *Star Ray*.

Star Ray was going to be the first ship to enter the area around what they were all hoping would be a fully seeded human culture. It was going to take the rest of the Starburst ships from ten hours up to three more weeks to reach the area. Thankfully, they would be there beside *Star Ray* in just fifteen hours.

But for now everyone was watching the feeds coming in.

Echo had no idea what might have happened to over one-hundred-and-eighty mother ships if they didn't find humans here.

"We have a galaxy ahead full of terra-formed planets," Jaden said.

Echo and Cole were watching the feeds. Behind them everyone in the command center stood silently, watching as well.

"The data doesn't look right," Cole said, shaking his head.

He glanced back at the command crew. "Get working on what they are sending us."

Everyone went to work instantly. Echo knew that each of them had a specific area of the data they would pore through quickly.

"The worlds appear to be dead," Lisa of *Star Ray* said softly. "Not like we had found before, but destroyed within a fairly recent period of time."

"There are a few human survivors scattered on the planets we are scanning," Jaden said. "Some planets are completely dead. No Gray or Cirrata that we can find at all still surviving."

Echo felt her stomach twist into a knot as *Star Ray* held position on the edge of the galaxy and launched hundreds of scout and military ships, all cloaked. She couldn't believe they were facing more dead human planets like the one she and Cole had worked on all those years before.

As the scout ships went to work quickly, staying shielded and moving in over various planets, the data really started to pour in.

"These were well-advanced human and Gray and Cirrata civilizations," JP said from behind them.

"When did this happen?" Echo asked as the images of cities came flooding in, most still standing but on closer look they were starting to deteriorate.

"When did this happen?" Cole repeated without turning from the big screen. "How long ago?"

"Recent," JP said. "Within one hundred years."

"We're leaving scout ships here and jumping at full speed to the home galaxy," Jaden said from *Star Ray.* "Our ships will track and observe the

Some Classic Dean Wesley Smith Stories
Available at your favorite booksellers.

survivors. We should be at the home galaxy in forty minutes."

"We will drop scout ships and military ships at each galaxy we pass," Lisa said. "We will continue feeds of all incoming data."

Echo just watched the big screen as more and more data started to pour in from the scout ships. Whatever had happened to these planets had happened galaxy wide to every terra-formed and inhabited planet.

Also there was no sign of any ships left in space or any stations left at all. Just floating debris where stations might have been.

And every galaxy *Star Ray* flashed past, the same story emerged. Complete destruction of what had been advanced and clearly stable human, Gray, and Cirrata cultures.

Recent destruction.

And that scared Echo even more than she wanted to admit.

And brought up horrid memories.

Chapter Twenty-Two

COLE STOOD BESIDE Echo in the command center and watched the big screen as *Star Ray* dropped into a holding position outside of the original seeded galaxy and launched hundreds of scout and military ships.

It was clear from first scans that the destruction was the same, only this had been far more recent. Within the last five years on one side of the galaxy. Some planets on the far edge of the galaxy where *Star Ray* had approached still had buildings burning and the data showed that those planets had been just recently attacked. Not more than a week before.

No Gray or Cirrata survivors, but hundreds of thousands of human survivors on almost every planet.

He glanced at Echo, who looked stunned. They both had been hit hard with the years on that destroyed planet trying to help that civilization recover. And that had been a natural disaster. Now, once again, they were looking at a planet with hundreds of thousands of human survivors among the ruins.

It took Cole a moment before he recognized this pattern of destruction across a galaxy. He had seen it before, hundreds of years ago.

The group of humans who had tried a biological experiment and created a race of rats that flooded a galaxy and destroyed everything before moving on. The original group of humans had used devices to move from one side of a galaxy to the other, destroying life on every planet infested with the rats.

So whoever or whatever was doing this was moving from one side of the galaxy to the next and then moving on to the next galaxy in line. And that meant the attackers were close.

And that the attackers were moving slowly.

"Star Trail," Cole said, "please contact the chairmen of *Star Ray*. Private channel."

Lisa and Jaden appeared on the main screen. Both looked white and clearly shocked.

They had not been involved with the war with the rats. They had become chairmen after that, so they might not have seen this pattern at once.

Cole quickly explained the pattern of destruction to them and how it fit from the earlier war, then said simply, "Whatever fleet is doing this, they are still close and headed to the next galaxy. From the looks of their movement, it will take them about four years to cover the distance between the two galaxies."

Beside Cole, Echo was nodding.

Both Lisa and Jaden were also nodding. "We are getting a call from Carrie and Matt. *Star Ray*, join them into this conversation."

The worried faces of Carrie and Matt appeared.

"Cole has just told us," Jaden said to them, "about this pattern of destruction being clear from the war with the rats."

Carrie and Matt both nodded.

"That is the reason we are calling," Carrie said. "Whoever did this is still close and moving at far slower speeds than we can move."

Jaden glanced at Lisa. Then he said, *"Star Ray,* launch a hundred military ships on a course for the closest seeded galaxy. And twenty each on courses to other nearby seeded galaxies. Have them stay shielded and report what they find. Do not have them engage or get close to anything they find."

"We'll all be beside you as quickly as we can," Cole said.

"Thank you," Lisa said. "We are going to need a complete conference as we get more information."

At that point they cut the connection.

Cole turned to his command crew. "Get answers, people. We need to know what we are getting into. What kind of weapon caused all this destruction?"

Then he turned back to Echo.

She clearly had something on her mind. He knew that look in her eyes.

"Star Trail," Echo said, "please show on the main screen the locations of each Starburst ship and their path headed toward *Star Ray's* position. Starburst ships in blinking green dots and their path in a green line."

The three-dimensional image of a few million galaxies appeared on the big screen. Nineteen green lines converged on one blinking green light.

"Now show in red the nearest possible seeded galaxies that might have been seeded on the way to the assumed new home for this group."

Cole watched as *Star Trail* showed a bunch of dots in red spreading away from *Star Ray's* location.

"Five Starburst ships are going close to some of those galaxies," Cole said. "A couple in just a few hours."

Echo nodded. "We're one of them. Exactly what I was thinking might be the case. Let's give Lisa and Jaden thirty minutes for their military ships to find something, then call a full conference."

Cole looked up at the big screen. *"Star Trail,* continue to update the location of the Starburst ships on that image."

"Understood," Star Trail said.

Cole just stared at the big screen. *Star Trail* was going to go within an hour of some possibly seeded galaxies in just five hours. There was no doubt they needed to see what had happened to them.

He wasn't sure he wanted to know.

Chapter Twenty-Three

ECHO LET THE next twenty minutes just drag past as everyone in the Command Center fought to find answers from the data pouring in now from hundreds of *Star Ray's* scout ships.

Then the data from the large military fleet that *Star Ray* had launched came through. *Star Ray's* ships had found the fleet of ships that must have caused the destruction.

Alien ships.

The first image appeared on the main screen and everyone in the Command Center gasped.

Completely alien ships.

Nothing at all like Seeder ships or Cirrata blimp-shaped ships or the Gray saucer-shaped craft.

These alien ships looked more like balls with spikes sticking out from all sides.

And there were a couple thousand of them. Some small, some about half the size of an old Seeder mother ship.

Clearly a fourth race had made it to a stable culture and found the speeds to cross between galaxies.

Echo forced herself to let out the breath she was holding, then from behind her JP said, "We are seeing something on planets in the first galaxy *Star Ray* found."

"Please put it on the big screen," Cole said.

"These are close-up images from a few of the planets destroyed almost a hundred years ago," JP said.

The images were of lush, green continents and some destroyed human cities near the bright blue ocean.

But something was off, very off.

From what Echo could see, it looked like the ground was moving and shifting all along the shoreline.

Then the image zoomed in and it was clear that what she was seeing was some sort of alien-looking bug. A cross between a crab and a spider. Black eyes on four stalks, sharp talons on front feet, four back feet, a hard shell of some sort with black patterns on them.

And there were billions of them in just the images they were seeing and they were all fighting each other, tearing each other apart as they swarmed out of the ocean and covered the land.

"The oceans have a much higher salt and nutrient base than we would have ever allow in terra-formed planets," J.P said. "The oceans have been altered and the oxygen levels of the atmospheres have been lowered as well to a more carbon-heavy combination."

"That's why almost no humans are left alive on these early destroyed planets," Cole said.

"With those creatures coming out of the oceans like that," Echo said, "the survivors or any animals on that planet won't last much longer anyway."

"The human survivors need to be evacuated," Cole said.

Echo nodded. From the reports coming in, *Star Ray* already had ships getting ready to do just that.

Were the swarming creatures the aliens? If so, what was happening?

Then Cole answered her unasked question with a statement that sent chills down her spine.

"Oh, shit," Cole said. "The aliens are seeding."

The deathly silence in the Command Center felt heavy with Cole's statement.

The images on the big screen were horrific. It looked almost like one creature swallowing up an entire planet.

"Star Trail," Echo said, "put the image of the map of Starburst ships and their locations back on the screen."

Cole nodded and turned around and thanked JP with a nod.

Echo couldn't get the images out of her mind. They had always known they might find aliens in all the billions of galaxies that would not be compatible in any fashion with humans. They had actually found many younger civilizations that had been spider or crab-like. But none of those had made it out of their own galaxy or even come close.

So this was clearly something that wasn't completely unexpected, except for the part of attacking advanced human and Gray and Cirrata cultures and wiping them out.

Cultures without defenses.

Seeded cultures usually cleared out their military as they advanced and stabilized. It had only been the war with the rats that had caused Seeders to bring back the military side of things in their ships. And right now Echo was very glad they had.

Very, very glad.

Chapter Twenty-Four

COLE COULDN'T BELIEVE what he had seen on those planets. Clearly the aliens had changed the oceans in some way and left eggs or some sort of device to create millions of aliens to swarm over the land.

He had no idea if those swarms looked like the aliens in the ships, but he was betting they did.

They scared him at a base level. He had seen images of many alien races over the years. Some had repulsed him, some scared him. These scared him more than any others had.

And something about the way they swarmed over everything and fought each other twisted his stomach.

"The Chairmen of the Star Ray are asking for a conference call," Star Trail said.

"Link us in," Echo said.

Cole took a deep breath and made himself calm down as much as possible.

A moment later the main screen cleared to show the other nineteen Starburst ships' chairmen and Ray and Tacita.

"We have only found the one fleet," Jaden said.

Cole was very relieved to hear that.

"The alien fleet is traveling at trans-tunnel twelve," Lisa said, "and will reach the next galaxy in just under four years. We have sent ships ahead and they will be reporting on the state of the next galaxy in the fleet's path within minutes."

Echo nodded, as did numbers of other chairmen on the big screen conference. They all liked the news that the alien ships were slow. That bought them time to study and make decisions.

"We believe we need to do a number of things almost at once," Jaden said.

Beside Jaden, Lisa nodded. "First, we need to backtrack and see where this alien fleet originated. That mission is already launched with three hundred military ships and three hundred scout ships."

"Second," Jaden said, "we need to scout all the possible surrounding galaxies that might have human cultures and check on their status."

"We understand that five of your ships will be approaching some possible seeded galaxies shortly," Lisa said. "We suggest you move toward those galaxies and explore as widely as you can while still making good speed. Watch for any possible alien home galaxy."

"Our military ships have the alien fleet surrounded completely and are staying shielded," Jaden said. "The aliens do not know we are there. We could stop them at a moment's notice, destroy them completely, but we feel we should study them as much as possible before taking any action."

Cole found himself nodding to that, as were most of the other chairmen.

"Third, we need to develop a map of exactly which human cultures are in this area," Lisa said, "how old they are, and where these aliens have seeded. It is clear they are seeding in the first destroyed human galaxies we came across. We will assume that seeding is their mission until other evidence supports a different theory."

"Then lastly," Jaden said, "we may need to send ahead a few ships toward the area we believe holds the new home of these human cultures. We need to see if any damage has happened in those areas."

"Anyone have any questions or suggestions?"

Carey of *Star Fall* said, "I do. We need to also look for evidence that this alien culture was human, Gray, or Cirrata created."

Cole again found himself nodding. Considering that many of them had fought a centuries-long war because of a human-created plague culture, that made complete sense.

"Agreed," Jaden said. "Ray and Tacita, we will need to have you in contact and updating the ancients in the Center on this. Have them searching their databases for anything in history like what we are seeing."

"We will do so," Tacita said.

"Another conference in six hours unless a major discovery happens ahead of then," Jaden said.

With that the conference ended.

Cole let out a breath he didn't realize he was holding. He was very happy that Lisa and Jaden had taken complete control of the situation. So now it was up to him and Echo and the crew of *Star Trail* to see what they could find over the next few hours in possible human-seeded galaxies.

He and Echo and JP, along with *Star Trail,* worked for the next fifteen minutes on which galaxies to go to first. They decided to set a course where they could scan hundreds of galaxies while still

moving at full speed toward a possible edge of human seeded space.

One hour later they found what Cole was hoping against hope they would not find.

An alien galaxy.

And not built in the remains of a human galaxy, but all on its own.

Chapter Twenty-Five

ECHO JUST STARED at the image of the spiral galaxy full of alien planets on the large screen. The idea of a complete alien galaxy just gave her shudders. The scene of the aliens swarming over the beaches and fighting had scared her at a very deep level. Far more than she wanted to admit to herself or to Cole.

"Star Trail, drop out of trans-tunnel near the galaxy," Cole said. "Make sure we and all scout and military ships are completely shielded. Send two hundred of both types of ship throughout the alien galaxy to gather up-close data."

Echo added, "Also send as many groups of fifty scout and military ships as needed ahead on our course to scout the next galaxies along our intended path."

"Holding position," Star Trail said. *"Ships launching."*

From what Echo could tell from the data starting to pour in, the galaxy was a fully-formed, galaxy-wide alien culture in a medium-sized spiral galaxy about the same size as the Milky Way. Millions of alien ships of all sizes were in flight between systems.

More and more information started to pour in almost immediately as the scout and military ships flashed to different points of the galaxy.

The alien culture seemed to exist half on the land and half in the seas on Earth-like planets around yellow stars. They clearly liked the same basic kinds of planets as humans, Gray, and Cirrata did.

Echo watched as the first images of the aliens appeared on the screen. They had the features of spiders combined with crabs, just larger versions of the ones swarming over those planets that *Star Ray* had found.

They were all black and gray, with hard shells and there seemed no way to tell them apart, which Echo knew meant nothing.

Again she barely contained a shudder.

"They are moving like ants," Cole said, watching one image coming in from what seemed to be a large city, but looked more like a giant pile of hardened dirt towering above the shore of an ocean.

"Hive mind?" Echo asked, now really worried. No alien culture that functioned as a hive mind that she had ever studied had managed to get off of their own planet. Let alone spread over a galaxy and to other galaxies.

As the next few minutes passed quickly and data poured in, the scout ships started to report that they had found the center of each planet, what appeared to be the main city on each planet.

And under the city was a vast network of partially flooded tunnels all leading to one massive creature in a huge underground cavern.

"Each planet has a queen," Cole said, his voice soft.

Echo was thinking the exact same thing, but they needed to be careful.

"We can't assume anything in an alien culture," Echo said. "We need to show this to the other chairmen and give the scientists time to look at all this data."

Cole nodded. *"Star Trail,* contact the other Starburst ship chairmen and Ray and Tacita. On the main screen please."

A moment later the faces of the other chairmen appeared. All of them looked very worried.

"We found an alien galaxy," Cole said. *"Star Trail*, send all Starburst ships and Chairmen Ray and Tacita the images we are getting from our scout ships.

"We believe we have also found what appears to be a queen of some sort on each planet," Echo said. "At first glance, the aliens seem to move as if controlled by a hive mind."

At that moment behind her JP said, "Scout ships reporting in from ahead."

Cole nodded. "Put those reports in the corner of the screen please, for everyone to see."

Echo glanced at the reports coming in from the scout ships they had sent ahead to other galaxies. Now she felt like she wanted to just sit down and put her head between her knees.

"Correction," she said. "We have found at least ten alien galaxies so far. None of which were built in the remains of a human-seeded culture."

"We are continuing the search for more," Cole said.

The stunned look on the other chairmen's faces was enough to tell the entire story.

Echo felt the same way exactly. None of them had any idea what to do next.

She wasn't sure there was anything they could do except protect the next human galaxy.

Section Five
The Aliens

Chapter Twenty-Six

FOR A MOMENT the conference was silent as everyone studied the data being sent by *Star Trail* to them. Cole did the same, stunned at the extent of the wide alien culture they were just beginning to find.

"We will send ships from here and determine the extent of the alien spread through the galaxies close to this one," Echo said to the other chairmen.

Cole nodded. That was going to be critical information.

"The ancients, the Gray, and the Cirrata," Ray said, "have no knowledge of such a culture existing, but they do not believe such a culture would be unusual."

"We are going to need to try to talk with these new aliens at some point," Tacita said. "So please keep that in mind. We will be studying here how to do so."

Cole was actually shocked at that idea, but Ray and a few other chairmen on the screen were nodding.

"The ancients," Ray said, "believe it is possible the aliens didn't even understand the human and Gray and Cirrata cultures on those planets."

Cole found that almost impossible to imagine, yet this was a completely alien culture.

"Hive mind," Tacita said, nodding. "If you are correct in that assumption, the aliens in the ships would only be workers without any ability to judge or think in a creative fashion."

"Just following orders," Ray said. "And thus not be able to recognize another culture."

All the chairmen were nodding now.

"So we need a vast amount of information yet," Cole said.

"Stay shielded everyone," Echo said. "We will report back as soon as we have a clearer image of the extent of this culture or during the next meeting *Star Ray* has set."

At that Echo cut the conference call and turned to look at Cole.

Cole reached over and hugged her with one arm, turning them both to face JP.

He was looking as shocked as Cole was feeling. And the silence in the command center spoke volumes on how everyone was feeling.

"Well," Cole said to everyone. "We joined onto this Starburst project to go explore and find stuff. Seems we have found a lot of stuff."

A couple of the crew laughed and JP just shook his head, smiling.

"Now let's figure out a way to quickly find the extent of this alien culture's spread."

"Star Trail," Echo said, turning back to face the big screen. "Show us a

three-dimensional image of a few thousand galaxies surrounding this galaxy."

The image appeared.

"Mark this galaxy red and all other known alien galaxies red," Cole said. "Adjust the scale to include the alien seeded galaxies *Star Ray* has found. And put in a blinking blue dot the location of the alien fleet."

To Cole the pattern was instantly clear. From the galaxy where they were, there was a clear path to the fleet.

"*Star Trail,*" Cole said, "Show a dotted straight line from this galaxy to the alien fleet."

The line appeared. Beside Cole, Echo nodded.

"*Star Trail,*" Echo said, "Extend that line back in the opposite direction from this galaxy, then show our path approaching this galaxy in an orange line."

"We came in sideways on this line of seeding," Cole said. "We have to go back along that line to see how far it goes."

"And if this is a hive mind at work," Echo said, "a galaxy-spanning hive mind, we need to find that original home with the original queen."

"And then what?" JP asked from behind them.

Cole could only shake his head. He had no idea.

None at all.

Chapter Twenty-Seven

ECHO SPENT SOME time talking with Cole about sending scout ships back, or if they should take *Star Trail* back along the clear trail of alien seeded galaxies. They really needed to find where these aliens all started.

Finally they decided that *Star Ray* would have enough help shortly from all the other Starburst ships headed there. *Star Trail* needed to find the start of this race, the alien home world. So they informed *Star Ray* to pull back the ships they had backtracking.

Then they sent the image of the line of seeding to all the chairmen.

Echo was starting to think that if this alien race really was a hive mind, there just might be one major queen that controlled it all.

"*Star Trail,*" Cole said, after he and Echo made sure all scout and military ships were accounted for and most were back on board, "follow along that extended line at full speed, scanning galaxies as we pass."

"Stop when you no longer find an alien-seeded galaxy," Echo said. "And show our path on the screen."

"*Engaging full trans-tunnel drive,*" *Star Trail* said.

Echo watched as dozens and dozens of galaxies flashed past, all with alien cultures.

Then, almost as quickly as it started, *Star Trail* dropped out of trans-tunnel drive.

"*Scanning a dozen galaxies ahead shows no sign of alien culture,*" *Star Trail* said.

"Return to the edge of the last alien galaxy," Cole said.

"Launch three hundred scout ships with military escorts to scout the galaxy," Echo said, "and another four hundred scout ships to scan all surrounding galaxies in groups of twenty."

A moment later *Star Trail* said, "*Near the last alien galaxy. Launching scout and military ships.*"

"Please show the path on the large screen with a dotted line from this galaxy to the alien fleet," Cole said.

Echo watched as the image appeared. "How many alien galaxies are along that path?"

"From two-hundred-and-sixty confirmed to five-hundred-and-ten possible," Star Trail said, *"depending on the results of galaxies along that line that have not been scanned."*

Echo stood beside Cole as both of them studied the data coming in from the scout ships. As with the previous galaxy, every planet seemed to have a queen center.

"Star Trail, is it possible to determine when this galaxy was settled by the aliens?" Cole asked.

"Approximately one-point-six million years ago," Star Trail said. *"With a possible variation of two hundred thousand years in either direction."*

"The Seeders were in this area of space first," Echo said, shocked at that information.

"Chances are they never got this far away from their home galaxy in this direction," Cole said. "At their speeds this galaxy and the first seeded human galaxy were over three hundred years travel time apart. No reason to come this way."

"And they were headed with seeding in the other direction," Echo said.

Now she understood that the human culture and the alien culture being this close had just been a bad piece of luck, and that the aliens seeding in the direction of the human galaxies had also just been a very bad piece of luck.

"Star Trail," Cole said, "is this is the oldest alien galaxy?"

"Of the ones scanned, yes, this is the oldest," Star Trail said.

"So now we need to find the original home world," Echo said.

The galaxy was a standard spiral galaxy, not large but not small either. It would have over a billion possible planets around yellow stars. Echo had no idea how they were going to narrow that down to find one home alien world.

But at least they had found the alien home galaxy.

That was a start.

Chapter Twenty-Eight

COLE WAS ABOUT to suggest to Echo that they call a conference when *Star Trail* informed them that Lisa and Jaden were calling a conference.

All nineteen Starburst ship's chairmen appeared on the large screen along with Ray and Tacita.

"We have some good news to report," Jaden said, starting right off. "The galaxy the alien ships are headed toward has a healthy and advanced human culture in it. No damage there or any sign any alien ship has even approached that galaxy."

"And the human populations of the billion-plus planets," Lisa said, "seem to have no idea they are within years of being destroyed."

Cole was very happy to hear all that.

Very happy and very relieved.

"We have found no other alien cultures off the line of seeding they are clearly traveling," Jaden said.

"Even better news," Lisa said. "Ancient-seeded human cultures have spread out as we had expected in a band of about fifty galaxies wide and the band seems to be moving in the direction of where we assume the center home worlds of this group of Seeders would be."

"So we have a pretty good idea what happened to all the mother ships," Jaden said. "They just kept on seeding."

"There seems to be no communication at all between the human galaxies," Lisa said. "Thus they would have no idea about the destruction that has happened or the threat."

Cole understood that. Seeded human galaxies tended to not expand outside of their own galaxy, even though they had the speed to do so with long missions. It was the Seeders, because of the last war, that had set up the breadcrumb networks both with Starburst ships and mother ships, but also between galaxies recently seeded. The idea was to try to pull the galaxy-wide cultures together.

It would be many centuries before the results of that would be clear, although faster ship speeds would certainly help that as well.

As Jaden paused, Echo said to the chairmen, "It appears we have found the original alien galaxy. We have not found their original home planet yet and the main queen, but given time we believe we can."

Cole told everyone the amount of time the aliens had been in existence and sent them all an updated map of the seeding trail of the aliens. "We have scout ships out making sure no other seeding lines were done by the aliens."

"This is all good news," Ray said, nodding.

"We will next need to figure out," Tacita said, "how the queens are communicating with the workers, if this actually is a hive mind culture. That needs to be the next priority."

"Agreed," Jaden said.

Cole nodded, as did Echo beside him and the other chairmen on the screen.

But then Matt from Starburst ship *Star Fall* said, "I think there may be more going on than we are seeing."

Beside him Carey nodded. Cole could tell they both looked very, very worried.

"Some of you chairmen," Matt said, "lived for a time on a planet in the Milky Way Galaxy that had a population destroyed by a radiation burst from space. That planet was our home planet."

Cole glanced at Echo who had gone a little white. They had spent six years there trying to help out the rebirth of that society, living and dealing with the dead. It had been a tough six years for both of them.

"We have been studying the data coming in from the planets just attacked by the aliens," Carey said. "There are survivors, but no dead."

"Those cities had millions of people in them and there isn't one sign that anyone in those cities died," Matt said.

"It was as if almost all of the population wasn't there," Carey said, "when the aliens arrived and started getting the planet ready for their seeding."

"Where could they have gone?" Ray asked.

The exact question that Cole was thinking. And he bet the same question that every chairman was asking.

Carey and Matt both shook their heads.

"The population of the planets seemed to be advanced and stabilized at around three billion per planet," Matt said. "We estimate around a billion human planets in the last galaxy."

Cole couldn't even do the math on that number of people, couldn't imagine it. And he really didn't want to think about that many people dying.

Silence over the large screen.

Finally it was Ray who said simply, "We all have a lot of work to do. Map out that entire area of space, make sure on everything, and see if you can find out what happened to all those people."

Tacita nodded and then cut their connection.

"Tomorrow morning at ten for another conference," Lisa said.

With that the conference ended.

Echo nodded to Cole and turned to face their command crew. "Miss no detail, people. We need to find that original alien home world and understand how this alien culture works."

"Star Trail," Cole said. "I want a search pattern in a one-hundred-galaxy radius of this galaxy completed quickly. Scout and military ships in bands of twenty each. Set it up and launch the ships as needed."

"That's going to be a lot of information coming in," Echo said to the command crew. "Set up teams to analyze every bit and fit it together."

Cole watched as his fantastic command crew nodded and set to work.

Echo turned back to him. "Come with me."

And a moment later they had jumped to their apartment.

"We need food," Echo said, moving to the kitchen area.

At that moment Cole realized he was hungry. And he couldn't even remember what meal they had had last.

Or even what time it was.

Chapter Twenty-Nine

ECHO COOKED THEM some simple hamburgers with fries and made them both a chocolate milkshake. Their three orange-and-white cats sort of watched from the edge of the living room, more surprised at the odd schedule than anything else.

While she cooked, Cole just sat at the dining table, clearly deep in thought. They often sat together, not talking.

Finally, as they were eating, she brought up what Carey and Matt had been talking about.

It had bothered Echo more than she wanted to admit and she needed to talk about it. Those years going into homes of the dead had made her understand just how unbelievably precious human life was.

And how fragile.

"What do you think happened to all those people on all those planets?" Echo asked. "Or their bodies? You think the aliens are to blame?"

Cole shook his head and kept eating, but she could tell the idea had bothered him as well.

She couldn't imagine how this was bothering Matt and Carey and a few of the other chairmen of Starburst ships who had spent time in the rescue there or in the rebuilding.

She knew that Jaden and Lisa were waiting for a few other Starburst ships to arrive before starting rescue operations of the surviving humans. But that would take another week or so. And Echo was very glad she and Cole were not involved in that kind of planning.

"Something purposeful had to have happened to them," Cole said after a moment. "On that planet in the Milky Way, over a million people had survived worldwide from a nasty natural disaster. But that left billions and billions dead, scattered everywhere. You don't just hide that many bodies in a few years."

"But where did they go then?" Echo asked, trying to wrap her mind around doing something with billions of people from a planet and then doing that on a billion planets.

Cole shook his head, again with the haunted look in his eyes. "The only logical conclusion is that the alien fleet did something to them. A weapon of some sort that dissolved them or broke the bodies down into a dust and only a few survived that."

Echo had come up with the same thought. But that would argue against the idea that the aliens might not even have noticed the civilizations on the planets they were preparing to seed.

"We need to find this alien home planet," Echo said, "and figure out what kind of weapons these aliens have and if we are in danger as well."

Cole nodded. "Not at all convinced our screens would protect us from something like that."

"I'm not convinced they don't know we are here," Echo said.

"Yeah," Cole said, "had that same thought."

The idea that their shields couldn't protect them scared Echo more than she wanted to admit.

Far, far more.

With that they both finished their meals.

Then Cole made them both large cups of coffee and jumped back to the command center while Echo gave their cats a treat and made sure their water supply was full.

Then she joined him, her coffee mug in hand, focused on finding the answer to what had happened to billions and billions of humans.

Something clearly had happened to them. She needed to know what had happened.

But she just wasn't sure she really wanted to know.

Chapter Thirty

COLE WAS SURPRISED that the next two weeks became a form of routine. He never would have thought it could, but it did.

Neither he nor Echo had gone back to exercising yet, so every morning after about six hours sleep and a quick breakfast, they found themselves in the command center.

That's where they both were now, with large cups of coffee, studying all the data coming over the large screen in front of them.

Twice a day they had conference calls with the other chairmen.

Every hour he and Echo got summary reports from all the areas of data coming in from the command crew.

They had yet to discover the original alien home world, but they felt they were narrowing it down.

The galaxies in a radius around this galaxy held no surprises at all and all scout ships not working inside the alien galaxy were now back on board.

The information about the aliens had been slowly growing. They were clearly a hive mind culture with one queen.

The aggressive nature that was evident when the aliens were young and coming out of the ocean was not evident at all with the adults of the race. Cole was very happy to hear that.

There seemed, at least from any human viewpoints, to not be any weapons or defenses on any of the planets.

The alien fleet seemed to have no weapons of any nature and beyond simple shields against dust and small particles, the alien ships seemed to have no defensive shields either.

Their trans-tunnel drives seemed to be basic and clearly alien-designed. No sign of human or Gray or Cirrata designs in the slightest.

And there was still no evidence at all on how the aliens communicated.

There were now six of the twenty Starburst ships with *Star Ray* and the others would be arriving over the next two weeks. The more ships that arrived in the area, the more comfortable Cole felt.

That was a lot of people working on the same problems and a lot of military might if needed.

The first conference call with the other chairmen was just over a half hour away when behind Cole, JP said, "We found it. We found the original planet and maybe the main queen."

"Details on the big screen," Echo said.

Cole could see that the original alien planet was located near the edge of the galaxy in one spiral arm. It orbited in a standard orbit that allowed for water

and oxygen and life to survive around a middle-aged yellow sun.

A massive alien city that looked more like a giant mountain filled the center of one large continent. And from all the scans the scout ships had taken, the largest living creature ever imagined filled the inside of that mountain.

"That queen is bigger than this ship," Echo said, her voice showing shock. "How is that possible?"

"From what we can tell," JP said, "It's far over a million years old as well."

Cole couldn't even grasp what he was seeing. The Gray, the Cirrata, and the humans were all small creatures with similar characteristics, even though very different.

But a creature larger than *Star Trail* and that old was truly alien in nature.

Cole was just shaking his head. Now what do they do?

"You are being contacted by the Sun Hawk chairmen," *Star Trail* said.

Echo glanced at Cole, a puzzled look on her face.

It took Cole a moment before the name sank in.

Sun Hawk was one of the Seeder mother ships they had been searching for from the first seeded area they had found.

What in the world were they doing here?

"Please, *Star Trail*," Cole said, "put them through on the big screen."

Behind them the command center went dead silent.

On the main screen was a man with a balding head and white hair and fairly dark skin. Beside him stood a woman with long gray hair, almost as long as Ray's, and pure white skin. Both of them looked like they were wearing comfortable shirts and jeans.

And both were smiling.

Behind them was what looked to be a massive command center, one level higher and about twice the size of the *Star Trail* command center. It was staffed by well over a hundred humans of various sizes and shapes and dress.

Except for the size of the command center, it looked pretty standard Seeder model.

"Chairmen Guinn and Lemmon," the man said, nodding. "It is an honor to meet you."

"We are Chairmen Sky Mead and Lennox Summerlin of *Sun Hawk*. Please call us Sky and Lennox."

Cole managed to open his mouth, but nothing came out.

Echo managed a little more.

"Please call us Echo and Cole," she said. "A pleasure and a vast surprise to meet you, to say the least."

Both smiled. "We have been following you for a while now and watching your movements and *Star Ray's* movements as well," Sky said. "We hoped to hold off contacting you for a little longer but since you have found the Karinos' home world, we felt it was critical we do so now."

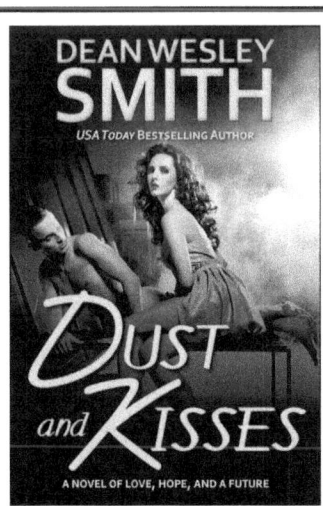

Now Available
from all your favorite booksellers in trade paper and electronic editions.

Cole again was almost too stunned to talk. Then he asked simply, "How long have you been watching us?"

Sky glanced at Lennox and he shrugged. "Honestly, we have had scout ships around all the Starburst ships since you all arrived in our old home areas of space. A very impressive mission to discover what happened to all of us."

"Commendable," Sky said.

"Yes, very much so," Lennox said.

"We need to ask you a favor," Sky said, getting serious before Cole or Echo could even say a word about what they had just heard.

"We need to ask you to withdraw your scout ships from around the Karinos' home planet and this galaxy before the great queen discovers you," Sky said.

Cole assumed she meant the massive queen they had just found, but they went on before he could ask.

"We have, as all Seeders have had, a very aggressive non-intervention and non-contact policy about alien races," Lennox said. "So if you don't mind, would you withdraw all your scout and military ships and we can move away from this galaxy a short distance and talk."

Echo glanced at Cole.

At this moment in time he was too shocked to even have any objection. The scout ships could always return if needed. He wasn't sure if they were being played in some fashion or another, but pulling in the scout and military ships wouldn't make much of a difference.

"*Star Trail,*" Cole said, "please issue an emergency recall of all ships around this galaxy and inform us when all ships are back on board."

"Thank you," Sky said, nodding.

"*Sun Hawk,*" Lennox said, "please send *Star Trail* a destination a number of galaxies away from any Karinos-seeded galaxies."

"Destination confirmed," Star Trail said.

"We will talk there," Lennox said, smiling. "In one hour."

"We assume you have a lot of questions to ask and we have some answers we can give you," Sky said.

With that they vanished.

"Star Trail," Cole said, "any sign of any human Seeder ship in our area?"

"No," Star Trail said simply.

"Any idea where that transmission originated?" Cole asked.

"No," Star Trail again said, simply.

Cole glanced at Echo who was looking puzzled and shocked.

"Any bets we were just played by the alien queen?" Cole asked.

"No bets at all," Echo said.

Section Six
The Real Surprise

Chapter Thirty-One

ECHO JUST FELT shocked.

And scared out of her mind. What kind of trap were they going to go into?

She and Cole had spent the next ten minutes studying all the data *Star Trail* had about the communication. It had been real, of that there was no doubt.

It had been recorded by *Star Trail*. But it hadn't come from anywhere in particular.

Star Trail said that it had been blocked completely with contact with *Sun Hawk*, if there really was a ship there.

"We need to tell the other chairmen what just happened," Cole finally said.

Echo agreed. At least if they were walking into a trap, the other chairmen would know what was happening.

As the chairmen finished coming onto the screen just slightly ahead of the regular meeting, Echo started off the news.

"First off, we found the alien home world," she said.

"But that is not why we called this meeting slightly early," Cole said. *"Star Trail,* play them the supposed meeting we had with the chairmen of the *Sun Hawk* within minutes of discovering the alien home world."

"Sun Hawk?" Ray asked, clearly stunned.

The rest of the chairmen's faces were just as stunned. It would have been funny if it wasn't so serious.

At that moment the meeting was starting to play for the chairmen. She and Cole could see all the faces of the other chairmen and Ray and Tacita's faces as well.

When Sky and Lennox appeared on the screen, both Ray and Tacita damn near burst into tears. Tacita actually moved backwards and sat down.

Echo always considered Tacita to be one of the toughest women she had ever met, so something about seeing images of Sky and Lennox had shaken her to her core.

What in the world would do that?

After the recording finished, Cole said, "All of our ships are coming on board now and will be in place in the next five minutes. The meeting point designated is less than ten minutes away."

"We are not sure if that was the alien queen staging that or if by some chance that was actually the chairmen of *Sun Hawk,"* Cole said.

"If it was *Sun Hawk,*" Echo said, "they have advanced farther than we have in technology and are at least as fast in travel speed."

"Those were two real people," Tacita said, her voice firm and now back under control. She had stood again as the recording of the meeting had ended.

"We know them very well from the first few seeding missions outside our first galaxy," Tacita said.

"We saw their names on the lists after all these years for the first time when we got the ancient's names with the seeding missions," Ray said. "We did not expect them to still be alive."

"They might not be," Cole said. "This alien culture must have a powerful form of telepathy to communicate from planet to planet and galaxy to galaxy. We have no idea what that kind of power is capable of doing."

Ray and Tacita nodded.

"Whatever or whoever is behind this," Echo said, "they effectively got us to remove our scout and military ships from that galaxy for the moment."

"So we are going to go find out who they really are and if they even exist," Cole said.

"*Star Trail,*" Echo said, "please set up a constant feed to all the other Starburst ships and Ray and Tacita of our movements and communications."

With that, Cole cut the conference and he and Echo turned to the command crew. "Everyone stay alert. Scan everything and if you see something off report it instantly."

The silent command crew nodded.

"*Star Trail,* are all ships on board?" Echo asked.

"*The last will be on board in thirty seconds,*" *Star Trail* said.

"At that point jump us to the designated meeting location," Cole said. "Full screens and full speed. Keep all military ships on high alert and ready to launch."

"On the main screen please scan ahead for anything waiting for us at that location," Echo said.

"*Entering trans-tunnel drive now,*" *Star Trail* said.

The main screen showed nothing at the designation point.

The distance was a full ten minutes away and Echo watched the scans of the empty passing galaxies as they flashed past.

Nothing.

That was the longest ten minutes Echo ever experienced.

Twice she had to force herself to breathe.

And not one word was spoken the entire time in the command center.

Not one.

Chapter Thirty-Two

"*DESTINATION POINT. DROPPING* out of trans-tunnel drive," *Star Trail* said.

"Hold position," Cole said.

The screen in front of them showed nothing. They were a short distance away from a small spiral galaxy that showed no life at all. This was empty space by any definition.

Cole glanced around at JP who just shook his head.

Nothing at all.

Finally, *Star Trail* said, "*We are being hailed by Sun Hawk.*"

"Please, on screen," Cole said. "And make sure this is streaming to all other Starburst ships."

If they were going to make a huge mistake here, he wanted to make sure none of the other Starburst ships would make the same one in the future.

"Thank you for believing us and pulling your scout ships," Lennox said as the two chairmen came on the screen.

Both Sky and Lennox were smiling. Cole could see that both actually showed a poise that must have come with age. Clearly these two were almost as old as Ray and Tacita. And Sky's long gray hair looked similar to Ray's long gray hair.

"We do not think that the Karinos queen felt any disturbance," Sky said.

Lennox nodded. "We are being very, very careful and studying the Karinos to figure out how or if we should ever contact them."

Cole understood that completely.

"So you promised us some answers," Echo said a moment before Cole could.

He was just stunned again at the two ancients facing him on the screen. They looked so normal and relaxed.

"And we will answer as honestly as we can," Lennox said, continuing to smile.

"Where exactly are you?" Echo said. "You can clearly see us but we can't seem to see you."

"We actually can't see you in any real fashion," Sky said. "We have just learned to trace shielded ships is all. As for where we are, we are very near you. *Sun Hawk*, please drop all screens except those used to protect the ship from debris."

A moment later, filling the screen, a massive ship in the standard Seeder bird shape shimmered into being. It looked sleek, yet massive, like a bird coasting in flight.

But to Cole something felt off about it.

It looked like a more advanced Seeder ship. Same standard shape, everything.

Information about the ship scrolled up the side of the big screen and suddenly Cole understood what felt off about the ship they were looking at.

It was a hundred times, if not more, larger than *Star Trail*.

Sun Hawk was so big, it could hold all twenty of the Starburst ships inside it and not even strain.

"Wow," Echo said, "*Sun Hawk* is a very large and beautiful ship."

"Thank you," Sky said, smiling. "We think so."

"*Star Trail*," Cole said, "please drop our visual and sensory screens, only leaving up the screens necessary for our protection."

Lennox nodded and smiled. "Seeder ships never do seem to change in look, do they?"

"Just size it seems," Cole said, smiling back. "How many souls do you have on board?"

"About two-hundred-million total of crew and families, plus military and scout ship crews and families," Sky said.

"Can I ask speed?" Cole asked.

"Not much faster than you appear to be," Lennox said. "Trans-tunnel forty-eight."

"Are you a Seeder ship?" Echo asked.

"No," Sky said. "At the moment we are one of a thousand ships this size that are being used to rescue humans from the planets in the way of the Karinos seeding. We have three more galaxies to deal with before the Karinos seeding ships move past settled human space and into empty galaxies."

So that was what had happened to the populations of those planets in that last galaxy. They had all been relocated.

"The Gray have about seven-hundred rescue ships," Sky said, "and the Cirrata have five hundred. Luckily, the other two alien races that make up our confederation, the Procyon and the Portia are not living on these early seeded planets."

"You have five races working together?" Echo asked.

"We have explored a great deal of space," Lennox said. "It seems six races that we know about have managed to escape the confines of their galaxies and gone exploring. Five live peacefully together on seeded planets in billions of galaxies and the Karinos are the sixth. To be honest, we have not yet figured out how to approach the Karinos."

"So they do not know you are here on these planets they are destroying?"

"No," Sky said. "At least as far as we know."

"Which is why we have these ships to evacuate populations," Lennox said. "We're starting on the next galaxy in line in a few weeks. We have been seeding and building their new home worlds now for a few thousand years. We started when we discovered the Karinos and the track they were seeding."

"A massive project," Echo said and Cole nodded.

At that moment *Star Trail* said only to Cole and Echo, *"Ray and Tacita would like to join the conversation."*

Echo glanced at Cole. "Why not?"

Echo smiled and turned back to address Lennox and Sky. "We would like to bring in two chairmen to this conversation that say they used to know you. If you don't mind."

"Our pleasure," Lennox said.

Sky looked puzzled.

"Star Trail, please add Chairmen Ray and Tacita to the conversation," Cole said.

Both Lennox and Sky jerked at the mention of those two names.

Then, as the two smiling faces of Ray and Tacita came on the screen, Sky stepped forward.

"Mom? Dad?" Sky asked, her voice not much more than a whisper.

Ray and Tacita just nodded, smiling the largest smiles Cole could ever imagine possible.

All he could do was stare at all four of them.

Chapter Thirty-Three

ECHO WATCHED THE family reunion clearly millions of years overdue.

After a short time, Sky asked where Ray and Tacita were. When Tacita told them they were in their original seeded area, Sky was very disappointed.

Echo would have been as well. But then Ray told Sky and Lennox they were on their way and would be there in two days.

That news shocked Sky and Lennox, so Ray had to explain the breadcrumb stations to them.

"We will be on our way shortly," Tacita said.

"We are so excited to see you again," Ray said.

With that Ray and Tacita cut out of the conversation, leaving Echo and Cole again facing the smiling faces of Sky and Lennox.

"Well, that was a surprise," Lennox said.

"To all of us as well," Cole said, laughing.

"You didn't know?" Sky asked.

"Ray and Tacita have been the leading figures for millions of years," Cole said, "in hundreds of thousands of galaxy seeding. They don't talk much."

Both Sky and Lennox laughed. "Yeah, that we remember as well."

"So what can our twenty Starburst ships do to help?" Echo asked, changing the subject.

"Besides stay out of the way," Cole said.

"Actually," Lennox said, "we were hoping you would offer."

"We need to focus on getting the main populations of over a billion planets to their new homes," Sky said.

Cole knew exactly where they were going. "You need help with the ones that wouldn't leave originally, but now might want to?"

"Exactly," Lennox said. "We have managed to get most of the stragglers off the planets where the Karinos are hatching their first wave."

"But not all," Cole said. "We were getting ready to try to help the remaining off some of those planets."

"We do not force anyone to leave their home," Sky said. "But seeing those Karinos hatchlings swarming the beaches might change some minds."

Now Available
from all your favorite booksellers in trade paper and electronic editions.

"It would change mine," Echo said.

"Let us talk with the other chairmen and get back with you," Cole said.

"And we will hold here until Ray and Tacita arrive through the breadcrumb network we have left behind us," Echo said, smiling.

"We will hold as well," Lennox said, nodding.

"And thank you for the wonderful surprise," Sky said.

"Wish we would have planned it," Echo said, smiling.

With that, the conversation ended.

"Star Trail," Cole said, "put on the main screen all the chairmen of the Starburst ships."

He had a hunch he knew how this was going to go. He couldn't imagine any of them not wanting to help.

But it was sure fun to see the faces appear on the screen laughing and smiling.

And behind every couple was a command center full of smiling faces as well.

It seems the mission they had all set out to do, find the ancients, was a complete success.

And Cole had to admit, that felt wonderful.

Epilogue

ECHO STOOD BESIDE Cole in the command center and watched on the big screen as the ground teams on dozens and dozens of planets worked to find humans still remaining. The images were of ruined buildings and dust covering everything. A horrid reminder of the six years on a planet she wished she could forget.

The new images were already starting to give her nightmares.

The two weeks since their first meeting with Lennox and Sky had gone quickly. All of the chairmen of the Starburst ships had agreed without discussion to try to save as many of the stragglers as possible.

All the Starburst ships had spent part of the two weeks setting up quarters for all the possible new arrivals. And getting to know Lennox and Sky's culture and the history of the last four million years for all these seeded groups.

It seemed that all but one of the groups had started the process to genetically alter entire populations to be born as Seeders.

But by the time it became clear that the lifespan of the new Seeders had fallen, the process was irreversible and the birthrate couldn't be increased. No amount of work could increase the birthrate of the Seeders and they all knew they were doomed.

So at a half million years and with sharply reduced and dwindling populations in each galaxy, they built new Seeder mother ships and used them as jumping points, their own bread-crumb trail, to get the populations to new worlds near the one seeded group that hadn't done the genetic manipulation.

So all that Echo and Cole and the others had speculated had happened. Every bit of it.

It was then that things really changed. Instead of having one hundred and eighty mother ships, they had closer to ten thousand to use.

So they moved mostly in one direction, seeding human galaxies as fast as they could.

Along the way the humans, Gray, and Cirrata met the Procyon, a raccoon-like race that had seeded about six galaxies. The Procyon built cities in large forests and loved the wet, damp jungles and forests around the equators of Earth-like planets.

The Procyon liked the way the humans, Gray, and Cirrata lived together on seeded planets and after a hundred thousand years or so of trade and negotiations, asked to join.

They had faster ships and other upgrades that helped everyone and they were welcomed. So from that point forward the four races all lived on and seeded the planets together.

And part of the growth of every planet was getting the races as they evolved to understand and live with the other.

As the seeding front wave neared the area of compact galaxies that they hoped to build a large center in, they discovered the Portia. They were a fist-sized spider-like race that had spread over almost fifty galaxies without ever changing a planet. They were colorful, likable, and horrific at the same time. They built small village-like cities around lakes. They hated the desert, the oceans, the mountains, and the jungles.

The images of them that Echo saw made her shudder. She had never much cared for spiders. But she had to admit their small village cities looked like fairy tale constructions of orange webs and bright blue sheets of walls that shimmered in the sunlight.

The Portia liked the other four races and were willing to trade and work with them almost from day one. Within fifty thousand years of meeting, they had joined into the seeding and were living in harmony with the other four races.

Now, almost four million years from the start, there were still over two thousand mother Seeder ships going in a hundred different directions from the massive cluster of galaxies called The Center.

Echo was impressed at the vast scale of it all and the history.

But now they were down to focusing on one human at a time. A very different, yet very important scale.

It was only a few of the humans who had decided to stay behind on each planet. All the Cirrata and Gray had left on the evacuation ships. Now, every hour, the images coming in reminded Echo of the six years she and Cole had spent helping clear out the dead and get a human society restarted on a planet in the Milky Way Galaxy. Only thankfully, this time, there were no bodies. Just people who had made a bad choice and were now willing and ready to leave.

And saving them felt great.

But something was missing. Something was starting to bother her.

She wanted to talk with Cole about it, but just as she was beginning he turned to her first and asked the question that pinpointed exactly what she was worried about.

"What are we going to do after we finish this?" he asked.

The job of rescuing survivors might take them another five to ten years. At most, before they would no longer be needed.

But during those years she desperately needed something else to focus on.

She looked up at the screen and then smiled. She knew the answer to that question. Knew it as clearly as any answer she had ever known.

"We go exploring again," she said.

Cole laughed. "Exactly what I was hoping you would say."

"Any bet that the other Starburst chairmen might feel the same way?" she asked, smiling at the man she loved more than anything.

"I would bet they all would," he said.

"So how about we have a conference call with them, suggest the idea, and get everyone planning," she said. "We only have a decade or so to get ready."

"Not a lot of time at all," he said, nodding. He pointed to the screen. "And a lot more fun than focusing on this."

Then he turned and kissed her.

She kissed him back.

"Thank you," she said.

He just smiled at her with that wonderful smile she never grew tired of, even after centuries.

Then she turned to face the big screen and all the images of ruined worlds. *"Star Trail,* please ask the other Starburst chairmen for a conference link. Tell them the topic is: *What are we going to explore next?"*

After a moment the smiling and laughing and nodding faces of the other chairmen started to push aside the images of the ruined planets.

One mission accomplished. They had found the ancients.

It was clearly time to figure out another mission for the Starburst ships.

And she had no doubt it would be fun.

—~—

Coming Next Issue in *Smith's Monthly*

Smith's MONTHLY

Number Thirty-Eight
November, 2016

Original Stories,
Novels, and Articles

Dean Wesley Smith

Heaven Painted as a Sunset

A Ghost of a Chance Novel

#1...October 2013

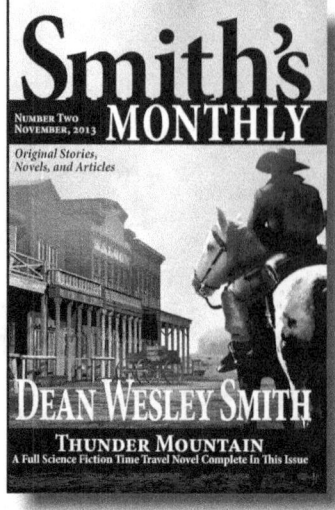

#2...November 2013

#3...December 2013

#4...January 2014

#5...February 2014

#6...March 2014

#7...April 2014

#8...May 2014

#9...June 2014

#10...July 2014

#11...August 2014

#12...September 2014

#13...October 2014

#14...November 2014

#15...December 2014

#16...January 2015

#17...February 2015

#18...March 2015

#19...April 2015

#20...May 2015

#21...June 2015

#22...July 2015

#23...August 2015

#24...September 2015

#25...October 2015

#26...November 2015

#27...December 2015

#28...January 2016

#29...February 2016

#30...March 2016

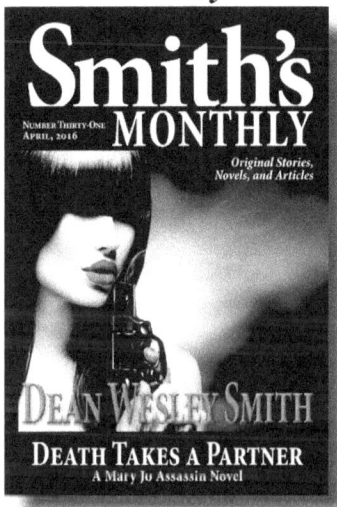

#31...April 2016

#32...May 2016

#33...June 2016

#34...July 2016

#35...August 2016

#36...September 2016

Thank You!!

I would like to thank the following wonderful people who support my blog and my work through Patreon. Your support is very important to me. Thanks!

Betsy Wilcox	Erick Lindman
Irette Y. Patterson	Christopher Ridge
Kathryn Rooney	Terry Mixon
Wendy Lee Maddox	James Husun
Jamie Curierre	Sherman Cox
Chris Cousino	Chong Go
Jane Lawson	Maria Grace
Shantnu Tiwari	Grondpom
Miguel Angel Alonso Pulido	Fen
Nancy Hendrickson	Robin Brande
Ryan M. Williams	J.R. Murdock
Jacob Proffitt	Kathleen McClure
Marian Goldeen	Gunnar Gunderson
Gary Speer	F.I. Goldhaber
Megan Bryce	Mary Jo Rabe
Michelle Tatam	John Kilgallon
Ann Tucker	Dave Hendrickson
Kari Wolfe	Jabberwocky
Albert Lemke	Eric Goebelbecker
Stacey Larson	Marsha Kessler
Diane Darcy	Scott Gordon
Krystle Jones	Martyn Folkes
Kari Gallagher	John
T. Thorn Coyle	Cj Lehi
Tasha Turner Lennhoff	Brenda Smith

Smith's
MONTHLY

Every Month Original
Novels, Stories, and Articles

USA Today Bestselling Writer
Dean Wesley Smith

TABLE OF CONTENTS

SHORT STORIES

FULL NOVEL

NONFICTION

The Writings and Opinions of
Dean Wesley Smith

Introduction
Some Schedule Fun

Those of you reading this a ways after this issue was published will wonder what I am talking about here. But let me say this simply. Even though it says November 2016 on the cover, the publication of this issue happened a good distance into 2017.

And that's fine, since this is my magazine. A number of people asked me why I just didn't skip the months I was behind. Just pretend I was on schedule again.

Honestly, I flat don't want to. In fact, by the time this magazine goes into its fifth year (Issue #49), I hope to be back on time, meaning the publication date on the cover will match the month the issue actually comes out.

But here in this introduction, I wanted to admit the fact that this is late and to thank a number of people for being so understanding while I went and did other things for a time.

All the subscribers to this magazine first off. Wonderful support and faith in a crazy project.

And also thanks to the Patreon supporters who also get this magazine every issue and support my blog every month.

Thank you one and all for sticking with me on this crazy idea of putting out a magazine of only my stuff every month.

Back when I came up with this idea almost four years ago, I told those around me that at times over the years I would get behind.

Actually, I said that after the first year, because I wasn't sure I could even fill my own magazine every month for a year. So after the first year, when I shifted my goal to getting this magazine to Issue #100, I warned people I would get behind at times as life got in the way.

But I also said I would always try to catch up.

So this is the first issue in getting caught up.

Thanks for the Support

Dean Wesley Smith

And this issue has some really fun stuff. Not only is there a new Ghost of a Chance novel, but the first story in a brand new Ghost of a Chance series starring Marble Grant, a former superhero.

Ghost of a Chance novels have attitude. Marble Grant stories take that attitude and multiply it a few hundred times. Hope you like them because every issue for the next ten issues will start with a new Marble Grant story.

And I hope you enjoy a lot of reading coming up. Over the next five months, as I get caught up, a bunch of these issues will be headed your way.

And once again, thanks for all the support.

Cheers.

—*Dean Wesley Smith*
May 18, 2017

Coming Next Issue in *Smith's Monthly*

ACE HIGH
A Cold Poker Gang Novel

Smith's

MONTHLY

NUMBER THIRTY-NINE
DECEMBER, 2016

*Original Stories,
Novels, and Articles*

DEAN WESLEY SMITH
ACE HIGH
A Cold Poker Gang Novel

Dying on a first date sucks. Dying on a blind date sucks even worse.

Marble Grant, superhero, finds herself suddenly dead in a disgustingly smelly back alley and not catching a white-beam ride to the other side of whatever.

As a superhero, she knew about Ghost Agents. Never met one, but knew they existed.

She never heard of superheroes making the transition to Ghost Agent before, either.

The first story in a new and fun Ghost of a Chance series, where ghosts solve problems and help people. And look damn sexy in the process.

Blind Date
A Marble Grant Story

One

DYING ON A first date sucks. Dying on a blind date sucks even worse.

Especially when your date dies with you. And then goes off through some tunnel of light into the next life or something, leaving you sitting alone, dead, in a dark alley, waiting for your own tunnel of light.

Hands down, the worst ending to any date in recorded history.

The alley we had been forced to go into was blacker than the inside of a latrine, and seeming how it smelled, I would have not been surprised to be in a latrine, but I knew I wasn't since it seemed that being dead meant I could see just fine in the dark.

And smell just fine as well. Holy crap. The nearby Chinese restaurant garbage smelled like my fridge after six days of feeling sorry for myself and laying on the couch and eating take-out without taking out the uneaten food. And no telling how many homeless and drunks had used this alley for a bathroom.

I was sitting on a big green dumpster owned by a nearby office, so thankfully it didn't have the odor of the other dumpsters coming up between my legs.

The scum with the greasy black hair and dirty ski parka that had killed us was going through my date's pockets as I sat and watched.

The guy looked skinny and no doubt drug-addicted. His motions were jerky, his eyes darting around him like a rat trying to find a way out of a maze.

My blind date, dear old Handsome Bob, as I had started to think of him for the full thirty minutes I had known him, had caused this mess by thinking he could be a macho asshole or something.

The scum with the greasy black hair had approached us on the sidewalk and Bob had shaken his head and said, "Not now."

We were headed down the street to a nice Italian restaurant that served the best red wine and bread plate this side of New York. And that was going some for the Old Towne section of Boise, Idaho.

Bob was dressed in a clearly expensive silk suit and no tie, while I didn't look so cheap myself. For the date I had put on dark slacks, a silk white blouse with pearls around my neck, and a thin see-through sweater. No bra because I wanted my date to get an occasional peak at what might be offered after dinner if things went right.

Sitting dead in an alley sure wasn't my idea of things going right.

The greasy jerk had pulled out a gun, his hands shaking. Dear old dead Handsome Bob had said, "You don't want to do that."

Bless him.

Clearly the druggie did want to do exactly what he was doing, but I didn't say that. I was busy ramping up one of my super powers.

You see, before I was so suddenly cut down, I had worked as a superhero in the housing and hotel industry. Over the last century I had worked both front desks of hotels and sold real estate. At the moment I was on the real estate side, trying to help out in the booming Boise real estate market.

Amazing the kind of crap that goes on in real estate when big money is involved.

I hit greasy-hair with a full dose of my calming power. The guy was so high on drugs my power actually didn't do anything but make him stop shaking so hard.

He pointed to the dark alley with the gun. "Get in there and then dig out your money."

"And if we say no?" Handsome Bob asked the guy.

Since Bob was almost a foot taller than the greasy-haired druggie, I suppose Bob thought he could bully the situation a little.

Bless dear old now-dead stupid Bob.

I hit the guy with another dose of calming power. I had enough power on a normal day to stop a shouting, irate, pissed-off hotel customer at a front desk and make them smile.

The guy with the gun got calmer, but his pea brain was still set on robbing us. At least I got him to not shoot us right there on the sidewalk because of Handsome Bob's stupidity.

"Let's just give him our stuff and he will let us go," I said to Bob.

"Smart woman," the guy said, smiling and showing a mouthful of rotted teach.

Actually, I had planned that when we got into the alley I would simply jump us away from this nut and then figure out something to tell dear old Bob.

Bob didn't know I was a one-hundred-year-old superhero and could just teleport anywhere I wanted. Not something you tell someone before a first blind date. Men tended to have sexual problems when they realized the woman they were with was over a hundred.

Bob nodded to me and we walked the twenty steps into the alley, Bob pushing me slightly ahead of him.

Then, as we stopped and turned at just about the point where the rotted Chinese food odor got the worst, Bob went to lunge at the guy.

Handsome Bob went to stupid Bob very quickly.

I was so surprised Bob would do something that idiotic, I didn't react fast enough to jump us out of there.

The guy fired, hitting Bob in the arm.

The bullet went through Bob's flesh and hit me square between the eyes.

Now that was a shocker, let me tell you.

One moment I am standing alive in the alley and the next I am a ghost sitting on a smelly dumpster watching dear old Handsome Bob hold his arm and swear.

The greasy-haired guy was now twitching again. He stared at my body lying there in the alley, clearly getting my wonderful blouse and sweater all stained up with my own blood.

Then he looked at Bob who was also staring at me, holding his wounded arm and looking sick to his stomach.

Then the guy did what any self-respecting murderer would do. He shot Bob.

Bob slumped to the ground and the guy fired one more shot into his head.

A moment later I watched Bob's ghost stand up, look around, then look up and float off into a white light.

"Nice meeting you jerk-face," I shouted after Bob.

I was pretty sure he didn't hear me.

As I said, the worst ending to a blind date ever.

Two

THE DRUGGIE WHO had killed me and my blind date started through Bob's pockets. He pulled out a money clip and then took Bob's watch. Then he rolled Bob over slightly and took out his wallet.

He pulled out a single-package condom and tossed it aside.

I just shook my head. "Damn, Bob, only one? Where was the confidence? If you had come back to my place, you would have needed at least three just to make it to breakfast."

The greasy murderer clearly didn't hear me. And I had a hunch dead Bob didn't either.

I glanced around. I was still the only ghost in the alley.

Where was my greeting party?

I figured I had become a Ghost Agent which was why I hadn't gotten the beam-of-light ride. I had never met a Ghost Agent, but I had heard from my best friend Patty that she and her boyfriend, Poker Boy, had worked with some Ghost Agents just lately to save the world. Seems Patty and her boyfriend were always saving the world, which I must admit I appreciated.

The guy stood and stepped toward my body.

"Hey, not so fast there, jerk-face," I said, jumping down from the dumpster and brushing off my pants.

The greasy-haired slime-ball picked up my clutch purse and went through it.

That I didn't much care about. I had a few hundred in there and that was that.

But then he looked around at the mouth of the alley and then looked back at me with that look I had seen scum like him get. Ghost or no ghost, he wasn't touching me, even if I did have a hole in the middle of my forehead.

This night had gone bad enough as it was.

The guy kneeled down beside my body and I took two quick steps at the guy and went to kick him clear across the alley.

Foot went right through him. Charlie Brown would have been proud of my form, though. I didn't end up on my back.

However, when my foot went through the guy, I got to read all of his thoughts.

All of what he was about to do to me.

So I closed my eyes and went inside the scum. Now I knew for a fact I was in a cesspool, swimming in the shit that this guy called thoughts. If I got out of here I would need about ten showers.

If ghosts took showers.

As he reached for my right breast, I shouted at the top of my lungs, "No!"

And trust me, I can be loud.

Just ask anyone who sat beside me at a Broncos' football game.

And I was inside the guy when I shouted.

Slime-bucket grabbed his head and rolled over backward, the intense pain striking everywhere.

As he rolled away, I managed to stand my ground and get out of his body. I shook myself, wishing I could forget the memories of what I had just seen in his mind.

It would take twenty showers before I would feel clean again.

The guy was holding his head and screaming and rolling on the ground. Blood was coming out of his ears.

Both ears.

"Wow, what did you do to him?" a voice behind me asked.

I turned around to see a handsome couple standing to one side looking shocked. Both were about my height of five-ten, both wore jeans, expensive shirts, and tennis shoes.

"The pervert was about to get his jollies on my dead body, so I climbed inside his head and shouted as loud as I could."

Both of them laughed.

Then the woman stepped forward. "I'm Jewel and this is Tommy. We came to help get you used to being a ghost, but guess you are doing just fine."

I shook both their hands, happy as hell I had company. "I'm Marble Grant. And got a hunch I'm going to need a lot of help. "

"Someone close to you?" Tommy asked, pointing at Handsome Bob?

"Knew him for thirty minutes," I said. "Blind date. But I had planned on getting much closer to him after dinner, if you get my drift."

Jewel laughed and Tommy actually blushed a little, which I loved. I had a feeling I was going to like these two.

"I suppose you two are Ghost Agents. Right?"

Both of them looked shocked.

"I was a superhero in the hospitality and real estate side of the world," I said. "Any chance you two know Patty Ledgerwood and Poker Boy?"

Now they both were looking shocked.

"We do," Jewel said.

"You know," I said, "I'm damn hungry and I assume there is a way ghosts eat, so any chance we could get out of this smell and grab a bite and you guys call Patty and have her meet us. I would kind of like to tell her about my sudden death myself, since she has been my best friend for a hundred years now, give or take."

Both of them just nodded.

"Anything we need to do with that guy?" I asked, looking down at the scum who had killed me and Handsome Bob before I had the chance to find out if the handsome part went all the way to Bob's southern regions.

Greasy hair was still rolling on the dirty concrete, holding his ears and screaming. He was losing a lot of blood through his fingers. I clearly had done some damage.

"I think he's finished," Tommy said, laughing.

"Yeah," Jewel said. "Got to remember that trick."

With that we jumped to a place I knew well and loved, the Golden Nugget Buffet in downtown Las Vegas.

Now I knew I was really going to like these two.

Three

THE GOLDEN NUGGET Buffet had been decorated in all warm brown cloth and polished brass. Plants ringed the outside of the side part of the dining room nearest the escalator and the tables were solid, as were the chairs.

My hand went right through a chair as I tried to pull it out and Jewel did it for me.

"You'll learn how to actually move some physical matter, but you don't want to do that too often because people start to get spooked.

"I'll bet," I said.

Tommy jumped away to find Patty and Jewel led me up to the wonderful smelling food. The images from the murderer's head were slowly fading, something I was very grateful for.

"Be careful to not run into anyone," Jewel said, indicating the six people around the large buffet area. "You end up reading their thoughts."

"Yeah, learned that with the guy who shot me," I said.

Jewel showed me how to pick up a plate, which was actually just the ghost component of the plate and how to take food from the buffet.

In five minutes of filling a ghost plate with ghost food, I managed to not run into anyone alive, which sort of felt like a victory. I called it the dance of the living. A living person came toward me, I stepped sideways and went around them.

Jewel did the same, seemingly without noticing.

Back at the table, I bit into a piece of prime rib and damn near had an orgasm right there at the table.

Jewel just smiled as I moaned and kept on eating the fantastic tasting food.

"I remember the food being good here," I said after a few bites, "but never this good."

"Everything is better when you are a ghost," Jewel said. "Food tastes better, emotions are more powerful, and the travel and living is easier."

"Sex?" I asked.

"As the joke goes," Jewel said, smiling, "it's to die for."

"Oh, no," I said. "I had enough trouble controlling myself when I was alive."

Jewel just laughed and at that moment Tommy appeared.

"Patty is in Poker Boy's office," Tommy said. "Let's just grab some food and jump there. She's expecting us but doesn't know why yet."

It dawned on me why Patty couldn't jump here. She was still alive. Anyone in the restaurant would see her arrive and then talk to no one. Not a good idea.

Tommy headed for the buffet. I really needed to pee, but instead I kept eating as we waited for him. Damn, the food was so good. I was going to be lucky to not gain a ton of weight now that I had died. I needed to remember to ask Jewel and Tommy how they stayed so thin.

After Tommy came back with a full plate of food, he jumped the three of us and our food and drink to what I assumed was Poker Boy's office, although I had never been there.

In fact, the place was like a legend.

But I had heard it was something special and I had heard right. The office wasn't really an office. It was more like a tile platform floating in the air a thousand feet over the Strip.

All four walls were freaking clear glass with a wood railing about waist high all the way around.

Without that railing, I would have been so afraid of falling off that slick checkered tile floor, I would have been clinging to the furniture and screaming like a ten-year-old girl not wanting to go see her uncle.

And I was dead, so pretty certain the fall wouldn't kill me again.

Still, scary damn place and now I really had to pee.

I made my heart stop racing and looked around.

In the very center of the room was this huge 1950s style diner booth, with a scarred tabletop and red vinyl booth seats on three sides. The thing was big enough to hold ten people if the people really liked each other.

There were a half-dozen chairs around the room that could be pulled up to the open end of the booth I suppose, but three of them just sat facing out over the incredible view of the city.

And wow, what a view. I had always loved the lights of Las Vegas. Just never seen them from the air like this before.

"Marble," Patty said as we appeared. "Tommy said you needed to talk with me. Everything all right? You could have just called you know?"

"Not sure I knew how exactly," I said, smiling at my best friend.

Jewel laughed as she set her food and mine on the booth table.

Patty was wearing her MGM Grand Front Desk uniform of dark slacks, tan blouse and a lighter tan vest. She had her long hair pulled back and was as stunning as ever.

Patty frowned, something I had rarely seen her do in a century.

I glanced at my food on the booth table, then turned back to my friend. "Got myself killed while on a blind date about thirty minutes ago."

Patty's eyes went totally round. "Are you all right?"

"Pretty sure I'm dead," I said, laughing. I pointed to my forehead. "Bullet right there did the trick."

Patty looked like she was about to cry.

"Can I hug her?" I asked, glancing back at Jewel?

"She's a superhero," Jewel said, "and she can see you, so sure don't know why not?"

I stepped toward Patty and she hugged me so hard, I wasn't sure I would be able to breathe.

And I hugged her back.

I guess, for the first time, it was sinking in that I had really died.

I was still here but I was dead.

That just sucked.

Except for the part about the food tasting so much better.

Four

AFTER WE GOT done with all the wonderful hugging, we all sat down in the big booth and I went back to eating and telling Patty about what happened with me and my idiot blind date, Handsome Bob.

"So what's next for me?" I asked after I was done eating and telling Patty everything. "Clearly the powers that be didn't want me to go with my blind date into the big beyond."

Jewel shook her head. "Honestly don't know. To my knowledge, there has never been a superhero become a Ghost Agent before."

"Training on your new ghost powers will be first priority, most likely," Tommy said.

"And seeing which of your superhero powers you still have," Jewel said.

I nodded and sort of sat back and looked at Patty. "Anyone around who might know why I am still sitting here in this diner in the sky?"

"I suppose I would know," Laverne said, appearing at the end of the booth.

She was smiling.

Thank the heavens she was smiling.

Now I had been a superhero for a hundred years, yet I had never met Laverne, the woman who ran it all.

Somehow, when I realized who she was, I managed to not pee my pants. Total victory at that moment.

Standing right beside me was the most powerful god in all of the world, Lady Luck herself, about to tell me why I had been spared from the tunnel to the next place.

"Thanks," Patty said as Laverne pulled over a chair to sit at the end of the table.

"Great timing as always," another woman said from behind me as she came around carrying some fantastic-smelling baskets of fries and massive milkshakes that could put a dragon into a diabetic coma.

"I'm Madge," the woman said to Marble.

"Nice meeting you," I managed to say as the woman in a far-too-tight blue uniform turned and headed for a door behind the booth.

"You too," the woman said over her shoulder and vanished through the door.

Laverne was already working on the fries in front of her. All I could do was stare at the shake in front of me.

There was absolutely no doubt I was going to gain a billion pounds being dead if I wasn't careful.

"So," Patty said as she grabbed a fry as well. "I assume it was just Marble's time. Right?"

Laverne nodded. "We all have our time to head on to whatever is on the other side. But the Powers That Be thought you, Marble, would make a good addition to the Ghost Agent ranks. So they held you back."

"Thanks," I said.

I couldn't believe I had actually said something to Lady Luck.

I bit into a hot fry and again just about had an orgasm right there in front of Lady Luck. Damn that would have been embarrassing. And more than likely messy since I really needed to pee and hadn't figured out where a restroom might be floating a thousand feet in the air.

"I had nothing to do with it," Laverne said. "But I tend to agree, I think a former superhero in the Ghost Agent ranks would be fantastic. We have a superhero teamed up with a Ghost Agent up in Oregon and that has been working wonderfully."

"I'm looking forward to seeing what I can do to help," I said. I wanted to take another fry, but didn't think I should risk it at the moment.

"Actually," Laverne said, glancing at Jewel and Tommy, "Marble, you won't be the only superhero headed to Ghost Agent status. You are going to get a partner."

"Oh, no," Patty said. "Who is dying?"

Laverne kept eating as if such a question was an everyday happening. I sort of sat stunned.

"Can't say," Laverne said. "Against just about every rule in the book."

Patty nodded and sat back, looking worried.

"But we will know just about when it happens," Jewel said. "We'll be there to help with the transition."

Laverne nodded and glanced at Patty. "And don't worry, it isn't any of Poker Boy's team."

Patty let out the air she had clearly been holding. "Thank you."

Laverne just smiled.

I was starting to think I might really like Lady Luck if I ever got the chance to know her better. I can say this floating office was starting to grow on me. I just wished it had a bathroom.

"We have some big challenges coming up," Lady Luck said. "A couple ex-superhero Ghost Agents just might be exactly the team we need to help out."

"So I need to get training until my partner arrives," I said.

Laverne nodded. "Exactly."

Laverne took one more fry and stood. "Welcome to the Ghost Agents side of things."

"Thank you," I said, nodding.

With that, Lady Luck vanished.

The four of us sat there for a moment in silence.

"At least I didn't lose you tonight," Patty said.

"Yeah, pretty happy about that myself," I said, smiling.

My best friend for the past hundred years smiled back.

"Tonight is a start," Jewel said. "A good start."

I laughed. "You know, when I became a superhero, I never had an origin story. I always thought every superhero should have an origin story. But for me it just sort of happened over a long period of time."

Patty smiled. "Yeah, same for me."

"But now that I am a superhero Ghost Agent, I guess tonight you would call my origin story."

The three of them laughed.

"From wanting sex with Handsome Bob to getting shot to meeting Lady Luck, an origin story to remember."

"That it is," Patty said, laughing. "That it is."

Then I smiled at my best friend. "I just don't want to add peeing in your boyfriend's office to the story. A restroom close by?"

Jewel laughed and said to Tommy. "We'll be right back. I've got an agent to train on how to use a restroom without actually touching anything."

"Don't eat my fries," I said to Patty, who just laughed.

And with that my Ghost Agent training started.

Potty training. Who knew?

Can't Get Enough of Poker Boy?
These stories and more are available at your favorite booksellers.

USA *Today* Bestselling Writer

DEAN WESLEY SMITH

THE THICKNESS OF A WARP

If time could be bent, how far could you bend it, and at what point would it break?

Professor Sid Munsey wanted his students to help him solve that impossible question.

He got far more than he expected.

A time travel story with a very unique twist. And a few loops as well.

The Thickness of a Warp

Einstein theorized that light and gravity, and thus time,
could be bent, which lead to the obvious question:
If time could be bent, how far could you bend it,
and at what point would it break?

—From the journals of Dr. R. E. Korsmeyer,
the "father" of modern time travel.

SID MUNSEY STARED at the famous Korsmeyer question as it floated in the air on the holo-screen where he had just put it for his entire class to see. Then he turned back to the twenty young college-aged faces staring at him. This class held its first meeting in the old-fashioned way, in person. This was critical to everything he was trying to accomplish. Two students had grumbled about that and he had dropped them at once.

He stared at the class, taking in one upturned face at a time, not letting even the faint-est bit of a smile out. The classroom was in the standard university half-amphitheater shape, with the stage he stood on facing the rows of climbing desks and chairs. Ten levels, with the main entrance up in the back.

Behind him, on the other side of a wall, was a large lab area, plus grad student housing he had set up just for this class. And back there was the center of his current experiment. These students would see it soon enough.

He had the temperature of the classroom set slightly low to keep the students alert. With what he intended to do today, he needed every student in front of him thinking clearly.

So far, he hadn't said a word. He had just appeared in front of the group out of seemingly thin air, a simple time-jump trick and an easy way to get from his lab and into the classroom. He had motioned for them to be silent, then had brought up the famous question in bright red floating letters for all to read.

If time could be bent, how far could you bend it,
and at what point would it break?

A question that had haunted him for his entire life, had made him successful and had led him to this point, this day in front of these brilliant student minds.

He knew his six-foot-six frame and long, bright green hair gave him an imposing look, added to by the old motion-tat streaming a bubbling red liquid across the side of his face, down his neck and under his collar. He needed the look right now, along with his reputation in the field of time travel, to bring these brilliant minds to him.

He was going to need them all.

In return, they had all fought hard to be here, since this was the first class he had decided to teach in eight years of doing research. And the title of the class had simply been "Warp Theory."

But he had a much larger plan for these minds who sat in front of him. They would either all soon be famous, or lost or dead.

He pointed at the words floating in the air above and behind him. It was time to start. "We're going to try to find the answer to that question in this class."

"Yeah, right," a young man two rows back said.

Instantly, from the information vid across his right eye, Sid knew the man's name was Brian Carrens, a trouble-maker who had slid through the six years it took to get to this course. Brilliant, but trouble. He wasn't needed in this first discussion, but would be later if things turned as ugly as Sid was afraid they might.

A few of the rest of the class turned slightly to only catch a glimpse of Brian vanishing. Brian would find himself two seconds before he left in a sealed containment area just behind the backdrop of the stage, in the living quarters set up off this classroom. Sid had planned on forcing out a few of the students as examples to the others in this first lecture, and Brian had been his most likely first target. He was glad Brian hadn't let him down.

"Now," Sid said, staring at the rest of the class of brilliant young minds, "anyone else doubt we can solve this age-old riddle in one simple class project?"

One young woman raised her hand.

"Yes, Miss Hackett."

Mella Hackett, physics and lightspeed major in her second year of graduate work. Beyond brilliant and very inventive, she was one of the few he wanted to keep on his side on this project at all costs.

"I'm not saying that I doubt you, Professor," she said, her orange and red mood dress changing to a pink tone of worry and carefulness. She had even had her hair mood-dyed and it faded from dark red to washed-out blonde.

Sid loved the new fashion mood dresses and pants that students wore these days. No emotion could be kept hidden. He would never put on an inch of a mood cloth himself. He was far too old-fashioned for that sort of fad.

"What are you saying, Miss Hackett?"

She stared at his moving tat as many did, almost hypnotized by it, then got to her point. "I am just wondering about the reality of a college class actually discovering the tensile strength of time."

Sid laughed. She had walked to exactly the place he wanted someone to go to in this opening session.

"Oh, Miss Hackett," he said, letting himself smile and emit a charming hormone in the air designed to relax his audience. "I never said anything about proving the tensile strength of time. I just said we were going to answer the very simple Korsmeyer question: *If time could be bent, how far can you bend it, and when will it break.*"

She opened her mouth to say something, then stopped, showing him a full double set of classic fang and chewing implants that were all the rage these days. She clearly had understood his meaning. Her hair went back to red, her clothes back to their original color.

Around the class a few other heads were nodding and clothes were changing colors faster than a vid screen losing depth settings.

Another hand went up, showing the older fad of adding fingers and an extra thumb. James Oliver Egglestone, the most brilliant of a class of brilliant minds. Maybe even more brilliant than Sid had been at Egglestone's age. The kid had no mood clothes on, only old-type jeans and a thick sweater that looked like it might have actually been knitted by hand.

"Yes, Mr. Egglestone?"

"It would seem, sir, that your own theory of the thickness of a warp would be in direct contention with what you are suggesting we will be looking to accomplish in this class."

Sid nodded. "You are correct. But can you explain to those who may not be following you, exactly how that might be?"

Egglestone shrugged. "Your theory, the one that made you famous and laid the groundwork for all modern time travel uses in transportation and teleportation, states clearly that the thickness of a time warp, or in other words, the time jammed in under the bend in time caused by the bend itself, determines and limits the amount of time that can be jumped."

"It does," Sid said, nodding.

He glanced around the glass. "I assume everyone in this room understands that basic issue. Take a piece of cloth and bend it. The cloth under the bend limits the amount the outer edge of the cloth can bend."

Everyone nodded.

"Good," Sid said. "Go on, Mr. Egglestone."

"In sixty-four years since you laid out that theory," Egglestone said, still slouching in the chair as if not really interested, "no one has been able to exceed a time warp thickness of more than three-point-seven-one seconds."

"And why exactly is that, in simple terms?" Sid asked, pushing the class and Mr. Egglestone to the last point he hoped to get to in this opening session.

Egglestone shrugged, as if answering a child's question. "No one has been able to drain the excess time away from under the warp, thus allowing the warp to bend farther around."

Suddenly Egglestone sat up, very interested. "Professor, are you saying you might have a way to do that, I mean, drain away the thickness of the warp? Is that what you've been working on for the past years?"

Sid laughed. "Past sixty years. If it was, would you be interested in staying in this class and helping me with the breakthrough?"

Egglestone laughed, showing normal teeth, more than likely capped for hardness, but still normal-looking. "Now I understand, Professor, why you brought this group of minds together. And blocked all our outside com-links."

Around the room, Sid watched as ten students suddenly went distant in their eyes, then came back with a slight look of panic. They hadn't actually noticed until that moment. Many of these kids hadn't been without the links for most of their lives.

"I didn't block your links," Sid said. "And Mr. Egglestone, you didn't answer my question. Would you be interested in helping me solve the question I have posed for this class?"

Sid again pointed at the floating words behind and above him.

"I would be interested, Professor," he said. "But I would also be interested in just how close you are to the discovery of draining away the time under a warp."

Again Sid laughed. "I didn't block your links. You tell me."

Egglestone opened his mouth as Miss Hackett had done, then also stopped.

"I am in contact with everyone else in the room except you, Professor," Hackett said. "I would assume there is a dampening field in the walls."

"Never assume and state a fact that you have not investigated, proven, then proven again," Sid said, staring at the young woman as her clothes and hair went to pink. "That will be one of the main rules this class must live by every moment of every second we are together."

Egglestone stood without a word, moved to the aisle, walked to the closed back door of the room, and opened it. He stood there for a moment, then nodded, closed the door, and returned to his seat.

Sid studied the kid, impressed at the lack of reaction. Clearly the kid had it figured out before he went to the door. The walk was just the first level of proof the kid needed.

Everyone stared at Egglestone.

"Mr. Egglestone," Sid said, smiling, "would you like to fill the rest of the class in on your theory and first level of proof you have just seen."

"You have solved the problem of draining time from under a warp."

The class actually gasped, which made Sid feel proud of his discovery.

"That much is clear from the evidence at hand," Egglestone said, "both with the sense of sight and my sensors and links and lack of downloads."

Sid made no move. "Go on."

The rest of the class's heads turned from Egglestone to him to Egglestone like watching an old-fashioned tennis match.

"So, to answer your first question, I would very much like to help you find the answer to Korsmeyer's question, but I fear you don't actually need our help in the actual solution. That will come naturally if I am right in my deduction. We are in the time warp jump now, which is why our links to the outside world don't work."

Now it was Sid's turn to be shocked, but he shouldn't be. Egglestone was brilliant. He had already figured out most of what was going on simply by going to the door.

"How long until the loops touch?" Egglestone asked. "Or do you think they will? You might as well tell us since you gathered us here to help you out of what you were sure was going to happen in your proof experiment."

"Loops touch?" Hackett said, her voice almost shrill. "Are you talking about a time loop, bending a warp completely around in a circle back to the same point?"

"The point of contact," Sid said to Egglestone, "should be that door. And my theory says it should be happening in sixteen seconds."

With that, Sid moved down from the low stage and up through the seats toward the back door of the classroom. The rest of the class got up and fell in behind him.

At exactly sixteen seconds, he opened the door, not really sure what he was going to be seeing. Nothingness of a time warp, or the closed door of the classroom as it had been when the loop started.

In a million theories, he did not expect to see what he saw.

He felt like he was looking into a million mirrors, only the images were not inverted.

He grabbed the edge of the door frame and a million other Sid's did the same thing in a million other door frames.

He stood there, door open, staring at himself, the class behind him in every one of those millions of images.

Hundreds and hundreds of millions of doors all facing in on the same point, fading off into unknown distances in all directions, all with himself and the class standing in the open door.

"Can you shut it down?" Egglestone asked from behind him.

"It just shut itself down," Sid said. "The moment the contact of a full circle was complete."

And Sid was sure he repeated those exact same words a million times in every door in front of him. He couldn't hear any of the others, but he was sure he had.

"Time loop," Hackett said softly behind him.

"Oh, no," Egglestone said, "the loops stretch off into infinity in all directions."

"It would seem so," Sid said, shutting the door on the sight of the millions of other copies of himself out there. He would bet that a million of "hims" shut the same door at the exact same moment.

"So," Egglestone said, "the reason for this class wasn't to solve the Korsmeyer question."

"It seems we just solved it," Sid said, trying to grasp completely what he had just seen. No theory he had worked out had the result he was seeing out there. Not one of them.

"How is it solved?" one student asked with a shaky voice.

Sid took a deep breath and faced the students, all who had worried looks on their faces. Even with the temperature lowered, the room suddenly felt very warm.

"The answer is that time can be bent into infinite loops, and can never break. That out there is our proof."

"As I said," Egglestone said, "we are not here to help solve the Korsmeyer question, except maybe as witnesses to its solution, but you were afraid you might need us to find a way to unravel this test and return if something like this went wrong."

Sid nodded. "I'm afraid that's true. For as long as it takes."

He moved down toward the front of the classroom and sat on the table there, facing the students who all went back to their chairs. A couple of them looked near panic. He wasn't so sure how he was feeling exactly either.

"For as long as it takes?" one woman asked. "How do you suggest we eat, sleep, and even work in this tight space?"

Sid pointed at the wall behind the stage. "Back there is a dorm and lab facility with everything we will need to live and work for decades if we have to. I made the bubble for this experiment in time very large, taking up two acres outside as well as this entire building. I made sure at the point of the start of the class, we were the only ones in the bubble."

"Besides all the rest of us through there," Hackett said, her dress and hair a flaming red, making her look really angry.

"I don't think they count," another student said. "Impossible to contact."

"But what about our families, our lives, our classes?" one of the lesser lights in the group asked.

Sid just shook his head, but the question bothered him at a deep level, a level he hadn't given any thought to.

Hackett turned on the poor kid, her clothes flaming her anger in bright reds. "Don't you understand anything about time travel? We solve this, it will be an entire class in less than a half hour of our real time. Maybe less. We just have to unravel this time loop."

Sid knew at once that she was wrong, and so it seems did Egglestone. There would be no forward movement in the class in real time. There never had been.

"Damn it," Sid said.

"You didn't think this might be the outcome?" Egglestone asked, his voice full of scorn. "Ten women, ten men, lots of food and water. You thought this through to some degree, didn't you?"

"Not for this problem. If I had, would I have started the loop?" Sid asked, staring at the words still floating in the air over the stage. "I planned that it would take time to figure out how to break out and return to the normal flow of time."

"So," Egglestone said, his voice clear with no sign of panic, "you hadn't realized that we would know before we started if we had made it." He waved his hand, as if erasing something from the air. "Of course we wouldn't know, because we return to the exact same time and place."

"What are you two talking about?" Hackett demanded. "You're starting to get me very, very worried."

Sid pointed at the door, but couldn't bring himself to say anything.

"We succeed, in some way or another, after maybe years, in getting back to the moment the time loop started," Egglestone said, shaking his head, clearly disgusted.

"And when was that?" one student asked.

"The moment I arrived in the room," Sid said, not really believing that he hadn't thought of what might happen with a complete bending of time.

"The loop goes around to that time and stops and we figure out a way to return to that point, but in the class, we start it right back up again. Clearly, from what we saw through that door, a large number of times."

"That's how all those other classes got out there," Egglestone said. "The experiment succeeded."

"And succeeded. And succeeded." Sid said.

"But why would we do that?" Hackett asked, her mood clothes going to flashing colors of puzzlement.

"So how do we get out of here? Get home?" one student asked, near panic.

"We don't," Egglestone said. "We're trapped in a time loop where we constantly listen to the same question, then stay in here until be figure out how to get back, solve the problem, go back, then loop again and do it all over again."

"Millions of times," Hackett said. "But that makes no sense. All we have to do is stop."

Sid couldn't say anything. He knew Egglestone was right. But something about what Hackett kept asking was bothering him a great deal.

"Maybe there was a good reason in nature for the thickness of a warp," Hackett said, sitting down, her mood clothes and hair going very dark.

Thickness of warp. Sid looked up at the famous question still floating in the air, then he knew the answer.

"All is not lost," he said. "We have to go ahead and find out how to get back."

"We've done that," Egglestone said. "Clearly a few million times."

"Why?" Hackett asked. "So we can get right back here again and again and again. You're going to have to come up with something better than a good grade to make me do that."

"Actually, yes," Sid said, standing and smiling. He pointed at the famous question still floating in the air. "Because that question, eventually, with millions of loops, will still win out."

"Now, for the first time, you have lost me," Egglestone said, sitting up and staring at Sid.

"Well," Sid said, "I'm glad I got something to teach you after all. Come with me. We have to check the level of the time vat."

He stood and headed across the stage toward the door from the classroom into the lab area.

"The what?" Hackett asked as everyone scrambled to their feet to follow him.

"If you drain off the thickness in the warp, you have to put that time/energy somewhere." Sid smiled at his class. "You know, the basic physics of conservation of energy and matter."

"You built a storage container for the time/energy you drained off under the warp?" Egglestone asked.

"Actually, a large one, with gauges to measure the amount of thickness of the warp it took for one loop. I figured that for any practical applications in the future, that number would need to be known exactly."

"But what difference does that make?" one student asked.

"A tank has only a limited volume."

"So when the tank fills up, the thickness can't be drained and the loop stops," Hackett said.

Sid nodded. "I put fail-safe devices in the tank in case of a problem like that, just in case the volume of a warp was greater than I had expected it to be."

"We fill the tank and then we can go home and pretend none of this happened?" one student asked.

Sid smiled, heading back for the area behind the stage. "Actually, you won't remember any of this, just like we don't remember the thousand or million times we have already been through this, made this discovery, and worked to go back one more time."

"Which explains the millions of us out there," Hackett said. "That explains why we figured out how to go back if all we were going to do was end up here again."

Sid held the door open to the lab area for the students to pass through. In a moment, they would see at what level the energy in the tank was, and to see just how many loops they were going to have to make to get this finished.

More than likely, it was thousands more, maybe millions. He had made the tank damn big. And if his first calculations were correct, the thickness of a warp just wasn't much.

But it would be enough.

In time.

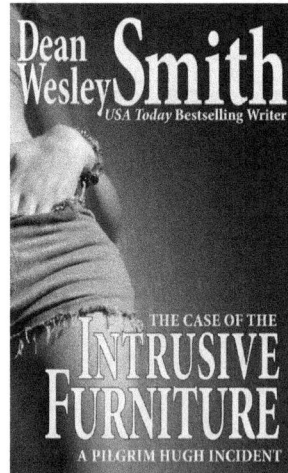

Looking for the latest Mary Jo Assassin novel?
It's available from all your favorite booksellers
in trade paper and electronic editions.

USA TODAY BESTSELLING AUTHOR

DEAN WESLEY SMITH

KILLING

THE **TOP 10**

Sacred Cows

OF PUBLISHING

A WMG WRITER'S GUIDE

The publishing world continues to evolve, but myths about who can make a living as a fiction writer maintain a life of their own. Whether you pursue traditional or indie publishing success, you need to know the pitfalls and traps that undermine many writers' careers.

In this WMG Writer's Guide, USA Today *bestselling author and former publisher Dean Wesley Smith addresses the ten most damaging myths that writers believe in modern publishing.*

Killing the Top Ten Sacred Cows of Publishing
A WMG Writer's Guide

Part 2 of 2
Sacred Cow #6

SELLING A NOVEL TO TRADITIONAL PUBLISHING WILL GUARANTEE THE NOVEL IS QUALITY; OR CONVERSELY, NOT SELLING A NOVEL TO TRADITIONAL PUBLISHING WILL MEAN THE NOVEL IS NOT QUALITY.

THIS MYTH IS so flat wrong in so many ways, I'm not sure where to begin. But wow do you hear this everywhere.

In fact, I have seen it even with successful indie-published writers. I have watched in horror as indie writers (making great money) have fallen for this myth by suddenly turning and selling to traditional publishers, even though they would make more money and get to more readers just by continuing on what they were doing.

So let me outline how I will attack this myth before giving some history, as I always do.

Here are the three main areas of thinking this myth falls into.

1) Because a book is bought by a large traditional publisher, the book is quality.

2) Because a book is not bought by a large traditional publisher, the book is not good enough to be published.

3) I am a new writer. How do I determine if my book is of "good enough" quality to be published?

Some History

Am I immune to this thinking of worrying about quality? Nope.

I was raised to read and was in school just as most of us were. In school, all books were things that had knowledge, were special, or (in the case of fiction I believed) were written by "gods" who took me to wonderful new places, strange planets, and fantastic spaceships. In fact, it never really dawned on me that real people wrote books until I owned a bookstore and started seeing so many thousands and thousands of books pour through. Some I liked, some I didn't, and some I wondered why anyone would even publish it.

We all were raised to think that something in a book is "important." And then (as we got older) we developed reading tastes. We discovered what kind of writing we liked, what our favorite genre was, and who our favorite writers were.

And we all bought books exactly the same as editors buy books. That's right, exactly the same.

We walk into a bookstore, pick up a book that looks interesting, read the back cover, then maybe read the first few pages and then (horrors) actually flip to the back to see how the book ended before we plunked down our money. We still do that now with electronic books by glancing at the blurb and cover, then reading the sample before buying. Same as in a bookstore.

In large traditional publishing, an editor gets a novel manuscript that looks interesting, reads the first few pages, flips to the proposal to see what the book is about, then reads to the end to see how the book ends. And then if the editor likes the book, she fights for it through the system of sales and art departments and so on. But the key is she has to like the book, just as you have to like a book before you spend money on it.

We are all editors editing for our own personal reading lists.

You may personally think Clive Cussler or Danielle Steele or Nora Roberts are bad writers, but millions of other independent editors don't agree with you.

You buy for what you think is quality writing and storytelling and what you enjoy reading. And what you think will differ from what I think and what millions of others will think. And what most traditional publishing editors will think as well.

Thankfully, that's the way it works. Always has.

The Limitations of Traditional Fiction Editors

Editors working for large traditional publishers are just people too. Heck, I've edited at times, remember.

Editors have huge restrictions on them that have nothing to do with the quality of a story. For example, the best story I ever got in the ten years editing for *Star Trek* was by a wonderful mystery writer named

Julie Hyzy. It was a story that I couldn't buy. All these years later that story is as clear to me as the day it knocked me out of my chair when I read it. But because no traditional publisher could buy that story, does that mean it was low quality?

Of course not. Julie was then, and still is, one of the best writers I know.

I couldn't buy it for reasons that had nothing to do with quality. Nothing at all. I couldn't buy the story because it didn't fit into the very narrow restrictions I had on what I could buy as an editor.

Every editor is exactly the same way, and these days, the restrictions are even narrower because of sales departments and publishers not wanting to take a chance on anything different or unusual. At this point, if you don't have something that is almost guaranteed to make money, publishers won't look. They are that scared.

So let me detail out the hurdles you have to jump through to get an editor to buy your book.

—*You must mail it to an editor, or get it through an agent to an editor who might buy it. (This step stops most writers these days.)*

—*The editor must love the book, meaning it must fit into the editor's taste area.*

—*The editor must think the book will fit in what the company publishes and what she can buy for her list.*

—*The editor must get someone in sales to think the book will sell.*

—*The editor must often get another editor to like the book*

—*The editor must get the publisher to sign off on the book in a corporate meeting.*

Wow, are there a lot of steps between a writer finishing a book and an editor making an offer. And don't forget that process often takes years.

And millions and millions of quality books (books that would find their share of readers if all things were equal) are eliminated by this process. (Luckily, with indie publishing, things are quickly becoming equal.)

So let me deal with the three major areas this myth hits that I outlined back at the beginning.

1) Because a novel is bought by a large traditional publisher, the book is quality.

This part of this myth is very, very deep inside all of us. We all think that because a large traditional publisher spent money and time to publish a book, it is automatically quality. I have heard this lately called "the stamp of approval" and "validation" by different writers.

The truth is that for the one house, the one editor, the book was quality. But I can't begin to point out the millions of examples of novels published for one reason or another by a traditional publisher that just sucked, were poorly written, and worse yet, poorly proofed and typeset and laid out.

In fact, I don't know if many of you have noticed, but at this point in time, the traditionally published books are much worse in format and proofing than what indie publishers are doing. Much, much worse.

Thinking of all traditional fiction publishers as one large great judge of books is just flat wrong.

A few people, sometimes less than two or three, are in charge of getting a traditionally published novel out to readers. Sure, there are others along the way, but only the editor, a sales person, and a publisher are the judges of quality of the book. And often one or two of them are missing in the equation.

An ugly secret: Very, very often the editor is the only person in a publishing company who has actually read the entire book.

Sorry, but true. The others have just read samples or pitches for the book the editor put together. Not kidding.

Another ugly secret... I know of a number of books that never got read at all by anyone in the publishing house, just sent in and published. (Yup, traditional publishers are great judges of work, especially when no one reads the book.)

When I learned this fact early on in my editing life, I actually was depressed. I had always believed that if a big traditional publisher put out a story, it was like the book was sent from some publishing god to the readers with some special secret stamp of approval.

To be honest, I hated the fact that I could pick a story as an editor and give that story some sort of special magical powers of sudden quality. And that story would get published and I would have been the only person to read it.

In the final result, all I was giving the story or book was very much like a reviewer gives a novel. I was saying I liked it. Nothing more.

Let me repeat that: NOTHING MORE.

Editors are humans who have likes and dislikes. Sure, we all try to pick the best stories, but they are always the stories we think are the best in our opinion.

And trust me, we can all be wrong. Very, very wrong.

And often are.

2) Because a book is not bought by a large traditional publisher, the book is not good enough to be published.

With the state of traditional publishing at the moment, with the slush outsourced, with editors tied by sales force demands, with companies barely holding on and trying to make changes to electronic sales, very few high-quality books with top stories are getting through. And it is often not the highest-quality story or novel that gets through, but instead it's the story that has the most marketability according to the opinion of a sales person. Who maybe only read a one-page summary of the book.

Thinking that a story isn't quality if it doesn't sell to a traditional publisher is just flat silly.

Let me give you a personal example: I have exactly two-hundred-and-fifty (250) rejections for different stories from five different editors of *Asimov's Science Fiction Magazine*. That's right, from the very beginning of the magazine I was pounding on that door and not once did I sell a story to them. Not once.

Should I think that all my stories are not quality because I can't sell to that magazine and those five different editors over three decades? Nope. They just didn't fit because my short stories tend to be slightly off of

center, to put it mildly. I have later sold almost all of those stories. But thankfully I never believed this part of this myth, or I wouldn't have kept the stories out there in the mail and eventually sold them.

3) I am a new writer. How do I determine if my book is of "good enough" quality to be published?

This is the difficult subject to talk about because all new writers must go through a learning curve to get craft up to certain "levels" that will allow readers to follow your story and stay involved with your story.

And trust me, for an experienced editor, it is easy to see at a glance a new writer who hasn't written enough words and studied enough to get craft up to a level anyone but family is going to want to read. What tips us off? Oh, easy things like no setting, no voice, characters you can't tell apart, walking from one part of the story to the other. All stuff that would make a reader put the book down and not buy it.

Notice I did not say sentence-by-sentence writing... At this point in history most everyone can write a decent sentence. Quality writing does not mean quality typing. It means quality storytelling.

The old method was to just write and submit and when your storytelling craft started climbing some of your stories started breaking through the editorial roadblocks and got to readers. That system was pretty clear for most, but wow did it fail writers with very unusual voices or stories that did not fit into certain genres. Those writers never did get through the system for the most part. Like I haven't got through the system yet at *Asimov's*.

But now we have a new world in which writers can publish their own stuff, and in a past blog, I talked about writers just publishing their own book and then mailing the trade paper book to traditional publishers as part of the submission package. I can't begin to tell you how many letters I got asking the question "How do I know if my book is good enough to be published?"

Back to #1 category above, writers think that just because a book is published, it has to be quality. So if the new writer publishes their own book in trade paper, it has to be quality before they dare do that. Right?

Nope. Just publish the thing and move on.

But how do they know if it is quality?

And the circular logic goes around and around and around.

HOW DOES ANY WRITER OF ANY LEVEL KNOW THAT A STORY IS QUALITY?

Short answer: They don't. We don't.

Long answer: They don't and never will, even if the story is published by a traditional publisher.

Being published by a traditional publisher means a book is liked by a few people. Put the book up on your own on Amazon and B&N and Smashwords and iBooks and Sony and Kobo and others and see how many people buy it.

In this new world, it is time to start trusting readers.

Why not do a POD version and use it as part of a submission package to a traditional publisher if that is still your goal?

Why not?

The answer to all this again comes down to writers and their belief systems. At this moment in history, most writers and all newer writers have no backbone.

Writers (as a class) do not believe that their work is their art. And they are not willing to defend it and keep learning from their mistakes and keep working to make their art better.

But, of course, my advice about "grow a backbone" has been ignored for years now in many of these chapters, so let me see if I can give a few more concrete guidelines. But realize, these are just my opinions and I am only one person.

How Do I Know if My Book Is "Good Enough" to Be Published?
(Dean's Opinion of What to Do)

1) How many words have you written in fiction since you started trying to write? Mystery Grand Master John D. McDonald used to say that all writers starting out had a million words of crap in them. I started selling stories just short of the million word mark and have sold some of my stories that I wrote between half-million and that first million. However, because of a house fire, I can't look back on any of the words before that.

But if you have a bunch of stories done, maybe a novel, and have been working at writing for a time, I think you are more than safe to let readers be the judge.

2) Realize that you may have paid your storytelling dues in other areas besides fiction. Say if you have written a couple dozen plays and had a couple produced, your storytelling skills are probably pretty good. If you've been a reporter or worked nonfiction. Things like that. Lots of other areas transfer over into fiction writing. In that case you might be writing quality fiction right from the first hundred thousand words.

3) How much are you studying writing to become a better storyteller? If you only have three how-to-write books on your shelf and have never even listened to a professional writer speak at a conference, you may be way ahead of yourself in thinking of publishing.

In other words, in short, what I am talking about is a learning period, and the learning must go hand-in-hand with the typing.

It's called "practice" in any other art. In writing you need to practice as well.

But you want my honest opinion?

Put the story up and let the readers decide. Right from the first story.

Writers are always the worst judges of their own work.

And readers who pay money always trump any other source of feedback.

So grow a backbone and trust your work and get it out there, either to a traditional publisher or electronically and POD published.

So What Is the Downside of Self-Publishing Too Early?

Nothing.

No one buys your book, it sinks like a stone because it is a poor story, and eventually (in a couple of years), as you keep learning, you pull it down and put it out of print.

Here is the problem that beginning writers have on this issue: *Beginning writers are staring at their own navels.*

What I mean by that is new beginning writers are so worried about sentences and pretty words and nifty grammar and pleasing their workshop that they forget they are storytellers. They are not working to become entertainers, but instead they just work on good sentences. Beginning writers just forget about readers and how readers are the real judges.

There are no repercussions for publishing a book in electronic or POD format and it not selling.

Well, maybe your oversized ego gets bumped some because you believed that you could be as good as Stephen King with your first novel and didn't have to do the decades of work and learning that King did. Get over it and get learning and practicing.

And what is even more frightening... If you publish a book that doesn't work, no one will come to your house and shoot you. No one will blackball you from all of publishing. No one will even notice, which is even worse than the first two. At least on the first two someone noticed your book.

You think people will notice; you think a bad book will ruin your career. Nope. You have no career to ruin as a new writer.

So what happens...

More WMG Writers' Guides
from all your favorite booksellers
in trade paper and electronic editions

You put up your own new book and it sucks. No one will buy it, and no one will notice and it will sink without a trace.

And you can promote it to your heart's content, sell it for 99 cents because Locke or someone else without a real belief in their own work did that, and still no one will buy it because they will look at the sample and think, "Nope this book isn't for me." And those readers will not buy it and they will not remember your name.

But if they like it.... Well, that's another story.

My Advice to Beginning Writers

1) Never stop writing and learning. Never think you know it all after a few sales. Never believe you are good enough. Learning in this business never, ever ends.

2) Keep your work for sale somewhere, either on editor's desks in New York or self-published or both. You are like an artist with your work hanging in an art gallery or a musician working a small bar. You are practicing and earning from your skill as it grows. It might not be much at first, but if you keep learning and practicing, the sales and the money will come with time.

3) Don't be in a hurry. This is an international business. You can't get there overnight. Put your work out for sale one way or another and then focus on the next book. Never look back. Leave the book up and alone. Have a five- and ten-year plan.

4) Grow a backbone. Believe in your own art without cutting off the learning. No writing is perfect and maybe a few people out there will think it works just fine and enjoy it. No book is perfect.

5) Never do anything that gets in the way of the writing. Stay away from stupid,

time-wasting self-promotion beyond your own website and tiny bit of social media, and just write the next story and the next book. In other words, be a writer, a person who writes. And rewriting is not writing.

6) And most of all, have fun. If you are not having fun while at the same time being scared to death, get off this roller coaster. The ride only gets more extreme and more fun the farther you go along the track.

Trust me, folks, you don't want to put all your hopes and fears and beliefs that a work is quality on the judgment of an editor somewhere.

Sacred Cow #7
TO SELL EITHER TO EDITORS OR READERS, YOU MUST WRITE WHAT IS HOT

THIS MYTH STOPS thousands and thousands of book sales and destroys careers.

And it's just stupid, even though the myth seems to have a logical base in publishing.

This myth spouts like a bad cold out of the mouths of top professionals all the time in one form or another, and usually with the best of intentions. And it has for as long as I have been in this business.

And beginning indie writers repeat this over and over like it's a bad chant from a long lost tribe of magic aliens.

But lately, with the advent of the slush-reading lower-level agents and with the indie publishing revolution, this myth has taken on very, very deadly consequences for many writers.

Why? Because they believe it.

Hook, line, and sinker.

So as I do in these chapters, let me take a look at the origin of this myth first.

It Came From the Editors

Actually, the origin is simple. It came about back in the dark old days of traditional-only publishing because editors and agents and publishers want to make an easy sale.

Yes, editors sell books as well. They sell a book they love to their publisher, they sell the book to a sales force, and they ultimately are responsible for selling a book to readers. Books that are different, that don't fit in what has been done before, are very, very difficult sales for editors and publishers and always have been.

And it has been proven that if a reader likes a certain type of book, they will look for that type of book.

Now remember, publishers need so many books per month in this churn of book lists, so they have to find books to buy, and when they can find an easy-sell book, it makes their job easier.

And it's human nature to want to have your job be easier.

Of course, easy-sell books are usually pretty flat. (Not always, but usually.) They are often following a trend. The books tend to do little if anything new, which is why they are easy sells. And never remembered.

Another book bought by a more gutsy editor has already paved the way. Easy-sell books are also easy to promote. "If you liked 'X Book' you're going to love 'X Book Almost-The-Same.'"

Easy sell. Editors and publishers and corporate sales forces love them.

Now understand, I wrote a ton of easy-sell books. Media books such as Star Trek have a pretty set audience a publisher can depend on. So when Pocket Books came to me to write some Star Trek novels, they knew exactly what the book would sell and so did I. Easy, no thought on the publisher's part.

What was a hard-sell book was *Star Trek: Strange New Worlds*. It took John Ordover years of fighting to get that series going and the fact that Pocket Books kept it going for ten years was not because of sales, but reasons of relationships with readers and Paramount.

Interestingly enough, over the history of publishing, the really monster books, the ones that people talk about and remember for decades, were not easy-sell books. Often they would have fifty or more rejections before finding an editor willing to work for the book and a publisher took a chance. Then (when the book became a hit) it was called new and fresh and readers loved it.

And hard-sell books are flat impossible to get through agents in this new world. Agents give up submitting books after four or five rejections and often drop clients who force them to submit books that are not easy-sell books. (Remember, these days agents work for publishers, not writers.)

And even worse, writers allow agents to have them rewrite their work to make it more of an easy-sell, thus killing any original work in the book.

And when somehow that fresh idea, fresh book does get through an editor and gets published, (in this new world, more than likely indie published first), it will spawn (like a bad horror movie) thousands of "easy sell" books.

But no one has made much of a long career writing only easy-sell books, because the target just keeps moving. One day one topic is hot, the next day the next topic is hot.

As a writer, if you try to chase that "hot-topic easy-sell" thinking, you might sell a few books, but you are lost in short order.

But then come editors and agents sitting on panels at writers' conferences telling new writers what they are looking for, what's selling, what isn't selling. In all honest truth, as an editor, I didn't know what I wanted to buy until I read it.

And as an editor for *Star Trek: Strange New Worlds* for ten years, I constantly told writers I hated the character "Q" from Next Generation. But I always ended up buying a "Q" story because some writer wrote one so well, with such a fun twist, that I couldn't not buy it.

Attempting to write what is hot isn't a new trend. It has been around since the beginning of this business. And the myth that you need to write what is hot, what is selling is as deadly today as it was fifty years ago. Honest, even in the new world of indie publishing, this myth will just kill your career and the fun in your writing fairly quickly.

So Why Is This Myth So Deadly?

The answer to that question is back in the writer's office. Each writer is different. Every chapter in this book I have been pounding that simple fact home.

Every writer is different.

Let me say that one more time:

Every Writer is Different!

And what makes your books interesting to readers is YOU.

I have also warned about taking the YOU out of your work over and over in these chapters as well. You can't see or hear your voice because to you it sounds dull because you hear it all the time. So when you rewrite something to death, you are taking the "you" out of your work.

And your ideas might seem dull because guess why? They are yours! Duh. They are as unique as you are, as how you write the ideas down.

But then you go trying to imitate some other writer, try to write what is "hot" because some editor or agent or writers' board told you that is what is selling. So what do you do? You take the YOU out of your work and it becomes mundane and just like everything else and won't sell.

Or if it does sell, it vanishes in the flood of sameness.

A SIMPLE RULE: In fiction, sameness and dullness do not sell.

Yet when a new writer hears an editor or agent or a bunch of writers on a writing board tell them what they "should" write to sell more, the young writer goes home and attempts to imitate the book everyone said they are looking for. They create nothing unique, nothing new, nothing of themselves. They write the same boring old crap that has already been done to death.

And this gets even worse in the circle-jerk thinking of places like online indie boards. You see talk about writing what is selling the most at the moment. That is the quickest way to writer death I have ever seen. It quickly forces a writer to get frustrated because "It was supposed to sell and make me millions, just like George R.R. Martin, but I only sold three copies last month."

So How Do You Solve This Problem?

Simple: Kick all the editor and agent and online board voices out of your writing office and write what makes you passionate or angry or excited.

Or as Stephen King has said, "Write what scares hell out of you."

Some basic guidelines on how to do this:

1) Never talk about your story with anyone ahead of time.

Their ideas, unless you are very experienced, will twist your original story into partially their story.

2) For heaven's sake, never, ever let anyone read a work-in-progress.

Totally stupid on so many levels I can't even begin to address. If you want to collaborate, make sure you have a collaboration agreement, otherwise, keep your work to yourself until finished.

And wow does this apply to workshops. Never show a work-in-progress. Ever. Trust yourself for heaven's sake and learn how to be an artist.

3) Never think of markets or selling when writing.

Enjoy the process of writing and creating a story. When the story is finished, then have someone read it and tell you what you wrote and then market it.

I get this question more than any other question. Should I write this to sell? Should I do this to have a career? And so on and so on. Folks, write what you want to write. Every writer is different, and if you celebrate that difference, you will eventually find an audience.

4) Follow Heinlein's Rules, especially #3 about never rewriting.

In other words, fix mistakes and then mail it and trust your own voice, your own work. Never rewrite to anyone's suggestions, especially a workshop.

And never use the word "polish" in front of me. When you take a unique piece of work and polish it, you make it look like all the others. And that's dull.

5) When an editor says they are looking for a certain type of book, ignore it.

They are just trying to be helpful to all the new writers looking for shortcuts to getting published. There are no shortcuts.

When agents say what they think will sell to editors, just laugh. I mean laugh really, really, really hard. They have less of a clue what will sell than anyone in the business, bar none. If agents really knew, they would write it themselves and keep all the millions.

I had an eye-opening moment one year when I asked a major agent what was the last book the agent read for pleasure. The agent couldn't remember because it had been years. The agent only had time to read what his/her clients were sending. Yet I heard this same person sit on a panel in front of a large group of beginning writers and go on about what the trends in reading were and what was selling in publishing. And yet they hadn't read a single book by anyone but their own clients. Yeah, trust that person's opinion to really make a career. Head-shaking it is so stupid.

6) Get passionate and protective of what you write.

It's your voice, your work, for heaven's sake, grow a backbone and stand up for it.

Sure, in the first million words you are going to need all sorts of help with craft and storytelling issues. Go learn that and take it in and study and practice and get feedback. And never stop learning. Make learning a regular part of your writing life.

But don't rewrite anything beyond fixing typos and mistakes. When you write a story or novel, trust yourself, trust your own art, and get it out to readers in one way or another.

Protect it from all who want you to write what they think you should have written.

Summary

So, in short, I am telling you flatly and bluntly to ignore any advice from any person about what is selling, what is hot, what you should write.

Write your own stories.

And if you do write your own stories, protect them from others, believe in them, and mail them to editors or get them up for readers to buy, you may be the next big thing and then thousands and thousands of writers will be trying to imitate you.

And they will fail, because there is only one of you.

Sacred Cow #8
YOU CAN'T MAKE A LIVING WITH YOUR FICTION

THIS MYTH "YOU can't make a living writing fiction" is so clearly hogwash, I shouldn't have to include it as a chapter in this book. All anyone has to do is look at a certain fantasy writer in England being richer than the Queen. And the number of fiction writers on the Forbes List every year. And that's not counting all the writers publishing their sales numbers each month just from Kindle alone.

But, alas, new writers hear this myth all the time, constantly, from every direction, and sometimes from longer-term professional writers.

It shouldn't be a myth at all, but it is.

Myth Origin

We have all seen the silly studies that an "average" fiction writer makes something like $2,345 per year. And, of course, people look at that and think "Oh, my, no one can make any money writing fiction." Of course, those who say that don't know how studies are taken, or what a number like that really means.

Most of the big studies ask every person who has a dream of someday writing a novel. The writers asked maybe have finished a few short stories, maybe even mailed a couple. They go to a writers' group regularly, and call themselves writers, because they are in the early days of learning their craft. They make no money. There are hundreds of thousands of this type of writer, all in the early days of learning.

Then, of course there are the writers who will never sell, a person with the best intentions, but no real drive to actually sell anything. Or if they do sell, it's to a small press that pays in copies or worse yet these days, they give their story away free to an online press and don't even get a copy.

Or they write poetry and are doing fantastic when they make a few hundred per year.

The studies ask all those writers how much they make, and the answer is almost always zero or not far above zero. Millions of "nothing" answers.

Then these studies include writers in organizations like SFWA, who lets a writer with three sales in the door. And Romance Writers, which has a huge chunk of membership that has never made a sale. All those thousands and thousands of unpublished or slightly published writers are included.

It's stunning to me that the average is so high, actually. But the truth is to get the final answer up to a few thousand, a lot of people have to be making a lot of money with their fiction writing to pull up all the beginning writers.

Writing, to my knowledge, is the only profession that takes studies this way.

It would be exactly like trying to figure out what an average lawyer makes by also including every undergraduate who is thinking of going to law school and every law student in the study about what they made working the law. Lawyers, in that type of study, would make less than two thousand average I'm betting.

Where Else Does This Myth Come From?

Duh? The answer is simple. It comes from all the people who are, for one reason or another, simply too afraid to try mailing out their fiction regularly to places who buy it. Or too afraid to put the stories up indie. Or only have one novel up and are wondering why they are not selling like Konrath. Or writers trapped in the agent myth, rewriting book after book for someone who wouldn't know what would sell if it slapped them.

For all those writers, it would be impossible to make a living at writing fiction. And thus, when you talk to them about making money, they are telling you the truth...

...From their viewpoint.

How about a writer who has sold three novels traditionally and for the first time understands how the money flows? Or has gotten five to ten stories up electronically. Those early writers are saying the same thing, of course. Selling one genre book a year is not enough to make a living writing. Putting up just a few books indie is not enough to make a living. Unless, you are fantastically lucky.

But most of us aren't that lucky, so a writer with one book a year, who has bought in to the writing-slow myth can't make a living, and they are telling other writers the truth as well...

...From their viewpoint.

So what about when you hear this myth spouted by a big name bestseller? I heard a *New York Times* bestseller in a keynote speech once tell 500 people there were only two hundred people in the nation making a living at fiction. Kris and I almost fell out of our chairs laughing, but we were just about the only people in the room laughing. Everyone else thought he was right. As it happens, I'm sitting next to him on a panel the very next hour, so as we were talking, I turned to him and said, "You know that 200 number is totally wrong."

He look sort of stunned and said, "That's what I had always heard." (The myth hits again and is repeated by big-name writer who is making millions.)

I said, "If that's the case, then don't you find it pretty amazing that there are seven of the two hundred on this one panel?"

He looked down the panel at the seven of us, all full-time fiction writers sitting on the panel. Then I asked the 100 people in the room how many were writers making at least $80,000 per year with their fiction writing. Five more people, two of whom I recognized, raised their hands. Twelve of us in the same room at a writers' convention. That stunned the keynote speaker, let me tell you, and we ended up spending the entire panel talking about this myth. And where that 200 number came from in the myth.

Turns out, there are about 200 NEW NAMES on the major bestseller lists every year. (There are 780 yearly slots on the *New York Times* list alone, not counting the same number on *Publishers Weekly* lists, same number on the *Wall Street Journal* lists, and the 2,600 spots on the *USA Today* Bestseller list in a year.) So there are about 200 NEW NAMES in fiction hitting the bestseller lists every year that have never been there before. That's just the top spots. I'm not talking extended lists.

And of course, in this new world, I'm not talking about the growing number of novelists making a living indie publishing. That number is growing by the day. But you get an idea where the silly idea of only 200 came from.

So, how many writers in the United States do make a living writing only fiction? Well, that depends on how you define "living." That's another shocker for me. For the longest time I figured over six figures gross per year was a living. At that level there are thousands and thousands of fiction writers making that much and a lot more.

But lately, I've been forced by discussions with other professional writers to look at reality a little bit more when it comes to "making a living."

A $2,000 mortgage, $1,000 for various insurance, $1,000 for various utilities, and $2,000 more for food and other details, like clothing, trips and such. $6,000 per month after taxes needed to survive. $72,000 per year, but if you are married and your spouse works, cut that number in half. Your half, to say you are making a living writing fiction only needs to be $38,000 per year. Slightly over $3,000 per month.

And many, many people I know make nice livings on less than that. A bunch less. So my number was way high when it came to "making a living" so I have no idea how many thousands and thousands and thousands of writers make a living.

It's a lot more than I even thought it was, to be honest.

How Do Fiction Writers Make Money?
(The Magic Bakery Metaphor)

Think of us (every writer) as a huge bakery and all we make are pies. Magic pies, that seem to just reform after we sell off (license) pieces of the pie to customers.

And each pie can be divided into thousands of pieces if we want.

The Magic Pie secret ingredient is called "Copyright."

Every story we write, every novel we write, is a magic pie full of copyright.

We can sell (license) parts of it to one publisher, other parts to another publisher, some parts to overseas markets, other parts to audio, or eBooks, or game companies, or Hollywood, or web publishers, and on and on and on. One professional writer I knew licensed over 100 different gaming rights to different places on one novel. He had a very sharp knife cutting that small section of his magic pie.

With indie publishing, most writers are only focused on one tiny aspect of their pies, the electronic rights. But interestingly enough, when a story or novel gets published electronically, it gets spread out to many, many stores, and sometimes other publishers see it and want to buy it for their project, or a movie producer sees it and options it, or a game designer sees it and makes an offer. So in this new world, getting stories up indie can help out other sales given time.

And indie published books are licensed in many other countries through Kindle and Kobo and iBooks. All different parts of the same pie.

And if you really understand copyright, you will understand those pieces are not even sold. They are simply licensed. But I am using "sold" for this article instead of "licensed" just because that's how most beginning writers think.

So each professional writer has this Magic Bakery, making magic pies that can be cut into as many pieces as we want and many of the pieces can return as if never taken, even after being sold (licensed) off. (You must learn copyright to really understand this... *The Copyright Handbook* out of Nolo Press would be a good start.)

Each Piece of the Pie Is a Cash Stream

And extending this metaphor just a little bit farther, you don't even have to have the same flavor of pie. Kris has Kristine Kathryn Rusch, Kris Nelscott, Kristine Grayson, Kris Rusch, Kristine Dexter, and others, not counting combining with me every-so-often as Kathryn Wesley or Sandy Schofield. And under her own name she writes articles, stories in all genres, and novels in many genres.

Each story, each novel is a pie. If you have a lot of product, you have a pretty consistent cash flow stream because you have so many cash flow streams working. (Think a bunch of small streams flowing together to form a river and you get the idea.)

Indie writers who are successful at this new world are saying this all the time. Joe Konrath constantly talks about getting up more work. I push writers to write more and more. And my *Smith's Monthly* is yet another way to blend a bunch of pies.

Indie writers are finally starting to see the advantage to having more and more product, more and more magic pies. Traditional publishers always did. They would have five or six new books per month per list, and they built those big buildings on lots and lots of small slices from many pies.

So, for you traditionally published writers, advances on novels are only one cash flow stream for a few pieces of a pie. That's why these days people say that hybrid writers, those who work both sides and all sides, are making the most money. See why?

Repeat: Each piece of the pie is a cash stream.

Let me try to explain this using just one piece of the pie.

Say you sold (licensed) the tiny piece of the pie called French Translation Rights, and your contract with the French publisher limited your book to trade paper only. (You could have also sold the piece of the pie that had French hardback rights, or French audio rights, or French mass market rights, or French film rights. You still have those in the pie and can sell them at any point as well. Get the idea?)

Your French publisher will have advances like your American publisher, and there will be royalties and so on. In other words, your French piece of the pie will flow money into your accounts just as your English novel sale does. And in this new world you don't need agents to sell these slices anymore. In fact, you'll sell them more often with just e-mail and direct contact.

And your German sale (license) would be the same. Your Russian. Your Italian. And so on and so on. Thousands and thousands of pieces of the magic pie can be licensed.

One more time: Each piece of the pie is a cash stream.

Say you went to ACX and put a story you had indie published into audio. Does using that one piece of the pie stop you from selling any other piece of the pie?

No.

And when the audio contract goes out of force, the audio rights piece of the pie suddenly appears back in your pie and you can license it again.

Magic!

You create the inventory, the pie, just once, but can license it for your entire life, having pieces you licensed keep coming back to the pie over and over, and your estate can keep taking and licensing parts of that pie for seventy years past your death. Nifty, huh?

Are you all starting to see why Kris and I are harping all the time about bad traditional publishing contracts? If you give too many rights to work away for too long, it never returns to your bakery to make you money. (Maybe in 35 years... again, study copyright.)

But Here Is the Problem Most Writers Face

A Magic Bakery owner who opens a shop and has only one new pie per year, only one flavor, has little chance of making enough money to make a living and keep his business open.

Just imagine (as a customer) walking into a mostly-empty store. You have a huge empty bakery that you have promoted everywhere, but you have only one pie on the shelf. All the rest of the shelves are empty.

Customer turns and leaves. (Would you trust a bakery with only one pie on the shelf?)

But imagine my store... I have shelves and shelves and shelves full of pies, walls full, twenty flavors, willing to do new flavors at any moment to customer demand, willing to license small slices of any pie at any time. I have a lot more chance of having a lot of customers and making a living than a store with only one or two pies.

When you step back and look at any retail store, what I am talking about is sort of basic business. I have inventory.

I have a crowded store and am making more inventory all the time to keep repeat customers happy.

Each piece of the pie is a cash stream. If I have four hundred pies in my shop, each with a thousand possible pieces, I have a huge inventory to make money from.

Each piece does not have to make me much money for it to add up.

Go back and look at my myth chapters about writing fast and about rewriting. See how it's all starting to fall together?

A Real Life Example:

One afternoon, while at a writers' retreat I wrote a short story called "In the Shade of the Slowboat Man." The story took me a few hours to write.

—Just a few hours to create that pie. It was rejected at the market I wrote it for, so I sold it to *F&SF Magazine.* Decent money.

—Then I sold another slice to the *Nebula Awards Anthology,* another small slice (nonexclusive anthology right) sold and then returned to the pie.

—Then I sold it to another reprint anthology (same right again), another small slice sold and returned to the pie magically for another person to buy.

—Then I sold the rights to an audio play made from the story, making more off of that slice than the other three before, and then I was hired with Kris to write the script from my story, so more money yet again.

—Now I have that story on Kindle, B&N, Sony, iBooks, Smashwords and other sites selling and making nice money each sale. And I have put it in a collection so it is making more that way each month as well.

I have made well over $10,000 income from one short story so far, and I still have the pie on my shelf in my Magic Bakery, still there for sale, even though it is selling electronically and in a paper version.

Say I decide to make a novel pie out of the story. Short story pie will remain and continue to make money, novel pie will be created and both will have thousands of slices to be sold.

I had Hollywood once give me $1,000 every six months for three years simply to give them the chance to buy a slice of one pie (story) on my shelf. That's right, I never SOLD anything from the pie. I simply said "Give me a thousand bucks every six months and I won't let anyone else buy that one small slice of that one pie."

They never touched the pie and I made six thousand bucks off of that option.

I love this business.

It Doesn't Take a Lot of Sales to Make a Living

Now understand, over thirty years I have published over 100 novels traditionally and hundreds of short stories. I have over 10 million copies of my books in print at last count a few years back. Yet many of you reading this have never read a single word of any book or story I have written. But somehow I have been making a living with my fiction for over 25 years now.

Why? Because I have a very full Magic Bakery, with a large number of pies to sell pieces from. You haven't read any of my fiction. Yet here I am, making a living with my Magic Bakery.

I sell one slice here, another slice there, a bunch of slices over here, and I keep selling them and the new stuff as well, over and over and over. I understand copyright completely, and I use that knowledge.

Can you make a living after writing only one or two novels and a few short stories?

The answer is no (without getting fantastically lucky).

You have a bakery with no inventory. An empty store.

You have nothing on your shelves. Nothing to really sell to customers, and even if they do buy a slice and decide they like your bakery and your goods, there is not much else for them to buy. So they won't come back. Duh.

But once you fill that Magic Bakery, once you have customers who know where to buy, know that your product is a good, quality product, then the money will come.

Each piece of the pie is a cash stream.

And a writer with a good inventory and the ability to sell the inventory to customers can make a large amount of money with fiction writing.

If I can do it, if I am one of the thousands and thousands of fiction writers making a living with our fiction writing, you can do it as well.

The Secret?

Just write, finish what you write, mail or publish what you write so someone can buy it. You know, Heinlein's Rules will build you one very nice Magic Bakery in a very short amount of time, actually.

And, oh, yeah, it's also a lot of fun.

Sacred Cow #9
TO BE GOOD, WRITING MUST BE HARD

THIS MYTH COMES in many forms and has many faces, but let me put it as plainly as I can to start.

Myth: To be Good, Fiction Writing Must Be Hard. (And it can't be fun.)

Total hogwash, of course, yet it is stunning how many new fiction writers believe this, and how readers, when they

bother to think about it, believe the myth as well. And, of course, almost everyone who teaches creative writing in a university program believes this as well, and teaches the myth.

Where Does This Myth Come From?

Answer: A thousand places, actually. But I think the best place to look first is at fiction writers themselves.

Fiction writers are people who sit alone in a room and make up stuff. By its very nature, one of the easiest tasks ever given to a human being. But, alas, fiction writers are people who make stuff up, and thus, making stuff up doesn't stop when our fingers leave the keys. We use words like "struggle" and "fought" in sentences describing the creation of a story. "I had to really struggle with that story." Or "I fought that story into existence."

Good, active writing. Who cares if the reality was you sat fairly still, in a comfortable chair, in a warm room, at a computer, and just made stuff up.

Don't forget that we fiction writers, by our nature, are drama queens, to say the least. Because our task is so easy and so much fun, we have to make it seem harder to those around us, and to ourselves, otherwise we get no credit for all the "hard work" we do every day.

Fiction writers play up this myth of "hard work" so much, we actually start believing it ourselves at times. If nothing else, fiction writers are the masters of self-delusion.

A second place to look for why this myth exists is the culture of publishing.

One manuscript page is about 250 words. This post is now a distance past that number of words right here. So if

I write one page, 250 words, per day, I would be done writing in about 10-15 minutes. Sometimes quicker, sometimes longer. If I did that 10-15 minutes every day for one year, I would complete a 91,000 word novel, about a normal length paperback book.

Oh, yeah, that's hard work, sitting silently for 15 minutes per day and moving my fingers. And the current culture would consider me a prolific writer if I did that every year for ten years. Heaven forbid I actually write 30 minutes per day and produce two books a year.

We fiction writers have to really hide this math, and we have to really do a lot of drama to keep the world believing that working fifteen minutes a day typing is hard work. Stunning how good of a job we have done in this scam, isn't it? As I said, we are masters of delusion, self-delusion, and just flat making stuff up.

Of course, there is always the "art" argument that comes flying in. Fiction writers who want to hold onto the myth that writing is hard work talk a great deal about the "art" and the "craft" of what they do, especially out in public. And of course, see my rewriting chapters about that part of the myth. But the truth is, when we are really creating art, we are doing it from the back of our brains, typing fast, buried in the story.

Oh, wow, does this chapter make fiction writers angry at me. I pull out all their excuses and pull back the curtain. Sorry.

How Did This Start?

In the beginning (I love starting a sentence like that), all fiction writers struggled over simple sentences, meaning back in the early days of learning how to talk and write as kids, writing was hard for all of us. I went all the way through college avoiding any kind of class that forced me to do a paper or essay. I hated writing. It was just too hard. Much easier for me to do a multiple-choice test.

Most people never get past those early, almost basic memories. So we grow up thinking that someone who can write a story, an article, or heavens, an entire novel, have a special super power and are working really, really hard to write. Some selling writers I know actually still believe this.

And, of course, the pulp writers, pounding out thousands of words a day, actually were working physically hard on those manual typewriters. Go ahead, don't believe me, try pounding out a single page on a manual typewriter as fast as you can. You'll be covered in White Out and your arms will ache.

But sitting here in my perfect chair with perfect arm support, letting my fingers try to stay up with my old brain, I'm not doing much work. In fact, if I didn't get out and do some exercise, some sort of movement in the real world, I would turn into a 500 pound blob with fingers. I was headed that way about three years ago. Now I'm down to 199 and still losing and exercising. That's right, I have to get up and move away from the writing to do any real work or exercise.

Also, the early days of trying to learn how to tell stories is difficult and very frustrating. The people around you think you are wasting time, your family talks in worried whispers behind your back, your workshop hates everything you type, editors give you form rejections, and even your cat won't go near your computer chair. Everything about learning how to write stories in the early professional days is hard. No argument.

The early days of trying to learn how to write professional-level fiction is an ugly extension and reminder of learning to write as a child. Very basic fear. It's a wonder any of us ever learn how to write novels, now that I think about it.

And of course there's Practice.

Don't even mention that ugly word to fiction writers. Fiction writers, unlike any other brand of art, think they don't need to practice. However, early days of trying to get published (and make decent sales indie) forces practice on all of us. No one buys our practice sessions and calls us brilliant, so we keep putting out stories and novels until someone does buy one or we get more than family buying our books.

And this, of course, is one main problem with indie publishing. Practice. You practice and publish, but you should have no expectations. Hard to do. Easier back in the day when all you got were rejections for years. Putting your practice sessions up on Amazon and making no sales is harder to deal with. Not as clear cut.

Practice is hard work for the most part. Anyone who played a sport or a musical instrument knows this fact. So when fiction writers are practicing in the early years, it is hard work.

Learning Is Uncomfortable by its Very Nature

When you are learning something new, it makes us all uneasy, makes us want to return to the status quo of not knowing something new.

We all like stability, but when learning fiction writing and the craft of storytelling, there is no stability. A fiction writer is constantly trying something new, constantly on edge, constantly learning, and thus it feels hard and uncomfortable for years at a time.

That's normal, just normal. And clearly not hard work, but because the learning and trying something new feels difficult, we think of it as hard work.

And this applies when we are struggling (nice word, huh?) through a story and it feels like it's not coming together. That, we say to other writers, is working. We had to "work" at the story, the plotting into an unknown place felt uncomfortable, therefore it felt hard and if it feels hard, it therefore must have been work.

As I said, fiction writers are great at self-delusion.

So the memory of working hard at writing still haunts all of us from our childhood. On my writing computer I have a novel to finish. But that feels like work, so I sit here at my internet computer, typing this instead. See, even I do it, still, after all the millions of words and over 100 plus traditionally published books.

So, as I do with every chapter in this book, let me try to outline in simple form where writing is actually hard, and where it isn't hard.

Where Writing Is Actually Hard

1) The business of fiction writing is hard.

No argument there at all. And that business comes flowing into the writing. Thoughts about selling or not selling stop most writers at times. That makes the typing hard. Just dealing with the myths around agents can drive a writer to a nap very quickly. To indie publish or not to indie publish? That can cause a writer to stop cold for months. Cash flow, doing proofs, doing covers, laying out books, and so on. Everything about the business is hard.

2) Discipline is hard.

Just carving out time to write fiction is hard. Really hard, actually. Especially in the early years when the feedback loop is so negative.

Simply finding time to get to the computer is hard when day job, kids, and bills get in the way. That's difficult for everyone and very hard work. The fun starts when you get to the chair with some time ahead, but getting there is hard work early on.

3) Writing more than six to eight hours a day is hard work.

I know, under novel deadlines, I have spent that many hours and many more at a computer. When you write for eight hours a day, you know you have physically worked at something. But fifteen minutes a day to write one novel a year. That's not work. Write ten thousand words a day for a couple of weeks and you will know real hard physical work in the area of writing.

Those are the only places I can think of that writing is actually difficult work.

Where Writing Is NOT Hard

1) Sitting in a chair for an hour or so a day, making up stuff, is not hard work.

It's just not. And no amount of whining or excuses from fiction writers will make me think any different.

2) Coming up with story ideas and novel ideas is not hard work.

In fact, after a while, professional fiction writers have far, far too many ideas to ever think about writing them all, and we are constantly coming up with new ideas every day. Coming up with story ideas actually becomes annoying because there are so many and it is so easy. (Fear of ideas not coming is something you learn your way past in the early days, the uncomfortable days. No worry. And if that scares you still, take the Ideas workshop.)

Where Writing Is Just Flat Fun

1) Sitting in a chair, making stuff up, while knowing that someone will pay you a lot of money for what you are making up.

Yup, that's fun.

2) Knowing that the typing you are doing today might still be read and earning you and your kids money seventy-five or more years from now.

No other job I know of has that wonderful aspect to it. That's fun.

3) Finishing and mailing or publishing stories is fun.

Some of you might call that work, the mailing process or the indie publishing process, but actually, it's fun. (If you think of it as hard work, if the fear is trying to stop you, you have other issues to get past.) Every time you mail something, or indie publish something, you are creating a potential, and that's exciting.

And these days, when you spend the time to learn how to put a book or story up electronically and/or publish it in paper yourself, you will discover that seeing that story sell two days after your wrote it or holding that paper book in your hand is nothing but fun. Great fun.

As an attorney friend of mine once said, when he goes to work, he gets so much per hour and then goes home. When I go to work, finish a story and mail it or publish it, every day I have the chance of making a lot of money and being read by a lot of people and making money with what I did that day for decades to come. That's exciting and fun.

4) I wrote that!

Yup, that's fun, great deals of fun, simply saying to someone, "Yes, I wrote that." I can't begin to tell you how much fun it was a while back at a conference spending a good hour and a half signing books as fast as I could sign. I have an ego, just as anyone else, and trust me, that's fun. Signing books for fans who love your work is not work. It's an honor and a ton of fun.

5) The challenge of the business.

Nothing is easy about becoming and staying a professional fiction writer. The business, the push to continue, the dealing with money is never easy. But the challenge itself is great fun.

If you aren't the type of person that goes at something that seems impossible and says, "Oh, why not, let's try...," then you might want to find another job to chase. If you feel that security is everything in your life, then go work for Enron. That should do the trick. (Oh, wait, that company and all its pension funds are so long gone, and most people won't remember that name. I rest my case.) But if you love challenges, there is no more fun challenge than this business and making up stories.

Suggestions on How to Make Writing More Fun

1) Take the pressure off.

Simply put, this is not brain surgery. No life is in your hands other than some made-up characters. And you can kill them if you want, since you are God in your story. Take off the pressure.

2) Take stock of how you feel when you get up from a good writing session, where you finished pages.

Do you feel good, excited, happy? Most of us do, sort of like just coming off a good carnival ride. Remember that feeling when you go back to write the next session or the next day.

3) Make mailing manuscripts to editors or indie publishing them fun. Mailing and the game of trying to match the right manuscript with the right editor at the right magazine or house is fun. Frustrating at times, sure. But the more you make that part of things into just a game to keep as much writing on the market as you can, the more fun you will have and the less rejection will bother you. (If you are still mailing stories to agents, you really, really need to catch a clue.)

And indie publishing, for those of you who have not yet started because of fear, is just flat a joy. It has an uncomfortable learning curve, yes. But I would never be doing this crazy challenge and *Smith's Monthly* without indie publishing.

4) Stop calling your writing work.

Stop thinking of writing as a grind. Stop complaining to other writers all the time how bad the week was and how little you got done. Just stop.

In other words... CHANGE YOUR ATTITUDE.

If you have an extra ten minutes, write something. If you are lucky and have a few hours, be excited about sitting down and exploring whatever world you are running around in with the story. Come at the writing with excitement, with expectations of fun, with delight.

As a mug I use for tea says on the side, "Attitude is everything."

Over the years I have allowed myself to fall into some pretty nasty traps around the business of writing and writing itself.

I let myself forget how much fun it is.

I let myself believe that some writing was better than other types of writing.

I let myself think that it was better to not write than write.

I have managed to escape all the traps, but I was not immune to them by any means. Heck, I quit writing a half dozen times along the way.

That's right, I figured the grass was always greener on the other side of some fence, so off I went to start a comic book store, or off I went to play professional poker, or off I went to try to play professional golf for a second time. And every time, at some point fairly quickly on those side roads, I realized I had left what I loved to do, that I had left the easiest job on the planet, and a job that paid the most: Writing fiction.

I had left a job I really enjoyed.

So now I write fiction for a living once again, and I enjoy it even more than I ever did.

More WMG Writers' Guides
from all your favorite booksellers
in trade paper and electronic editions.

I sit alone, in a room, and make stuff up. That's my job description. I have, without a doubt, the easiest and best job in the world.

It is a giant myth that my job is hard work.

Sacred Cow #10
IF I DO (THIS OR THAT), I WILL KILL MY CAREER

THIS MYTH JUST gets more and more annoying by the day. So I figured it was time to take a hammer to the myth in this last chapter of this book.

If you catch some hints of annoyance on my part through this chapter, it's because I think this is flat out the stupidest myth there is. And one of the most dangerous because it causes writers to act in head-shakingly stupid ways. It also shows no understanding of the business of publishing, or the business of indie publishing. So please be patient with me. I'll try not to be grumpy.

If I Do "This or That," I Will Kill My Career

Now, of course, beginning writers are the ones saying this. You never hear long-term professionals like me or Kris or anyone else who has gotten a half dozen years making a living say this. Ever.

Why? Because we know it's just not possible. It really isn't.

Professional writers don't worry about mistakes killing careers, we worry about mistakes that will cost money or get us screwed or signing bad contracts or letting some agent rip us off.

Who can kill a career?

The writer who believes this myth can kill their own career simply by believing it. Sort of Zen, but true. Any writer that stops writing and just becomes an "author," (a person who has written) will kill their own career. That's how careers are killed. A writer stops writing.

What is a "Career"?

My good old dictionary defines the term as "An occupation, a way of making a living."

I suppose by that definition it could be said I have a career. I write for a living, I sell books and stories. I helped start a new publishing company four years ago and now sell most of my stories to that company. And for years I was a part-time editor and still edit an occasional anthology. I have a reputation under this name and I have done so many things to this name, it's stunning the name is still alive, including telling people how fast I write and doing these Killing the Sacred Cow blogs.

Kris has many pen names. Do Kris Nelscott and Kristine Grayson and Kristine Dexter have careers? Or are they all part of Kristine Kathryn Rusch?

I think all pen names are just part of the career of the writer. But on the other side, it can be thought that each pen name has a career. Your choice how you look at it.

I find it wonderful that I can get the income from five or ten other careers (pen names). I did for years and years. That's a very cool thing about writing. Just like Evan Hunter got all the money from Ed McBain's career. Nifty how that works, huh?

And that writing under other names is just one thing that makes careers in writing impossible to destroy.

Why? Because even in the worst situations and after the worst mistakes, we can all just change our names and keep writing, that's why. Unlike any other profession, we are free to just be as many people as we want to be.

A business person tied to a resume can kill a career with a bad action or choice. An actor can kill a career because they are tied to their face. A doctor can make a mistake and kill a career by actually killing a patient.

A writer can decide to stop writing, which kills a writing career eventually. But again, that's self-inflicted.

But if the writer can clear out the ego and change names when sales drop or things go wrong, there is nothing to stop that writer from writing until the moment they die.

Writing careers can NOT be killed unless the writer stops writing.

Wait, let me say this one more time:

Writing careers can NOT be killed unless the writer stops writing.

But the belief that a career can be killed by a mistake is often terminal for

---

a writer. This myth can be very danger- ous if you believe it. The myth itself will cause you to stop writing and thus kill your own career.

Let me give a couple of main exam- ples and some minor ones of how this myth rears its ugly head these days.

Mail a Novel to an Editor Against Guidelines

Yup, I know that all guidelines say "Agented Submissions." And for decades before that all guidelines said "No Unsolicited Manuscripts."

So? Who cares? (What are you all? Sheep?)

Editors need manuscripts, they are looking for good novels that they think will sell. And in this new world, agents will just get in your way and mostly they work for publishers. So why deal with them?

You send an editor a great few-page sample of your novel with a good cover letter, a short synopsis and a SASE and they will look at it. They might send you their form letter saying "get an agent." Fine, but they will look at it for the most part. And if you are close, the editor will write you a letter, and if your book is good and it fits, they will make you an offer on it. (Then you need to deal with an attorney and bad contract terms, but that's another topic.)

So, you all remember editors? The people who can buy books at publishing houses? Remember?

So sending a manuscript directly to an editor will not kill your career.

Why?

1) The editor won't remember your book if they didn't buy it.

I know many of you think you are the center of the universe, but honestly, the editors don't remember manuscripts or authors they don't read.

2) There is no such thing as a blacklist unless you threaten the editor with a gun.

3) Honestly, the editor can't come to your house and yell at you. Honestly, they just won't care if it doesn't fit their line.

4) The worst they can do is just toss your manuscript away and not respond, which some of the younger, rude editors do at times. You are out a few bucks post- age. Shrug.

Yet I have heard hundreds of writers say "If I mail my book directly against guide- lines to an editor, I will kill my career."

You won't!

But you might sell a book and actu- ally start a career.

If I Indie Publish a Bad Story... I Will Kill My Career

I love this from new writers who think they actually know what makes a good story or a bad one. Of course they don't.

And to be honest, when it comes to my own stories, I don't know either. No writer is a good judge of his or her own work. None.

Any writer who thinks they are a good judge of their own work has far too much ego, or has spent far too much time in creative writing classes in college.

Professional writers can spot when another person's story works or doesn't work and why, but on our own stuff, we suck. Nature of how the brain works and again a topic for another post.

And indie publishing something really, really, really bad will not kill a career. No one will buy it. And thus not care.

Really is that simple.

You know... Trust the readers.

And if you are really afraid of a story, put it under a pen name (called a burner name) and don't tell anyone. Just let it sit there.

Publishing a story you think sucks won't kill your career!

It might make you a little money, however.

More Silly Thinking

Example... Kris got a letter the other day from a writer flat believing that if he self-published anything it would completely kill his career. Of course, he was a beginning writer, wasn't selling anything, and thus had no career. But he was convinced.

Example... I have heard many, many times from writers that if you don't have an agent, it will kill your career.

I haven't had an agent for eight years. I keep selling and making money. Interestingly enough, it's always beginning writers or someone with only one or two novels published that tell me this. We have talked about this myth already bunches of times in other comment sections, but it is always framed by "...if you don't have an agent, it will kill your career."

Truth: *These days having an agent can do more damage to your income and long-term copyrights and income stream than not having one. Far, far more. Honest.*

Example... I have received many letters over the last few years from writers afraid to negotiate contracts for fear it will kill their careers.

Kris and I have walked away from many, many contracts that had bad clauses that we just wouldn't sign and we negotiate everything and we still make our living at this business of fiction writing.

In fact, if all writers as a group suddenly grew a pair, we actually might get royalty rates for electronic publishing moved upward. But this fear of "killing a career" by negotiating a contract hurts us all.

And even worse, writers let agents do the negotiating, agents without legal degrees who can't practice law but do so anyway, and who are more concerned about keeping the publisher happy then helping the writer. Yeah, that gets us good clauses in contracts.

Any wonder contracts have been getting worse and worse over the last five years? It's all because writers are afraid of killing their careers. Most don't even have careers in the first place, because they aren't making a living at their fiction.

And why aren't they?

Because fear never gets you anywhere in business, folks.

I asked a few other professionals about other examples of where they hear this silly myth and I got hordes and hordes of stories, all funny to me and the other professionals, but all very real and believed by the young writers spouting the myth.

And these stories range all over the map.

Example... A writer who thought that if he didn't rewrite a manuscript at least ten times, he would kill his career. Hadn't sold anything yet for some reason. (grin)

Example... Another beginning writer was convinced that a bad cover on a book (he thought bad) would kill his career. His first novel from a traditional publisher and he thought he knew more than the art department in the publishing company and was trying to get another cover his friend drew to replace the cover. He did far more damage to his reputation than a hundred bad covers could have done. But he was convinced a bad cover would kill his career.

Not even that kind of stupidity would kill his career, but it didn't do him any good with that one publisher, that's for sure.

Folks, I have had more bad covers than I can count over the decades. I'm still making a living.

Example... Another writer swore that if he didn't have at least three people proof his story or novel before he indie published it, it would kill his career. He actually said he wanted his story perfect, to which the professional telling me the story laughed and said, "Yeah, as if there is ever a perfect story in publishing."

Summary

There is only one way for a writer to kill a career: Stop writing.

It really is that simple.

But if you go into everything you do in publishing believing the myth that you can make a mistake and kill your career, you will make all your decisions from a position of fear. And you will make horrid decisions.

And if you don't believe me on this, just ask any long-term professional writer, a writer who has been around for over twenty years, how many mistakes they have made. The professional will laugh and then more than likely ask which year? Or which dozen do you want first? Something like that.

And most beginning writers would tell me that writing a series like *Killing the Top Ten Sacred Cows of Publishing* would kill my career because I have said so many things that are against "common stupidity...I mean knowledge."

Hah, fooled you. I'm still here and selling and making a very nice living.

If you never stop writing, gain some courage, and stop worrying about killing your career, you might be stunned at what you can manage in this business. You will be writing and enjoying the writing until the day you die.

And that's a great reward.

So stop worrying and go have fun.

~

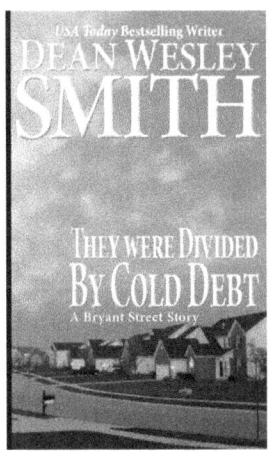

USA *Today* Bestselling Writer

DEAN WESLEY SMITH

UNLOCKED GATE

Cindy Kemp loved St. Patrick's Day in Chicago. Especially as a student and a bartender.

Green beer, green drinks, and lots of eligible guys to take the edge off of far too many weeks of no sex. The St. Patrick's party beat all parties.

But when the green starts to drain from everything, including the beer, Cindy discovers a world far beyond the bar.

A fantasy story with a twist. And a green beer.

Unlocked Gate

CINDY KEMP WOULD have sworn on her dead uncle's favorite Chevy, even bet that she wouldn't go shopping for an entire week, that the color green couldn't be drained from anything. Especially beer.

Okay, she would have been wrong, so it was damn lucky no one thought to bet her before all the green drainin' started.

"Incoming!" she shouted over the nasty beat of someone doing ugly things to a Neil Diamond song, not that she liked Neil Diamond. God forbid.

She slid the glass of green beer down the highly polished oak bar like a puck in a shuffleboard game. Ben and Wolf-Boy, two regulars sitting at the bar quickly got their beers out of the way as the new one slid past.

She held the poised follow-through of an expert beer-slider, her hand high over her head, her wrist twisted slightly to the left, as the glass with the perfect head of green foam stopped exactly in front of the goofy-looking guy with thick hair and a long nose.

Not a drop spilled.

Man, she was good!

The customers crowded against the bar applauded.

Wolf-Boy gave her his famous wolf-whistle, which even turned heads on the dance floor. Every time he did that, she expected bottles on the back bar to shatter like a bad television commercial.

She bowed and then winked at the other bartender, Judy, who just shook her head, her long red hair flapping around in a ponytail behind her back.

The guy with the long nose gave her a beaming smile that made Cindy's stomach queasy and his nose seem even longer, if that was possible. The guy's father must be a cobbler.

She turned quickly to the well and began work on a drink using Crème de Menthe and rum for the trashy blonde woman beside him. The bar went through gallons of the smelly green Crème de Menthe once a year. The rest of the time the bottle just sat on the back bar growing mold, as if anyone would even notice with the green color.

God, she loved St. Patrick's Day in Chicago. It was still early in the evening, yet Peter's Place was jamming. The music hugged her like her best winter coat, its bass beat rattling the bottles. The music was the party and all she did was push things along with tons of green beer and ugly green drinks.

With the music jammed up so loud, she could barely hear drink orders unless she bent forward, giving the guys at the bar the perfect hint of the tops of her breasts. She figured it never hurt to tease a little, toss out a little bait just to see who might take the hook. Of course, if someone like the guy with the long nose took the bait, she would toss him back. She had her standards after all, even though she was damned horny and had been for weeks now.

St. Patrick's Day brought more than just the regulars out to play, especially since Peter's Place was so close to the University of Chicago tucked dab smack in the middle of a street of shops that stretched for blocks. Students jammed around the long bar three deep, covering just about every foot of Peter's Place's hardwood floors. Some of the regulars had gotten in early and claimed the dozen stools. Everyone else stood, drinking, eating peanuts, and shouting over the music.

Huge barrels of salted-in-the-shell peanuts were scattered around the room. She had a hunch that some of the poorer students used a glass of beer and a few bowls of peanuts for dinner more often than not. Peter, the owner didn't seem to care or notice. The salty peanuts kept the floor a white dusty color and people drinking. On New Year's Eve, right at the tick of midnight, everyone threw peanuts. So far no one had been seriously hurt. She just kept thanking the work-force gods that her job didn't include sweeping the place.

She pulled her blouse away from her chest a couple of quick times, letting cooler air inside her shirt. The fans hanging down from the tall ceiling tried their best to keep the air moving, but she had no doubt that by midnight, she would be sweating like after a good workout. The music already had a good thirty people on the small dance floor in the right corner, which wasn't helping the heating factor either, especially the way some of them were jumping around.

She glanced over at the goofy guy with the nose. There was just something about that nose that kept her staring at it. Maybe it promised other large body parts. She tried to imagine a wild night with that nose and the idea just made her laugh. If there was ever an argument for plastic surgery, the poor guy had it sticking to the front of his face. He should offer to do ads for a plastic surgeon. The before and after pictures would be enough to convince anyone.

Again she fanned her blouse opened and closed a few times. Maybe she shouldn't have worn silk tonight. She had bought the green blouse two days before in the thrift shop off The Loop. The rich from the Lake Shore area gave away some of the best designer clothes and she wasn't above buying them at a tiny fraction of the price. Even though she was a working student, that didn't mean she couldn't dress in the style. It just took a little more creativity and patience in the thrift stores.

Tonight, she had on a really hot green skirt with the light-green silk blouse, unbuttoned two buttons down, and dark green silk tie that she kept loose and tossed over her shoulder when dealing with dirty glasses. The green shamrock post earrings and the green ribbon holding her long brown hair in place added a put-together touch to the outfit.

She was "hot green" and she knew it.

She finished the Crème de Menthe drink that smelled like Listerine and glanced at the guy with the nose. He had turned and was talking to the blonde who had ordered the drink.

The woman had no sense of taste in clothing. She wore a green thin cotton blouse tucked into Levi's two sizes too small. Rolls of fat flopped over the tops of her jeans, straining the poor blouse, pulling it tight against her tits, which sagged some and needed to have a bra covering them.

Cindy almost felt sorry for the blouse. On the right woman, with the right stuff under it, the blouse would look nice

Mr. Long-Nose was sure interested in what that poor blouse was straining to hold in. He stared at the blonde's chest like her eyes were there. Cindy sat the drink down in front of the blonde and waited for Mr. Long-Nose to turn away from the peep show long enough to pay for it.

If he bought two more of those drinks for that blonde, he was going to be very sorry later. Crème de Menthe tasted like thick mouthwash going down. Cindy couldn't imagine what it tasted like coming back up, but she knew for a fact it smelled horrid. She had seen a few too many women in the bathroom realize just how bad that green stuff really was for them. Every St. Patrick's Day she thanked the work force gods that her job didn't include cleaning up the bathrooms either.

In front of Cindy, a large guy with a football jersey shoved his way through the crowd and slammed his half-full glass on the bar between Wolf-Boy and Ben. Both Wolf-Boy and Ben were math majors who loved to drink. And they often kept her entertained with fast one-liners and catty looks at others.

Now, both looked at him over their glasses, giving Jock-Boy the "annoyed look" the two had perfected for jerks at the bar. But the big jock wasn't into noticing anything but himself.

"How come I didn't get a green beer?" he shouted over the music.

"You're too tall," Wolf-Boy said, just loud enough for Cindy to barely hear.

"Too stupid," Ben said.

Jock-Boy ignored them and held up his glass for her to see.

It was full of regular-colored beer, or something that looked like it. Whatever it was, it hadn't come from any of their taps, since every keg they had on line had been filled with green food coloring.

No doubt the guy was pulling some sort of scam on her to get a free beer, but it didn't matter. Nothing was going to ruin her good mood tonight. It was St. Patrick's Day and if she was lucky, she would cut a prime candidate out of the crowd and get laid before breakfast.

Jock-Boy set the glass down again and said, "Well?"

"Don't touch that!" Wolf-Boy said, leaning away from the yellow beer in mock horror, like it might blow up.

Ben leaned the other way, also showing mock horror. "It's been…recycled."

She laughed and then pretending to be very careful, took Jock-Boy's glass between two fingers like she was holding a dead frog and poured out whatever was in there. She got him a clean glass and pulled him a green beer, again making sure the head was perfect on the top.

She placed the beer in front of him. Before he could pick it up and turn away, the green vanished like it had never been there.

"Not funny!" the guy shouted over the loud music at her.

Both Wolf-Boy and Ben were now very seriously studying the golden-filled glass, clearly as stunned as she was feeling.

Jock-Boy hadn't touched it. No one had but her. Something must be going wrong with the food coloring Peter had put in the kegs.

She glanced down at Judy, but her partner behind the bar was busy at the second well and hadn't noticed anything going wrong. Typical. The woman could ignore a fight, a fire in a garbage can, and two women slapping each other at the bar all at the same time. And had.

Suddenly, the green beer Wolf-Boy had been sipping on lost its green. Then Ben's did the same.

"Okay, now that's something!" Wolf-Boy said, bending down and studying his glass up close.

Ben looked almost afraid of his beer. Maybe this would be what they both needed to slow down the drinking. Two math majors who were so damned smart that they were bored with school, so they drank and ate peanuts and kept her entertained every night.

Maybe this was a joke they were pulling? They could do such a thing. Maybe they had set up Jock-Boy. That was possible, too.

"Nice trick, guys," she said, smiling at the three of them.

All of them looked at her with far better poker faces than any three college boys could ever have.

Oh, shit, they hadn't done it.

Suddenly, the green vanished from the Crème de Menthe the blonde was drinking, leaving an ugly white liquid in her glass.

Okay, this was going beyond funny, beyond a trick. She didn't like this and she had no idea what was happening. She hated not being in control and knowing what was happening.

Color just didn't drain out of drinks like that. Someone was playing a really great prank, or she had just stepped into an old Twilight Zone episode. If Burgess Meredith walked up to the bar, she was going to run for the back door, right down the top of the bar if she had to. She had watched far too many of those old episodes while dating Danny, a Star Trek geek majoring in physics.

If he hadn't been so damn good in bed and so damn good looking, she would have left him after about the thirtieth episode in a row of The Twilight Zone. But not even the good sex had

Missed the latest Thunder Mountain novel?
It's available from all your favorite booksellers
in trade paper and electronic editions.

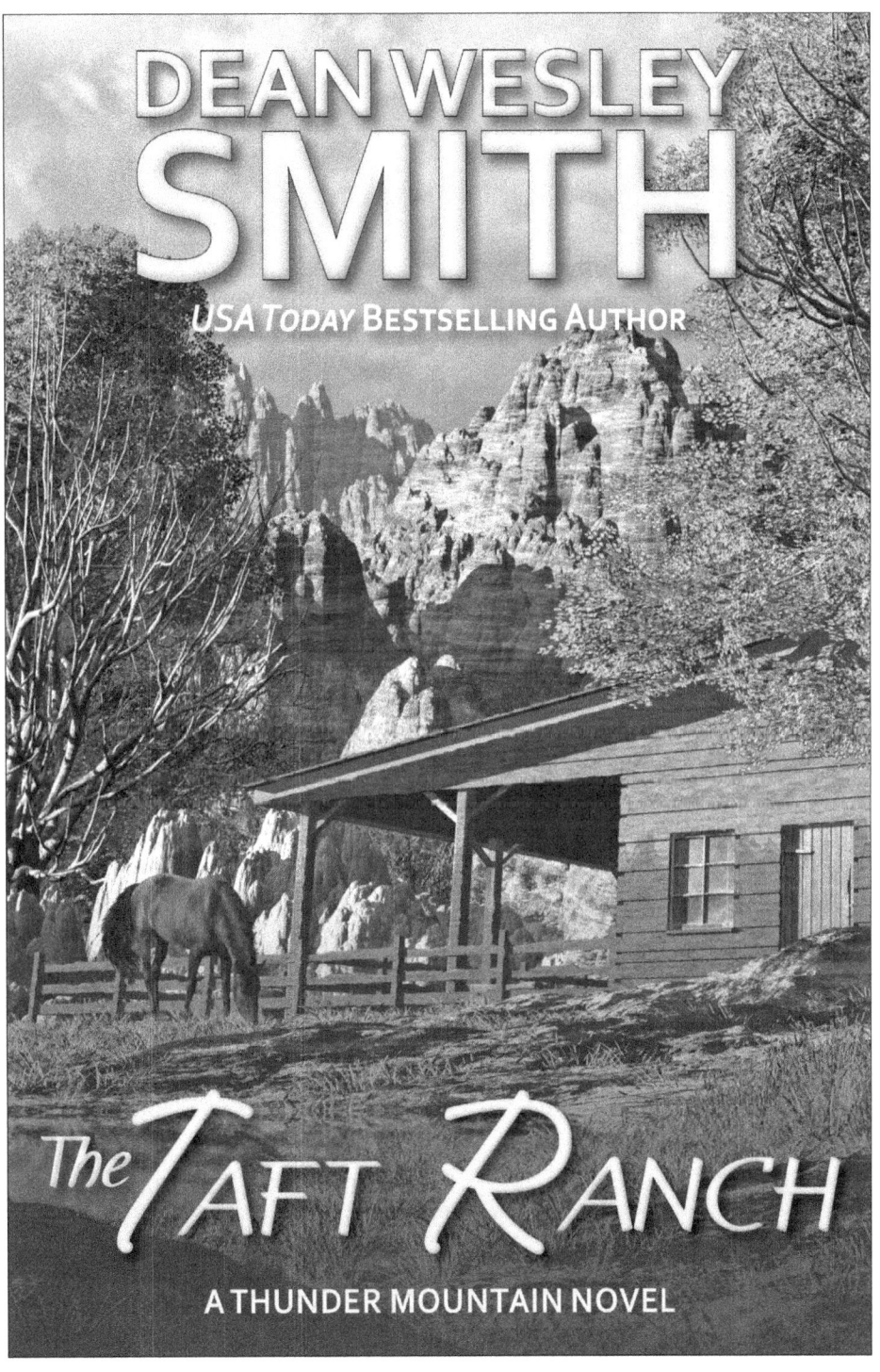

been enough for her to stay after the night he came to bed wearing pointed ears, a red shirt, and no pants, muttering about his need to Pon Far, or Prom Fart, or something like that.

That had been two months ago, and now she asked every man she met if he was a Trekkie before ever thinking of jumping into bed with him. Sometimes even great sex wasn't worth pointed ears.

Cindy made herself take a deep breath and just stop, taking stock of all the regular colored drinks in front of her. Even the jerk in the football shirt wasn't doing anything but staring.

Suddenly, the blonde's green blouse went pure clear, as if the light green color had been sucked out through the edge of her sleeve. Her blouse was now completely see-through and Mr. Long Nose almost dropped his glass of now golden beer as he stared at the blonde's tits.

The blonde, who clearly already had one-too-many Crème de Menthes didn't seem to even notice, but Cindy and everyone else along the bar sure did. Now it was clear the woman needed to lose a lot more than twenty pounds. Through the clear shirt, you could now see her butt crack and thong underwear.

Shit, those things had to hurt, especially sitting on a bar stool for hours.

Cindy shuddered and turned away as fast as she could, but she knew that image was going to haunt her. A butt crack ghost, more frightening than any real ghost.

Out of the corner of her eye, she caught a glimpse of something on top of the bar, moving back toward her well.

Mist.

A green, sort of odd-shaped cloud of green mist moved over the golden beers and then past her well, sucking the green out of all the limes in her fruit tray.

She rubbed her eyes and the green mist seemed to vanish.

"I think I need a drink," she said.

"I need a god-damned green beer, with no tricks," Jock-Boy shouted.

She grabbed another glass and poured him a green beer, not caring that it really didn't have a good head on it.

It was simply too damn early in the night to lose it. She wasn't even tired yet. Hot, yes. But tired, no. So this couldn't be happening.

But it was.

Along the bar on the other side of her well, the customer's beers and drinks started losing their green color. And a guy wearing a green hat with a big "O" on it suddenly found himself with a pure white hat on his head.

Damn, this would be funny if it wasn't so damn scary.

She could feel her heart pounding like a dozen muggers were coming after her trying to get her cell phone and purse.

She stepped back away from the bar, hoping that her wonderful green outfit kept its color. She had never been one to wear white, except as an accent to some bright color or another. And she had paid thirty bucks for the green silk blouse and the color fit with two of her other outfits, so she sure didn't want it ruined.

"Squeeze the pimple," she said to herself softly. "Squeeze the pimple."

She relaxed.

It always worked, cleared her head. She had taken almost two years of self-defense classes and another year of martial arts training, and the one thing her instructor had taught her was that fear never helped in any situation. If she started feeling afraid, started feeling her heart race, she needed to drain that fear out of mind like draining a big old white-head pimple.

From that moment on, every time Cindy had felt afraid, she just muttered "squeeze the pimple" and the fear just went away.

"It's the drainin' of the green!" one short woman shouted over the music, her eyes wide. She dropped her golden-colored beer and the glass shattered on the floor. Beer and salt and peanut shells always made for a nice mess for the bouncers to clean up.

Cindy stared at the women as the poor thing, clearly two drinks beyond reason, backed away from the bar with a horror-movie look on her face.

Now Cindy was sure she was in a *Twilight Zone* episode. Or a really nifty hidden camera show.

That had to be it.

She made sure her hair was out of her face, that her blouse was adjusted, her tie down and in place, and looked around for the hidden cameras. There were none that she could see, but that didn't mean they weren't there.

Again, out of the corner of her eye, Cindy caught a glimpse of some "thing" that was green on the bar. This time it looked like more than just a cloud. It had a human shape. A green mist-filled human shape.

Real short.

And that short, green-mist thing was going from person-to-person along the bar, draining the green from everything.

Suddenly, as if coming out of thin air, an old guy with a white beard and balding head appeared near the bar in front of Green Mist Man. He had on a long gray trench coat that made him look like a flasher waiting for a flashee. He carried a staff-like stick in one hand and moved through the crowd like it didn't exist.

"Let's go," the old guy said to Green Mist Man.

None of the other patrons around the old guy seemed to notice anything different. They were either holding up their drinks, or pointing to something that had been green and was now a pale white color.

Cindy intently watched the old guy as the music changed to a punked-up version of Greensleeves that actually had a danceable beat. Every year the DJ played that song and every year she had hated it. At the moment, she was too weirded-out to even think about hating it.

The old guy ignored her and the music and all the people around him and kept his attention on Green Mist Man standing on the bar.

Cindy moved over closer to the old guy in the trench coat, ignoring the complaints of the customers. She needed to hear what the old guy was saying over the loud music.

Cindy stared at his eyes. They were a deep blue, and seemed to show an intellect and intensity she didn't see much in the college guys she dated. He would have made a great Gandalf if he were about six inches taller, tossed out the ugly trench coat for a white robe, and let his beard grow just a little longer.

"No arguments," the old guy said again to Green Mist Man on the bar. "You've already caused enough problems here."

The Green Mist Man seemed to shrug, but the mist was swirling so much, Cindy wasn't sure if it was a shrug or a "get screwed" sign.

"Yeah, I know you just got started," the old guy said, seemingly having a conversation with a cloud of the color that had been drained from the drinks. "But this is where it stops. You know you don't belong here, no matter what today is."

The old man grabbed into the Green Mist Man, clearly making contact with what looked like a misty arm about two feet above the bar. He then turned and started for the door.

She had to be seeing things, but now, after all this, she had to know for sure. She grabbed her black police baton that she kept behind the bar for emergencies. It could knock a guy coming over the bar at her out cold before he had time to even duck. So far, she or any of the other women bartenders hadn't had reason or need to use it, but she felt better with it in her hand.

She quickly moved down the bar to where Judy stood talking to a customer, ignoring completely the strangeness going on around her as Judy could do so well.

"Cover for me. I'll be right back."

Cindy ducked under the lowered bar entrance at the cocktail station, not giving Judy any time to answer. Somehow, Cindy managed to stay with the old man through the crowd. From what she could tell, the old guy seemed to be dragging Green Mist Man along, talking with him all the way.

Clearly the old guy was nuts and she was buying into his weird hallucination.

Normally she wasn't the type to follow nutty old men who carried a big stick and looked like a flasher. She liked her men young, driven, and well dressed. But before tonight, nothing had ever happened to the color green in her bar. It seemed like it was going to be a night of firsts.

Cindy managed to get out the door right behind the old guy. She nodded to the bouncer, and then followed the old man in the trench coat and little Green Mist Man up the street like she was a peeping tom sneaking along behind two lovers.

"You're not going to tell me how you got in, are you?" the old man said, keeping up the conversation with his misty companion.

There was a pause, and then the old guy laughed, sort of a crackling-of-brittle-paper sound. "I figured as much."

It was like listening to one side of a really stupid phone conversation.

As the old man walked down the sidewalk and past the alley that went in behind the bar, Cindy stopped, about to turn back to have the bouncer report the old guy to the cops. Suddenly two things happened at once.

First, the air started to shimmer just inside the mouth of the alley. The old man stopped, then shoved the little Green Mist Man at the hole with a shout of, "Don't come back!"

Then, from the other direction, two guys just appeared out of the air over the street about ten feet behind the old man, stumbling for a second as if they didn't expect a step down.

There wasn't a step in the middle of the street.

And those two couldn't have come out of thin air.

"You're losing it," she muttered to herself.

Could she still be at home dreaming? Maybe it was from serving the food coloring. She had read that dye could cause people to see strange things. Or maybe she was just going nuts from not enough sex in the month since she and Twilight Zone Boy had broken up.

Both men sort of staggered toward the old guy who had his back turned to them. They both carried bats, but they sure didn't look like baseball players. Something about them looked off, like they had been sleeping in a dumpster the night before. Their clothes were soiled, their ugly plaid shirts not tucked in, their shoes untied and caked in a thick mud. They squished when they walked and Cindy couldn't tell if they were squishing or if the mud was.

She forced herself to really look at them, even though everything about them revolted her. One guy had a leg that was turned directly away from his body to the right. The other had two left hands.

And one had an ear-looking thing glued to the middle of his forehead with a dangling earring made of beads hanging down over his nose. It looked liked a woman's ear.

"Now that's gross," she said out loud.

Even from twenty steps away, they smelled like a dumpster behind a fish place in August. Suddenly before Cindy could even guess what they intended to do, they raised their bats and stepped toward the old man.

They clearly meant to hit him hard on the side of the head and back.

"Hey!" Cindy shouted. "Watch out!"

Her voice echoed down the street and she saw the bouncers turn toward her. They were too far away to really help, so she started toward the very one-sided fight.

The old guy spun and managed to get his long stick up to ward off one blow, but the other blow landed solidly. She didn't like the sound of that at all.

She had no idea what she would do against two weird guys with bats except maybe distract them, but she just couldn't let them beat up an old guy.

"Squeeze the pimple," she muttered as she ran. "Squeeze it hard!"

The old guy was on his knees, his hands and arms trying to cover his head. His big stick rattled on the pavement and rolled away from him.

She reached the two and planted the baton against the side of the guy with the third ear stuck in the middle of his forehead. He staggered away, but the other smelly guy hit the old man once more before the two of them turned away as she swung at them.

They half-ran, half-staggered back into the street. A moment later they vanished into thin air like they had never been there.

The shimmering that was still in the air at the mouth of the alley vanished as well as the old man slumped to the ground.

This Saint Patrick's Day was sure not turning out to be as much fun as she had hoped, and a whole lot weirder than she ever imagined possible.

Cindy shouted to the bouncer to call for help as she knelt beside the old guy, trying to not get his blood on her skirt. Bright green skirts just didn't come along very often.

"Hold on, mister," Cindy said. "Help's on the way."

The old guy focused his gaze on Cindy. "You're the bartender who was following me."

Cindy didn't need to be Nurse Betty to tell the old guy was in intense pain.

"Don't talk."

She flipped her green tie over her shoulder and eased closer to him as he fought to focus on her. He had a broken arm, and who knew what kind of internal injuries. It was amazing he was talking at all, considering how much blood he was losing from a cut on the side of his head.

"Did you see the shimmering in the alley?" the old guy demanded, staring up at Cindy. The guy had a gaze that could stop a speeding train and Cindy knew she had to answer him.

"Yeah, I saw it."

"And I knew you were watching me in the bar through my shield. You have a natural power, young woman. Someday you may make a good candidate."

"For what?" she asked.

"The Knight Watchmen, of course," he said, closing his eyes in pain."

"Rest. You need to save your strength." Cindy glanced up as the bouncer signaled her that help was on the way. A half dozen people were standing around in the street and on the sidewalk, watching and whispering.

The old guy chuckled. "You'd think after five hundred years, I'd learn to watch my back a little better."

Cindy ignored the five hundred years comment, now knowing for sure that the guy had escaped from a special home somewhere.

"They came out of nowhere at you," Cindy said, wishing like hell that the help that was coming would hurry up.

"Actually, they didn't," the old guy said, then coughed again, this time spitting up blood on his white beard.

That couldn't be good. Cindy knew that much from watching movies.

"I should have seen them coming," the old guy went on. "Just getting too old for this."

"Easy," Cindy said. "Just hang on."

"We got him, kid," a man said, shoving Cindy aside.

Cindy fell backward onto her butt on the curb of the sidewalk, then got up quickly and brushed off her skirt.

The two new arrivals crowded over the old guy.

She took a deep breath and focused on the night and the street around her. The air felt intense, crisp. For some reason the smells of the night air were sharper. Something about helping someone made everything feel more intense, almost like the sex had been with Twilight Zone Boy.

"He's going to make it," one man said, glancing around as he kneeled over the old guy.

Cindy finally looked at the two guys who shoved her aside. They were not medics. They both carried long wooden staffs and both were also wearing long trench coats. One was older than the other, but for some reason, she couldn't really see them clearly. Maybe they had all belonged to the same convention of flashers.

But she could see energy in and around both of the men, and strange carvings on the big sticks that were constantly in motion. Both men seemed to almost glow like soft lights.

"Glad to hear that," Cindy said.

"You can see us?"

She pointed up the street at the crowd. "I think most everyone saw what happened."

Slowly like an out-of-focus camera viewfinder coming into focus, the two of them came clear.

One of the guys was about her age and really cute. Far too cute to be wearing a stupid trench coat.

The other looked very old, only with no white beard like the dead guy. He looked like the type that would flash a person on a street corner and then just laugh.

The cute guy stared at Cindy and smiled. "Seems we have a future recruit."

Cindy didn't let his smile flutter her heart for more than a second, maybe two, even though it was an amazingly lust-filled smile. Or at least that was what she wanted it to be at that moment.

He stood and offered her his hand, pulling her to her feet. His touch sent electric shivers through her entire body and her knees felt like they might not hold.

God he was good-looking, glowing like he had a lot of light coming through his skin. He was taller than she was by a few inches and had thick, wide shoulders. His thick, brown hair was just the kind she liked to run her fingers through. She started to raise her hands to do just that, then stopped herself. His facial features all worked together, nothing too long or too short. And his smile reached his wonderful green eyes that seemed to see right through her.

If someone last week would have asked her to describe her perfect man, she would have described the guy in front of her.

Oh, no, he couldn't be gay, could he? Maybe if she jumped him right here in the street, she would find out.

She shook her head yet again and the intense feeling eased just a little. She had to get herself under control. The old guy getting beat up shouldn't be shaking her up this much.

"Squeeze the pimple," she said, softly.

"Excuse me?" the guy said, touching his face near his nose.

"Nothing," she said. She took a deep breath and forced herself to think. The fantastically good-looking guy in the trench coat just stared at her.

She had to say something, get to know this guy. But what could she say? After a long moment the need to say something overwhelmed her and she said the first thing that came to her mind.

"I'm not going to be a flasher."

Oh, God, how lame was that?

Both men laughed and the older one said, "I think with your body, the world will be sad about that."

The young guy's laugh was as good as his looks, and again she thought about just jumping his golden-glowing body right there in front of the crowd around the old guy, who still hadn't come to yet. Now that might make the paper.

And no doubt it would make the Internet as well. Not the way she wanted to be famous. Damn, she had been horny before, but never like this. What the hell was going on?

A siren in the distance broke that thought.

Get it together. Ignore the fact that he smells like freshly baked rolls, that his skin glows like a perfect sun tan, that his laugh is infectious, and his green eyes show he's smart, damn smart.

Ignore all that.

He's wearing a trench coat for God's sake.

What other bad habits does he have?

Actually, she more than anything wanted to see exactly what was under that trench coat, but managed to not say that out loud as well.

"I've got to get back to work," Cindy managed to finally say. "Sorry about your friend there."

"First," the cute guy said, "could you tell us what happened?"

"She saved my life, that's what," the old guy said, opening his eyes.

"Glad to see you coming around," she said.

"Thanks to you," he said. "I was getting a leprechaun out of the bar and she somehow saw us and followed me out here. I got attacked from behind by a couple of trolls pretending to be zombies, clearly run by the Unseelie Court, and she beat them away from me before they could kill me."

Both of the other men in trench coats nodded, very serious looks on their faces.

Cindy stared at them. It wasn't a convention of flashers. It was a convention of nut cases.

The sirens were getting louder. Help was almost here.

The guy helped the old man to his feet while the younger guy handed him back his staff.

"Hey," Cindy said. "Aren't you disturbing a crime scene?"

They all laughed, which made the old guy cough.

She was getting damned tired of them just laughing at everything she said. If she wanted to do stand-up, she'd go down the street to the local comedy club. At least there, the audience wouldn't be flashers. Or at least not all of them.

"I'll take care of our friend and the crowd," the cute guy said to the other.

"Thank you, young woman," the old guy said as the other guy helped him toward a spinning hole in the air that had just opened. "I owe you."

Then the old guy and the other guy were gone, leaving Cindy standing beside the cute guy. Her heart fluttered with both excitement and panic.

"So what was all that?" she asked, hoping her voice sounded as firm as she wanted it to sound.

"We belong to a group of men and women called The Knight Watchmen. We protect humanity from all the fairies, trolls, and other creatures that live in dimensions among humans. We are like the policemen of the Unseen World."

"Yeah," she said, shaking her head. "And I'm Alice and I've fallen through a rabbit hole.

He laughed and extended his hand. "My name is Sean. Sean Ballard. I'm from Seattle originally, but that was a while back now. You wouldn't believe me just how long ago."

Cindy almost didn't take his hand, then she remembered how nice his touch felt. "Cindy Kemp. Student and bartender from Chicago, now living in the Twilight Zone."

Again electricity seemed to flow through their touch, and he seemed to light up again with that golden tan glow.

Maybe she should start calling herself "Electric Girl" because of the way she kept lighting up Cute-Flasher Boy.

He actually held her hand a little longer than he should have. She didn't mind one damned bit. A very large part of her wanted to not be angry, but instead to just learn everything about this wonderful hunk. But somehow her anger won the fight and she pulled her hand away.

"So really, what is going on?"

"Did you see the *Men in Black* movie?" he asked. "We're the magical version of the guys from that movie. And we've been around a lot longer."

"Cute," Cindy said. The feeling of wanting to jump his bones vanished like toilet paper flushing down the drain. "So next you're going to do a flashie-thing to me and I won't remember any of this."

"Yeah, I'm afraid so," he said, looking slightly sad. "But you have natural power like I did. The Knight Watchmen have noticed you now. When your power comes in full, you will be recruited and we can meet again."

She stared at him. The crazy things he was saying made as much sense as anything for what she had seen, but she still wasn't going to believe it.

"Come on," he said, gently taking her by the arm and turning her back toward the bar. The sirens were getting close, real close.

"One more question," she asked as they walked the short distance back toward the crowd, letting the electricity flash between them. She wanted to jump him so bad, she almost couldn't control herself. And he smelled so much like fresh baked bread, she wanted to just lick his skin. "Why do you smell so good?"

He smiled. "All good magic smells wonderful. Bad magic, like those trolls, smells awful."

She shook her head and again the voice cleared. "Smelly magic," she muttered to herself. "Great, what's next?"

"For now, nothing I'm afraid. But maybe in the future we'll meet again. I can hope. And maybe, if you are strong enough, you'll remember me."

Her heart actually skipped a beat and her breath got short.

Then he raised that stupid long stick of his and banged it into the ground and everything went white.

* * *

"So what happened out there?" Judy, the other bartender asked as Cindy ducked under the gate and headed back to her station.

"Just the first fight of the night," Cindy said, putting the black baton back where it belonged under the bar. "They all ran off before the cops got there."

Suddenly Judy leaned over toward Cindy, sniffing. "Wow, what have you been eating?"

Cindy glanced at Judy who had followed her down the bar, sniffing. Had her partner behind the bar lost her last brain cell? "Nothing, why?"

"You smell like freshly baked bread."

In front of her both Ben and Wolf-Boy nodded.

"You do!" Ben shouted over the noise of the bar.

Everyone had lost it and she needed to get back to work.

"It's a new perfume," she shouted back at them. "Called Magic."

And when she said that, for just a moment, the most handsome man she could ever imagine appeared in her mind, laughing.

Damn, she was so horny, she might have to call Twilight Zone Boy if she didn't find someone tonight.

But the party for St. Patrick's Day was just getting started. She just might meet someone yet. Anything was possible on St. Patrick's Day.

~

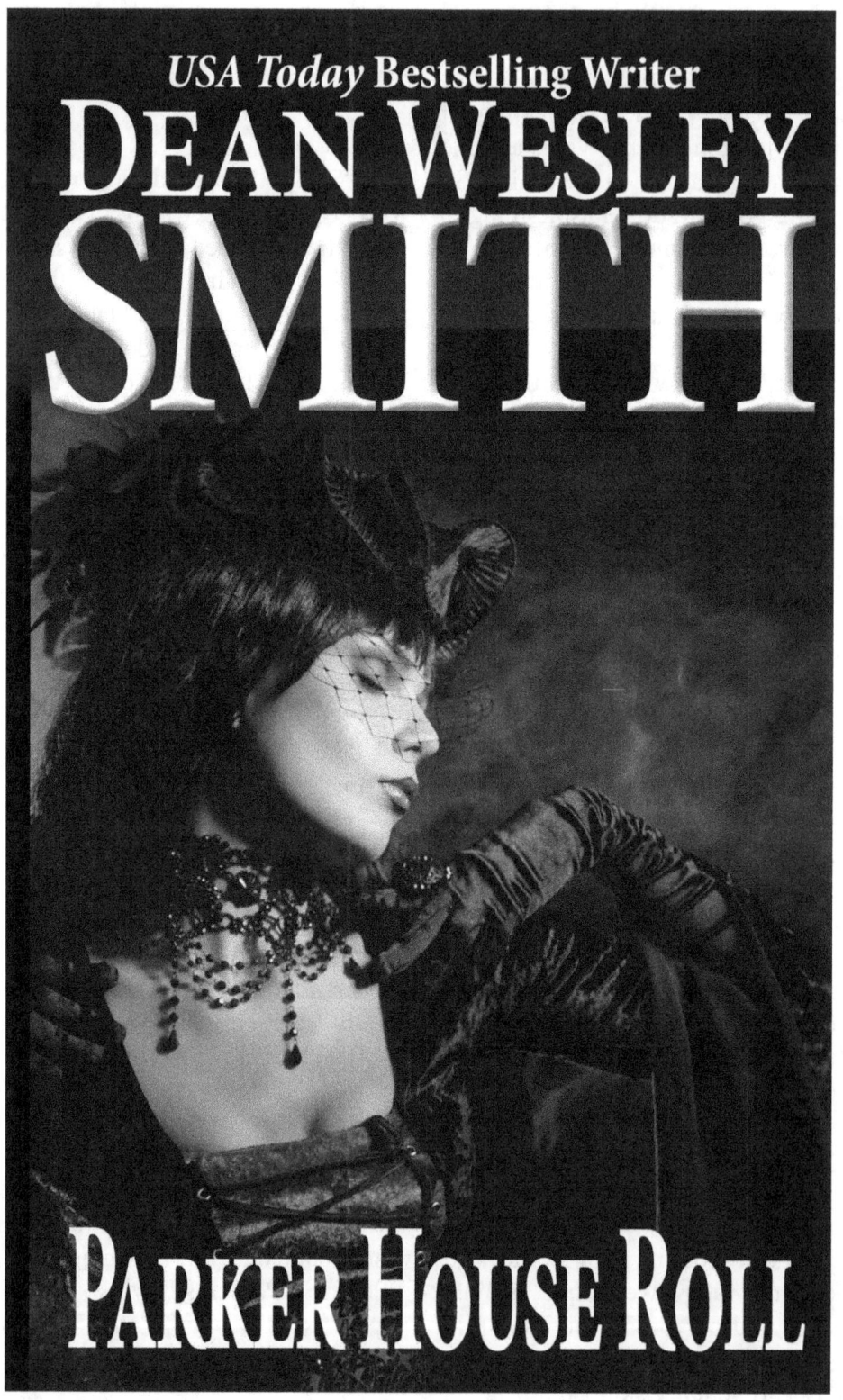

USA *Today* Bestselling Writer
DEAN WESLEY
SMITH

PARKER HOUSE ROLL

Buckey the Space Pirate needs a lesson on costumes.

Who better to teach it than Fred, his talking oak tree friend?

Buckey will even listen to Fred's limericks to get Fred to be quiet in front of Buckey's new girlfriend.

But the lesson on costumes quickly becomes more than just a lesson on clothing.

A Parker House Roll
A Buckey the Space Pirate Story

WHEN YOUR BEST friend is a four year old, time-traveling talking oak tree named Fred, you don't introduce him around to your other friends. And especially to a girl you are trying to impress.

So when Sally, my new girl, and I spent the June afternoon in my mother's backyard, under a huge orange beach umbrella, talking about what costumes we were going to design for the next science fiction convention, Fred had strict instructions to not say a word.

My mother's house was one of those standard subdivision square things with a patch of grass, a bunch of bushes, and about five small trees in the back yard, one of which was Fred.

I had figured it was the safest place to plant him. I planted Little Fred and when he started talking just like his older version had, I convinced my mom to put up a seven foot wood fence all the way around the yard. I told her it was for privacy, but mostly it was because I got too many stares from the neighbors because I would stand in the snow talking to a small tree.

I suppose that if one of the neighbors talked to trees, I would have stared, too.

The fence turned out to have added benefits in the summer, especially when I wanted to have a girl over. And my mom sure didn't seem to mind me hanging around, since I mostly spent my nights in my apartment near the university.

But the fence didn't solve the problem of Fred. He had already cost me two girl friends. Whenever he spoke they just wouldn't believe that what was talking was the baby oak tree. They always thought it was me playing some sort of stupid joke on them. And since Fred usually insulted them, convincing them it wasn't me had proven to be very, very difficult.

So that morning, before Sally arrived, I stood in the back yard and sternly lectured the young tree to behave himself. I even went so far as to tell him that if he said a word in front of Sally, I would never listen to another one of his stupid limericks.

The threat had worked. Not one word from the tree. For two hours Sally and I laughed, drank cold, fresh-squeezed lemonade mom made and planned our costumes.

Fred kept quiet. But as I came back into the yard after walking Sally to her car, Fred quickly started off with his revenge.

"There was a young girl of Oak Knoll,
Who thought it exceedingly droll,
At a masquerade ball,
Dressed in nothing at all,
To back in as a Parker House roll."

I dropped down onto the lawn chair and pretended to not pay attention to the six-foot tall oak tree with fifty-seven leaves. Fred had told me that number one day last week just to impress me with his growth. It had now been over four years since I had taken an acorn from the first talking Fred, Big Fred I liked to call him, and conceived Little Fred.

"You do know what a Parker House roll is, don't you?" Fred asked, his voice seeming to come from everywhere around the little tree.

Actually one day Fred and I figured out that he was really projecting his voice inside people's heads. But it always seemed that his voice was coming from the air around the tree. It had taken me two days of climbing in the huge branches of Big Fred before I believed the talking wasn't just a practical joke of some kind or another.

"That limerick dates from the early 1940s. Its history is interesting."

Again I just sipped on the cold lemonade and stared at the notes and sketches Sally and I had been making. He knew I hated learning about the limericks almost as much as I hated hearing them.

"You know," Fred said, pretending that I wasn't pretending to ignore him, "that you two have no real costume sense at all."

I laughed. "Yeah, as if a tree knows anything about costumes."

"Actually," Fred said, his voice taking on a British accent and sounding very formal. "I know a great deal. Many a costumed human has reposed under oak trees over the centuries. Remember you were dressed in a very strange manner on the night we first met."

"How could I forget?" My date and I had left a costume party and gone looking for a little fun in an outdoor private place. I was dressed as Bucky the Space Pirate and she was dressed as the Moon Queen.

We ended up under the old limbs of Big Fred, down in the corner of Center Park. Just as we were getting, as they say, "down to it," Big Fred decided to talk to us with a limerick insulting a part of my date's private anatomy. She never believed it wasn't me doing the talking, even though my mouth was in a place that made talking somewhat difficult.

We never went out again.

And I have hated Fred's limericks ever since.

"That is nothing," Fred said, going on as if it really mattered to me, "when we think of the humans of previous centuries. Their normal dress would function very well for costumes today. There is a long tradition of that, too, as you well know."

He paused for a moment. "If you want to see a real costume, hold onto one of my limbs and I can take you to the tree that Queen Elizabeth was sitting under when she was told her sister died and she was Queen of England. She had on a very fancy dress that day. It would make a wonderful Martian Goddess design for Sally."

"Thanks," I said, "but I think—"

"In fact, I even know what Elizabeth was reading at the time. I wouldn't mind taking you to see."

I shook my head and went back to studying the sketches of costumes we had talked about.

Oak trees had this ability to move back and forth through time along, for lack of a better way of putting it, their family trees. To prove that to me Big Fred had convinced me to climb into his limbs. He took me all the way back to the dinosaurs, where it seemed as if one of them was trying to knock me out of the tree. Scared me so bad I had never had the courage to try it again.

"You know," Fred went on as if being silent for the two hours had dammed up a flood of words, "actually what the early British kings wore would make a much better choice of costume for you. In fact, poor young King Edward VI dressed most times very much like your Bucky costume. Only with more class."

"Not a chance," I said. "If anything Bucky dresses more like a Musketeer."

Fred laughed. "As if you would know. Come on. Grab a branch and I'll take you back to see poor little King Edward. He was poisoned, you know. That's why he died before he turned sixteen."

I stared at the little tree, its leaves drooping in the heat of the afternoon. Damn him. He knew I loved a good mystery. And he knew I was interested in the history of that period of Britain. He had me.

"How would you know that?"

Again Fred just laughed. "Only way you're going to believe me is if I show you."

I dropped the notebook on the grass. "Damn it, Fred. After that ride back to the dinosaurs, the last thing I want to do is have you whisk me into the past again. It isn't a normal thing to do."

"As if what you did with Sally the other night was?"

"Fred! How could you see? It was dark out here."

Fred didn't say a word, so I grabbed my lemonade and went back into the house. Mom was off running errands. No way some stupid little tree was going to get the best of me.

Twenty minutes later I found myself sitting on the ground at Fred's base, holding onto his lowest little branch.

At least Fred had the decency to not laugh.

"Hold on tight," Fred said.

The world went black for a full second, then the shock of cold, winter-like air slapped me.

I gripped onto the rough, cold bark of the huge oak limb I found myself straddling and glanced quickly around at the limbs and other trees.

Damn this felt so real. Fred had always promised me that I would really never leave my backyard. Yet when Big Fred had taken me back to the dinosaurs, I swore I felt that dinosaur hit the tree.

And right now I would swear that I was holding onto a very large limb in a very cold forest, God knew where.

My heart pounded in my chest and the blood rushed through my ears so fast I could barely hear. All I wanted to do was cry for Fred to take me back.

What the hell had I been thinking?

Man wasn't made to go riding oak trees through time.

There was a rustling noise and I glanced down.

I was about fifteen feet above the ground in what looked to be a pretty thick forest. Below me were two men, one bent over working at something in the low brush. The man standing looked to be of a higher class. He wore breeches, with a white blouse-like shirt and a cloth coat and hat.

The man working the brush was obviously a beggar of some sort. His rough clothes were filthy and all the way up in the tree I could smell the man's odor. Layers of sweat and onions. Rotted onions.

As I looked closer it became clear that even the standing man's clothes were dirty and his hair under his hat looked as if it hadn't been washed in a year. I guessed that both their odors were mixing to make it up in the tree this far. My eyes were going to start watering in a minute.

"Fred!" I whispered. "Get me out of here."

But Fred didn't answer.

The man on his knees stood, his hands covered with dirt. He handed something carefully to the other man, who looked at it for a moment, nodded and then placed it in a small cloth bag. He flipped

the beggar a coin and turned and walked away through the woods.

The beggar quickly stuck the coin in a dark place in his coat and headed the other direction down the path. Neither looked back.

After they were out of sight I looked around to make sure no one else was in sight, then asked, "Fred? Who were they? What were they doing? Now that I have seen this, can I go back? It's colder than hell out here."

Fred's laugh came softly, as if from a long distance. "Actually who they are doesn't really matter. But what they were doing most definitely does. Notice down where they were in the bushes. See the mushrooms in the fairy ring configuration? That is what they were picking."

"So?" I asked.

"Those are Panther Mushrooms, or as they are scientifically called, *Amanita pantherina*. Sometimes they are called Fly Agaric, because they are used to kill flies."

"Poison?"

"Very much so. Hang on. Off to the next stop."

"Wait. I don't—" But it was too late.

There was a second of darkness and I found myself on a much smaller limb, with much less to hang onto. And it seemed even colder, if that was possible.

This oak tree occupied a solo position on the edge of a huge expanse of lawn and hedges on the edge of a cobblestone road. The road seemed to be the main entrance to a huge palace or whatever they were called in Britain. The same man who had pocketed the mushrooms rode up the road and under the branch I sat on. I noticed after he passed that he had been the one who smelled of rotten onions.

"This is where King Edward VI is staying at the moment," Fred said. "Hang on."

Again there was a second of blackness and I found myself in another oak tree on what seemed to be the exact opposite side of the same huge building. The sun was brighter and the air seemed slightly warmer.

"It's two days later," Fred said, his voice almost a whisper. "Watch."

"Why are you whispering?" I asked Fred.

But he didn't have time to answer.

A small boy, white-skinned and thin, walked up and sat on a stone bench below the very limb I clung to. He was dressed in green tights, an ornate jeweled vest of a dark green color, and bright-jeweled shoes, also dark green.

Fred was right. It would make a great costume for a science fiction convention. But it needed a hat. The king wasn't wearing one.

A man dressed completely in black with a white powdered wig that didn't even pretend to hide his black hair walked slowly up to the boy and handed him a brown-looking drink in an ornate chalice.

The boy stared at the drink for a moment, then took a big gulp and made a face. If the stuff tasted as bad as it looked, it was amazing the kid was drinking it.

"Medicine," Fred whispered. "Made up of nine spoonfuls of a liquid distilled from spearmint and red fennel, liverwort and turnip, dates and raisins, an ounce of mace, two sticks of celery, and the quarters of a sow nine days old. Of course, it also is laced with a small amount of the ground up mushrooms."

"You're kidding?" I said, my voice almost breaking out of a whisper. The young king and his doctor didn't seem to notice.

"I'm not," Fred said. "The king will be dead by early July. Poisoned from the medicine he was taking to get better."

"But who? Who wanted him dead? Who is the guy giving it to him?"

"That is just one of his doctors," Fred said. "He doesn't know, I will wager. But thousands want the young king dead. This is the time of the great fights between Protestant reformers and Catholics. Actually most who know the king was poisoned think it was the Duke of Northumberland who did it. He had the young king sign a Devise for Succession right before he died to give the crown to his wife, a Lady Jane Grey."

"But Northumberland was beheaded by Bloody Mary. Right?" I felt proud remembering that much of my English history.

"Correct," Fred said.

Below me the young king handed back the chalice to the doctor and stood. "Dost thou hear voices?" he asked, his voice thin and high.

The doctor shook his head no.

The king looked around for a moment, then shrugged and moved off toward the palace at a slow walk.

"Can he hear us?" I asked. "Please tell me he can't hear us."

"Well," Fred said, "did you get enough information for a new costume. Did you notice the detail of the neck-line and how—"

"He could hear us, couldn't he?"

"The king? Yes, I suppose he could. But did you also get a good look at how he did the tights with those shoes?"

"Damn it, Fred. You said I wasn't really here."

Fred laughed. "Actually you are and you aren't. If someone was to look in the backyard they would see you sitting beside me for about five seconds. That's all the time we will be gone."

"But what happened if I had fallen out of this tree right on his head?"

I looked down at the stone bench where the King of England had just been sitting. I was going to be sick.

Fred laughed. "I suppose you would have changed history. There has been a great deal of speculation as to how things would have changed if Edward had lived. But no scenarios worked out with someone falling out of a tree and killing him."

Again Fred laughed.

"This is NOT funny," I screamed at him.

Across the lawn both the king and the doctor turned and looked back in my direction. Then the king started back and the doctor clapped his hands to summon someone from near the palace.

"Fred! Get me out of here."

"But this would be such an interesting occurrence, don't you think?"

"No! I don't!" I screamed again. Then in the lowest, meanest voice I could manage I said, "Now get me out of here."

The world went black and then everything came back to light. But I was still sitting in a damn oak tree in England.

And it was still cold.

"Fred!" I said, my voice as mean and as mad as I could make it sound. "I want to go home. Now!"

"In a moment," Fred said.

I took a deep breath and looked around.

Across an open square from the tree was the famous Tower Hill I had seen hundreds of times in pictures. A crowd filled the open area and there were three men on a raised platform, all dressed in black. One appeared to be a priest. And as I watched one man with his hands tied behind his back kneeled and put his head in what looked to be a trough.

The third man, with very little hesitation, swung a huge ax and cut the kneeling man's head off.

I couldn't believe my eyes.

The man's head rolled into a basket and the executioner reached down and picked it up for the cheering crowd to see.

Can't Get Enough of Buckey and Fred?
These stories and more are
available at your favorite booksellers.

Blood still squirted from the headless body as the heart kept pumping and still more blood dripped from the head.

I felt dizzy and sick as I gripped the rough bark of the oak. "Fred," I whispered. "Who was that?"

"Northumberland," Fred said. "Just thought you would want the entire story of what happened to the man who poisoned a British King."

"Home? Please?"

"Your wish is my command, oh Master," Fred said.

The summer heat washed over me and the second I felt the ground under my butt I let go of Fred's little limb and lay back on the warm grass.

The sun felt heavenly against my face and my hands tingled as they warmed up.

"Well," Fred said. "Did you get some good ideas for costumes? You do that King Edward one and you will really impress that Sally friend of yours."

I sat up and stared at the little oak tree. "Fred, why isn't the poisoning of Edward in the history books?"

"For the same reason a lot of crimes go unpunished. No proof. You would be amazed at what we trees have seen you humans do to each other over the years. In fact, you know the skeleton that was found by the lake last week?"

"Yeah," I said, not really wanting to know what Fred was going to say.

"He was killed. Twenty-one years ago. Grab a limb and I'll show you who did it."

I scooted back on the grass a few more feet away from the little tree.

"I think I will pass on that one."

I could just see myself trying to explain to the police how I knew what happened in a twenty-one year old murder. Better in this case to just not know.

"Suit yourself," Fred said. "You want to hear another limerick? It's about costumes again."

I groaned and lay back on the grass so that the hot sun on my face would chase the cold and the picture of that young king from my mind.

"Oh, good," Fred said, his voice bubbling with happiness. "This limerick is also from the early forties and is very similar to the other one I told you this afternoon."

Again all I could do was groan.

"A nudist girl wearing three raisins,
A masquerade prize was her goal,
The judges said, 'Lookie,
From the front she's a cookie,
From the back she's a Parker House roll.'"

"You do know what a Parker House roll is, don't you?"

No way was I going to tell the damn little tree that I didn't.

~

DEAN WESLEY SMITH

USA TODAY BESTSELLING AUTHOR

GHOST
AGENT

THE DEEP SUNSET

A GHOST OF A CHANCE NOVEL

WITH POKER BOY

Attorney Gail Kelly dies suddenly on her way to dinner and within minutes meets Dan Carson, aka Sunset.

A Ghost Agent for over a hundred years, Sunset offers to help train Gail. But somewhere in their lust for each other (yes, ghosts can be horny) they stumble onto a plan that could destroy the world.

Dan and Gail and other Ghost Agents must join up with Poker Boy and his team and a bunch of gods to try to save the world just one more time.

USA Today *bestselling author Dean Wesley Smith brings you the fifth book in the crazy Ghost of a Chance series.*

The Deep Sunset
A Ghost of a Chance Novel

PART ONE
A Meet Cute But Dead

One

YOU NEVER PLAN on dying.

Well, at least when you are young you never plan on it.

Gail Kelly sure hadn't. She was twenty-eight, still slim and single, and still very happy in her job as a prosecuting attorney in a small Oregon coastal county. And she was really good at it as well.

Dying was a long ways from her thinking. In fact, marriage and kids were still a long ways from her thinking. She didn't even have a steady boyfriend.

So when that chip truck came across the center line on a curve on Highway 101 and hit her before she could even blink, she didn't have time to think about dying then either.

It just happened so fast.

One minute she was driving her wonderful red BMW convertible, headed south to meet some friends for some drinks and dinner, the next she was sitting on the soft hillside next to the highway.

A very friendly woman about Gail's age was kneeling next to her, smiling. And a handsome man stood on the highway, watching. Standing beside him was a short guy dressed in a purple jogging suit who looked completely out of place on the rough Oregon coast.

Both the man and the woman looked comfortable, dressed in jeans and expensive shirts and running shoes.

"Go slow," the woman next to her said.

"So what happened?" Gail asked, trying to look around, but only seeing the three people and the edge of the highway. The pine forest around her and the ocean below seemed to be a blur.

"You were in an accident," the woman said.

Gail looked down at herself, her legs, her arms. Nothing seemed to be bleeding.

She had on a blue silk blouse with a jogging bra under it, jeans, and her best Nike running shoes. There didn't seem to be a mark or scratch anywhere. The road was a good ten feet below her. Why she would have climbed up here was beyond her.

And she felt fine.

Gail stood and the woman helped her up with a gentle touch on her arm. The two of them went down the soft hillside and through a slight ditch to where the handsome man and the guy in purple stood on the pavement.

"I'm Jewel," the woman said. "This is my partner, Tommy."

The good-looking man nodded and smiled slightly at Gail. He had short military-cut brown hair and broad shoulders. Gail could see in his eyes that he was worried about her.

"This is K.J.," Jewel said, indicating the short man with the purple jogging suit. Now that Gail was closer, she could also see that the man's hair was purple and his shoes were purple and he wore purple fingernail polish. Wow, she hoped he wasn't going into any bars along this coast. He didn't fit. In fact, she had a hunch this K.J. person didn't fit anywhere outside of San Francisco.

K.J. just nodded and smiled, showing purple caps on his teeth.

Gail looked around, trying to focus, but actually not seeing anything but the hill and some trees and the blue of the ocean beyond.

"I must have bumped my head," Gail said. "I'm having trouble focusing."

"That will pass," Jewel said.

"How do you know?" Gail asked staring into the woman's green eyes. "Are you a doctor?"

"Actually, she is," the guy in purple said. "But that's not why it will pass."

"Then why?" Gail asked, slowly starting to get angry.

"Because you're dead, that's why," a voice said from behind her.

She turned to look into the dark brown eyes of the most handsome man she had ever seen. He looked like he had come right out of court and had just taken off his tie. He had perfectly styled brown hair and those large brown eyes were places to get lost in. His dark suit was made of silk, as clearly was his shirt, and he had on expensive shoes Gail was convinced were not sold anywhere in Oregon.

"I'm Dan, but a lot of my friends just call me Sunset."

Gail was convinced those brown eyes of his were seeing right through her. Because of that, it took her a moment to realize what he had said.

"Dead?"

"Oh, nice timing, Sunset," the guy in purple said, clearly disgusted.

The handsome man nodded to Gail, ignoring the guy in purple. "Afraid so. But trust me, you're going to love it."

Sunset smiled at her as he took her elbow and turned her up the road. Suddenly, everything came into clear focus around her.

The evening still had some light as the sun had just set over the ocean. The forest was on her left, the sea down a steep cliff on her right. She could see what was left of her wonderful convertible under the front of a large truck right in the middle of the two-lane highway.

Someone was hosing the entire thing down with a fire extinguisher and a number of others were standing to one side, most with their hands over their mouths.

She could see part of her body twisted in an unnatural way against the grill of the truck. And the truck driver had come about halfway through the window of his truck and was still just hanging there. He looked dead or almost dead.

The sight was so horrific, it took her a moment to realize that was her against the front of the truck.

Holy shit, Sunset was right.

She was dead.

How could that even be possible?

She turned to face him and her knees started to give out.

Sunset and Jewel caught her and eased her to the ground.

"So, Sunset, what are you doing here?" K.J asked.

Jewel held Gail's arm and Tommy, her partner had stepped back.

"Here to train Gail," Sunset said.

Gail had her head down and was focusing on just breathing. She knew this feeling from having too many drinks and she knew just solid breaths of air would help.

"Jewel and Tommy train the new recruits," K.J. said.

"Not this time," Sunset said.

"Train me to do what?" Gail asked, finally letting the anger come out as she stood. She didn't need any training.

Jewel patted Gail's shoulder and stepped back.

"To be dead and worthwhile," Sunset said, smiling at her.

"How about I be *not* dead?" Gail said.

"Not really possible," Sunset said, pointing in the direction of the wreck. "It was your time. See the truck driver? It's almost his time as well. Watch."

Sunset turned her toward the wreck again as suddenly the truck driver sort of moved away from the cab of his truck while his body still remained sticking out of the window.

For a moment he seemed perfectly healthy even though his body in the window clearly wasn't.

Then the driver looked upward and sort of floated in the air and after a moment was gone.

"So how come I don't float out of here?" Gail asked. "And get away from you nut-jobs."

She was angry and scared, but mostly angry, and when angry, she pulled no punches.

"The powers-that-be think you would be a good help in saving people," Jewel said, her voice gentle.

"I don't save people," Gail said, her voice stern. "I put people in jail."

"Sometimes that's saving people," Sunset said, smiling at her and clearly ignoring her anger. "You hungry?"

That question surprised her. "I thought you said I was dead."

"Oh, you are," Sunset said. "And from here on out, the food tastes better."

"You are just confusing Gail," Jewel said, stepping up and putting herself between Gail and those amazing brown eyes.

"I did just fine when I died," Sunset said.

"That's not what I heard," K.J. said.

Gail glanced over. The little guy in purple clearly had some issues with Sunset.

Sunset was about to say something when Jewel raised her hand. "Not here, not now. You can help in Gail's training, if she wants help, but not until I say so."

Gail was impressed. Jewel clearly was the one in charge here.

Sunset looked at Jewel who clearly wasn't backing down.

Finally he nodded to Jewel and smiled at Gail. "See you soon I hope."

Gail was so confused, all she could do was nod.

Then Sunset just vanished right in front of her eyes.

"I'm having the weirdest damn dream," Gail said, deciding to sit down once again on the pavement.

Jewel helped her down and then looked at K.J. "Find out what that was all about. We'll be at the Golden Nugget having dinner."

K.J. nodded and then the little guy in purple also just vanished.

"I haven't even had a drink yet," Gail said, shaking her head.

Then she looked up at her twisted body against the front of the truck and wondered if she would ever drink again.

Two

SUNSET APPEARED ON his favorite stool at the Sushi bar in Fong's Restaurant just off Broadway in Portland. He was angry at himself. He had screwed up something awful with that introduction and he knew better than to go up against Jewel and Tommy and K.J.

Sunset had been a Ghost of a Chance agent as long as K.J. Actually, slightly longer since Sunset died in 1901 and K.J. hadn't shown up until a few years later.

But Jewel and Tommy were already forces in the agency, even though they were fairly new. They had worked with

Poker Boy and others, which was far more than Sunset had ever done. Up until just a few years ago, he hadn't even known the superhero part of all this existed.

Sunset always liked to work alone and he had done just fine that way for over a hundred years. But now, the powers-that-be had told him he was getting a partner even though he had no desire for one.

He hadn't expected his new partner to be so beautiful. That had caught him by surprise, but was still no excuse for him being a jerk. He had figured she could just stand the blunt truth.

He knew she was smart. He had researched her life a little and knew she was still single, a prosecuting attorney with almost a perfect record, and she liked her drinks.

Sunset liked his drinks as well, which is how he had gotten his name. He loved to drink tequila sunsets, which was basically like a tequila sunrise with tequila and orange juice, only instead of the sweet red grenadine syrup that sunk to the bottom of the orange juice, a red soda water was put on the top, holding the red to the top of glass.

And it was a lot less sweet than a sunrise. He had started drinking them back when he worked the New York area after the Second World War. No bar out west served them regularly, so he made them in his Portland condo for himself. He never seemed to tire of them.

He grabbed a plate of California rolls as a waitress carried it past and started to work on them. He loved how, as a ghost, he could eat the ghost part of any meal and no one knew he was doing it.

And the ghost part of a meal tasted so much better than a regular meal ever had when he was alive.

He sat eating and thinking about Gail and how they were going to have to work together and how, now after seeing her, he actually wanted to try to work with her.

Damn, he wished he hadn't screwed up the introduction.

He needed to do something about his mistake and do it now.

He pushed what was left of the sushi roll aside and stood.

"Come on, Sunset. You can do humility. Honestly you can."

With that he jumped to the Golden Nugget Buffet in Las Vegas. He was going to apologize and see if he could help in her training, see if he and Gail really could be a team.

He didn't do apologies that often. As a Ghost Agent, working alone, he had never really needed to. But he had a hunch with Gail, it would be worth taking his pride down a few notches.

Three

ONE MINUTE GAIL had been on the main coastal highway in Oregon looking at an ugly wreck that she had supposedly been in, then she found herself standing near a wooden table in a well-lit buffet.

The smell of fresh beef and baking bread surrounded her and a low level of talking filled the air.

The buffet was all in brown wood tones and bright polished brass. It was a huge place and the table they were beside was in one corner and a distance away from any other people.

The place was comfortable, even though impossible. Gail knew for a fact she couldn't be here.

Yet it seemed she was.

It sure felt and smelled and sounded like she was.

Jewel and Tommy were both standing beside her.

"How did we get here and where is here?" Gail asked after looking around.

"The Golden Nugget Buffet in downtown Las Vegas," Jewel said, indicating that Gail should take a seat. Jewel pulled the chair out slightly for her. "We jumped you here from Oregon."

"I'll get us some water," Tommy said and turned away.

Gail sat down facing the buffet area and Jewel sat beside her at the four-person square table.

"This is the strangest dream I have ever had," Gail said, shaking her head.

None of this was making any sense to her. Not a bit of it. She hadn't even had dinner yet, so it couldn't be something she ate. And she really didn't know anyone or had even been to Las Vegas before, so a place her dream would take her shouldn't be here.

"We all think this is a dream at first," Jewel said. "I know I did."

"So did I," Tommy said, handing Gail a glass of water and then giving Jewel one as well.

Gail made herself take a long drink. The water tasted pure and fresh and wonderful. Best glass of plain water she had ever had.

Now she knew she was dreaming when water tasted good.

Jewel must have been reading her expression. "You think that was good, wait until you taste the food."

"So the Sunset guy was right?" Gail asked.

"He was," Jewel said.

Right at that moment Gail noticed that Jewel had a classically beautiful face and eyes that seemed to really show kindness. And clearly she and Tommy, who also had a classic handsomeness about him, were a team.

"Who is he?" Gail asked as Sunset's handsome face and perfectly dressed body came clearly back to her mind.

"He's another Ghost Agent like we are," Jewel said. "Like you'll be if you decide to stay after you learn everything."

Gail just shook her head. "You know how silly that sounds?"

Jewel nodded and smiled. "Very silly. But very serious at the same time."

"Okay," Gail said, ignoring that her stomach was rumbling just twenty minutes after she had supposedly died, "until I wake up, I'll play along. What do Ghost Agents do?"

"We save people," Jewel said.

Beside her Tommy just nodded.

"Yet we are ghosts?" Gail asked.

Jewel and Tommy both nodded.

Gail shook her head. All this silliness was impossible to believe. She must have caught a horrid bug and was feverish and in a hospital somewhere. Fever dreams were the only thing that could make any of this make sense.

And if she was having a bad fever dream she would think of dying. That made sense.

"Let me see if I can show you a few things," Tommy said.

He stood, then walked right through the table in front of Gail as if it wasn't there.

Then he walked over to a couple starting to leave and let them walk through him.

Then he came back and sat down. He was frowning and Jewel noticed it as well.

Jewel reached over and put her hand on Tommy's arm.

"That older couple that went through me just had their last meal," Tommy said.

"They have used the last of their money. They have a gun in their car."

Gail felt stunned. "How do you know that?"

"When you touch a living person, you can read their thoughts," Jewel said, not looking away from Tommy.

"I'm going to follow them," Tommy said, standing. "See if I can figure out something to do."

"What can he do?" Gail asked.

"So many things," Jewel said. "And so few at the same time."

At that moment Sunset arrived, standing to one side of the table. His silk suit was perfect, his shirt open under the suit jacket, and he had a slight look of worry in his large brown eyes.

Gail felt a jolt go through her as she looked up at him. She had never had that reaction to a man before, ever. More than likely part of her fever dream.

And he looked slightly startled as well, then nodded to her and turned to Jewel. "If I apologize for my boorish behavior on the coast, and promise to behave myself and help where I can, may I join you?"

Jewel nodded and smiled, indicating he should take a seat next to Gail.

Then Jewel stood. "Tommy's going to need my help with that couple. I'll be back when I can."

And she vanished.

"What couple?" Sunset asked.

"An elderly couple that walked through Tommy when he was trying to convince me I'm not dreaming," Gail said. "Tommy said the couple had just had their last meal and were out of money and he wasn't sure what they were going to do next."

"Oh, no," Sunset said softly.

"Is that what you ghosts do? Save old folks from themselves?"

Sunset nodded, clearly serious. "Sometimes that, sometimes more. Jewel and Tommy and K.J., along with a superhero and his team and a few of the gods helped save the world just three months ago."

"Saved the world?" Gail asked, ignoring the gods and the superhero part.

Sunset nodded and looked at her for the first time since she sat down. "Jewel will tell you all about it at some point. But I want to apologize for my first meeting. I hope you will give me a second chance to get off on the right foot."

Gail smiled and offered her hand.

"I'm Gail," she said.

He took her hand and instantly she felt a surge of pleasurable electrical force going through her.

"I'm Sunset," he said, clearly noticing the connection.

They sat there for a moment like that, holding the handshake, then he pulled his hand away and looked down.

She felt instant disappointment.

They sat in silence for a long moment, then she finally said, "How do I wake up from this?"

He looked at her, was about to say something, then clearly changed his mind.

"We need food," he said, offering his hand to her as he stood. "Let me show you how ghosts get our food."

"Ghosts are hungry?" she asked, glad he was again holding her hand. If this was a dream, she might as well enjoy it.

"We get hungry, we sleep, and we have to use the bathroom," he said. "Nothing changes on any of that except that no one can see us except other Ghost Agents."

"And we can read people's thoughts?" she asked.

"That," he said, leading her toward the buffet, "and so much more. You'll see. Jewel will train you."

"You're not going to help?" she asked.

"I'll help as much as you would like me to," he said.

"I would like you to," she said.

He nodded and smiled.

"I'll do my best."

And with that, once again they returned to silence. But he was still holding her hand as they made their way around all the tables toward the buffet.

And that felt right.

Oh, oh so right.

Four

SUNSET WAS EXCITED that maybe he had made up for some of his behavior out on the highway. And he was stunned at the connection he and Gail had. Her touch had sent shivers through him like no other ever had in a hundred years.

That was exciting all by itself. He couldn't believe how attracted he was to her.

As they got near the buffet, he said to her, "Be careful not to touch anyone else."

"Read their thoughts?" she asked.

"Just give it some time before you do that. Let Jewel be here to help you through some of those issues."

"Have you ever trained anyone?" she asked. Then she laughed. "I'm acting as if this dream is all real."

"Pretending for the moment it is real," Sunset said, "the answer is no."

They stopped in front of the plates. There was one plate sitting to one side of a stack of others.

"Pick that one up," he said, pointing to the single plate.

She did, holding a plate in her hand.

He pointed at the plate also still sitting there.

"How?" Gail said, looking at the plate in her hand and then the one on the counter.

"You are holding the ghost version of that plate," Sunset said. "Everything has a ghost version."

She stared at the plate in her hand. "It feels real."

"It is, except no one can see it. And if you put it down, after a half day or so it will vanish."

She just nodded and he moved them along to where there were some pizza slices that looked pretty good. He took one slice and she just stared at where the slice still remained on the serving tray.

And yet there was the same exact slice on his plate.

It was at that moment, when neither of them had been paying any attention, that a solid, middle-aged woman who smelled faintly of cigarettes came right up behind them and at the pizza.

The woman plowed right through Sunset and Gail.

Sunset quickly pulled Gail aside, but not before they both knew the woman's full history, about her affair with an office worker, her divorce, about her inability to stop eating and smoking and gaining weight since the divorce, and how her two children really hated her for causing the divorce.

One romp in the hay had cost the woman everything she treasured and she had no idea how to even start to get it back.

That wasn't supposed to have happened. Not without Jewel here to train Gail.

Sunset put the plates they had been carrying down and took Gail's hand and led her back to the table.

Gail seemed to be in shock. He had to be careful, very careful to not be an idiot.

When they sat down, Sunset pushed the glass of water toward her. "Take a drink, it will help."

She did, then nodded. She came back into her eyes a little.

Then she looked up at him. "I'm not sure I want to see inside people's heads, into their lives, into their secrets."

Sunset nodded, thinking carefully, as if in a courtroom and every word mattered. And it really did. "I understand that. Thankfully, what we saw will fade quickly from our minds."

Silence.

Sunset let the silence go on as Gail worked over in her mind what had happened. He knew she was smart. He needed to trust her ability to think things through right now.

"This isn't really a dream, is it?" Gail asked after a long moment of staring at the heavy-set woman they knew so much about.

"No, it's not," he said.

"I'm really dead?" Gail asked, looking directly at him. "That accident on the highway really happened?"

"It did," Sunset said, his tone as gentle and understanding as he could make it. "But you now get a very rare chance of living an even better life, a very long life if you want, and help others at the same time."

She nodded.

Sunset couldn't think of one other thing to say. He really sucked at this training stuff.

Five

ONCE GAIL ACCEPTED that she was dead, she wanted to know more about this crazy new world she found herself in. Part of her still didn't believe it, but for the moment she was going to just stop fighting it.

Sunset struggled a few times, in a very cute way, to try to explain a few things, and then looked massively relieved when Jewel and Tommy returned.

Damn he was cute.

Sunset asked them how it had gone and Jewel explained.

Gail was impressed that they had gotten the elderly couple to toss away the gun and call their children and tell them what was happening.

It seemed their children were very well off and had been worried about the couple. But the couple was too proud to say anything about not having any money left at all.

Gail was stunned at how Jewel and Tommy had literally saved lives. But Tommy had been a cop, Jewel a doctor.

How did Gail being a prosecuting attorney help?

When she asked that question, Sunset had said that only time would tell. He had been an attorney as well and he had been doing fine.

So Gail had agreed to training with Jewel and Tommy, with Sunset helping every day, but taking only a supporting role.

Over the next month, Gail stayed in Jewel and Tommy's home in Las Vegas in their guest room and they trained in the casinos, helping people where they could.

Finally, after a month, as the four of them were eating breakfast back in the Golden Nugget Buffet, Jewel turned to Gail and said simply, "You ready to find your own place?"

Gail had known that was coming, but it worried her because she didn't know what she should do. She wanted to go back to Oregon, but she was fairly certain she didn't want to return to the coast. Portland was the only town she liked, but Sunset lived there and she didn't want to be too forward. They were both very attracted to each other, but so far during her training had kept arms distance.

And she was going to have to work with him, so having an affair with a partner might not be such a hot idea, even though she wanted to. She had a hunch they would decide that later.

Gail pushed her waffle away and sat back.

Jewel just smiled and Tommy kept eating.

"I own this wonderful penthouse condo in Portland that is just sitting empty," Sunset said. "You can have it if you would like."

"You own it?" Gail asked. "How do you do that?"

"Actually a corporation I formed owns it," Sunset said. "I'll explain how all that is possible someday down the road on a really long and boring day."

"And you are willing to give the condo to me?" Gail asked.

"No problem," Sunset said, shrugging. "Money is never much of an issue for us ghosts, you know."

Sunset turned to Jewel. "Could you get some of your superhero friends to move some real furniture into the place. Furniture Gail picks out if she wants to take it?"

"Glad to," Jewel said, smiling.

Gail smiled at Jewel. "Thanks."

She couldn't believe how lucky she felt right now to be with these three wonderful people. And to have this exciting new life ahead of her, even though she was actually dead. She felt alive, more than she had ever felt when actually living.

Then Gail looked back at Sunset, her future partner, who was smiling. "That's very kind of you and I accept. Thank you."

Sunset nodded.

Gail turned back to Jewel. "Does this mean I'm done with my training?"

"Sunset can take it from here," Jewel said. "But we'll always be here if you need us for anything. We all work together you know."

Gail nodded.

"One condition to all this," Sunset said, smiling at her. "Once you are all moved in, you throw a party. I'll make the tequila sunsets."

"You're damn lucky I love that drink," Gail said, laughing.

"Yeah," Sunset said, "I think I am."

Gail pulled her waffle back toward her and took another bite, savoring the rich maple syrup flavor.

Around her the wonderful sounds of the morning in the Golden Nugget Buffet went on.

People talking. People laughing.

People being alive.

She hadn't planned to die on that highway on her way to dinner a month ago.

No one expects to die.

But now, sitting here with other Ghost Agents in a restaurant full of the living that she knew she might be able to help if they needed it, dying didn't seem so bad.

And sitting beside Sunset just made it all the better.

Oh wow did it make it better.

She had to die to meet the man of her dreams. She had a hunch it was going to be worth it.

PART TWO
A First Big Job

Six

THE WILDEST FIVE months Gail could ever have imagined had just passed. Now she sat at her kitchen table in her beautiful condo overlooking downtown Portland and watched as Sunset scanned through his morning news on an iPad sitting on the kitchen table.

She was still learning to make her touch firm enough to control a computer or even move something on a table. Every day she felt she got closer. Sunset had told her that things took time to learn. After all, she had only been dead five months.

Hard to believe that just five months ago she had been a successful prosecuting attorney on the Oregon Coast. Before her wonderful red BMV lost an unfair fight with a large truck.

Just as with every morning, Sunset looked like he had come right out of court and had just taken off his tie. He always wore a dark suit made of silk and a silk shirt. Plus he always wore perfectly polished expensive shoes. He dressed the same every morning and she sort of liked that about him. He was, by far, the most handsome man Gail had ever seen.

She was dressed in what made her feel comfortable. Dark dress slacks, comfortable matching shoes with short heels, a silk blouse and silk bra under it.

She and Sunset made a perfect power couple, but so far they were just partners even though she was flat out in lust with him.

She watched him work at the computer for a moment longer, then turned to stare out the large windows. Outside her wonderful penthouse condo, the Portland skies were gray. The fall had been beautiful, but now heading into November the season was changing, the air getting a bite to it, and the leaves on the trees turning stunning shades of orange, red, and brown.

She actually loved the fall and winter in Oregon. This was going to be her first winter as a ghost, so she didn't know what to expect, exactly.

Sunset, when he had been alive, had been a lawyer in private practice and had spent a lot of time in the last decade helping out in poor areas and giving free legal advice at a clinic in the northeast side of Portland.

He had died over a hundred years ago in a boating accident on the Willamette River. As he had freely told her, he had had one too many tequila sunsets and he had fallen out and hit his head on the side of the boat.

He said he sat on the bank for an hour watching them search for his body after trying to wave them down before he realized he was a ghost. No one had been there the moment he died as he and three other Ghost Agents had been for her. It wasn't until an hour later that someone from the Ghost of a Chance agency showed up and tried to start explaining things.

As Sunset said, they didn't get off well together right from the start.

Gail, on the other hand had been met the moment she died in the car wreck by Jewel and Tommy and K.J. and Sunset and then trained. Where Sunset had learned most things himself about being a Ghost Agent, Gail couldn't imagine doing that.

So, now as a ghost for the hundred-plus years, Sunset had tried to help those that seemed to need some help. When Gail asked him his record, he shrugged. "Some are beyond help."

The condo they were in was owned by a corporation that Sunset had started. He had done that by going inside the body of a live lawyer and getting the lawyer to do the work, then clearing out any memory of what that lawyer had done.

And not leaving any record of the lawyer on the documents either.

Sunset had learned to be an expert in computers and legal issues involving computers and how to leave no trail. Gail had a hunch she hadn't seen the level of his expertise yet. She had asked him about it once and he had laughed and said, "When you have been around as long as I have, you get ahead of the new stuff coming in."

Sunset had hired a "record firm" to be the address of record for the corporation who owned this condo and other properties around town, again just going inside a person in the firm to set it up.

Money to buy this condo and others had come easily from a few scams that he had busted. He drained the accounts of the bad guys and made sure that the money could never be traced out of the country and then back into his corporation. He used the money to buy land and places like this condo he had given her. Often with the land and buildings he bought he lowered the rent for social services, trying to help them out.

Gail had been stunned over and over the last few months at how Sunset, who

had come off brash and pushy at first, spent most of his days trying to figure out ways to help others.

After her training, they had taken to meeting every morning in her place to plan the day. So far, they both had managed to hold the physical part of the relationship at bay, but she wanted to change that and change that soon. Who knew a ghost could get so horny?

Being a ghost and being able to be inside a live person had been one of the more stunning things Gail had learned. At first she hated it, but as her training had gone on, she got good at directing a live person and sometimes helping them.

And, of course, the live person never knew Gail was there.

"So how about we tackle something larger today?" Sunset said, staring at the iPad. "Now that there are two of us, we might be able to."

"What are you thinking?" she asked, moving over and putting her hand on his shoulder and leaning down to see the screen better. She loved touching Sunset and she loved when Sunset touched her as well.

She pushed the thought aside about taking him into the bedroom and focused on the computer screen in front of her.

"Out in Gresham there's an investment firm that is starting to get complaints," Sunset said, pointing to an article. "Got a hunch they might be thinking of covering their tracks here shortly if we don't do something to help out the police."

Gail smiled. "White collar crime. That's my favorite type."

He laughed. "Me too.

"Let's go see what we can see," she said, looking at the address of the main office. "You want me to jump us there or you want to do it?"

"I don't think you need the practice, but what the hell, go ahead," Sunset said.

She took his hand and a moment later they were standing to one side of a fairly busy office on the main floor of the three-story building. The office was bright and had large windows along one wall. Doors into smaller offices lined the far wall and one sidewall. Twenty desks with cubical walls around them filled the space, all with a person at the desk behind a computer, talking with someone on the phone over a headset.

They all looked relaxed and busy.

The place didn't feel like it had just had a negative article written about it. It felt like an active business on just a normal day.

"Did I get us to the right spot?" Gail asked, glancing around as two people walked by, laughing at some conversation.

Sunset nodded. "This is the right spot but this is not at all what I was expecting. Not at all."

She could only agree with that. Something was wrong. Very, very wrong.

Seven

SUNSET FELT STUNNED at the big office in front of them. This place should be a stress-filled office with workers huddled whispering and panicked looks on manager's faces. That article this morning in the paper had been damaging to say the least and would be fatal to a business playing a scam as this one clearly was.

But nothing seemed to be wrong here. Maybe the article had just been a revenge piece from someone who had lost money here. But it hadn't felt that way. It had been done by a major reporter for the paper and clearly had the backing of the editors of the paper.

In his years as a live attorney, or his years as a Ghost Agent, Sunset had seen the pattern of a scam investment company numbers of times once the rock they had been hiding under was lifted. They fled like bugs afraid of the light.

No one in this room was fleeing or even seeming to be worried about their job or the company they worked for.

"This is off," he said to Gail.

"Way, way off," Gail said, nodding.

Over the last five months, Sunset had come to really respect Gail's opinions. She was smart, more than likely smarter than he was about many things. And she was the best-looking woman he had ever met. They were just settling into working together, but what he really wanted was for them to take the partnership to a relationship.

And soon.

Real soon.

Across the room was a guy in an expensive gray suit without a tie smiling at some other manager type.

"I'm going to see what he is thinking," Sunset said, pointing to the expensive suit.

Gail nodded. "I'll see what the brunette here at this first desk is worried about."

Sunset jumped over beside the guy in the suit and merged inside of him, making sure to be very careful that the guy didn't know Sunset had joined him in any fashion. Most people didn't notice when a ghost was riding along in their minds, but a few, a very few, could sense something different.

Sunset didn't need to worry about this guy. His mind was mostly a blank slate.

His entire focus was to sell the many forms of securities this company was selling. And he really, really believed that this company was helping people.

Sunset stayed inside the guy's mind. It felt as off as the entire office felt. Almost as if Sunset was inside an empty gym. Most people's minds were full of a thousand thoughts, all jumbled.

In this guy, all that was gone.

Slowly, digging back into the guy's past, working through memories of his wife and kids, Sunset finally found what he feared.

This guy had been run through a therapy brainwashing system of some sort. It had been quick and complete, of that there was no doubt.

Sunset eased out of the guy and jumped back to where Gail had gone inside the brunette sitting in front of one of the desks.

After a moment Gail appeared, looking shocked.

And angry.

In the few short months, Sunset had never seen Gail angry and he had a hunch she would be a power to get out of the way of when she did get angry.

"The poor thing was brainwashed," Gail said. "So much so that she left her boyfriend of three years, moved in with two other women working here, and all they talk about is how fantastic this work is."

"So was the boss," Sunset said.

"We have to figure out how far this spreads," Gail said.

Sunset agreed completely. They quickly split up the building. She would take the rest of the main floor, going into random people to see what was going on with them, he would go to the second floor and check that. They would meet near the elevator on the second floor and both check out the top floor at the same time, where they expected the bosses to be.

Thirty minutes later they stood in front of the president of the company's office. He had been as brainwashed as everyone else in the entire building.

That fact had shocked Sunset more than he wanted to admit.

The big evil of this place didn't work here.

"So now what do we do?" Gail asked, shaking her head. Sunset could see anger was clearly still there

Sunset was angry as well, but it was covered by a feeling of sadness for the almost two hundred people in this building.

Sunset looked at Gail. "We need lunch, then we need a lot more research on this company."

"How about we do a little research before lunch?" Gail said. "How about we go visit that reporter who wrote the article this morning, see what he has already dug up."

Sunset smiled. "Really, really good idea."

This time he took her hand, something he loved doing, and jumped them both to the reporter's office on the second floor of the city's major newspaper.

Eight

GAIL WAS BARELY controlling the anger she felt at how all those people were being controlled.

And being used to hurt other people.

Whoever was behind this was the scum of the earth. And in Gail's training, Jewel had shown Gail a few tricks to make the really ugly people suffer.

Gail just hoped she remembered a few of those when she met the person or people who were behind this.

The reporter was a solid man, about forty, with a beer gut. He wore jeans and a plain T-shirt and a Cubs baseball cap that more than likely covered a bald spot.

His office was a messy control center and when they arrived he was sitting behind his computer, typing.

They both nodded to each other and went inside him together, still holding hands.

The guy's name was Ryan and he was a bubbling mass of anger. The article he was working on was about the company they had just visited, about how much money the company scam had taken for worthless property and investments. All from innocent investors who bought into the sales line.

The guy had really done his research. The company in Oregon was nothing more than a shell company. All the money came in and vanished into overseas accounts. And his article had done nothing at all to dent their business and that was why he was angry.

He wanted to take them down and hard and fast.

Gail agreed with that completely.

His focus on the new article he was writing was the investors, warning them away, trying to convince them to sell their investments and try to get some of their money back.

Sunset had no real hope anyone would get any money back. In fact, he knew, without a doubt, this one was within one week of shutting down. That was the pattern.

But in one week a lot of people could and would still be hurt.

The reporter flat didn't understand why even the president of the company was just giving him the company line, even though there was a chance the guy would end up in prison.

Gail knew. Everyone, including the president had been brainwashed in such an effective manner as to be frightening. Every person in that building totally believed to their core they were doing good for people and their money.

Gail and Sunset stepped out of the reporter's body and then Sunset jumped them to a wonderful deli-style restaurant in the Pearl District. They grabbed a few ghost sandwiches a couple of customers had ordered and then jumped back to her condo to eat at the table, since the weather was too cold to eat out on the deli's outside space.

She got some plates and bottles of water. Then they ate in silence for a few minutes, both thinking. She liked that about being with Sunset. He had no problem with silence.

Finally she looked at him and asked the question she didn't know the answer to.

"Think we can clear their minds?"

Sunset nodded. "One at a time," he said, "but we can do it."

"How?" she asked.

"We go into their minds and simply wipe out the few hours of brainwashing sessions. We erase it."

Gail was shocked. "We can erase someone's memories? Jewel never said a word about being able to do that."

Sunset nodded, looking slightly pained. "I learned how to do it with a rape survivor who couldn't stop wanting to kill herself. The memories she had were so vivid, it was as if she was living them again and again every day. I finally went in and not only dulled the memories, but erased most of them. It gave the poor kid a chance to find a way to recover."

Gail nodded, not wanting to imagine how hard that must have been for Sunset to do.

"So you can show me how?" she asked.

Sunset nodded. "But I am suggesting we erase not only the memories of the brainwashing, but the memories of the months working for the company. The longest is about five months that I saw."

"That would leave a big hole in all their lives," Gail said, stunned that he suggested that.

Sunset nodded. "Better that than those poor people living with the guilt of what they did to others. Suicide would be a choice a number of them would make with that kind of guilt."

Damn, he was right. It would be better to have a person just sort of wake up and learn about what they had been doing from others than remember it and regret it deeply.

She and Sunset finished their sandwiches, talking over the plan of how to cover the entire building. They were both worried about how bosses would react, how workers would react, and how the people they hadn't gotten to yet would deal with others suddenly stopping what they were doing. There were over two hundred people in that building and there just was no way to clear them all quickly.

And Gail had no doubt they couldn't do it before five when everyone went home.

Finally, Gail said simply, "We can't do this alone. We need help."

Sunset nodded, clearly agreeing.

Gail sort of looked up at the ceiling, focusing on the two that had trained her and said, "Jewel? Tommy? We need your help."

She and Sunset had gotten into a case too big for them to deal with in the first few months of their partnership.

Didn't that just figure?

Nine

SUNSET REALLY HAD come to like and admire Jewel and Tommy during Gail's training. And the four of them had had a lot of fun meals together over the months as well.

Jewel and Tommy appeared in just moments after Gail asked for them. Both of them were wearing their normal jeans and dress shirts and running shoes. Tommy kept his dark brown hair cut short and Jewel had her brown hair pulled back as she seemed to always do.

They had quickly proven to the powers running everything that they were the best at what they did. Sunset had learned some things from them as well during Gail's training.

"You guys ever not dress up?" Tommy asked.

Sunset glanced at Gail's business suit and then at his own silk suit.

"Our working clothes," Gail said, smiling.

Tommy had teased them about how they always looked like they were fresh out of court. Sunset didn't mind. It made him feel comfortable.

"Problems?" Jewel asked.

Sunset indicated that Gail explain what they had found. And what they needed help doing.

When she was done, Jewel looked at Sunset. "You can cut out that much memory permanently from a person?"

"I can," Sunset said, nodding. "I can show you how. Some of these people will be dealing with doctors and such trying to regain their memory of the months, but they never will."

"We figure that would be better than the guilt they will experience," Gail said. "This financial scam has hurt thousands, will take many families entire savings. I would have trouble living with a memory of doing that to anyone."

Jewel and Tommy both nodded.

Sunset was glad they agreed.

"No sign of who is in charge?" Tommy asked.

"Going to be spending a lot of time on digging out that worm," Sunset said, "once we stop this and stop more people from getting hurt. But the reporter who dug all this up knows that the money is vanishing into overseas accounts. He just can't confirm that yet."

"So the key right now is stopping this," Jewel said. "Lay out your plan for us."

"We clear the brainwashing of the officers and board members and upper management, but leave the memories," Gail said. "They will be able to help prosecutors and also, more than likely, end up in jail. At least they will know why they are there."

Sunset nodded. "The rest of them we go in and just cut out everything that happened from the moment they were put under control of whoever is doing this to the present."

Jewel and Tommy nodded.

"I have one question," Sunset said. "You ever hear of anyone being able to do this kind of mind control at this level?"

"Besides one of us when we are inside someone," Jewel said. "No. But when we are finished I will ask some of the superheroes if they have heard of such a thing."

Sunset was afraid of that. "We will be researching that after we get this done. So anything from any of these victims that we can get today as to how this was done will help as well."

They all nodded. Sunset doubted they would find anything. Of the people whose minds he had been in, the brainwashing had happened seemingly instantly as they sat in front of a computer screen answering a few basic questions.

Something on that screen had gotten to them, implanted this belief about this scam company being the greatest. More than likely the people really behind this scam weren't even in this country.

They certainly weren't in that building. Eventually, they would be found, but that wasn't going to be today. Today they had to stop this cancer right here in Portland.

"Be careful around that moment of brainwashing," Gail said. "We don't want any of us getting hit with it."

Sunset and Jewel and Tommy all nodded to that as well and until one in the afternoon, when employees would be returning from lunch, the four of them planned their attack on the two-hundred-plus people in the three-story building.

Ten

GAIL FELT TERRIFIED at what they were about to do.

All four of them jumped to a back room on the lower floor of the building and all four of them went into one poor man's head.

He was a mailroom guy named Stanley who was fresh out of an MBA degree. He had only been working for the company for a month. His goal was to work his way up in this fantastic company and maybe someday own stock in it as well.

Sunset quickly, using this guy as an example, showed Gail and Jewel and Tommy how he removed a section of the man's memory.

Gail was surprised at how simple it was. Sunset simply put a clear mental box around the memory and then just shrunk the space inside the box until the box was nothing more than a dot.

Instantly the guy seemed confused as to where he was and what he had been doing.

Sunset gave him some calming thoughts and told him to just go home.

Then Jewel and Tommy and Sunset and Gail left the guy's mind as the poor MBA grad left the building.

"We're going to have to plant some memories," Jewel said, "in people as to where they parked their car, where they live if they moved while working here, things like that."

"And calming thoughts," Gail said. "I want to try to keep these people calm because it's going to feel like they are just waking up."

All three of them nodded to her suggestion. That would take them all more time, but it would be worth it for the people they were saving.

"So here we go," Sunset said. "Let's get the officers first. Just clear the brainwashing in the same way. A mental box around only the time they were at that computer, squeeze it down to nothing."

Gail took a deep breath and a moment later they were walking into the plush offices on the third floor.

It took the four of them about thirty minutes to clear the brainwashing from the officers and then erase the memories of the support staff working upstairs. Gail dealt with two women who had been with the company since the start. She calmed them as much as she could and gave them the suggestion to just get their coat and things and leave.

Then Gail and Sunset and Jewel and Tommy went to the second floor.

They started with the managers first, then worked their way through each room. In one hour they had that floor cleared.

The ground floor was looking a little frightened as everyone upstairs seemed to be going out the front door, looking confused.

Again the four of them started with the managers of the room and by four in the afternoon, the building seemed empty.

Gail had so many people's memories and thoughts in her head, she felt a little confused herself. But a few deep breaths and things seemed to sort out some.

The four of them had done it before five.

They spent the next thirty minutes making sure they hadn't missed anyone. By that point, Gail felt a lot better. The only people left in the building were the officers of the company upstairs, huddling together, talking about what they should do.

One man was just sitting in his office crying.

Gail hated to see that and pointed the guy out to Sunset who went into the crying man and a moment later the guy stopped, stood, squared his shoulders, and went to talk with the other officers.

"I just gave the guy a backbone is all," Sunset said, smiling at Gail as he appeared next to her.

"I'm going to go tell the reporter to check the building now," Sunset said. "Maybe contact the officers. You guys up for dinner?"

"I'm sort of missing the buffet dinner at the Golden Nugget in Vegas," Gail said. That was the restaurant that the four of them had eaten in the most during her months of training.

And today, this had felt like a lot more training.

"Wonderful idea," Sunset said, smiling at her. "I'll meet you all there."

He vanished.

"Great by us," Jewel said.

Jewel and Tommy smiled and vanished.

Gail stopped and looked around the now empty main room full of desks and computers. The four of them had saved a lot of people a lot of grief and lost money this afternoon.

They had shut down a scam. As a prosecuting attorney, that had always felt good to her.

She had been dead now for five months. And as each day went by, she felt more and more useful.

And that felt wonderful.

She nodded to the empty room and jumped to join her friends and the man she was head-over-heels in lust with.

Maybe after a good dinner in Las Vegas, she and Sunset could come back to her apartment, have a few drinks, watch a movie, and then end up in her big bed in celebration of a job well done.

She would like that.

Far more than she wanted to think about before dinner.

PART THREE
A Much Bigger Problem

Eleven

SUNSET WOKE UP next to Gail in her huge bed. The light from the late fall sunrise was flowing in through her bedroom window and in the distance he could see the cars crossing one of the many Portland bridges.

Beside him she lay sprawled, her normally perfectly-combed brown hair sticking out in all directions. Her face was so beautiful, he could stare at her all day and never get tired of it. He loved her pointed yet short nose, her thin eyebrows that seemed to express her every emotion, and that small mouth, still red from all the kissing last night.

Her wonderful body was half-exposed and she looked like a goddess. How in the world had he gotten so lucky after a hundred years of being dead.

They had finally taken their partnership to a relationship last night and it had been better than he had even imagined it might be. And for the last five months, since first seeing her, his imagination had been very active.

But they just seemed to fit together in all ways and all likes.

As he stared at her, she stirred and opened one eye. Then she closed her eye and sighed.

"Damn, glad that wasn't a dream."

"You have dreams like that?" he asked.

She smiled. "About you, I had a few like that, only not that good. And don't let that go to your head."

He laughed and kissed her and she turned and moved into his arms.

And once again they just sort of fit together.

In all ways.

Thirty minutes later he finally crawled out of the bed and headed for the shower, leaving her sprawled naked on the bed. That was an image he would not ever be able to forget, he had no doubt about that.

She joined him in the bathroom as he was drying off. She kissed him with a smile and then, without a word, got into the shower.

"I'll get coffee," he said.

"Oh, that would be heaven," she said.

"I think I'm already in heaven," he said, laughing.

"Yeah, thinking the same thing," she said.

Thirty minutes later they were both dressed and sipping on their coffee and eating slices of toast while Sunset pulled up the story on the investment firm in the paper. It was the lead article.

And as they both knew, none of the officers had any idea what had happened or who was behind the company. And the reporter agreed with them. And until someone figured out where all the money had gone to in the scam, none of the investors were going to get much if anything back.

"Seems we know what we need to do next," Sunset said.

"Find the worm behind all that," Gail said.

"And find out how they brainwashed all those people," Sunset said. "That has me the most worried. I can't imagine that anyone smart enough to do this would leave evidence on any computer. So it had to come in over the cloud somehow."

Gail nodded. "I noticed the program the people were watching when the brainwashing happened. It was a company orientation video they had to log on to get."

"Yeah, saw the same thing," Sunset said.

"You know anyone good enough to trace something like that back to a source? If it would be even possible."

Sunset smiled at her and nodded. "I'm not sure it is possible, but if it is, it's going to take pulling some strings for us to find someone good enough to do it."

"You know someone like that?"

He nodded. He didn't really know the person, but had heard rumors as computers became a thing over the last thirty years. The best there was, the actual god of computers and programming. And all the good and bad that went along with them.

But he had never met a god or even much realized the gods existed until just lately. He had always thought this person, called a god, to be a rumor. Now he wasn't so sure. But it might be the best shot. The skill to trace something like this was far beyond his abilities, he knew that for sure.

Gail just stared at him like he had lost a marble. "Not some kid we just take over, huh?"

Sunset laughed. "Nope, on something like this we need the best."

"And the best is?"

"From what I have heard, she used to go by the name Pheme," Sunset said. "Not a clue what name she is using these days. But I think a friend of Jewel and Tommy's might be able to help."

"Pheme as in fame?"

"Spelled with a ph and an e," Sunset said. "Again, all rumor, but lately I'm starting to think some of these rumors actually exist."

Gail nodded. "Strange name."

Sunset just laughed. "From what I have heard, that's only the start of it."

Twelve

GAIL LOVED THE fact that she and Sunset had finally taken their partnership and flirting to a relationship. It felt right, felt comfortable, and had been an amazing amount of fun, both last night and this morning when they woke up.

And now, from the sounds of it, they were off on an adventure to find someone to help them track that mind-altering program those poor people at the company had been subjected to.

"You want me to call Jewel and Tommy?" Gail asked.

They had both finished their coffee and toast and had finished reading the morning articles about the scam they had broken up yesterday.

Outside the penthouse windows the morning sun was breaking through the clouds, promising a nice fall day in Portland.

"Please," Sunset said.

Gail focused on Jewel and Tommy and called their names. The she said, "Need a little help when you have a minute."

Less than a minute later Jewel and Tommy both appeared. Gail knew that at this time of the day in Las Vegas, they both would have been eating breakfast at the Golden Nugget buffet. They would have already done their morning runs and then showered.

They were very much people of schedule.

"Sorry for the interruption," Gail said to them after Sunset offered Jewel and Tommy coffee and they both shook their heads. "We think we might need a little help tracing the computer program back to a source."

"We figured as much," Jewel said, smiling. She turned to Sunset. "You thinking of trying to find Pheme?"

Sunset nodded. "I'm only guessing she actually exists. But if she does, her reputation tells me she might have a chance of tracing something like that through just about anything. I did a little work yesterday after I cleared one person who was pretty good at computers. I had him try to trace back the training program. It didn't exist on his or any computer in that firm. Or on the firm's cloud storage in any form."

Gail was impressed that Sunset had done that. She had tried a little of the same, but didn't get as far as he had.

"So it didn't really exist," Tommy said. "But it came from somewhere? I got the same results when I tried to have someone trace it yesterday."

"Exactly," Sunset said.

"We have already called Poker Boy," Jewel said. "He and a couple of his team are waiting for us in his office."

Gail looked at Sunset who was nodding, then at Jewel and Tommy. She had

no idea what kind of name Poker Boy was, but that was the second time in her five months of being dead she had heard the name. Looked like she was about to find out.

"Never been there or met him," Sunset said. "So do the honors and jump us there."

Jewel nodded and a moment later Gail found herself standing in one of the strangest offices she had ever seen. It was basically a square with windows for walls on all four sides and a glass ceiling. The only furniture in the entire room was a huge booth that looked like it was right out of a 1950s diner. Red leather bench seats around three sides, a scarred Formica tabletop, and a few wooden chairs scattered around the open end.

Outside the glass walls it was clear the room was floating a thousand feet in the air right over the Las Vegas strip. A large airliner making an approach to the airport went past far too close for Gail's tastes.

Not possible.

This room wasn't possible. It must be some sort of illusion.

A wooden railing at waist high went all the way around the room, otherwise Gail would have felt she would slip on the checkered tile floor and fall off of the office.

She forced herself to take a deep breath and try to just look around.

The morning outside those windows was stunning. The air clear, the mountains in the distance on three sides sharp and looking like they were very close. Jaw-dropping view and she bet her mouth was open at the moment staring.

Beside her Sunset's mouth was open as he stared out of the windows as well.

"Jewel, Tommy," a voice said from behind them.

Sunset and Gail turned around to see Tommy and Jewel hugging a guy in a black leather coat, jeans, and a black fedora-like hat. The guy seemed to be about the same age as the rest of them and had a smile that could charm an entire room.

Behind him a stunning woman with long brown hair and wearing an MGM Grand uniform slid out of the booth, also smiling.

Staying in the booth was a guy in a gray cardigan sweater and an older guy who looked like anyone's classic grandfather, right down to the wire-rimmed glasses perched on his nose.

The woman hugged both Jewel and Tommy, then Jewel did the honors of the introductions.

"This is Gail and Sunset," Jewel said.

Jewel indicated the guy with the hat and black leather coat. "This is Poker Boy."

He nodded and smiled.

"This is Patty, aka Front Desk Girl."

She smiled and nodded at both of them.

"In the sweater is Stan, the God of Poker and beside him is Ben, the God of Libraries."

Gail wanted to open her mouth and ask about a dozen stupid questions, but for the moment she decided to just wait and ask later. If she hadn't been dead and standing in a glass office floating a thousand feet above Las Vegas, she might have questioned the idea she was meeting gods.

But she had been dead now for five months and so far every day had surprised her. Today was just a little larger surprise than most.

"Join us," Poker Boy said, indicating the booth. "You two just came from court or something?"

"That is how they always dress," Tommy said.

"Best dressed people ever to see this dump," Poker Boy said, shaking his head.

They all moved toward the booth as Poker Boy said to Sunset, "Heard a lot of good things about you since someone filled me in on the Ghost of a Chance agents."

"Thanks," Sunset said. "I didn't know all of you existed until a few years ago and since then heard nothing but good about you and your team."

Patty touched Gail's shoulder as she and Sunset took a seat facing the booth and Jewel and Tommy scooted into the booth after Stan and Sunset moved farther in.

With Patty's touch Gail felt much calmer. Clearly some sort of power or magic. Either way, Gail appreciated it and nodded thanks to Patty.

"Sorry to hear about your accident," Patty said to Gail. "But very glad you could join the team and work with Sunset."

"Thank you," Gail said. "It's been an adventure so far."

Gail was actually more stunned at Patty's mentioning of the accident. Not a person had mentioned it before that moment and Gail had honestly spent no time thinking about it or her lost life on the coast. No grief, nothing.

She found that odd, now that she thought about it. She would have to ask Sunset about that later.

"So how can we help you?" Poker Boy asked.

Sunset and Jewel took turns explaining about the scam company and what they had found and about the brainwashing program that vanished from the computers.

"So you really can erase areas of a person's memory?" Patty asked.

"Only if we have to in order to keep the person either sane or alive," Sunset said.

"But yes, we can and we had to do it in this case. Both to get rid of the brainwashing and to help them through the recovery."

Jewel and Tommy were both nodding.

"Wow," Poker Boy said, nodding. "That's a skill that might come in real handy at times."

"So you want to find a way to trace that program back to the source?" Stan asked.

Sunset nodded. "We're thinking Pheme might be able to help."

"Who?" Poker Boy asked.

Ben had sat back, shaking his head and closing his eyes. Stan just looked like a frozen statue.

"Oh, shit," Patty said softly.

Gail just looked at the reaction among the gods and Poker Boy's puzzled look. This clearly might not be a good idea.

Not good at all.

Thirteen

SUNSET WAS STUNNED at the reaction of the team of gods. He had heard that Pheme was a problem, but not one that would cause these kinds of reactions.

"Okay," Poker Boy said, clearly not happy. "Who is this Pheme and why the reaction?"

Stan just shook his head. Then he said simply, "Laverne?"

A moment later a thin woman in a silk blue pants suit and a white blouse appeared. She had her dark brown hair pulled back tight off her face, giving her a stark and commanding look.

Sunset immediately stood and stepped back, pulling the stunned Gail with him as he went. He had no idea how he managed to stay on his feet, but he did.

The woman smiled and stuck out her hand toward him. "Sunset, wonderful to meet you finally after all these years."

Sunset shook Laverne's hand. He couldn't believe he was actually shaking the hand of Lady Luck herself, the most powerful god among all gods, the god who ran everything.

He was so stunned he couldn't even get a word out.

Laverne didn't seem to notice. She turned to Gail. "Welcome to the other side of things, Gail. I'm Laverne."

Gail nodded and said, "Wonderful to meet you."

Laverne laughed, then glanced at Sunset. "She has no idea who I am, does she?"

Sunset smiled. "Not a clue."

"Explain it to her later," Laverne said, smiling. "Come on and sit back down. Madge is bringing up fries and some shakes."

Sunset managed to get Gail back to their chairs and make room for Lady Luck to sit beside them. Somehow he managed that without tripping over a chair or shaking too much.

After all, it was Lady Luck who had just joined them.

A moment later a woman five sizes too large in all ways for her 1950s waitress uniform appeared from behind the booth and served them all milkshakes and the most fantastic-smelling French fries he had ever seen.

"I'm Madge," the woman said to Sunset and Gail as she slid the fries in front of everyone and then put a massive chocolate milkshake in a tall, heavy glass in front of them.

"I figured you two could split one to start with," Madge said. "But if you want more, just shout."

"Thanks, Madge," Laverne said as the large woman moved around behind the booth and went through a door there.

Sunset had no idea where a door would lead considering they were in a room floating high above Las Vegas, but it had to go somewhere.

"So," Poker Boy said, "the ghost crew here thinks a person by the name of Pheme might be able to help them trace a computer problem. I have no idea who that is."

Laverne munched on a fry and nodded. "If anyone can trace anything through computer networks of any kind, real or magical, Pheme can do it. But she doesn't go by Pheme anymore. She has been Dottie now for centuries."

"So these three had a reaction when the name Pheme was mentioned," Poker Boy said. "And then they called you. What has she done to cause that?"

Lady Luck smiled and Sunset could feel it. He had a hunch people down on the Strip below could feel it. And the smile was a fond one.

"Pheme has a reputation of being wild and going her own way," Lady Luck said. "That's all."

The old man named Ben just shook his head and looked down at the fries in front of him.

Stan, the God of Poker, actually smiled.

Sunset had a hunch Laverne was glossing over some of the issues with Pheme, or Dottie, or whatever she was now called.

"Have you seen Pheme lately?" Patty asked.

Laverne again smiled and her gaze got distant. Again it was a warm and fond smile. "We meet every Tuesday for lunch."

Silence filled the office and no one said a word around the booth as Laverne sat there, a distant look in her eyes, a fond smile on her face. If Sunset had to guess, Laverne and Dottie were doing more than having lunch every week.

More Ghost of a Chance Novels
Available at your favorite booksellers.

But no way in hell was he going to ask Lady Luck a question like that.

Nope.

Not a chance.

No damn way.

Fourteen

GAIL WAS COMPLETELY startled by Sunset's response when the attractive, thin woman in the silk suit appeared. Clearly the woman was powerful, but she also seemed very nice.

So far today, Gail had met five very nice people, or gods, or whatever they were, and one waitress who really should be pulled aside and talked to about how to pick clothes that fit.

And now it was clear that this woman by the name of Laverne and Pheme, or Dottie, were very close. More than likely affair close. And it seemed that everyone but Poker Boy and she and Sunset had known that.

"So do you think Dottie can help these agents get a trace on this scammer?" Poker Boy asked.

Laverne shrugged, still smiling. "Let's ask her. Dottie, could you join us for a moment?"

A second later a very short, thin woman who looked to be about thirty appeared next to Laverne. She had short blonde hair that was clearly styled and wore jeans, tennis shoes, and a tan blouse that had an Apple Computers logo on it.

"Was just going to take a break," the woman said. She smiled at the table. "Great finally meeting all of you. I'm Dottie."

Laverne went quickly around the table doing introductions, then when she got to the four Ghost Agents, Dottie got very excited.

"Always heard rumors there was a ghost crew working on helping people," Dottie said. "Great to finally meet some of you."

"The pleasure is ours," Jewel said, smiling.

"Pull up a chair and grab a fry," Laverne said. "They have a favor to ask of you."

"Oh, fun," Dottie said, bringing a chair up beside Laverne.

Gail could tell that Laverne and Dottie were clearly very close just by how they sat touching shoulders.

Jewel quickly told Dottie the story of the scam and how they had saved the people in the building but couldn't trace the program. The entire time Dottie sat munching on some fries.

Gail hadn't touched the fries or the milkshake in front of her and neither had Sunset. She didn't feel like eating at the moment.

"Wow," Dottie said. "That's a damned dangerous program."

Everyone at the table nodded, including Laverne.

"I'm fairly sure I can trace the program back through whatever it bounced through," Dottie said. "But what we find on the other side has me a lot worried."

"That kind of programming could be used for all sorts of things," Laverne said, nodding. "From suicide defenders to forms of brainwashing anyone who comes at the people behind this."

"No protection against anything like this?" Poker Boy asked.

"It's been a while since anything like this," Laverne said. "Ben, have you any ideas?"

The older-looking god shook his head. "Rumors of something like it still existing back in the Atlantis days. Used on criminals."

"Of course," Laverne said as both she and Dottie nodded at the same time. "The Necklace Stone."

Gail did not much like the sound of that and around the table everyone frowned.

"Haven't seen old H in decades," Dottie said.

"She's here in Vegas," Laverne said.

"No shit," Dottie said, taking another fry. "She working as a hooker?"

Laverne laughed, but she was the only one. The rest of them just sat silent.

Gail could tell instantly there was bad blood between Dottie and whoever the "H" person was.

"No," Laverne said, "she actually is working as a counselor at a local high school and going by the name of Harmony."

"Well good for her," Dottie said, still munching on a fry.

Laverne turned to the four Ghost Agents. "I have a hunch it might be better if you four approached Harmony."

Dottie laughed and kept eating.

Gail was certain that Laverne was right about that. But she had no desire to meet someone these two women were feuding with.

"For fear of asking one of my amazingly stupid questions," Poker Boy said, "any chance the rest of us can be filled in."

"Ancient history," Dottie said.

Laverne said nothing, clearly answering Poker Boy's question.

At that point Dottie looked directly at the four Ghost Agents and said, "When you need me to track that program, just shout my name. But first find out what happened to that necklace. You need to see if we can use it for protection or not, and then we need to figure out exactly what we are dealing with."

Then Dottie smiled at Laverne. "Thanks for the fries. My break is almost over. Got to get back to work. See you Tuesday?"

Laverne smiled and nodded. "Tuesday it is."

"Call me when you are ready," Dottie said to the four Ghost Agents.

And Dottie was gone.

All Gail could do was sit and stare at where she had been. And wonder exactly what the hell was going on.

Fifteen

SUNSET SAT SILENT along with everyone else for a moment after Dottie vanished. He was as confused as everyone seemed to be at the moment. They had come to find help with a computer trace and ended up seemingly in the middle of something larger and much older.

"Ben," Laverne said. "Explain to everyone what they are facing and dealing with if it is the Necklace Stone and what it protects against."

The older man at the table nodded and Laverne vanished.

"Well, that was interesting," Poker Boy said. He grabbed a fry and looked at Ben. "How long a story is this going to be?"

Ben shook his head. "Not long, actually. The Necklace Stone they are talking about didn't start off to be a necklace. It was a crystal, blue and green in hue, and about three inches long. It actually was an ancient technology we got from the Titans in that war. It had the capability to block the control of minds."

"So it was magic?" Sunset asked.

"No," Ben said, shaking his head. "Magic only exists in the dark form. Computers and televisions would look like magic to someone from just a few hundred years ago. This crystal was actually an advanced ancient alien technology."

For some reason that made Sunset feel better. And beside him Gail was nodding as well.

"Someone mounted the crystal on a necklace?" Patty asked.

"Harmonia did that," Ben said. "Or Harmony as I guess she is called in this time. From that point forward it became known as the Necklace Stone. She kept the necklace close to make sure it wouldn't fall into the wrong hands. But it was supposedly lost in the fall of Atlantis."

"You all were around during Atlantis?" Sunset asked. "Atlantis was a real thing?"

"Very real," Ben said, nodding.

"I'm not that old by a long ways," Poker Boy said, shaking his head.

"Neither am I," Patty said.

"We were both there," Ben said, indicating himself and Stan who had been sitting quietly, sipping on a chocolate milkshake. "Laverne and Dottie were both there as well."

"Wow," Gail said softly.

Sunset felt the same way exactly. He felt like he had been around a long time being a Ghost Agent for a hundred years, but compared to these folks, he was a baby. He could only imagine how Gail was feeling right now. They would have to talk about it later.

"So there is bad blood between Dottie and Harmony?" Poker Boy asked.

Ben nodded. "They were married for almost a thousand years. A complete love match in their time."

"Oh," Patty said.

"Didn't end well I take it?" Poker Boy asked.

Sunset was starting to really like Poker Boy. He just said what he was thinking. Sunset sometimes wished he could do that.

"They got separated during the destruction of Atlantis," Ben said. "Dottie never stopped looking for her and by the time Dottie discovered Harmony was still alive, five hundred years had passed and Harmony was married to Cadmus and living in Greece. They had a pack of kids as well."

"Let me guess," Poker Boy said, "They haven't spoken since."

Ben just sort of nodded and said nothing.

"How many years are we talking about?" Sunset asked.

"Five thousand or so," Ben said. "Give or take a few centuries."

Sunset couldn't believe how silly this entire case had become. And deadly serious at the same time.

"So," Gail said, "Our best bet on tracking this brainwashing program and the person or people behind it is Dottie. And Dottie won't even try it unless she has the protection of a Necklace Stone from her ex-spouse whom she hasn't talked to in centuries. And the stone might be lost anyway. Do I have that right?"

Jewel nodded. "I'm reading that the same way.

"Sounds to me like a typical day around here," Poker Boy said, munching on a fry. "I'm up for helping if you want me?"

"Please," Sunset said. Gail, Jewel, and Tommy nodded.

"Call me if you need help," Stan said and vanished.

"I think I should go with you as well," Ben said. "Harmony was a good friend of mine."

"That would help," Sunset said.

"Sorry I can't join the fun," Patty said, "but work calls."

She kissed Poker Boy on the cheek and also vanished.

So now they were down to six.

Jewel glanced at Sunset and Gail. "I think Tommy and I should fade back on this one as well. Too many ghosts might overwhelm the poor woman."

"I'll call you when we get some answers," Gail said.

Jewel and Tommy vanished and then they were four.

Sunset just had to smile. His partners were a brand new ghost, a famous super-hero, and an old god. That was too stupid for even a television sitcom.

Sixteen

GAIL AND SUNSET jumped with Poker Boy and the older Ben to a small room that smelled faintly of unwashed gym socks. The place was clearly a wait-ing room with a dozen chairs and two windows, one that looked out at an empty school hallway and the other that looked out over a street lined with parked cars.

The floor was scuffed tile and a wooden desk sat on one side facing the chairs. The desk didn't look used at all.

The sound of kids laughing and talking came from outside the windows of the room in the hallway.

Gail didn't know how she felt other than numb. This was all happening so fast. In five months she had barely gotten used to the fact that she was a ghost and could help people, now she was learn-ing that gods really did exist and some

of them had been around for a very, very long time.

And they just worked regular jobs. Clearly both Patty and Dottie worked. Gail couldn't quite grasp that the god of computers worked as a clerk at an Apple store.

Gail hadn't gotten a chance to ask Sunset who the thin, powerful woman was who had appeared first in Poker Boy's diner-slash-office. Clearly she was someone very powerful and used to being in control of things. But Gail had never heard of a god named Laverne before.

But Gail had heard of Harmonia, a Greek goddess who seemed to now be going by the name of Harmony and work-ing at a local high school in Las Vegas. All this was going to take some getting used to.

Ben moved over to a closed inner door in the small waiting room and knocked.

A woman's voice on the other side said, "Come in."

Ben glanced at the rest of them and opened the door, moving into the small office beyond.

The woman sitting at the large wooden desk looked to be no more than thirty, with short blonde hair and green eyes. She glanced up with a smile as if greeting a student.

The office felt comfortable, with shelves of books behind the desk and two chairs in front. A large window had the blinds open allowing the morning sun to shine in.

It took a moment, then the woman beamed and said, "Ben!"

She jumped up and moved around the desk and hugged Ben and he hugged her back.

Harmony was wearing dress slacks and a cloth blouse and tennis shoes. Gail liked how Harmony dressed for her job. Comfortable, yet business.

"Been far too long," she said, smiling at Ben.

"It has been," Ben said. "And that's on me."

"I heard you moved over from the lamplighters to library work," she said. "A perfect fit for you."

"It is," Ben said. "And I want you to meet the person responsible for saving me from fading away to nothingness. This is Poker Boy."

Again, Harmony beamed as she shook Poker Boy's hand. "I have heard some wonderful things about you and your team. Everyone owes you more than just thank you for saving the world so many times."

"Appreciate that," Poker Boy said, smiling in return. "We couldn't do much of what we do without Ben helping us, though."

"And that's no surprise," Harmony said.

Ben just smiled and shook his head. Then he turned to Sunset and Gail. "Harmony, I'd like you to meet two of the Ghost of a Chance agents. This is Sunset and this is Gail."

Harmony looked puzzled. "Who?"

Gail glanced at Sunset. Clearly Harmony couldn't see them.

"Oh, sorry," Ben said. "Forgot. Laverne, a little help."

A moment later Harmony stepped back as clearly she could suddenly see the two Ghost Agents.

"Well, that was strange," Harmony said, smiling. "Until this moment I didn't know the Ghost of a Chance agents were anything more than a myth."

"We've worked with the agents a number of times," Poker Boy said. "They are great."

"Well, happy meeting you as well," Harmony said. "Do all Ghost Agents dress so well?"

Sunset laughed and said, "Just habits from when we were alive."

Harmony nodded and turned and moved around behind her desk, indicating that Ben and Poker Boy should sit in the two chairs.

"So I assume the four of you are here for a reason," Harmony said, settling back in her chair as if ready to listen to a student.

Gail stood beside Sunset and watched and listened as Ben and Poker Boy explained the problem of the brainwashing program and what they were trying to do."

"Let me guess," Harmony said, "You want Dottie to track the program back to the controller."

Ben nodded. "She said she didn't really want to attempt it without some protection."

Harmony nodded, sitting back and thinking. "The Necklace Stone."

Ben simply said, "Yes. Does it still exist?"

"It does," Harmony said.

Gail couldn't even begin to imagine what Harmony was thinking. Or if the bad blood with Dottie still existed after so many centuries on Harmony's side. There was clearly still some bitterness on Dottie's side.

"That program as dangerous as it seems?" Harmony asked.

"We think so," Sunset said.

Gail nodded. "We believe the company they took over could very well be a test run of some sort. Something much larger."

"That kind of power would make sense that it would be tested like that," Harmony said. "And no computer program can do that."

Gail and Ben both nodded to that. Gail had no doubt that something outside of programming was going on and clearly so did Dottie and now Harmony when they heard about it.

"The technology that could do that was owned by the Atlantis Head Council," Harmony said. "It was called the Mind Stone. It was only used on the worst criminals of the time. How did you all free the employees from the affects of the Mind Stone?"

Gail wasn't surprised that it had a name. She and Sunset explained how they could go inside of live people and had just erased the memory of the brainwashing."

"Wow, Ghost Agents can do that?" Harmony said, nodding. "No wonder you are teaming with them, Poker Boy."

He laughed. "Just learned that tidbit about erasing parts myself this morning."

"A good skill to have," Harmony said. "Especially handy in counseling in trauma cases."

"Used it a few times for exactly that," Sunset said, nodding. "I'll be glad to volunteer if you ever need my help on

something. Or to just get to the bottom of a problem in a person's mind."

"I will be glad to help as well," Gail said.

"Thank you," Harmony said. "I really do appreciate that and more than likely will ask for that kind of help at times."

She sat thinking for a moment, then she looked at Ben. "Dottie thinks she can trace this attacker?"

"She does," Ben said, nodding.

"And she's right that she would need the Necklace Stone if she came face-to-face with someone wielding the Mind Stone against her."

Ben nodded.

Gail just sat and watched.

After a moment Harmony nodded. "I'll go with her, but we will need you two Ghost Agents to go along as well. We might need you to control who we find on the other side. And Poker Boy, you and one of your team should also go. The necklace, through me, can protect us all."

More Ghost of a Chance Novels
Available at your favorite booksellers.

Ben and Poker Boy both nodded.

"Tell Dottie it will be good to see her again," Harmony said. "I'll be off in two hours. We need to get this done before anything worse happens with that Mind Stone."

"Thanks," Ben said. "We'll be in Poker Boy's office when you are ready."

"Yes, thank you," Gail said as Poker Boy and Ben stood.

A moment later they were back in Poker Boy's office.

A second later the woman named Laverne appeared. "She agreed?"

"She did," Ben said. "Two hours and we'll jump from here. You want to tell Dottie or you want me to."

Laverne smiled. "I'll tell her. This could be fun. Get a fast laptop hooked up here to the Internet. Dottie's going to need that."

Laverne vanished and Poker Boy sat down in the booth laughing.

Gail looked around at the fantastic view of Las Vegas and the mountains around the valley. What in the world were they facing?

In the next two hours, she really needed some answers to that question.

Seventeen

SUNSET SAT WITH Gail and Ben and Poker Boy in the huge booth in the floating office above Las Vegas. They sat where Stan the God of Poker had been sitting earlier, leaving the end of the booth open. This was not at all how he had imagined his day was going go. Especially after the wonderful start of waking up next to Gail.

In front of them were two wonderful cheeseburgers and a basket of fries and a milkshake. And spread out around them the fantastic view of Las Vegas on a clear, sunny day.

Both Poker Boy and Ben were stunned as they watched Sunset and Gail eat. Poker Boy and Ben could see the Ghost Agents eat, yet the main food never moved from its spot on the table.

"Does that taste thinner?" Poker Boy asked as Sunset took a bite of the ghost part of the cheeseburger, leaving the real cheeseburger sitting on the plate untouched.

"Actually a thousand times better," Gail said before he could answer. "It's like we are eating the very essence, the pure flavor of food."

"Everything is better as a ghost," Sunset said. He smiled at Gail and she blushed. He loved that.

As the next hour went by, he and Gail and Poker Boy asked questions of Ben about the Mind Stone and the Necklace Stone that was supposed to protect them from being brainwashed.

"Both were far-advanced tech," Ben said. "The Mind Stone was used in the war with the Titans and helped turn the outcome of the battle. The stone on the necklace was used by those wielding the Mind Stone to protect themselves from its powers."

Poker Boy looked startled. "So the person using the Mind Stone might have a stone similar to what is on Harmony's necklace?"

"Yes," Ben said, nodding.

Sunset didn't like the sound of that at all.

"Is the person or persons on the other side going to be able to see me and Sunset?" Gail asked.

"More than likely not," Ben said. "The only reason we can see you is that Laverne gave us the power to be able to do that."

"So who exactly is Laverne?" Gail asked.

Poker Boy laughed.

Sunset just put his hand on her leg and smiled. Gail was going to have a very hard time with this one.

"Laverne," Sunset said, "is Lady Luck."

"She pretty much runs everything," Poker Boy said.

Gail looked first at Poker Boy, then at Sunset, clearly wanting to say something, but then changing her mind.

Sunset leaned over and kissed her on the cheek. "Being a ghost is never dull, is it?"

She just laughed and said, "Never."

At that moment Laverne and Dottie appeared. And as they did Madge, the waitress in the far-too-tight fifties diner uniform came out of a back door to the office carrying a laptop computer.

Laverne and Dottie pulled up chairs to the booth table and sat down.

Dottie opened the laptop and got it going, then turned to Sunset. "When we are ready, I'm going to need you to be in my head to show me exactly what you saw in that office and the computer connection you tried to trace."

Sunset nodded. He couldn't imagine being inside a god's head, but he would do what he could do.

Dottie laughed at Sunset. "Don't worry kid, I won't let you see anything you're not supposed to see in there."

"Appreciate that," Sunset said, smiling at her.

Dottie turned to Gail. "You are going to need to be riding along inside Harmony's mind, showing her the same thing. Can the two of you be linked up while in two different people's minds?"

"If you and Harmony are holding hands," Sunset said. "That way Gail and I can know what both of you are doing at the same time."

"And we can keep the two of you connected as well," Gail said.

Dottie frowned, but said nothing, instead focusing on the computer in front of her.

Laverne just smiled and Poker Boy managed to keep a complete poker face.

Sunset had no doubt what they were about to do was going to be interesting, to say the least.

Eighteen

TENSE DIDN'T BEGIN to describe the moment when Harmony arrived. At first she did what Gail guessed most visitors to this office did the first time. Harmony gasped and looked around.

Then she turned and saw Dottie and Harmony's face turned white.

Dottie glanced up from the computer and over her shoulder. "Hi, H. How you been?"

Then Dottie turned back to what she was doing on the computer.

Gail watched as Harmony took a deep breath and came toward the table. She sat down on the other side of Laverne.

Silence filled the office, a tense, uneasy silence until finally Dottie said, "Sunset. Need you to give me what you saw on those computers in that office."

Sunset nodded, glanced at Gail and then moved over and vanished into Dottie.

"Okay," Poker Boy said, shaking his head. "No matter how often I watch that it doesn't get any less creepy."

Gail watched as Dottie nodded and her fingers seemed to become a blur on the keyboard.

Then Dottie said, "Gail, need you in H. Poker Boy, you and Ben ready to go?"

Laverne stood and stepped back and Harmony moved over beside Dottie.

"Ready?" Gail asked.

Harmony nodded and Gail moved over and went inside her.

Harmony had most of her brain walled off. Gail found a spot that felt like she was standing off to one side of Harmony's mind and then said simply, "I'm here."

"Understood," Harmony said out loud.

"Put your hand on my shoulder and don't let go," Dottie said to Harmony.

Harmony did and Gail was almost overwhelmed by the emotion of love and missing Dottie that Harmony felt before she could get it under control.

Sunset said, "You here, Gail?"

Gail imagined herself moving up into Harmony's shoulder and reaching across to hold Sunset's hand.

"We're ready," Sunset said to Dottie.

Harmony extended the screen around them from the stone on the necklace she was wearing.

"We're ready as well," Gail said.

Poker Boy and Ben had moved out of the booth and were touching Dottie and Harmony's shoulders.

"Here we go," Dottie said. "Laverne, track us as much as you can."

With that Gail felt Dottie jump them.

They ended up standing in a large, ornate, oak-shelved office. A massive number of books filled the walls and a gigantic oak desk filled one side of the room, empty.

The ceiling had to be twenty feet overhead and looked to be inlaid in some sort of gold.

Decorative rugs in gold and browns covered the floor under couches and a few chairs all faced the desk.

Gail had never seen a room like it.

There was no one in the room and no sign at all of computers.

"Jump us back!" Harmony shouted. "Now!"

The panic in Harmony's mind was almost too much for Gail to handle and she put up screens against the waves of emotion.

Sunset was having the same problem with panic coming from Dottie.

"I can't," Dottie said. "My computer didn't come with me."

"Wouldn't work here anyway," Harmony said.

"Someone want to explain where we are?" Poker Boy asked as Ben moved over and dropped down onto a chair. He looked completely defeated.

Outside the room sirens were wailing.

Gail read from Harmony's mind that those were warning sirens, telling everyone to take cover.

Then Gail realized what Harmony was thinking.

She stepped out of Harmony at the same instant that Sunset stepped out of Dottie.

"What happened?" Poker Boy asked. "Where are we?"

Gail reached over and held onto Sunset's hand.

Harmony kept her hand on Dottie's shoulder.

"Not so much as to where we are," Ben said from the chair he had sat down in. "It's when."

"When?" Poker Boy asked.

Gail knew the answer because both Harmony and Dottie had recognized the room instantly.

"This is the High Chancellor of Atlantis's office," Ben said. "And those sirens mean Atlantis is breaking apart as we stand here."

"That can't be possible," Poker Boy said.

But Gail knew it was.

And she knew the history that Harmony and Dottie had had in this office.

"What have we done?" Harmony said.

"It seems we are about to repeat our own past," Dottie said.

Harmony nodded.

She took her hand away from Dottie and looked directly at Poker Boy and Ben. "The four of us need to hide. Gail, Ben, you two stay and watch what happens next for us."

"Why?" Poker Boy asked.

"Because if this really is what it seems to be," Harmony said, "Dottie and I are about to rob this place."

Dottie laughed. "Interesting we came back to the scene of the crime, isn't it?"

"Very," Harmony said. "Back to the beginning of our end."

Nineteen

SUNSET KNEW THAT something wasn't right the moment both Dottie and Harmony got upset.

Somehow, they believed that they were back at the end of Atlantis. But that couldn't be possible any more than the employees of that scam investment firm thought they were selling good investments.

As the four live people scrambled for a door out the back of the large room, Sunset turned to Gail who was looking shocked and a little panicked.

"We're not really here," Sunset said. "We're being duped just as those people in that firm were duped."

"Are you sure?" Gail said, indicating the room around them. "This sure feels real."

"It sure does," Sunset said. "Would you let me into your mind, see if I can find the spot where we were brainwashed?"

"Please," Gail said. "Anything to make this end."

Sunset took her hand and a moment later he was in her mind, something he hadn't ever done with another Ghost Agent before.

He could instantly see how much she cared about him, which made him happy.

"Hurry, someone's coming," Gail said.

Through her he could hear the door starting to open.

He focused on the last few seconds right before they jumped away from Poker Boy's office and made the entire thing slow down, like watching everything in slow motion.

And the moment he did that, he saw the issue. They had never really jumped anywhere.

He carefully took that moment around that jump point in Gail's mind and blocked it off and shrank it down.

"What?" she asked, suddenly back inside of Harmony.

Sunset quickly showed her what he had done and had her do the same for him, cutting out the mind control that made him think they had jumped back in time.

Then they carefully, at the same time, did the same for Dottie and Harmony.

Then they left their minds, stepping back into Poker Boy's office.

"What happened?" Laverne said. "None of you jumped."

Dottie slammed the lid on the computer closed and stood up. "Whoever is behind this got us before we could even move. The moment I linked into the origin site."

"The stone didn't protect us," Harmony said softly.

"It did," Dottie said. "Just not in the right way at the right moment. We were not ready for that kind of attack."

"Thank you," Harmony said turning to Sunset and Gail. "I assume you saved us by cutting out the brain control moment."

"We did," Sunset said.

"That damned office was like returning to a nightmare," Dottie said.

"What office?" Laverne asked.

"The Atlantis Chancellor's office right before the moment of destruction," Dottie said.

"Oh," Laverne said.

"I think Sunset and I need to clear Ben and Poker Boy," Gail said.

Laverne laughed as the five of them looked at the frozen faces of Poker Boy and Ben still standing where they had been before the jump.

"You take Ben," Sunset said to Gail. "I'll get Poker Boy back."

Gail nodded.

A moment later he had the brainwashing moment out of Poker Boy's mind and stepped away.

"Damn am I glad that wasn't real," Poker Boy said.

Ben only nodded. "Not a place I ever wanted to return to."

Sunset looked at Dottie and Harmony and Ben. That was it. Sunset now knew how they could figure out who was behind this.

"Who would know that room would torture all three of you?" Ben asked.

Gail nodded. "Or that it even existed?"

"And have enough power to stage an instant attack the moment you linked up?" Sunset asked.

Dottie and Laverne and Ben all looked blank, but Harmony shook her head, then said, "Damn him all to hell."

And with that she turned and moved over to the edge of the room and stared out at the city below.

"Damn who?" Laverne asked.

Harmony shook her head slowly, keeping her back to all of them.

Dottie moved over to Harmony and put a hand gently on her shoulder. "Who could do this?"

"That bastard ex-husband of mine," Harmony said. "The one who brainwashed me into marrying him instead of continuing to look for you."

"He did what?" Dottie asked.

"Cadmus?" Laverne said, her voice low and mean.

Harmony nodded. "He told me the Mind Stone that went along with the Necklace Stone was destroyed, but I always half believed he had it and had used it on me."

Then Harmony spun around and looked at Sunset and Gail. "Could you two dig out an ancient brainwashing if it really did happen?"

Sunset looked at Gail, then turned back to Harmony. "If you wouldn't mind opening up to us, we could try."

"You were brain controlled by Cadmus?" Dottie asked, her voice soft.

"Let's find the hell out, shall we?" Harmony said.

She moved over and sat down in a chair facing the booth.

Sunset just looked at Gail, who was looking as worried as he was feeling.

They were going to dig back through the memories of thousands of years of a god.

What could possibly go wrong?

Twenty

THE TENSION IN Poker Boy's floating office felt so heavy, it was amazing the thing stayed in the air.

Gail took a deep breath and smiled at Sunset, who was looking as concerned as she was feeling.

"Harmony," Gail said. "Can you focus on the time and place you think you changed?"

Harmony nodded. "Haven't wanted to think about it for centuries, but I can do that."

Gail took Sunset's hand.

"We'll see what we can find," Sunset said.

Then the two of them stepped inside Harmony.

Gail was stunned at the anger Harmony was feeling. And the emotions she blocked out trying to focus on the time.

"We find where she was still looking for Dottie," Sunset said. "Then moved forward in time from there."

"Right here," Gail said, seeing clearly the intensity of Harmony's search. The world at that point was in ruins with pockets of the old civilization that had been Atlantis fading back into the dark ages.

Gail moved them forward through time in Harmony's mind like fast-forwarding through a movie until Harmony met Cadmus. He seemed handsome, kind, and wanted to help. He had built a city and a large compound on a hillside and had all the modern things she loved about Atlantis protected and still in use.

But Harmony knew she couldn't stay there long. She had to keep searching.

Sunset moved them forward a few more days and Harmony had decided to stay with Cadmus.

"In those two days," Gail said.

"Agreed," Sunset said.

Gail moved them back in time in Harmony's memories, again like a movie running quickly in reverse, images just flashing past, and then forward until a dinner with Cadmus on the night before Harmony planned on leaving.

And there it was. Clear as day.

He had altered her mind to forget her quest and stay with him.

What a bastard.

Cadmus had basically raped Harmony's mind.

Now Gail felt angry and she could tell that Sunset was as well.

"You stay here at this spot in the memory," Gail said. "I'm going to step out and ask Harmony exactly what she wants us to do."

Sunset let go of her hand and Gail stepped out of Harmony and back into the light of Poker Boy's office.

If she thought the tension was thick before they went into Harmony's mind, now it was suffocating.

Harmony and Dottie both looked at Gail like she was about to tell them they were going to die.

"The night you were having a last dinner with Cadmus," Gail said to Harmony, "before going back on your search for Dottie, Cadmus brainwashed you with the Mind Stone. We have the exact moment and time."

"I will kill that bastard," Harmony said, her voice low and mean.

"I will help you," Dottie said.

"What would you like us to do?" Gail asked. "Blocking off that brainwashing moment now will not change the history, but it might change how you view the memories of him and your five children with him."

"He held me prisoner against my will," Harmony said. "Cut that moment out and I will live with the rest. Clear the brainwashing."

Gail nodded and stepped back into Harmony and beside Sunset.

"I got this," Sunset said, taking Gail's hand.

A white bubble formed around the entire moment when Cadmus used the stone to brainwash Harmony. And Sunset then tightened the bubble down harder and harder until that entire moment of brainwashing was now gone from Harmony's mind.

Then they stepped out of Harmony.

She was blinking, as if just waking up from a long nap.

Then she slowly turned to Dottie as tears started to run down Harmony's face.

"I am so, so sorry," Harmony said, sobbing.

With that the two ancient gods were in each other's arms crying.

Love derailed thousands of years before now clearly still existed.

How wonderful was that?

PART FOUR
A God Fight

Twenty-One

SUNSET WATCHED HARMONY and Dottie hug and cry for a moment, then started watching Laverne, the most powerful god of them all.

In the floating office the tension was thick. Very, very thick. Almost to the point the air felt heavy and hard to breathe.

Clearly Laverne was not happy.

In fact, Lady Luck was radiating anger.

Sunset bet that passengers on the planes coming into the Las Vegas airport could feel it and more than likely fights were breaking out in the casinos below.

It was that powerful of an anger.

Poker Boy and Ben sat in the booth and tried to pretend they were not there.

Finally Harmony turned to Sunset and Gail. "Thank you for freeing me."

"You are more than welcome," Gail said.

Sunset just let himself nod and bow slightly.

"So now we have a major problem to deal with named Cadmus," Laverne said.

Sunset almost shivered because Laverne's words were so cold and angry.

Making Lady Luck angry was never, ever a good plan.

"Do you know where Cadmus is?" Dottie asked.

"No," Laverne said. "He is blocking me."

"He has a compound in the hills of Greece," Harmony said. "He was always trying to get me to talk with him and come back and live with him."

"That compound can't be breached in any conventional way," Laverne said, nodding. "I know of the place. I would not doubt he has a small army inside it and let's not forget his powers without the Mind Stone."

"What are his powers?" Poker Boy asked.

"Too much for most of us," Dottie said and Poker Boy just nodded.

Sunset glanced at Gail who nodded. They were clearly thinking along the same lines.

"Let the Ghost Agents go in," Sunset said.

"Will he be able to see us?" Gail asked.

"No," Laverne said. "I am the only one who knows how to make a Ghost Agent visible to a god or superhero."

"Will he sense them?" Poker Boy asked. "We did this once before but the god could sense the Ghost Agents."

Sunset would have to ask Poker Boy about that when he had a chance.

"We can attack him at the same time and keep him busy if he can sense you," Dottie said, pointing at the computer.

"He's so arrogant that I doubt he would consider anyone actually coming at him from inside his compound," Harmony said.

Dottie and Laverne both nodded to that.

Sunset turned to Ben. "Would you be able to get exact plans and location of his compound for us?"

Ben nodded. "It will be in the records. I will get them now."

He vanished.

"So what will you be able to do to him?" Poker Boy asked.

"If we can get inside his body," Sunset said, smiling. "Just about anything."

"Oh," Poker Boy said, not breaking his poker face.

"We will need Jewel and Tommy on this as well," Gail said.

Laverne turned to Harmony. "You know him better than anyone. Could this work?"

"If he was distracted, yes," Harmony said.

Laverne took a deep breath. "All right. We have two missions here. One is to get the Mind Stone from him and get it to safety in my office."

Sunset nodded as everyone else did. After seeing what that Mind Stone could do to an entire office of people as well as Harmony, he wanted it out of commission completely.

"Second, we capture Cadmus. Let me deal with him under the rules."

Sunset swore that when Lady Luck said the words 'the rules' the entire floating office shook.

Poker Boy actually looked like his face went white with that.

Dottie and Harmony both just nodded.

"We would like a say in Cadmus's fate," Harmony said, touching Dottie.

"And you will have it," Laverne said.

She turned to Poker Boy and Sunset and Gail. "You three along with Jewel and Tommy develop a plan with Ben when he gets back. I want to be ready to move on this in two hours."

All three of them nodded like their heads were being pulled by the same string. Sunset had never had a direct order from Lady Luck before. It carried the weight of a train hitting you.

"You two come with me," Laverne said to Dottie and Harmony. "We have some history to discuss."

With that, the three gods vanished.

"Well, this is going to be interesting," Poker Boy said, shaking his head.

Sunset could only nod to that massive understatement.

Twenty-Two

GAIL WATCHED AS Madge put some fresh fries and milkshakes on the table in front of all of them. The fries smelled wonderful and looked like they were perfectly salted.

Madge also put some glasses of water on the table and Gail went for one of those first. Something about roaming around in a god's mind in ancient pre-history had made her thirsty. Or maybe it was because she felt so far, far out of her depth here it wasn't even funny.

Less than a year ago she had been a happy prosecuting attorney on the Oregon Coast, trying to make her little coastal towns safer. Dealing with gods

and ghosts and superheroes sure never would have crossed her mind. Not even in a fever dream.

Jewel and Tommy had returned and Ben had returned with the plans of the Cadmus compound.

Around the large booth in the floating office in the sky were Poker Boy, Ben, Jewel and Tommy, and Sunset and her. And there was enough room in the booth for a couple more, the booth was so big.

Jewel and Tommy told them about the last time they had tried this with another god named Numa inside of another compound. It seemed that gods liked compounds or something.

Gail didn't like the part of the story where the god had trapped the Ghost Agents in his own body. So Jewel and Tommy had a plan this time to avoid that, which Gail was very happy to hear.

It seemed that they had taken on Numa and now were using his entire compound as a headquarters for Ghost Agents. Plus it had made all of the Ghost Agents very rich. Jewel and Tommy had said nothing about that, and since Sunset had already made himself rich in real world money, it had never occurred to Gail to ask.

After this mission, she would.

When Sunset heard about all the other agents, he asked if it might not be a good idea to bring them in as well. Jewel shook her head.

"We would have to get them up to speed on the Mind Stone and besides," Jewel said, "I would rather have them as backup."

Gail liked the sound of that a lot, actually.

By the time the two hours were up, they had a plan. Only Sunset would go into Cadmus's body first. Jewel and Tommy would be inside household staff and military, getting them close to

Cadmus and getting ready to make them stand down and leave the compound. But not until Cadmus was out of the picture.

Gail would stay with Dottie and Harmony on the direct attack.

"More than likely," Poker Boy said, "Cadmus has all his people under some sort of Mind Stone control. You are going to need to break that before they will do anything."

"Like we did in the office building," Tommy said.

"We can do that," Sunset said, nodding.

Gail just hoped they could. Dealing with brainwashed office workers was one thing, going against the military and staff of a god might be another level of brainwashing.

"We're going to have to walk in," Jewel said, looking at the plans of the massive compound.

Tommy nodded. "More than likely his protective screens will be up around the complex, only allowing certain people through. The three of us will have to be nothing more than a dot in one of

---

those people moving inside. It was us transporting through a screen and also getting Numa's people to stand down before we got to Numa that alerted him to our presence."

Gail nodded to that.

Thankfully, Tommy and Jewel had some experience with this. Gail had a hunch this was going to be very different, but at least it felt like they knew what they were doing going in.

Gail really wanted to ask if ghosts could die. It had not once come up in the training, but it was clear that ghosts could be trapped from what happened the last time Jewel and Tommy tried this. And being trapped for eternity scared Gail a lot more than dying again.

She decided to hold off that death question until after this was all over. No point in scaring herself anymore than she already was.

At that moment Laverne and Dottie and Harmony appeared. All three of them took chairs at the end of the large booth and Dottie put her laptop on top of the table, but didn't open it.

All three of them were determined.

"We are fairly certain that Cadmus does not know Harmony and Dottie and Ben and Poker Boy escaped that last trap," Laverne said.

"So I'm going to ride us in over the top of what he did last time to us," Dottie said. "When you are all in position."

Laverne looked at the four Ghost Agents. "Are you ready?"

"We are," Jewel said.

Gail managed to nod.

"We have a set timeline worked out," Poker Boy said. "At exactly one hour, you start the computer attack. Ben and I will ride with you on that."

Laverne nodded.

"We will need one of you to stay with us," Dottie said to the four Ghost Agents.

"I will be doing that," Gail said. "Sunset and I have a connection so I will know if they are in trouble. And I can help you in case the Mind Stone traps you again."

"Get the shields down on that compound," Laverne said to Tommy and Jewel and Sunset. "The moment that happens I will deal with Cadmus."

Gail managed to not shudder. Lady Luck really had a way with radiating power.

And right now she was pissed.

Wow.

Twenty-Three

SUNSET AND TOMMY and Jewel jumped to a spot just outside of Cadmus's main compound gate.

Sunset was surprised. The air was hot and very dry and the light felt even more intense and bright than it had in Las Vegas. Around them were rocky hills covered in some sort of blue-green tree and brush. In front of the three of them was an ancient stone wall with a gate.

But nothing ancient about the men standing with guns in guard stations on the walls.

The walls wound over the hills in both directions and the main compound inside could not be seen from this point.

A truck was parked at the gate and the driver and a guard were talking, checking papers. Then two of the guards checked the cargo of the truck. From what Sunset could tell it was fruits and other food items.

"The driver," Tommy said.

They moved quickly to him and climbed up into the cab and vanished inside him. Then all three of them made themselves as small as they could, tucked back in the man's head so that they could see through him where they were going, but with luck not be noticed.

The guy's name was Meletios and he had a wife, three kids, and a thriving delivery business. He delivered to this compound twice every day and always had to go through the same process, which he found annoying and stupid.

Sunset and Tommy and Jewel watched for any signs that their presence had been spotted as Meletios drove his truck in and over a slight ridge on the two-lane paved road, heading toward a large compound tucked against one hill.

The compound was huge and clearly opulent. Meletios thought it was gaudy and stupid and a waste of wealth.

The main home in the back and on the highest point had the kitchen he was delivering his cargo to. On the left were large stone buildings that housed hundreds of soldiers and on the right large modern office buildings Meletios had never been allowed to go near.

Those buildings worried Sunset and he whispered that to Tommy and Jewel and they both nodded.

Why this god would take the time and energy to brainwash an investment firm in Portland, Oregon, was making less and less sense. There was a lot going on here they hadn't discovered yet.

Meletios pulled his truck up to the service entrance to the main building and went inside with his inventory clipboard to get help unloading.

At that moment, once inside the walls of the building, Sunset and Tommy and Jewel stepped out of their ride.

They moved past the modern kitchen area that looked like it could have been right out of any restaurant in Las Vegas and into the main part of the house.

The corridor had high ceilings with thick wood beams spaced along them. Some sort of stucco walls were decorated with tapestries and art of all colors and the floors were polished stone.

The place felt and looked like a palace.

A man who looked like a house cleaner came past and Tommy motioned for Sunset and Jewel to stay put and he slid inside the man. A moment later Tommy came out.

"This way," he said.

Sunset followed Tommy and Jewel, moving quickly through the wide corridor.

Until they found one large wooden door.

"Cadmus has a suite behind this door," Tommy said.

At that moment two men in New York style business suits came from the other direction down the hallway and started to go through the door.

"Good luck," Tommy said as Sunset went into one and Jewel into the other.

Sunset was instantly stunned at who he was riding inside. The man's name was Loman Foley and he was head of an investment bank out of Las Angeles. The man Jewel was in was his partner.

The buildings on the grounds were investment companies. And they were moving billions, slowly taking over more and more of the world's resources.

The small investment firm in Portland was only a tiny tip of a massive iceberg.

Sunset went into the man's history and found where the Mind Stone had brainwashed the man.

Sunset put a field around the entire thing and the memory of the last three years, but did nothing.

The two men knocked on Cadmus's office door and someone on the other side they recognized as Cadmus said, "Enter."

Sunset knew that Loman and his partner were there to give Cadmus his daily briefing on the progress they were making.

"Now!" Sunset said through the connection he had with Gail back in Poker Boy's office.

Gail said simply, "Moving."

As the two men stopped in front of Cadmus, Sunset was shocked at what the ancient god looked like. He had been expecting some sort of Zeus figure, but instead Cadmus looked to be no more than forty and blonde, with a chiseled chin and bright green eyes. He had on a silk dress shirt and no tie.

Just as with Laverne, the man radiated power.

He sat behind a massive wooden desk with computers on it. The walls were filled with what looked to be ancient books and on one wall a large stone fireplace was in front of a group of chairs and a dark couch.

The two men in suits stopped in front of Cadmus's large desk and Cadmus sat back in his large office chair, ready to listen.

As Lowman was about to start his report, Cadmus suddenly leaned forward toward his computer.

"That is not possible."

Clearly Cadmus had gotten an alarm about Dottie's attack.

At that moment Sunset shrunk the bubble around Lowman's brainwashing and gave him the instruction to just stand still until otherwise ordered.

Then Sunset stepped out of Lowman just as Tommy vanished inside of Cadmus.

Beside Sunset, Jewel appeared and instantly went with Tommy inside of Cadmus.

All Sunset could do was be their backup in case something went wrong.

The ancient god had his fingers poised on the computer screen when suddenly he tipped over to his side and rolled out of his chair. His head cracked the stone floor, which was going to hurt if he ever woke up.

He lay sprawled on the stone on his back, legs apart. His eyes were open and staring at the ceiling.

An instant later Laverne appeared in the room alongside Dottie and Harmony.

Dottie had her arm around Harmony who looked like she was going to be sick when she saw the ancient god on the floor.

Gail was with them and Sunset couldn't remember being so happy to see someone in a long time. And they had only been apart for an hour.

Gail hugged him and he hugged her back.

"Glad you are safe," Gail said.

Tommy and Jewel appeared from Cadmus, smiling.

The two men looked at Laverne with puzzled looks on their faces.

"They remember nothing about the last five years," Jewel said. "We left commands that they are to do as told."

Laverne nodded. "Please go home to your families and say nothing about this to anyone. Understood?"

Both men nodded and just about ran from the room.

Sunset tried not to smile at that.

"What did you do to him?" Laverne asked, indicating Cadmus.

Jewel smiled. "We shrunk his entire mind down inside of a small ball and disconnected control from his entire body. "He will continue to live fine, but he has no control of anything."

"Can you bring his mind back?" Laverne asked.

"At any point," Tommy said. "He is still in there and can hear everything that is being said by you right now. And his mind can feel the pain and everything his body needs, but he cannot control or react."

"But he feels the pain?" Dottie asked.

"He does," Tommy said. "He has a bad headache from hitting his head on the stone. And right now I bet he is getting very, very angry."

"You put his mind in jail, basically," Harmony said.

"Yes," Jewel said.

"There is no way he can get out of that jail, either," Tommy said. "But he will still need to be watched and one of us will need to check on him at times."

Laverne nodded.

Sunset liked the sound of that.

Harmony walked over to Cadmus and bent down and opened up his shirt. On a chain under his shirt was a pendant. She yanked it off, not caring that it ripped skin.

Sunset figured that was the Mind Stone.

Then Harmony stood and took off the pendant she wore and handed both to Laverne.

Laverne looked at both and nodded, then put Cadmus's Mind Stone in her pocket and handed the other one back to Harmony.

Sunset watched as Harmony nodded thanks, then put her pendant back around her neck. At some point Sunset was going to need to ask why Laverne had done that.

Then Harmony bent over Cadmus again.

"You imprisoned me for centuries," she said, her voice mean and level. "You being imprisoned like this only suits your crime against me."

Harmony stood. "Under the rules, how long can you keep him like this?"

Laverne got an evil smile on her face. "He looks healthy to me. We will put him in a prison cell and feed him and take care of his needs. I am sure for a few centuries at least. That will be enough to follow the rules for his crimes not only against you, but for what he has done now. At least the crimes we know about now. If we discover more, the time might stretch."

"Thank you," Harmony said.

Then as Sunset watched, Harmony turned back to Cadmus. "And for all the pain you inflicted on me with that thing between your legs, expect me to visit you every few months to help in your healing."

With that she kicked him as hard as she could in the groin.

Sunset flinched, as did Tommy, but Cadmus just lay there, his eyes open, starting at the ceiling.

Wow, that had to hurt.

Then Harmony turned to Laverne, smiling. "I hope that helped his healing."

Laverne smiled and nodded. "I am sure it did. And I am sure he will look forward to his regular treatment."

Harmony laughed. "I know I will."

PART FIVE
Stopping the Unstoppable

Twenty-Four

GAIL COULD NOT believe how worried she had been about Sunset. She was so much in love with him, it amazed her. She had never felt like that for anyone before.

And she liked it. Not the worry part, the love.

Right now, more than anything, she wanted them to be back in their wonderful condo in Portland celebrating the success they had just had. But she had a hunch they had a much, much larger problem now. She didn't know exactly what, but she could sense from Sunset the problem was immediate.

Just as Laverne and Harmony and Dottie were about to leave with Cadmus, Jewel stopped them.

"We have a very large problem to solve yet," Jewel said.

Gail watched as Sunset and Tommy both nodded.

Laverne looked puzzled.

"Those two office buildings here on the grounds are headquarters for a massive threat to civilization," Tommy said.

Gail almost gasped at that kind of language coming from Tommy. In her time training with them, neither he nor Jewel had been people who exaggerated.

Laverne actually raised one eyebrow at that.

"The two men who were here were major bankers, investment bankers," Sunset said, "and they both had been controlled by a Mind Stone.

"We cleared them," Jewel said, "but there are thousands in those two major buildings and maybe upwards of a million more around the world, many controlled by Mind Stone programming, all working to bring down the world economy by pulling massive amounts of money from it."

Gail actually felt sick to her stomach. The small scam they had discovered in Portland had only been a tiny tip of a massive problem.

"What can be done?" Laverne asked.

All three Ghost Agents shook their heads.

Laverne stared at them for a moment, then nodded. "Find out how far and wide this spreads," she said. "And how it is being spread. And where the money is going."

Gail nodded with Sunset and Tommy and Jewel.

Laverne turned to Dottie and Harmony. "I am going to need you both to be tracing through the computer world the Mind Stone programs and stopping them where you can."

Dottie and Harmony both nodded.

"I will get Poker Boy and his team working from their side on this as well," Laverne said. "Everyone feed his team information as you have it. We meet in his office tomorrow at lunch to figure out what we can do to clean up Cadmus's mess."

Everyone nodded and with that the four gods left the four Ghost Agents standing in the massive, plush office.

Gail turned to look at Sunset. "Is it really that bad?"

Sunset nodded. "Worse."

Gail felt shocked. "How can it be worse?"

"We aren't sure yet," Jewel said, "but there might be more Mind Stones."

Gail thought she might be sick.

"It didn't feel like Cadmus was actually in control," Tommy said. "He thought he was, but it didn't feel like it."

"And I got that same sense from the man I was in," Sunset said, nodding. "But he didn't know who actually was."

"Oh," was all Gail could think to say.

This was a long way from over and that scared her more than she wanted to admit.

Twenty-Five

SUNSET KEPT HIS arm around Gail as the four of them stood in the lush office of Cadmus and planned their next move.

Jewel and Tommy decided that the four of them should stick together and not try to clear anyone, just find out any information they could. Sunset liked that idea and so did Gail.

"We need to see if there are more Mind Stones," Tommy said. "And who has them, without tipping our hand at any of this."

Sunset nodded.

So with that they jumped to the top floor of the tallest building inside Cadmus's compound.

The offices here were larger than Cadmus's office and very modern. Lush blue carpet covered the floors and a bank of computers filled the back wall of the largest office.

And one guy seemed to have that large office and be in control, at least here. He seemed to be in his forties, dressed in a silk suit, and a chiseled face and chin, like he had modeled when younger.

He radiated control, so they all four decided to climb inside him to get the same information before spreading out.

The guy's name was Kenyon and from what Sunset could tell the guy was president and CEO of about twenty different investment firms and banks around the world. And each investment firm ran or controlled hundreds of other corporations.

It was like a giant web of businesses with Kenyon sitting at the top of them all. And running it from this office.

He was rich beyond even his own imaginings. But that wasn't stopping him or even slowing him down.

Sunset slowly realized that Kenyon was only in charge of this branch. From what Sunset could tell, there were six other branches of banks, investment firms, and corporations as large.

Three women and four men ran the seven major businesses.

And they reported to a group of three, of which Cadmus had been one.

Kenyon hated Cadmus, thought him an idiot.

Their names of the other two were Rhesus and Sinon. Both lived together as a couple in the United States just outside of Las Vegas.

"Can anyone see the reason behind all of this?" Tommy asked.

"No," Gail said. "But Kenyon has been brainwashed."

"I see that," Jewel said.

"Can anyone see exactly what they are doing?"

"Everything I can see," Tommy said, "appears to be a normal business structure. No scams at any point, that at least Kenyon knows about."

"From what I can tell from him," Jewel said, "Kenyon would be mortified if he had a scam like the one in Portland anywhere along his command."

"I agree," Gail said.

Sunset had to agree as well. Everything he was seeing through Kenyon made this all appear to be a very legitimate business.

"So why was this guy brainwashed with a Mind Stone?" Jewel asked. "I'm going to go exploring back in his memories before the brainwashing."

When she came back a moment later she said, "Let's get out of this guy's head and talk."

All four of them stepped back into the plush office as Kenyon kept working on a merger document he had been reading between a firm in Sweden and one based in Germany.

"This guy is no different before the brainwashing than after," Jewel said.

"So why is it there?" Gail asked.

Sunset knew the answer almost instantly. "It's a time bomb."

Jewel nodded. "That's my guess also. But we need to see if Kenyon is the only one who is the same before and after that lump of brainwashing."

They all nodded and headed for different offices.

Twenty minutes later they were standing in the wide hallway near a receptionist desk and a bank of elevators.

"They are all the same before and after," Tommy said.

Sunset agreed. "And I tried to get near one of the lumps of brainwashing. My sense is if triggered, it will expand and just shut down the person."

"I saw the same thing," Jewel said. "Everyone will simply fall over, not dead, but trapped in their own minds as we did with Cadmus."

"Why?" Gail asked.

"These seven major businesses control a vast number of the world's banking and investments and corporations," Tommy said.

"Everyone running them falls over," Sunset said, "it will send the world's economies into the dark ages."

"Not counting the panic of just having that many people suddenly appear sick," Jewel said.

"Oh, we are so screwed," Gail said.

Sunset could only agree to that.

Twenty-Six

GAIL SAT NEXT TO Sunset in the booth in Poker Boy's floating office. Tommy and Jewel sat on chairs at the end of the table, leaving room for Laverne on one side. They were the only four there at the moment.

After realizing what might happen, she and Sunset and Jewel and Tommy had spread out through the two buildings, making sure that nothing was different.

And then they had gone to the other six business headquarters and gone inside the heads of the other six presidents. All were the same as Kenyon.

All had what appeared to be a ticking time bomb in their heads, ready to go off and shut them down instantly.

So after four hours, they all decided it was time to tell Poker Boy and Laverne what they had found, see if any of them had any ideas.

Gail was flat scared for what would happen if something triggered all those planted bombs, as they were calling them. They had no idea how all of them would

be triggered. From what they could tell, it had taken years and years to plant them all.

But there must have been a reason.

Madge brought the four of them burgers and fries and shakes, which looked amazing and smelled even better. As they were digging into the food, Poker Boy arrived with Ben and sat across from her and Sunset.

Poker Boy never seemed to take off the leather coat and black fedora-like hat.

"Wow, those smell wonderful," Poker Boy said.

"Help yourself," Sunset said. "We're only eating the ghost elements, remember?"

Sunset pulled the entire cheeseburger ghost plate and burger toward him, leaving the original.

"Oh, yeah," Poker Boy said, smiling, taking the original and pulling it closer.

Ben just took a few fries and sat back, saying nothing.

At that moment Laverne appeared and sat down, taking one of Gail's fries.

"So how bad is it?" she asked, looking sideways at Jewel and Tommy.

"Bad," Tommy said.

"Really bad," Jewel said.

Gail found herself nodding to that.

Jewel told Laverne what each person that they had seen had in their heads.

"Time bombs?" Poker Boy asked.

"That's what we are calling it," Gail said.

"It will do to each person who has it inside," Sunset said, "when triggered, basically what we did to Cadmus."

Laverne just shook her head and Poker Boy sat there not showing any emotion at all.

"So how did these all get implanted?" Laverne asked.

"A computer program of some sort," Jewel said. "From what we can tell. But it is not altering in any way the person's thoughts or activities. It is just sitting there dormant."

"So a lot of people not working for those companies might have it as well," Poker Boy said.

The four Ghost Agents just nodded. That was something they had figured out fairly quickly that this might have spread far, far beyond the businesses.

"We think," Jewel said, turning slightly in her chair so that she could face Laverne, "that there are more Mind Stones out there."

Laverne slowly nodded. "I have been afraid of that for more centuries than I want to count."

"We believe that Cadmus had two partners in all this," Jewel said, going on. "Two men by the name of Rhesus and Sinon."

Laverne blinked.

From what Gail could tell, Lady Luck was actually surprised.

"Ben," Laverne said. "Do you know those two names?"

Ben nodded. "Lower level workers on Olympus. They have been a couple since before Atlantis. They were support in the fight against the Titans."

Laverne turned back to Jewel. "You are sure those are the names?"

Jewel nodded.

Gail found herself nodding as well.

"The three of them were the brains and money behind the entire seven massive businesses," Tommy said. "From what we can tell, they have been building these businesses for most of the last century and through this century."

"They were in the fight with the Titans," Ben said. "As was everyone from Olympus. So they might have obtained Mind Stones. But I doubt they would have had the power to use them."

"Cadmus might have trained them," Poker Boy said. "Is that possible?"

Laverne nodded slowly.

"Would it take a Mind Stone to trigger the shut-down reaction?" Poker Boy asked.

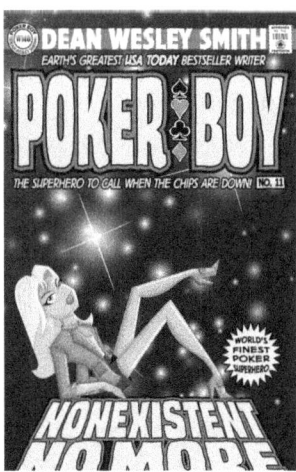

Can't Get Enough of Poker Boy?
These stories and more are available at your favorite booksellers.

Ben shrugged.

"I honestly don't know," Laverne said. "But I will find out."

Gail wasn't happy with the sound of that.

Laverne looked at Jewel and Tommy. "Would it be possible for me to get inside Cadmus's head, talk with him, without you releasing him?"

It took a moment, but slowly Gail and Tommy both nodded.

"We could take you in," Jewel said.

"Then we need to do that now," Laverne said, standing.

She looked at Ben. "Tell Gail and Sunset and Poker Boy about those two others, find their location, and scout them out. We need to know if they have Mind Stones as well. And if they really are connected with all this."

Jewel and Tommy stood and a moment later the three of them were gone.

Heavy silence filled the floating office and the large booth.

Gail did not envy Jewel and Tommy having Laverne ride along with them into the head of another very angry god.

Gail had only been a Ghost Agent for a very short time and already so much of this was so far over her head. Doing something like that would scare her silly.

She would do it if she had to. But she was really glad she didn't have to.

Twenty-Seven

SUNSET WENT BACK to working on his burger and fries and milkshake while Poker Boy jumped Ben to his office to get information on Rhesus and Sinon. There had been a number of things in that conversation that Sunset had desperately

wanted to ask about. But the time wasn't right, clearly.

Gail leaned against him for a moment, then also went back to eating. With the way things were going, there was no telling when they would be able to eat again, so they might as well do it now while they had a break.

Sunset hadn't gotten more than a few bites into his burger when Poker Boy and Ben returned.

"I was remembering them right," Ben said as they slid into the booth and Poker Boy went back to eating as well. "Rhesus and Sinon are low-level gods who have been here since the beginning. They have made no trouble at all and just stayed together and to themselves, only coming forward to help when asked."

"So this sort of plan to drop the world back into the dark ages isn't their style?" Poker Boy asked.

"Sure doesn't seem like it would be," Sunset said.

"I agree," Ben said. "But over centuries people do change."

Sunset just shook his head at that. He had been a ghost for over a hundred years. He still couldn't imagine centuries.

Beside him Gail was staring at her fries and just shaking her head, clearly having the same trouble.

"So do you think they will remember you?" Poker Boy asked Ben.

"I would imagine they would, yes," Ben said.

"So why don't we all four just go talk with them," Poker Boy said. "Ben, you and I from the outside, Gail and Sunset from the inside."

"Seems like as good an idea as any," Ben said.

Sunset and Gail and Poker Boy all took one last bite of their burgers while Ben took another fry.

Then they jumped into the warm Las Vegas air.

In front of them was a walled compound with a wide driveway leading through a high metal gate. The grounds were beautiful, from what Sunset could see through the gate, decorated in that desert rock and sand, with low-water plants everywhere and a number of large trees up closer to the main house inside the walls.

Poker Boy went over and hit the call button on the wall. A moment later a voice came back with simply "Yes."

"Ben and Poker Boy here to see Rhesus and Sinon."

There was silence for a moment, then the gate clicked. "Please, come in."

The four of them walked up the wide driveway toward the large brown stucco home covering a small hilltop. It was a massive mansion, but there were bigger in Las Vegas. And even though this showed money, it didn't shout it as Cadmus's compound had.

A man in silk slacks and a pink golf shirt and no shoes met them at the massive front door to the mansion. His hair was colored blonde and swept back off his forehead. He had to have two rings, at least, on each finger. Not cheap rings, either.

He was smiling showing perfect teeth and clearly surprised and happy to see Ben and Poker Boy.

"Rhesus," Ben said, "I'd like you to meet Poker Boy."

Poker Boy nodded, bowing slightly. "Pleasure is all mine."

"Oh, heavens, no, it is our honor," Rhesus said, almost giggling. "Come in. Come in. Sinon is so flustered he had to run and change clothes. I told him he looked fine but he would have none of it."

Sunset and Gail stood off to one side, saying nothing, as Rhesus let Poker Boy and Ben into the vast mansion.

Then Sunset and Gail followed.

The ceilings of the place were so high and the entrance so large, with large stone columns and stone floors, the place almost echoed like a canyon.

Sunset took Gail's hand and they stepped into Rhesus.

Sunset was shocked. He wasn't sure what he was expecting, but Rhesus was on the inside exactly how he presented on the outside. He and Sinon had been a couple for more centuries than Sunset wanted to look at.

And they didn't care at all about money. They made enough to live in their style of comfort and that was it.

And there was a time bomb in him as well.

"This guy isn't smart enough to do this sort of major plot," Gail said after a moment.

"We saw that Kenyon and the other six corporation heads were reporting to them," Sunset said. "But I see no evidence at all that is the case."

"And I see no sign at all," Gail said, "that they know what a Mind Stone is."

"They are being used," Sunset said. "Just as Cadmus was being used."

Rhesus had shown Poker Boy and Sunset into a massive library with large couches and chairs and a massive stone fireplace. The shelves were all dark maple and every shelf seemed to be jammed with ancient books.

"It is so unusual that we get guests," Rhesus said.

"We need to go all the way back in this guy's mind to see if we are missing something," Sunset said.

"I agree," Gail said. "Look for any sign of the Mind Stones being with them."

Like pealing an onion, Sunset drifted back into the depths of Rhesus's memories, back before Atlantis, back to the fight with the Titans to save Earth.

Turns out the Titans were aliens. And the gods were not yet gods, but more of a major ship's crew.

"Here," Gail said.

Sunset went to her.

It was in a memory, right after the Titans had been defeated, that Rhesus picked up two Mind Stones. He did not know what they were, but thought them attractive. So he kept them.

The necklaces, along with all the other jewelry of Rhesus and Sinon, moved with them for centuries, finally ending up, as far as Rhesus knew, in their vault under the house. He had no idea what they were and had not given them a thought.

"Got a hunch they are not in the vault," Gail said.

"Got a hunch you are right," Sunset said. "Shall we go tell Ben and Poker Boy what we have found?"

They emerged from Rhesus just as Sinon made his entrance. And an entrance he made. Some of the best drag queens in all of Las Vegas would be jealous of Sinon.

His thick makeup was perfect, his long brown hair pulled up and tucked on his head, his jewelry stunning and large. He looked to be about five-foot even, including his heels which he walked in without a problem. He wore thinning silk slacks, a frilly silk blouse, and a scarf of rainbow colors around his neck.

Ben and Poker Boy both stood when he entered and introduced themselves.

As Sinon was working to offer Ben and Poker Boy a snack from a tray of small pastries on a nearby mantle, Sunset told Ben and Poker Boy what they had found.

"We'll check Sinon now," Gail said, "but I am not expecting anything to be different. They did not know what the Mind Stones were when they found them."

Sunset followed Gail into Sinon and found exactly the same thing as they had found in Rhesus. The two had been together for more centuries than Sunset could imagine and that impressed him.

As the four live humans were finally getting settled on the couches facing each other, Sunset and Gail stepped out of Sinon.

"The same as expected," Sunset said and then he and Gail stepped back.

"To what do we owe this honor?" Rhesus asked.

"Actually," Ben said, "we believe you might help us track down two pendants that are required in a fight we are waging at the moment. We believe you might have found them back right after the war with the Titans."

"A terrible time," Sinon said, fanning himself with an imaginary fan.

"We picked up a lot of trinkets and jewelry after that war," Rhesus said.

Ben went on to describe the two Mind Stones and Rhesus nodded.

"We have two of them," Rhesus said.

"Would it be possible for us to borrow them?" Poker Boy asked.

"If it will help your team and Laverne save the world yet again," Rhesus said, "I am sure we can part with them."

"Oh, heavens yes," Sinon said, standing. "They are in the vault. I will lead the way."

Rhesus smiled fondly as he and Ben and Poker Boy stood and followed Sinon.

They took a hidden elevator down three floors. It was behind what looked like a normal hallway panel of wood with an original Picasso on it.

A large stone chamber was at the bottom of the elevator, lined with shelves and full of furniture and pottery of various types.

A large vault door was against the far wall and Rhesus took only a moment to open it, leading all of them into a massive bank-like vault full of drawers and drawers of jewelry and stones.

All Sunset could do was shake his head. Amazing what collecting could do if a person could manage it for thousands and thousands of years.

"They are here," Rhesus said, pulling open one drawer about halfway down the room.

The drawer was empty, as both Sunset and Gail expected it would be.

Rhesus just stared.

Sinon took one look in the drawer and fainted dead away.

The Mind Stones were gone.

Twenty-Eight

GAIL WATCHED AS Rhesus tried to help Sinon back to his feet on those heels he wore. Not an easy task.

"We'll see if we can figure out what happened," Gail said to Poker Boy and Ben.

"I'll take Rhesus," Sunset said.

Gail nodded and a moment later was inside Sinon. But instead of looking generally at things, she focused down on any access he might have done with the vault, or with anyone else in the vault.

Gail could tell that the two had been very careful. Not even their employees knew how to get into the vault. And almost no one knew it was even there.

But a god like Cadmus, if they knew where the vault was, could teleport inside and get the stones and take them.

Gail worked her way back through Sinon's mind, ignoring all the lifestyle things she flat didn't want to know about, and focusing on the vault.

As far as Sinon was concerned, no one had been in that vault since they built it fifty years before. And the stones were there at that point because he had put them there.

As the four live humans returned to the library, Gail left Sinon.

A moment later Sunset appeared from Rhesus.

"I have nothing," Gail said.

"They had not thought of those two stones since they built the vault," Sunset said, "and no one but someone who could teleport could have gotten in there."

Ben and Poker Boy both nodded. "I'm afraid we need to get going. We now must find out who stole your pendants."

"Please do," Rhesus said as he comforted Sinon who had dropped into a chair and looked faint again.

"Thank you for your time," Ben said.

"Yes, thank you," Poker Boy said, bowing to both gods slightly.

Then they vanished.

Sunset and Gail stayed for a moment longer, until Sinon burst into tears and started sobbing about how much of a fool they had made of themselves.

The noise was like a bad actor on a stage thinking he had to project the sobs to the back row.

"You want to help them?" Sunset asked.

Gail shook her head. "This is their relationship. Rhesus will take care of it."

Sunset just shook his head. "Poor man."

"It's worked for them for more centuries than I can imagine," Gail said.

Again Sunset just shook his head as Sinon kept sobbing, getting snot all over his perfect outfit.

Gail took Sunset by the hand and a moment later they were in Poker Boy's office and away from the sobbing god.

And the silence was wonderful.

Twenty-Nine

SUNSET AND GAIL slid back into the giant diner booth across from Poker Boy and Ben. Sunset just stared through the windows of the floating office and out over Las Vegas. The sky was a deep blue and the distant mountains looked closer because the air was so clear.

A couple of airliners were circling for approach into McCarran and a small plane was climbing away toward Lake Mead in the distance.

A beautiful day, and one he and Gail would have enjoyed if the world didn't feel like it was about to end.

Madge hadn't taken away the basket of fries, so both he and Gail started munching on them. They were almost as good cold as warm.

Poker Boy and Ben just sat silently, clearly lost in their own thoughts.

Finally Poker Boy said, "Not a bit of this makes sense."

With that, Sunset agreed. Nothing at all about any of this made sense.

"So correct me if I am wrong," Poker Boy said. "We have seven major businesses, as far as we can tell, completely legit. Right?"

Sunset nodded. "Yes, and we have checked them all. They are all aboveboard and report to two people called Rhesus and Sinon, but clearly not the originals."

"And there are two more Mind Stones, right?" Poker Boy asked. "Stolen from that vault."

Gail and Sunset both nodded to that.

"And the only way to take anything from that vault would be to teleport in there and get them," Poker Boy said. "And yet no one really knew they were there. Just makes no sense."

"And what is making even less sense to me," Sunset said, "is where did the vast amounts of money come from to start up these two major conglomerates?"

"And for what reason?" Gail said.

Can't Get Enough of Poker Boy?
These stories and more are available at your favorite booksellers.

"Not a bit of sense at all," Poker Boy said again, shaking his head and going back to staring off into space.

Sunset munched on a fry and did the same thing.

"The key," Ben said, speaking up for the first time, "is who knew Rhesis and Sinon had those stones."

Poker Boy nodded. "And knew them well enough that they could safely be used as patsies."

At that moment Laverne and Jewel and Tommy appeared and sat down in the chairs facing the large table.

Sunset was shocked at how shaken all three seemed.

"Cadmus knew about the other two Mind Stones," Laverne said, her voice cold and angry. "He was the one who jumped into their vault and stole them."

"That answers that one question," Poker Boy said.

Sunset just nodded.

"He does not know where they are now," Jewel said. "He lost control of them forty years ago."

"This has been building for that long?" Poker Boy asked, sounding as shocked as Sunset felt.

"Yes," Laverne said.

"Wow, talk about a long game," Poker Boy said, sitting back.

Sunset looked at Laverne, who also seemed to be lost in thought. But he needed to know the big answer.

"Do you know who Cadmus gave the Mind Stones to?"

Laverne nodded, along with Jewel and Tommy.

"He gave them to Alecto and Demeter."

"Oh, no," Ben said softly.

"Two of the Furies?" Gail asked, clearly shocked.

Laverne nodded.

Sunset had no idea who they were, but from Ben's reaction and Gail's question, it didn't sound good.

"So why the time bombs in people's heads?" Sunset asked.

"Revenge," Laverne said simply. "I imprisoned them for a few thousand years. They plan on getting back at me by destroying the world I help defend."

"Oh," was all Sunset could think of to say.

Thirty

GAIL WATCHED AS Laverne vanished, saying she was going to check on any progress Dottie and Harmony were making.

"Someone want to fill me in on the history of Alecto and Demeter?" Poker Boy asked.

Gail knew the Greek history of the two, but from what she had been learning just the last day or so, the history often shadowed but was not exactly accurate when it came to gods.

"There were three of them originally, sisters called The Furies," Ben said. "One was killed in the battle with the Titans and that turned the other two angry, to say the least. They blamed their sister's death on Zeus and Laverne for even getting them into the war."

"So how did they end up in prison?" Sunset asked a moment before Gail could.

"When Atlantis fell," Ben said, "they profited from the pain and death and set up massive estates in central Germany. Laverne jailed them. They were released by the Fates about five hundred years ago and vanished."

Gail glanced at Jewel and Tommy, who were being very quiet after their experience in Cadmus's mind.

"Does Cadmus know where they are located?" Gail asked.

Both Jewel and Tommy shook their heads.

"And he does not know about the time bombs they planted either," Tommy said. "He thought it was all about making money and getting control of a vast part of the world's businesses."

"So how do we first find them and then stop them?" Poker Boy asked.

Silence met that question around the floating office.

Finally Ben said simply, "If we find them, we get the Mind Stones. Without the Mind Stones, they should not be able to trigger the time bombs in people's heads."

"So we go after the Mind Stones," Poker Boy said.

Gail liked how Poker Boy always seemed to be in charge without ever really acting like he was in charge. A trait of a true leader.

Then Gail heard herself think the word charge and had a thought. "Ben, since we have one Mind Stone, would the stones be linked in some sort of power connection in any way?"

"Something we could trace?" Sunset asked, following exactly what she was thinking.

Ben sat for a moment. Silence filled the office.

Then he said, "It's an alien technology, so I don't know for certain. But it might be possible. Laverne?"

Laverne appeared standing at the end of the table. Ben quickly told her Gail's question.

Laverne nodded after a moment. "It might be possible. What would you need to figure that out?"

"I'll need to run some tests on Olympus," Ben said.

Laverne nodded. "Do it. Stan, please jump with Ben to Olympus."

Stan, the God of Poker, appeared a moment later and then he and Ben vanished.

"I will tell Dottie and Harmony what they are doing," Laverne said, and vanished.

That left the four ghosts and Poker Boy at the table.

Gail looked at Poker Boy. "Olympus still exists?"

Poker Boy just shook his head. "You wouldn't believe me if I told you."

Gail laughed. "After the last few days, you would be surprised at what I would believe."

Sunset, Jewel, and Tommy all nodded to that as Madge appeared from behind the booth carrying new batches of hot French fries and cheeseburgers.

And the wonderful smell changed the topic perfectly.

Thirty-One

AFTER FIFTEEN MORE minutes of talking, they had come up with nothing more, so Poker Boy said he was going to go try to explain to Patty what had happened.

Jewel and Tommy jumped home to rest and Sunset jumped Gail and himself back to their condo in Portland.

The day there was as beautiful as it was in Las Vegas. Only greener.

The rivers were glistening in the sunlight and the view just stopped him cold. Amazing how being threatened with the end of civilization made him appreciate it even more.

They both climbed into the shower and then into bed, mostly without talking. They both needed a nap and the next thing Sunset realized, Gail was bringing him a cup of coffee that smelled wonderful.

She had gotten up and dressed and gone down to the Starbucks on the corner to get coffee and some pastries for both of them.

They sat in her dining area, staring out at the view. The sun was already low enough now in the west to put much of the downtown Portland area in shadows. But Mt. Hood, with the early winter snow, was bright white in the sunlight.

The coffee and pastry helped and as he was about to finish the last bite, Gail said, "Another thing makes no sense."

"Add it to the list in this craziness," Sunset said, laughing. "So what is our new addition?"

"Why use a Mind Stone for basically a small job like was done in this investment company here? It doesn't fit the pattern we are uncovering at all."

Sunset sat back, feeling slightly stunned. She was right. It didn't fit the pattern, yet when Harmony and Dottie tried to trace it, they had been trapped by Cadmus in a memory of Atlantis.

"Harmony and Dottie knew what had been used was a Mind Stone," Sunset said, forcing himself to think this through. "And they figured they needed the thing that Harmony had to block the powers. Right?"

"They called it the Necklace Stone," Gail said, nodding.

"So maybe this Necklace can stop this, if there are more of them," Sunset said. "But we just have no idea what it does."

"It seemed very important and then all of us sort of forgot it," Gail said. "Seems like we need to remind people of it."

"It does seem that way."

Gail called Jewel and Tommy and a moment later they appeared. They both looked refreshed as well.

It only took a minute to explain to them what they were wondering about the Necklace Stone.

"Laverne," Jewel said looking slightly upward at the ceiling on the condo. "We have an idea, but need a few answers first."

Laverne's voice came back strong. "Poker Boy's office."

The four of them jumped there instantly.

From a fantastic view overlooking the green and water of Portland, Oregon, to an even more fantastic view overlooking the brown desert and mountains around Las Vegas, it was just late enough in the day that the lights of the Strip were starting to take over from the daylight.

Poker Boy and Ben were sitting in the booth when they arrived and a moment later Laverne appeared. Clearly Ben had managed to finish his research.

After they were all seated, Sunset decided he was going to get right to the point. He looked at Laverne and said simply, "Why was the Necklace Stone so important when we first started this? What does it do?"

"And how many of them are there?" Gail asked.

Laverne actually frowned.

Poker Boy shook his head and muttered, "Forgot all about that."

"The Necklace Stone is a name for an ancient alien device that blocks the powers of the Mind Stones," Ben said. "Which are also alien devices. There was only one Necklace Stone known to exist."

"But until today there was only one Mind Stone known to exist, correct?" Poker Boy asked.

Laverne nodded.

"So why do the scam in Portland?" Sunset asked, deciding to continue directly at the topic that bothered him. "What purpose did that do?"

"It brought the Necklace Stone out of hiding," Poker Boy said.

"Shit!" Laverne said and vanished.

Silence filled the office.

Deadly silence.

When Lady Luck herself swears, you know something is very, very wrong.

A few long moments later she appeared with Dottie and Harmony, both looking a little shocked.

"Is the Necklace Stone still on you?" Laverne asked Harmony.

She nodded and showed Laverne, who looked visibly relieved.

She indicated that the two ancient gods should join them at the table and Sunset and Gail scooted clear around to the back of the booth to let Jewel and Tommy into the booth.

Sunset was having trouble coming to terms that he was not only dealing with Poker Boy, but there were four ancient gods sitting in this old diner booth with him.

Laverne tuned to Ben. "What did your research on Olympus discover about the Mind Stones?"

"Nothing new, I'm afraid," Ben said. "The Necklace Stone can block the effect."

"Can we produce more Necklaces?" Sunset asked, speaking before he realized even what he was thinking.

Silence filled the office again as Ben looked at Sunset, then slowly nodded. "I think we can. Yes."

"So what kind of area will the Necklace protect?" Poker Boy asked.

"I honestly don't know," Ben said. "But I did discover that the Necklace Stone gives off a very specific signal.

From Olympus, I should be able to track if there are more of them."

Sunset understood devices far, far better than he understood what some of the gods could do, so it was a relief to him that they were talking about the Necklace Stone as nothing more than a screening device.

"If that signal the Necklace Stone is emitting could be expanded," Sunset said, "or enough Necklace Stones produced, to cover the globe with their blocking signal, we would not have to ever worry about the time bombs in people's minds being triggered by the Mind Stones."

Laverne nodded. "Ben, do you and a few others need Harmony's Necklace Stone to do the research to find out if what Sunset suggested is possible?"

"No," Ben said. "But I do have a way that using Harmony's Necklace Stone, you might be able to trace other Necklace Stones. But I think it is something only our Ghost Agent friends here will be able to see."

Ben smiled at the shocked look on Sunset's face.

"Harmony, would you take your Necklace and hold it out?" Ben asked.

Harmony did, holding out the flat long crystal stone in her hand and leaving the cord around her neck.

"Now," Ben said. "My understanding is that Ghost Agents can see auras, correct?"

"Yes, but we keep it dampened most of the time," Jewel said. "Too distracting."

Sunset agreed with that. If he didn't dampen his vision of people's auras, he would have gone crazy a century before.

"Turn it back on now," Ben said.

Sunset did as Ben suggested, at first blinded by the huge and intense and powerfully bright aura of Laverne.

All four Ghost Agents shielded their eyes.

"Laverne," Jewel said. "Could you and Dottie please move around behind the booth for a moment."

Dottie and Laverne did, leaving only the very bright aura of Harmony, shimmering in bright gold and green colors.

Stunningly beautiful.

But then Sunset looked at the Harmony stone and he could see the web of energy coming off of it, expanding like a web over the entire office.

"It is clear," Jewel said. "Like a net over all of us."

"See if you can see a string of the energy leaving the localized net," Ben said.

Jewel and Tommy both stood and then both of them floated up and out through the office walls, just seeming to stand out in the air, studying everything.

Silence once again as Sunset watched. He didn't know that Ghost Agents could float like that. Clearly something he and Gail needed to learn.

After a full minute of everyone watching them through the windows, they came back inside.

"There are hundreds of lines of power leaving this net in all directions," Jewel said.

"Maybe upward of three hundred by my quick count," Tommy said.

"You think they all lead to other Necklace Stones?" Laverne asked.

Ben nodded. "I do. I think every Necklace Stone is connected to every other Necklace Stone."

"Oh, wow, we might not need to produce more," Jewel said.

Sunset could only hope she was right.

Thirty-Two

GAIL WAS STUNNED when Jewel and Tommy just sort of floated out into the air a thousand feet above Las Vegas Boulevard. That must have been something to feel.

Clearly floating like that was something that hadn't been in her training. But she wanted it to be and soon. She had always dreamed of flying and she had a hunch that is exactly what that would feel like.

When Jewel and Tommy came back and reported a possible hundreds more Necklace Stones, she actually felt excited.

Laverne nodded to the news. She turned to Ben. "Get Stan and head back to Olympus and figure out how to expand the protection of the Necklace Stones."

Ben nodded and a moment later Stan appeared and then the two of them vanished.

Laverne turned to Dottie and Harmony. "I would like you two to keep working on the computer side of things. We still need to know where Alecto and Demeter are. And protect that Necklace Stone. But don't go just yet. I need the Ghost Agents to follow the trail from your Necklace Stone to others first."

Both nodded.

Then Laverne turned to Poker Boy. "Put all of your team on alert. You are going to be getting the Necklace Stones when the Ghost Agents locate them. We might need them at a moment's notice."

He nodded. "Back in five minutes." Then he vanished.

Laverne turned to Gail and the other three Ghost Agents. "I need you four to spread out and follow those energy lines to other Necklace Stones. Then tell Poker Boy to bring them back here. I will collect them and keep them safe until Ben figures out how to use them."

The four Ghost Agents nodded.

They all stood as Madge brought burgers and fries and vanilla milkshakes for Laverne, Dottie, and Harmony.

"Gail and I have a problem," Sunset said to Jewel and Tommy as they moved toward the edge of the office. "We don't know how to fly like that yet."

Gail was very happy Sunset had told them instead of her.

Jewel and Tommy both smiled and nodded.

"There is no trick to it," Tommy said. "You know how you were able to jump to a new place by just imagine being there?"

Gail nodded.

"Just imagine yourself lifting off the ground, being lighter than air," Jewel said. "Same thing."

"Remember we are ghosts," Tommy said. "We don't really exist in any form other than what we imagine. We can transport, walk through things, so we can float as well."

Gail nodded and just focused and imagined herself lifting into the air from the floor.

Next thing she knew she was going through the glass ceiling of Poker Boy's office and out into the warm air of the desert. There was a pretty good wind, but it didn't seem to affect her at all, even though she could feel it.

It felt so wonderful to just float in the sky, she just wanted to shout for joy. She had no fear at all.

Sunset floated up right beside her, a smile on his face so wide he looked like a kid. She imagined she was smiling just as much.

Tommy and Jewel joined them, also both smiling.

"Fun, isn't it?" Tommy asked.

All Gail could do was nod, enjoying the feeling of floating like a kid's balloon.

As all four of them floated there, Jewel pointed back at the office below them. "See the web of bright white lines around everything?"

Gail looked and nodded. It was as if the floating office had a bright fisherman's net around it.

And moving away from the net were hundreds of lines going in all directions.

Five actually went down to different spots in the Las Vegas area.

"Let's all four follow that one," Tommy said, pointing to one that dropped toward the downtown area. "See what is at the other end."

As one they flew along the white energy line. Gail had no doubt that they could go faster, but even going slowly, they reached the other end of the line within a few seconds.

The Necklace Stone was being used as decoration in a landscaping area near a sidewalk in the Golden Nugget Pool area. It had a large net radiating out around it as well.

And hundreds and hundreds of power lines radiating off from it as well.

"Poker Boy," Jewel said into the air as the four of them stood around the Necklace Stone. "Can you jump to me?"

A moment later Poker Boy appeared in the pool area and Gail noticed that he had formed a pocket of time around himself and them, making everyone in the pool area seem to freeze. She had heard he could do that, seemingly stop time. It was creepy because all sound suddenly stopped.

And all the people around the pool were frozen in bizarre postures.

She knew Poker Boy had to do that to make sure the cameras and all the people around in the pool area didn't just see him appear.

Jewel bent down and pointed at the stone that was almost too bright to look at.

Poker Boy picked it up and studied it. Gail turned off her aura vision so she could actually see it as well. It was long and shaped like a crystal and sort of a gray color.

"They sure don't look like much, do they?" he said.

Gail had to agree, they didn't.

He nodded and vanished, letting time crash back in around the four Ghost Agents.

The sounds of the living hit hard. Amazing how you don't notice sounds until there was a complete lack of sound.

Gail turned back on her aura vision and all the white lines that had come off the Necklace Stone were gone.

"Back to Poker Boy's office to plan this," Jewel said.

When they appeared in Poker Boy's office, the net around the place had doubled and the lines leading off to other stones were now much brighter.

Gail could only imagine what this place would look like when they had hundreds of those stones here.

She just hoped that nothing would go wrong with that many stones that close together.

Thirty-Three

THREE HOURS LATER, Sunset found his sixtieth stone on a rocky beach just along the English coast. The weather there was cold and the wind biting.

He quickly called for Poker Boy, who appeared, took the stone Sunset was pointing to and vanished, all within ten seconds.

Sunset jumped back to floating above Poker Boy's office just as Gail appeared.

"Traced another one under water," she said. "That's six for me under water."

"Eight," Sunset said.

They had been discovering that many of the stones were in lakes or deep in oceans. They could go in and down into depths, but none of the gods could follow them to actually pick up the stones. So they were going to wait until Sunset figured out what was possible before trying to retrieve those. Both Tommy and

Jewel were convinced that if they needed to, they could pick up the stones and get them to the surface.

Sunset was convinced he couldn't. He could barely move a plate on a table, let along pick up something and try to bring it up through water.

A moment later Jewel appeared and then a moment after that, Tommy. All four of them floated about two hundred feet above Poker Boy's office.

There were so many Necklace Stones in Poker Boy's office, with their aura vision turned on there was a glow around the office that glowed almost as bright as a sun.

"I think we have every one not under water," Tommy said.

Gail nodded.

"I bet Poker Boy is exhausted," Sunset said, smiling.

"Let's go find out," Jewel said.

They jumped back inside the office. Sunset made sure his aura vision was off because he flat didn't want to see what it looked like in there with that many Necklace Stones.

"We're sure the rest are all under water," Jewel said to Laverne as the four Ghost Agents scooted into the booth. Dottie and Harmony were gone. A large wicker basket full of Necklace Stones sat beside Laverne. All of them looked exactly the same dull gray.

Poker Boy was sitting in the booth drinking a milkshake and working on a hamburger.

A moment later Madge appeared with burgers and fries and milkshakes for the four of them as well. The food smelled fantastic and he didn't realize how hungry he had become.

At that moment Ben and Stan appeared and joined Poker Boy on the other side of the booth.

Ben saw the basket of stones and nodded. "Any luck?" Laverne asked.

Ben nodded. "As far as I can tell, there are only three Mind Stones and I think I have a way to trace them now from their energy signal."

"Fantastic," Laverne said, nodding.

"Were you able to get all of the Necklace Stones?" Ben asked.

"No," Laverne said. "About thirty are in oceans and lakes. By my count we have two-hundred and sixty-three in this basket, plus the one Harmony is wearing."

Ben nodded. "That will be enough. We need two-hundred and sixty."

"To do what exactly?" Laverne asked.

"We will need to put the stones we have in exact places along all the major energy lay lines around the planet," Ben said. "I have the exact locations each would need to be placed. Then from Olympus, I should be able to power them up using the lay lines to expand the Necklace Stones' protective area."

"Will it be enough?" Laverne asked.

Ben nodded. "It will form a shield around the planet that will basically make the Mind Stones worthless. But I would not suggest we go after the Mind Stones until we have that in place."

Laverne nodded.

Laverne turned to the Ghost Agents. "Go get some rest. We're going to need you as soon as we have the shield in place."

Sunset found himself nodding along with Gail and Tommy and Jewel.

Then Laverne turned to Poker Boy. "Get every one of your team who can teleport and have them meet here in ten minutes. I will call Harmony and Dottie to help. We will take the stones to their locations one at a time."

With that Poker Boy and Stan both vanished.

Sunset reached over and took Gail's hand and a moment later they were in their condo in Portland.

The nightlights of the city were beautiful.

You up for a movie?" Gail asked after a moment of both of them just standing in their living room staring at the lights.

"I'll jump down to the theater to get us some popcorn," Sunset said.

Thirty seconds later he was back with a large bucket of the best-smelling popcorn as Gail managed to get a streaming movie going with the remote. She was actually getting better at moving real-world things than he was. And that came in real handy at times.

PART SIX
Pure Evil Does Exist

Thirty-Four

GAIL WOKE FIRST. She and Sunset had both fallen asleep watching a comedy about old guys robbing a bank. Now the screen was just showing other possible movies for them to watch.

The half-eaten bucket of theater popcorn was still on the coffee table, so they hadn't been asleep that long or it would have vanished. It was still dark outside the windows, with the lights of Portland shining bright.

She untangled herself slowly from Sunset and stood, stretching. The clock on the wall in the kitchen said it was just after two in the morning. They had been back in the apartment for six hours.

She had a hunch that was going to be enough time for Poker Boy and his team to set the stones. So they were going to be needed shortly.

She gently woke up Sunset and he sat up straight and yawned as she punched a few buttons on the remote to turn off the television.

They both splashed water on their faces and changed shirts, then jumped to an all-night restaurant just outside of downtown that served a good bar-rush crowd, so there would be lots of choices for them to pick from.

The place smelled wonderful of fresh coffee and bacon. She was surprised at how hungry she was.

She ended up with three eggs, toast, and bacon while he got a plate of pancakes and ham. They found a booth in an area that looked closed and settled in, drinking coffee and eating breakfast.

They had just finished when Jewel and Tommy appeared and slid into the booth with them.

"Laverne says it will be another hour before the protective net goes live," Jewel said. "We wanted to make sure you two were up and ready."

"Ready as we can be considering we have no idea what we are getting into," Gail said.

"Food's good here," Sunset said, pointing at his empty plate.

"Already ate," Tommy said, "but that coffee smells wonderful."

He stood and headed to get him and Jewel a couple cups of coffee.

Gail waited for Tommy to get back, then asked, "You both were in Cadmus's head. He knows Alecto and Demeter. Any idea what we are getting into?"

Jewel glanced at Tommy, then sighed. "Total evil," she said.

"Powerful evil," Tommy said. "I doubt we are going to be able to get to them like we did Cadmus. At least not easily."

"Cadmus was afraid of both of them," Jewel said. "Terrified."

Tommy nodded.

"I'm amazed the gods don't have some sort of police system to take care of their own getting out of line," Sunset said.

"We are the police force," Jewel said.

Tommy nodded. "Laverne runs everything, is the most powerful god of them all, but even she has limits. That's why Poker Boy and his team are there with her and why she is also using us now when we can be helpful."

Gail just shook her head. "She really is Lady Luck?"

"She is," Jewel said. "And she is that powerful."

Gail forced herself to not think about that. At least not at the moment.

"Any idea where this Olympus they keep talking about is at?" Sunset asked.

"Not a clue," Jewel said and Tommy nodded.

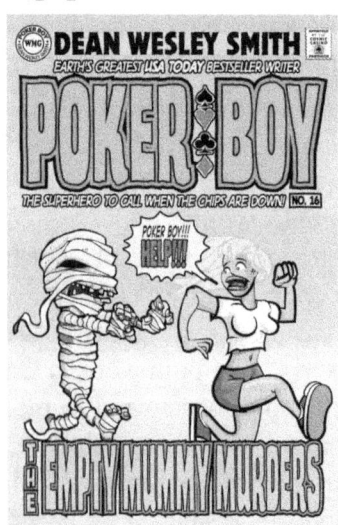
"It's not on this planet," Laverne said, appearing in front of the table and grabbing a chair and pulling it over.

Gail glanced around. Everyone in the restaurant had frozen in place, so Laverne had taken them into a space between moments in time where no one would see her.

Gail was surprised that Laverne didn't look tired or even frazzled in the slightest, even though they must have been working through the entire night.

"Are we ready to go?" Jewel asked.

Laverne nodded. "The Necklace Stone net is in place and turned on. No Mind Stone can work now."

"How long will that network hold together and be powered up?"

"Centuries," Laverne said. "Everyone who has had a time bomb planted in their heads will be long dead by the time that network stops protecting them."

"Wonderful," Sunset said.

Gail nodded to that, feeling a massive sense of relief.

"So have you found Alecto and Demeter?" Tommy asked.

"No," Laverne said. "We will need you four for that to trace the Mind Stone power lines. Once we find them, we will figure out what we can do."

Gail felt her stomach twist.

"Where do we start?" Jewel asked.

"Let's go to Poker Boy's office," Laverne said. "I have a suspicion those two are not far away."

A moment later they were back in Poker Boy's office.

The lights of Las Vegas were bright below them and the mountains dark around the valley. The night sky was clear and a lot of stars could be seen through the glass ceiling.

Poker Boy and Patty, his girlfriend and superhero, sat against each other in the booth, both looking exhausted. There was no one else there.

Gail took Sunset's hand and the four of them stood, waiting for instructions from Lady Luck.

But she hadn't jumped back here with them. She must have had another stop along the way.

So they stood there, the four of them, staring out at the view, waiting.

Thirty-Five

SUNSET JUST WAITED with Gail, holding her hand, feeling comfort in having her beside him. He couldn't imagine doing any of this stuff without her, even though he had been alone for almost a hundred years. Now, in a very few months, being alone seemed like an impossible, alien thing.

Laverne took almost two minutes to appear. With her were Dottie and Harmony, both clearly sleepy. Laverne must have woken them up.

Dottie carried her computer to the booth table and immediately sat down and opened it up.

Harmony stood beside her, hand on her shoulder.

Laverne watched them get ready as both Poker Boy and Patty perked up, working to wake up as well.

"Ben and Stan are on Olympus, monitoring the safety net," Laverne said. "If we need a certain type of help, they will be able to give it from there."

Poker Boy and Patty and both older gods nodded.

Sunset had no idea exactly what Laverne was talking about, but it sounded positive at least.

Laverne then turned to the four Ghost Agents. She took the Mind Stone they had taken from Cadmus out of her pocket and held it in her hand.

"This should have an energy radiating from it as the Necklace Stones did," she said. "We believe the Mind Stones will be linked as well."

"We are not going to be able to see the lines of energy with you holding it," Jewel said. "Your aura is far too bright."

Laverne nodded and set the Mind Stone on a chair, then stepped away.

Sunset moved over between the stone and Laverne and turned on his aura sight.

Laverne was right, it had a red tone around it and two red lines left the stone and went out through the window at a downward angle.

"Red power lines," Jewel said. "Two of them aiming downward toward the north. The lines are basically together."

"I suspected they would be here," Laverne said, nodding. "Gail, Sunset, would you two follow the lines. Do not engage, just come back and tell us exactly what you find."

Jewel was about to object, but Laverne held up her hand.

"We'll be right back," Sunset said, taking Gail's hand.

He understood completely what Laverne was thinking. He and Gail were the least experienced and the most expendable if they ran into trouble. She would need Jewel and Tommy's help to get him and Gail out of trouble if they found it and got stuck somehow.

He and Gail floated out into the cool night air and down along the red line. It was much fainter than the white lines now blanketing everything and a couple of times the red lines seemed to stop at a white Necklace Stone line.

It took them almost a full minute before they found where the red lines ended.

They carefully eased down into what looked like a massive gated mansion on a rock bluff to the north of the city. Guards patrolled the grounds and the paved road coming in was patrolled as well.

They slowly floated down along the red line, hand in hand, drifting first down through the roof and then through an attic until they were floating near a high ceiling in a massive bedroom.

The room was faintly lit and decorated in expensive Southwestern-style furniture.

Two women were sleeping together in a huge bed. The two red lines ended on each woman's chest.

Sunset squeezed Gail's hand and a moment later they were back in Poker Boy's office.

Sunset let out the breath he was holding for some reason and beside him Gail did the same.

"They are in an estate to the north of town, well guarded," Gail said.

"The two stones are being worn by two women who are sleeping at the moment," Sunset said.

"Those stones will protect them from you entering their minds," Laverne said, shaking her head.

Sunset looked at the stone still sitting on the chair, then back at Laverne as she frowned, trying to figure out something to do.

"You said you could get help from Olympus," Sunset said. "Would it be possible to send a burst of energy along those power lines to heat up those stones, force them to take them off?"

Laverne looked at Sunset for a moment, picked up the Mind Stone from the chair, then nodded and vanished.

"Might as well grab a seat," Poker Boy said. "She might be a while."

All four of them sat down in the booth facing the tired faces of Patty and Poker Boy as Madge appeared with a carafe of coffee and six cups.

"I thought all you served was milkshakes," Poker Boy said, smiling and nodding his thanks as Madge poured him and Pattie both a cup.

"Not even you wants a milkshake at four in the morning," Madge said.

With that she set the pot full of coffee down in front of the four Ghost Agents and vanished behind the booth.

"She is amazing," Gail said.

Sunset had to agree with that.

Poker Boy just laughed. "You have no idea."

Thirty-Six

GAIL SAT WITH Sunset for the hour it took until Laverne returned. Outside the floating office, the sun was just starting to color the distant mountains with a faint pink tint.

When Laverne showed up she said, "You four Ghost Agents get to their bedroom. The power is going to hit those Mind Stones in less than three minutes."

Gail felt her stomach tighten around the coffee. If this didn't get those two gods to take off those stones, they might be alerted that what they were doing had been discovered. Then it would be up to the Necklace Stone shield to work and none of them wanted to really trust that.

Laverne then turned to Poker Boy. "You and Patty be ready to jump the moment you get the call from the Ghost Agents."

"I will be with Harmony and Dottie making sure that any signal is blocked coming out of there."

With that she vanished.

"Good luck," Poker Boy said as Gail and Sunset and Jewel and Tommy jumped into the bedroom of the two sleeping gods.

They stood silently off to one side and the two women didn't seem to know they were being watched. Thankfully.

Both women seemed to be in their late thirties. Both had blonde hair and thin faces.

Gail had heard that sometimes gods could sense a Ghost Agent. Clearly these two did not, at least not enough to wake them up.

The red lines between the two Mind Stones around the women's necks were clear as well as the red lines coming in from the other Mind Stone.

Suddenly that red line coming in through the roof to the two stones seemed to glow an intense red. After a moment it was so bright, Gail had to shut down her aura vision and beside her Sunset at first turned away, then shut down his vision as well.

The two gods on the bed jerked, as if being hit with an intense electrical current.

Their hands grabbed for the Mind Stones on their chests, but the stones seemed to be almost stuck there.

Clearly the stones were getting hot, as the skin around the stones on the women's chests started to turn black.

Gail was shocked. This was not what she had imagined would happen.

Then with one final burst of bright hot light, the energy cut off.

The two gods lay silent, clearly unconscious.

But the stones were still on their chests, so none of them could enter their minds.

"We need help." Jewel said. "They are knocked out and still wearing the Mind Stones."

Poker Boy and Patty instantly appeared and moved to the side of the two gods. They carefully worked to take the stones off the women.

"This looks like it hurt some," Poker Boy said as he peeled the stone off one of the women's chest, taking black skin with it.

Patty was having trouble with the other because it was stuck so hard to the skin.

But the moment Poker Boy had the Mind Stone off of the one woman, Jewel and Tommy went inside her.

Less than three seconds later they reappeared.

"She is dead," they said at the same time.

"Laverne!" Poker Boy said as he moved around to help Patty take the other stone off of the second woman. It made a sound Gail didn't want to ever hear again when they pulled it loose.

Laverne appeared just as Jewel and Tommy went into the second woman.

They reappeared a few seconds later.

"She is dead as well."

Laverne just nodded and said nothing.

Poker Boy handed her the two Mind Stones and what was left of the skin of the two women on the stones vanished.

Laverne put the two stones in her pocket.

"Ghost Agents, check everyone in this house for any kind of information," she said. "And first of all, find their computer area."

Gail nodded with Sunset.

"Poker Boy and Patty, guard these two and make sure nothing changes," Laverne said.

Poker Boy nodded, not looking happy with the task.

"I will get Dottie and Harmony and we will be ready to check out the computers here to make sure nothing is set as an automatic trigger."

With that she was gone.

"Computer room first," Jewel said. "Let's split up and find it. Sunset, you and Gail take the kitchen staff area. We'll take the business area."

The next moment Gail was standing beside Sunset in a large kitchen that smelled of fresh coffee, bacon, and fresh bread.

Five minutes later the four Ghost Agents were standing in the large computer area, making sure the two men and two women sitting at stations were not doing anything that needed to be stopped instantly.

They were not. But they had been brainwashed very much like the ones back in Portland, to believe what they were doing was wonderful.

Gail cleared out the brainwashing on one woman back two years and told her to go home to her husband and children the job had caused her to neglect.

As the last worker left the room, Laverne and Dottie and Harmony appeared and got down to work.

And Sunset and Gail went back to checking everyone they could see and clearing out some brainwashing where they could.

Three full hours later Laverne called them into the computer room to a smiling Dottie and Harmony. Poker Boy and Patty were standing there, holding hands.

"All clear," Harmony said. "We have set worm programs that will spread around the world and destroy the time bombs in people's heads as they see the program."

"It won't get everyone," Dottie said. "But in just a week or so the threat will be over."

"I have taken care of our two deceased problems," Laverne said. "They have already been sent on a path into the sun."

"So once again the team-up of ghosts and superheroes and gods help save the world," Poker Boy said.

He smiled at the four Ghost Agents. "Kinda fun, huh?"

All Gail could do was shake her head and laugh. She wasn't so certain about the fun part, but is sure did feel good.

Real good.

Thirty-Seven

SUNSET WATCHED AS Gail wound her way back through the wood and brass tables at the Golden Nugget Buffet, carrying a plate of food. She looked radiant, even though tired.

He couldn't believe how much in love with her he was. It now seemed like she had always been a part of his life, and always will be. At least he was going to do his best to be on his best behavior to always have her with him.

She set her plate down, leaned over and kissed him, and then sat down to start to dig in.

He had already started eating.

Jewel and Tommy were still at the buffet filling their plates, dodging around the few live humans in the restaurant.

"How about we sleep until noon," Sunset said, "then just lounge around all day."

"I was kind of thinking we might spend part of the afternoon in bed not sleeping," she said, smiling at him.

"I like that idea a lot," he said, smiling back at her.

She looked directly at him, suddenly serious, and said simply, "Thank you."

He was shocked, but smiled. "We haven't spent the afternoon yet. I might be thanking you."

She laughed. "I am sure you will be. But I wanted to thank you for believing in me, training me, letting me become your first partner after a hundred years of working alone."

Sunset reached toward her and took her hand. "It has been my honor."

"This is sure a long way from that coast highway and the front bumper of that truck," she said.

He could tell she was still having trouble grasping the last day or so. Actually, he was as well. They had both learned and seen so much. It was going to take months to talk it all out, he was sure of that.

Jewel and Tommy sat down across from them and started to eat.

"Did we really just save the world?" Gail asked.

Sunset felt the exact same way, shocked at the very idea.

Tommy smiled as he worked on a piece of ham and Jewel nodded.

"We really did," Jewel said.

"And chances are it won't be the last time," Tommy said.

"Yeah," Jewel said, "This is our second or third time in just a year."

"It's not getting old," Tommy said and they all laughed.

Sunset had heard a few comments about the last time. "Wasn't the last saving of the world around Christmas?"

Jewel nodded and smiled again.

"So tell us what happened," Gail said a moment before Sunset could ask the same question.

"Well," Tommy said, "you know how it was hard to understand that there were gods and superheroes over the last day?"

"Let's not forget the fact that Atlantis existed and Olympus is somewhere out in space," Gail said. "Yeah, pretty tough."

"Pretty crazy day," Sunset said. "To use a wild understatement."

"Well imagine our surprise," Jewel said, "when we discovered Santa Claus was real as well."

"Nope," Gail said, shaking her head. "That's just one step too many."

Sunset felt the same way, but he laughed with Tommy and Jewel. It was too silly to even comprehend.

"You'll meet him at the Christmas party," Tommy said.

Jewel nodded. "He likes us because we saved him."

"So we save the world and get to meet Santa Claus," Gail said. "Now I know for sure that I really am dead."

"And still dreaming," Sunset said, smiling at the woman he loved. For months that had been a standing joke between them.

"Of course I'm dreaming," Gail said. "I'm going back to a beautiful condo in Portland and make love to the most handsome man I have ever met. Santa Claus is just going to be a bonus."

Jewel and Tommy and Sunset all laughed so hard Sunset was sure that even the live people in the early morning breakfast buffet could hear them.

Gail just kept on eating.

In over a hundred years of being dead and trying to help people, he had never felt this good.

This much in love.

And this much alive.

And after a long nap, later that afternoon Gail made him feel even more alive.

She had been right. He did end up thanking her.

~

Coming Next Issue in *Smith's Monthly*

#1...October 2013

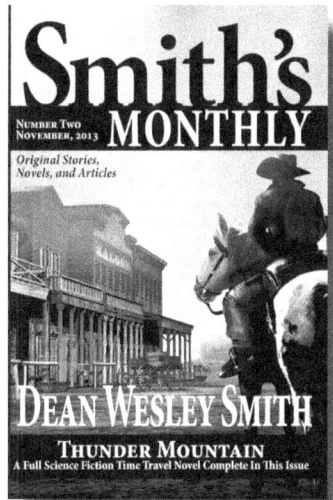

#2...November 2013

#3...December 2013

#4...January 2014

#5...February 2014

#6...March 2014

Don't Miss an Issue!

Subscribe

Electronic Subscription:

6 Issues... $29.99

12 Issues... $49.99

Paper Subscription:

6 Issues... $59.99

12 Issues... $99.99

For Full Subscription Information Go To:

www.SmithsMonthly.com

**All Issues Also Available
at Your Favorite Bookstore**

#7...April 2014

#8...May 2014

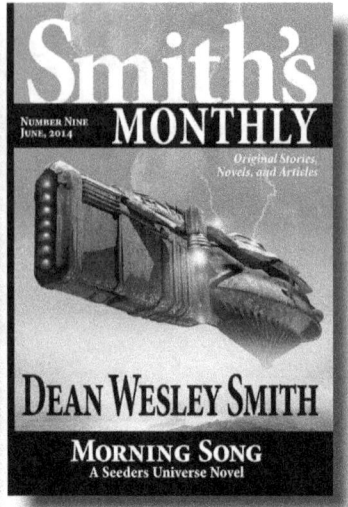

#9...June 2014

#10...July 2014

#11...August 2014

#12...September 2014

#13...October 2014

#14...November 2014

#15...December 2014

#16...January 2015

#17...February 2015

#18...March 2015

#19...April 2015

#20...May 2015

#21....June 2015

#22...July 2015

#23...August 2015

#24...September 2015

#25...October 2015

#26...November 2015

#27...December 2015

#28...January 2016

#29...February 2016

#30...March 2016

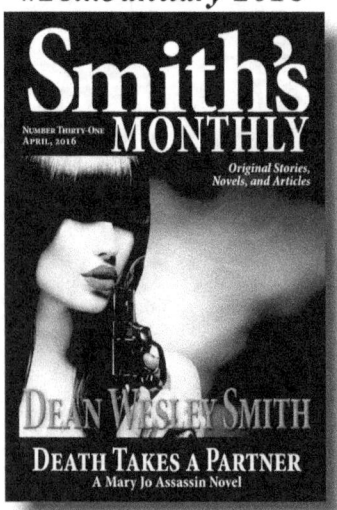

#31...April 2016

#32...May 2016

#33...June 2016

#34...July 2016

#35...August 2016

#36...September 2016

#37...October 2016

#38...November 2016

#39...December 2016

Thank You!!

I would like to thank the following wonderful people who support my blog and my work through Patreon. Your support is very important to me. Thanks!

Irette Y Patterson
Kathryn Rooney
Erick Lindman
Christopher Ridge
Raphael Husbands
James Gotaas
milady133
Danica Oakley
Kenny Norris
Kate MacLeod
Leah Cutter
Leigh Anderson
Robert J. McCarter
Jennette Heikes
Jamie Curierre
Albert Lemke
Marsha Kessler
Diane Darcy
Robin Brande
James Husum
Terry Mixon
Shantnu Tiwari
Chong Go
Maria Grace
Gnondpom
David Hendrickson
Fen

Sherman Cox
Miguel Angel Alonso Pulido
Marian Goldeen
Michelle Tatam
J.R. Murdock
Gunnar Gunderson
Jesse P Thurston
coraa
Martin Barkawitz
David Beers
Leslie Claire Walker
Nancy Hendrickson
F.I. Goldhaber
Michael J Lawrence
Barbara G. Tarn
Anthony St. Clair
Ann Tucker
Karl Gallagher
T. Thorn Coyle
Cristof Jones Harrison
Tasha Turner Lennhoff
Brenda Smith
Kari Wolfe
Mary Jo Rabe

And a very special thank you to
Betsey Wilcox.

www.ingramcontent.com/pod-product-compliance
Lightning Source LLC
Chambersburg PA
CBHW081152170626
46813CB00009B/3164